WRONG FOREST

A NOVEL BY
E. GALE BUCK

ISBN: 978-1-7360230-7-5 (paperback)

This is a work of fiction.
    Mystery; Thriller; Suspense; Action & Adventure;
    Suitable for Young Adult - Adult

Keywords: Camping; Mystery; Hijacking; Thriller; Marriage

Cover image taken by author at Morris Hill Campground,
    George Washington & Jefferson National Forest. Near
    Covington, Virginia

Published April, 2025 by
Speurach Press
all things magical but not yet understood
an imprint of
The Silver Wreath
Martinsville, Virginia
www.woodsmanstories.com

Printed in United States of America by
Ingram Lightning Source

Other Titles by E. Gale Buck

<u>From Speurach Press</u>
Vrenessbith - two parts
  - Awakening
  - Catharachd
Treasured Adversaries
The Thirstday Cognizance Brigade
Lost Finder

From The Silver Wreath
<u>Christmas / Woodsman</u>
The Woodsman's Tale
Finding Nicholas
Secret Stories of Santa
A Quiet Service - four volumes
        a scandinavian legacy
        exploring a new world
        passion beyond misfortune
        reaching beyond tomorrow
Lessons of Christmas

<u>Faith / Inspirational</u>
Secret of the Turquins
Excuse me, My Name is God, do you have a minute or two to
        talk

For Children - <u>Tales from the North Pole</u>
(Illustrated by Christiana J. Buck)
        How Santa's Reindeer Got Their Bells
        The Bethlehem Tree
        First to Fly
        Joy Ride

All titles available through Amazon, Bookshop.ORG, and other
fine bookstores.

For information on new projects follow The Silver Wreath on
Facebook.

Acknowledgments

What can you say about a writing colleague who repeatedly says, "Your going the wrong way."? I can't thank Jeff Mansour enough for "sticking to his guns," even though he did not see where this story was going until it got there. The true value of another's opinion can never be fully expressed for it shapes the story to come. Had I tried to write this story without Jeff's comments, it would have been a very different story. Thank You.

Then there is my life companion, my bride, my best friend, and "partner in crime," Christy. She also challenged fine details and pushed me to "get it right." Saying "Thank You" to this wondrous lady does not begin to express my gratitude for her tireless work on my crazed creations. She appreciates what I do well and hounds me until I get the mistakes corrected. Still Love You.

"Matt, your phone is ringing," Barbara announced as she carried her personal duffle bag to the car.

"Yes, I know. I've ignored the last two calls, any reason I should answer this one?" Matthew replied, taking the bag from his wife and placing it strategically among others in the back end of their Dodge Durango. "I'm on vacation and don't care to be bothered by anything that might ruin my mood."

"It could be important. You want me to get it?"

"If you must. Is this the last bag?"

"Need to bring out the food."

"I'll put that in the camper." Matt then closed the back of the car, stepped over the trailer hitch, and strolled to the door near the rear of their camper.

Twice each year, Barbara and Matthew escaped the rigors of everyday life in the city. This time they were heading for a small out of the way campground in the mountains. Six hours on the highway for four days of peace and quiet. Living comfortably in their twenty-four-foot ultra-light camper, their biggest decisions would be where to wander each day. That is if wandering fit their mood of the moment.

"It's your boss. They have a crisis." Barb relayed the dreaded information as she held Matt's phone out to him.

Matt heaved a heavy sigh as he raised the phone to his ear. "Yel-oh." After listening intently for nearly a minute, he responded with a heavy and discontented sigh. "Okay. I'll be there in about twenty minutes." Lowering the phone to his waist, he pressed "End Call" and looked to his wife. "Safety breach in a secondary lab. Wilson is out sick, or so he claims, and nobody on site is qualified to handle it. I'll be back as soon as I can." His face crumpling into a frustrated scowl, he raised his arm to throw the phone as far as he could, preferably into an oncoming train; if only there were one available.

Barb stepped over to her husband of thirty years and kissed him gently. "I'll load the food and the rest of the stuff into the camper. We'll leave as soon as you get back. Take my car and drive carefully. Please."

After clipping the evil vacation wrecker onto his belt, Matt wrapped his arms around his wife and let all his frustrations and anger subside. "Thank you." He then kissed her lovingly and climbed into her Subaru Legacy. That was nine fourteen on a cool Tuesday morning in late April.

"So, what was the emergency?" Barbara asked her husband as they pulled out onto the westbound highway.

"New man in the lab, who was not qualified nor cleared to change gas tanks, didn't want to wait for one of my staff. Screwed the valve on incorrectly. When gas began to leak, he knocked two empty tanks into one of those big bottles of cleaning acid, which had just been delivered and not stored properly. Acid all over the floor, which is now quite clean, and gas seeping from the tank. Nothing volatile, just a big unpleasant mess. My crew had already responded and taken care of most of it before I arrived. While they finished cleanup, I interviewed the idiot, then inspected everything. Most of my time was spent doing all that required paperwork. When I get my hands on Wilson, he'll . . ."

"Hey, it's over," Barbara interrupted, soothing her husband's rekindling anger. "We are now on the road with peace and quiet waiting at the other end . . . and no phone reception." A minute later she asked, "Any idea what time we'll get there?"

"Well, traveling this time of day, traffic will be heavier so maybe six and a half hours. Not quite two o'clock now, so eight-thirty, with an ounce of luck."

"That's only four hours late. I think we'll survive."

Tires hummed on the highway beneath them as they left the metropolitan area and found better scenery of a rural flavor. The CD player added relaxing tones, which were frequently drowned out by trucks rolling past them. Wrapping around another metropolis on the westbound bypass, Matt noticed that shadows from the trees were growing. He pulled his visor down to block the sun as it slid slowly toward treetops and hills rising before him. After a brief stop in a rest area, Matt and Barb joined commuters rushing home and the highway became increasingly more difficult to manage.

"You about ready for a supper break?" Barb asked, sensing Matt's growing tension.

"Funny you should ask that. I was just thinking that Bobby would be asking for a burger break about now."

Their youngest son, Bobby, had been killed in an auto
accident four years ago. He was seventeen and off with
teammates celebrating victory at a regional track meet. The
driver, Bobby's best friend, stopped abruptly for a yellow light.
The truck behind them didn't. Four young lives were snuffed out
in that instant, all wearing golden medals won earlier that day.

Bobby always wanted hamburgers while driving to
campgrounds. Angela, who was two and a half years older than
Bobby, could not stand cheap burgers. They were fine when thick
and juicy and required two hands, but not the thin cheap patties
found at most fast food chains. Angela preferred fried chicken
when traveling, as did her young husband. The last time they
visited "home," Matt thought he was at a chicken restaurant
when he opened their car door. Angela never cared much for
camping, either. Steven, the eldest of three children, preferred
backpacking to trailer camping. "Don't choke me with a
bathhouse and neighbors," he would say. "Give me a wide-open
mountain range and enough room to roll out my sleeping bag,
surrounded by nature." Steven moved to the west coast for a job
and outdoor opportunities.

"Tell you what," Matt replied to Barb's suggestion, "traffic
should lighten in a few more miles, after we pass this city. We
can stop for a burger, or whatever, then."

"Sounds good."

At five-thirty, they pulled off the highway to get supper.
Rather than enjoy a relaxed meal, as they often did on these trips,
they grabbed hamburgers and kept driving. Matt groaned as
mayonnaise laden white lettuce dripped onto his shirt. Barb
chuckled, but said nothing. An hour later, with dusk stealing the
last rays of sunlight, a loud rumbling sound came from the rear
of the Durango. The driver's side rear tire was flat.

Changing tires on a tow vehicle is the same as any other car,
except when it is a back tire you have to disconnect the trailer
and roll the car forward so you can raise the rear end. Making the
job a bit more difficult, tools and access to the spare tire are
hidden in a well at the back end of this particular model
Durango. Matt fumed silently as he handed bags to Barb so they
could lift the well cover, then removed the gear he had stored in
the well.

"Whoever designed this system should be shot!" Matt raged as he lowered the spare to the ground. Dropping the spare beside the flat, he looked down the highway and wondered if they were safe enough in the fading light. "Barb, would you please drop a flare behind the camper. I don't want to deal with any more accidents today."

Barb dug two flares out of a safety kit Matt had removed from the storage well and lit one, dropping it fifteen feet behind their trailer, clearly visible from the hilltop a quarter mile back. Commuters and truckers all pulled into the left lane when they saw the flare, removing most of the danger from Matt's work. All but one. Two truckers crested the hill running side by side and well over the posted speed limit. Fortunately Matt was rolling the spare tire behind the car when they blew past. Thirty minutes after dropping the spare, he was cranking the flat tire into its storage area beneath the vehicle.

Darkness now surrounding them, Matt retrieved a flashlight from the camper and searched the area around the back of the car for anything small that might have been left before closing the tailgate. He then climbed into the driver's seat and slowly backed up to reconnect the camper.

"Well, that only took an hour," Barb chirped as they pulled back onto the road.

"Closer to ninety minutes. Guess we'll spend tomorrow getting the tire repaired," Matt replied. His voice was now extremely tense and tired. Checking his rearview, he noticed the flare flickering out.

The last ten miles of their journey was a two-lane country road. Not a highway, just a country road decorated with farmhouses, a few mobile homes, and lots of dark shadows that would have been beautiful trees had they arrived before supper. Reaching the gate into the forest, which at a quarter till ten was surrounded by darkness, Matt was pleasantly surprised to find the gate still open; the campground was a mile and a half beyond. Grateful, he pulled through and slowly continued down the narrow rough paved road. One hundred yards beyond the gate, he was stopped by a man walking with a dog. Matt rolled his window down so they could talk.

"Evening folks, I'm Bart, your Campground Host. You have reservations?"

"Yes, site fifteen."

"Nice site, 'cept we have a power problem on it. Why don't you folks take the next site, number seventeen instead? Top o' the hill beyond fifteen. Just as nice and right across from the shower house, if that matters."

Matt shrugged his shoulders in passive agreement. The campground host patted the car. "Well, it's late so I'll not be bothering you tonight. Nobody else in that area, but please keep the noise down as you set up. I think two groups on the upper loop have already turned in for the night. They're a good ways off, but you know how sound travels at night in the forest. I'll check with you in the morning. G'night." As he started to walk away, he called to the spaniel walking with him, "Come on Miranda, past time to close the gate."

Rolling slowly down a road barely wide enough for two cars, Matt looked at darkened evergreen trees looming on the left side of the road. To the right was a five-foot drop into the forest. Reaching the campsite loop, he paid no attention to the sign warning about bears, poisonous snakes, and other dangerous wildlife. It was too dark to read the sign, anyway. A faint smell of burning wood drifted through the trees on a slight breeze into Matt's open window. The roadway was now gravel and a single lane as it wove through a forest of evergreens and leafing hardwoods. Reaching their assigned site, he stopped to let Barb out.

Weary from the long drive, Barb climbed from their truck and guided Matt as he backed their camper into its resting place. Unable to see anything in the dark other than Barb's waving flashlight, Matt turned the steering wheel sparingly and gently pressed the gas pedal. Experience paid off as both campers worked efficiently together to level and stabilize the trailer. Their camper situated and ready for use, Matthew took Barbara by the hand and they walked to the bathhouse. Neither said a word as they parted company at doors marked MEN and WOMEN. Returning after a few moments, Barbara found Matt staring across the campground soaking in the quiet.

Looking to the sky as she approached her husband, Barb commented, "Stars are pretty tonight."

Matt looked up. A crescent moon hung near the horizon with dots of light scattered across the blackness. Wisps of clouds drifting past temporarily hid some stars. "Yes. Be better without the light on the bathhouse . . . still, better'n we get at home. Can't see any lights in the campground . . . Bart was right, looks like we are the only ones here," Matt commented as they walked.

"Is that bad?" Barb replied, affectionately squeezing her husband's hand.

Two

Day One

Waking as a new day began to dawn, after a fitful sleep, Matt stepped out of his camper and turned toward the bathhouse, beginning this day as his last had ended. Reaching the front of his SUV he stopped and opened his eyes wide, placing one hand on the car's hood to steady himself. A hickory tree, nearly a foot in diameter, stood six feet in front of him, blocking his SUV. Looking further into the dim light, he could not find the road which they had driven in on, nor was there any sign of a bathhouse. Spinning around he saw nothing but silhouettes of trees, a mature forest void of any mark of mankind . . . other than his vehicle and camper.

Now fully awake, he felt a damp chill in the air. Placing both hands on the hood of his Durango, he felt the cold metal. *Yes*, he thought, *I am awake. This car is real and I can see the camper right where it should be. . . . But, this is not where we parked last night.* Suddenly, his bladder began to scream.

"This is just a trick of the morning light; I've got to get to the bathhouse!" He mumbled aloud to himself, walking briskly. Arriving at where he believed the bathhouse had stood the night before, he spun around, searching the ground for a structure of some sort. A foundation, a hole, anything. Distracted by the absence of the building he had visited just hours before, Matt tried to reconcile his problem. "The bathhouse was here. Now it isn't. There is no way this can be happening. I have got to be caught in a nightmare of some kind . . ." Once again his bladder cried out in pain, assuring Matt that he was indeed awake or if this were a dream it was incredibly real. Raising his eyes, he scanned the forest for other campers and thought, *Oh, what the hell . . .* Still trying to figure out where he was or possibilities of what might have happened, he unzipped his fly and relieved himself.

"MATTHEW! What are you doing?" Barb cried out.

"I'm answering nature's call," Matt replied, meekly.

"Shouldn't you have used the toilet in the camper or at least gone to the bathhouse?"

"I'm there, but it's not here," he responded, zipping his pants closed.

"What do you mean, 'not here'?"

Returning to his wife's side, next to their car, he put his hands on her shoulders. "Barbara, my love, something tells me we're not in Kansas anymore."

"What?" Barbara stared at her husband with total confusion.

"Look around, what do you see?" he asked as he put an arm around her shoulders, his voice tense. "There is no road, no bathhouse, no other campers, and trees have grown up where we backed in last night. It doesn't make any sense."

Both Matt and Barb turned a full three hundred sixty degrees. Sunlight just beginning to pierce the forest crown from the horizon, they could see they were surrounded by mature oaks and hickories pushing out tender new light green leaves. Hemlock provided darker green colors and smaller cedars were scattered through the sparse undergrowth. Three dogwood trees were in full bloom with white crowns, glowing on the top as the sun's first rays touched them. Rhododendron clusters were abundant. Surveying their immediate campsite, Barb noticed two small trees growing between their Durango and their camper, each over six inches in diameter.

"Matthew, where are we?" Barb's voice was shaky, and she brought her hands to her mouth in total disbelief.

"Haven't a clue." Matt struggled to keep his calm, however his heart was pounding in his ears, making it difficult to think clearly. Seeking some normalcy, he took a deep breath and continued, "Maybe the GPS on my phone will tell us something." He then returned to the camper to retrieve his phone. Barb waited outside, surveying the forest for some sign of life. She was not relieved when all she saw were three squirrels. Exiting the camper, Matt fiddled with his phone and called, "Barb, check your phone. Mine's deader'n a doornail."

"I think I left it in the car. Bop the doors, please."

Matt stepped back into the camper, returning seconds later pressing a button on a car fob.

"Doesn't seem to be working. Let's go 'old school' and use a key." Desperation overtaking fear, he raced over to the car and fumbling with a ring of keys, unlocked the front passenger door. Reaching inside the center console he retrieved his wife's phone and handed it to her. As she tried to turn her phone on, he pressed the unlock button on the door. "Nothing. Car seems to be dead, too." Growing increasingly exasperated with the situation, Matt closed the passenger side door and walked around to the driver's door. Unlocking it with the metal key, he slid behind the wheel and tried to start the engine. Nothing.

"What about the batteries in the camper? Can we charge the phones in the camper?" Barb asked, hopefully.

"If there's any juice, yes we can. Or I think we can . . . no . . . YES! I do remember charging them in the camper on our last trip. Let's find out."

His mind racing through the facts as he understood them, Matt ran back to the door of the camper, jumped in, and pressed a light switch on the roof. "Nothing, well practically nothing." Pressing the button to off, he continued. "We have a glimmer of power. Not enough to charge or do anything. I'm not sure our flashlights will work, either." Reaching into a cabinet by the door, he retrieved a flashlight and hesitantly pressed the button. "IT WORKS! Bright as day! Flashlights work."

Her heart in her throat and tears welling up, Barb asked, "Don't you have one of those emergency recharge packs for your phone?"

"Yes! Thank you! Now, where did I put it?" Having a fixed task with a predictable outcome, a sense of reason began to seep into Matt's confused mind. "I remember unplugging it when my phone began to ring yesterday morning. Where did I put it?" Matt stood outside the door to their camper and thought. "Glove compartment . . . no, back well. I was just starting to store stuff in the back and dropped it in the rear well."

Barb wasted no time trying to open the back end of the Durango, only to find it still locked. "Needs a key," Matt reminded her as he inserted his key into the lock. Seconds later, the rear gate was up and both were removing bags left in the car until needed. Raising the lid to the well and holding it up with his hand, Matt looked for his charger. Tools and bags were strewn around from changing the flat tire on the way to the campground. "Where did I put it?" he asked himself. "This doesn't make a bit of sense." He then began shifting every tool, frantically checking every box and bag. Lifting a small socket set, he breathed a sigh of relief. A dark grey device the size of a normal cell phone waited to be discovered. "Gotcha. Not where I remember putting you, but at least we got ya. Now, do you have any juice to share?" Both Matt and Barb held their breath as he pressed the power button. "100 Percent! We have power for the phones!" he exclaimed jubilantly.

Wrapping his arm around his wife, Matt kissed her passionately before returning to the camper and his phone. Plugging his phone into the quick charge cable on the power pack, he suggested, "We should give it a chance to charge a bit before turning it back on. How about breakfast?"

"Sounds good," Barb replied, her voice void of any enthusiasm. This was not the camping trip she had been anticipating for the past three weeks. She pulled bacon, eggs, and butter from their camper refrigerator, which was not as cool as she had expected.

"No gas!" Matt exclaimed, one hand holding an iron skillet and the other on a knob on the stove. "First, no power; now, no gas!"

"Did you open the gas last night or just fall in bed?"

"Good point. Maybe I should open the gas tank. I'll start the fridge after breakfast."

"You turn on the gas and fix breakfast. I'll start the fridge." Barb smiled for the first time that morning.

Matt quickly exited the camper and went to the front. After opening the gas, he went back inside and lit a match, which he held to a stove burner as he opened that burner to high. Escaping air caused the match to burn quickly and Matt had to turn the gas off. Striking a second match, he broke it and ground his teeth. Opening the burner again, after igniting a third match, he sighed when the stove lit after only two seconds. Turning to the sink, he tried to fill their kettle with water. Nothing happened and Barb exclaimed, "Matt, I can't get the fridge going!"

"I'll take a look at it after breakfast. Right now, we don't have water for coffee. I filled the fresh water tank before we left, so I know we have water." Holding the kettle in one hand and leaning against the counter with the other, Matt closed his eyes in an effort to think more clearly. "Ah, no power for the pump, therefor no pressure." Squatting down, he opened the cabinet beneath the sink and began working a pump handle. After a minute, he stood and tried the water, again. Water now flowed smoothly, albeit with little force. "We have water and soon hot coffee!" he exclaimed.

"Eggs are good. Thank you for the first normal thing of the day," Barb said as she used her last bite of bread to mop up remaining egg yolk.

Sighing and smiling at his wife, Matt replied. "Yes. Breakfast was good. Now, let's see if my phone can tell us where we are."

Stepping outside, Matt surveyed the forest. Nothing had changed. Whatever had started this odd nightmare still had them in the wrong forest. Sighing with frustration, he pressed the power button on his phone, relieved to see the power meter register 100%. That relief faded quickly, however, when the phone reported, "No Service." Out of desperation, he drilled down to his apps list. Finding Maps, he tapped *Open* then touched the locator icon. Nearly a minute passed before a map appeared, pinpointing their location. Cautiously, Matt widened the area of the map until he found something he recognized.

"Good news and not-so-good news. We appear to be right where we are supposed to be. Map says we are in Hemlock Bluffs Campground."

"And what's the 'not-so-good' news?" Barb asked, not certain she really wanted to know.

"Well . . . the map shows rivers that I expected, but no highways. No cities or towns. According to this map we are where we should be . . . but that is now in the middle of nowhere."

"Do you see any way out of nowhere?"

"No, not really. There is no place to go. Like I said, no cities or towns or roads. Just forest going on forever."

Barb sat quietly digesting this information. "This doesn't make any sense. The bathhouse is gone. The campground is gone, no matter what your map says. The campground is gone! Trees are growing where we DROVE last night! I'm beginning to think we're caught in an episode of 'The Twilight Zone'."

Bob smiled as he answered, attempting to be reassuring. "Hey, we wanted to get away from it all. Looks like we finally made it."

Barb's expression went blank, as if to say, *You've got to be kidding.*

Matt drew a deep breath and made a suggestion. "Okay, joking aside, I do have an idea. We've camped here before, not on this site but in this campground. And while we were here, we did a lot of hiking. Behind us is a mountain, and then another mountain. In front of us is a river. We crossed it shortly after turning off the main highway last night and we have hiked there in the past. Maybe five or six miles. As I recall, there is a country store less than a mile down the road from the river crossing. What say, after we cleanup, we wander toward the river and see if we can get a cold drink at that store?"

"And maybe a few answers?" Barb added, agreeing with her husband.

"Not sure they'll have any answers, but I do remember the steak we bought there last time. And if they don't have steak, we can grill burgers when we get back."

"Get back?" Barbara retorted. "We get to that store I don't know that I'll be coming back!"

Matt didn't reply. Instead, he turned on the water. Water flowed smoothly then quickly turned into a trickle. His brain went into overdrive, analyzing aloud, as he considered why. "The hand pump doesn't build enough pressure to complete a meal." He stood thinking quietly. "Hey, didn't we buy a solar cell not too long ago?"

"Yes!" Barb exclaimed as she jumped up from the table and squeezed past Matt. "Under the bed. Give me a hand."

Together they lifted the bed and found a box containing a solar battery charger. Matt held the bed while Barb retrieved it. When Matt dropped the bed, Barb handed him the box. "I'll take care of the water heater, you go be Mister Science and figure out how to connect this thing."

"Forgot to start the water heater, too, didn't I," Matt sighed as he took the box.

"Just like the fridge," Barb chided.

Matt took the box outside, and began reading instructions on the back. Barb quickly joined him with more bad news. "Water heater needs power to ignite. So, when you get that thing hooked up, maybe we can solve quite a few problems. You might want to read the instructions inside the box."

Eyeing his wife with an ounce of contempt and a pound of love, Matt opened the box and spread the contents in the rear of the SUV. After a quick review, he stepped back and looked around.

"What's wrong?" Barb asked.

"Need sunshine, direct sunshine." Matt then retrieved a wad of wire and began unwrapping it.

"How much wire do you have?"

"Not sure. About to find out."

Stretching the wire to its fullest extent, Matt connected one end to the battery terminals and the other to the back of the solar panel. It was two feet short of a patch of direct sunlight, however the controller did come on showing one-third power.

Looking at the controller screen, Matt announced, "Well, I guess it will charge the battery, but may take a while. What say we go find the river. Should have enough power to start the water heater and pump when we get back."

"Just a minute," Barb replied and stepped back into the camper. She emerged seconds later with a hat, backpack, and a bottle of water. "Water heater is working. You'll be able to wash dishes when we get back."

"What about the fridge?"

"I started it, too."

Three

Barb took a quick swig of water from her bottle and stuffed it into the pouch on the side of her daypack. She paused briefly, thinking, *I wonder how long our water supply will last? We have twenty or so bottles, and the tank, but what if we can't find a source of clean water before we get out of this mess? For that matter, what if we can't get out of this mess? . . . That's silly, we're heading out right now. We'll be okay.*

Matt stood on the other side of the tree blocking their Durango, trying to sight a path with Bobby's compass, which they found in the camper. His plan was to travel due east until they found the river. Looking out, he realized the first part of this path would take him down a densely forested hill. He could not see the next hilltop nor any clearly identifiable landmarks. They would have to rely on the compass to maintain their direction.

Shifting her daypack, Barb asked, "Why can't we take the car? It has four wheel drive."

"Yes, I thought about that. Problem is, no pathway of any kind. Look out there," Matt pointed the direction he wanted to travel. "Nothing but trees, we'd be stuck before we really got started. Besides that, battery is dead. Car won't start."

Barb looked out across the forest and sighed. "Okay. I guess you're right. Let's get going, I can almost taste that cold soda."

Grabbing two walking sticks leaning against the tree in front of the car, Matthew handed one to Barbara and took her free hand. Together they struck out over the hill toward a new adventure.

"How'd you sleep last night?" Barb asked Matt as they trudged through the forest.

"Not so good. A bit restless, but then I usually do sleep a bit off our first night out. Just getting used to the mattress, I guess. You?"

"Same as you, I suppose." . . . "Woke up with a headache. Not bad, just kind of numbing the back of my brain."

"Me, too. Didn't really think about it till you said something." . . . "Let me help you over this log." Matt offered his wife his hand to support her as they climbed over a fallen tree.

"Thanks. No sign of any forest management, is there?"

"Not as far as I can see. Almost looks like virgin forest."

"Almost?" Barb challenged.

"Well, do they still exist? Virgin forests, I mean."

Both chuckled at Matt's attempt at humor. At the next hilltop, he paused to check their compass and find a new landmark, across a small meadow to the north side of a clump of rhododendron near the top of the next hill. Behind and all around them the forest was a mix of primarily oak and hickory spaced ten to twenty feet apart. Dogwoods adorned with white crowns filled gaps. The ground was covered with layers of old leaves and fallen branches. The terrain rolled up and down with occasional areas that were flat, like groves. Small clearings filled with grass were not uncommon. When he could see the next hilltop, Matt would sight to something on that hilltop, otherwise his line went to a tree or bush as far off as he could certain a straight line.

Stepping off again, Barb touched Matt's arm then pointed off toward the southeast. A small herd of deer was grazing at the southern edge of the meadow, near another rhododendron cluster. A buck and three does, two of which appeared to be pregnant, looked back at them. The deer watched as Matt and Barb resumed their journey, but did not run.

An hour into their journey, Barb dropped her pack so she could get her water while Matt sighted the next eastbound leg. He helped her situate her pack before they continued.

"Matt, do you really think we'll find a way out when we get to this river?"

"I've got to, don't you?"

"I hope so, but let's get real for a minute. Have you seen any sign of man since we woke this morning?"

"I've seen a beautiful woman, does that count?"

"Get serious! I haven't seen a single sign of civilization. NOT ONE!"

"No, I haven't, but we didn't see signs of man on the Appalachian Trail, either."

"Yes we did, all over the place. Trail markers, shelters, overlooks with safety rails, even a bit of trash. That trail was a city scape compared to this place."

Matt drew a deep breath and smiled meekly at his wife; his frustration was sliding into concern as well. "Look, it's a beautiful day and we're in a beautiful forest. We'll deal with the bad news when we have to. Not before." He rubbed the back of his head and neck, trying to relieve muscles knotted with tension.

"I thought you were always prepared for any potential outcome."

"Barbara, . . ." Matt couldn't finish his thought. Instead, he turned and marched with a more determined pace. Barb struggled to keep up.

Matt stopped to sight a new line, two hours into their journey - about 10:40 in the morning. Standing next to a berry bush about to burst into a thousand tiny blossoms, his walking stick in the crux of his left elbow, he lowered the compass and softly said, "Barb, I think I hear the river. Listen." He then put his hand out to her, planted the end of his stick firmly into the ground, and pushed off. They stepped more lively through the trees, using their walking sticks to push briars aside. Anticipating a shallow river of chilling cold water bouncing over a stone bed, they practically danced with delight.

Arriving at the riverbank, their delight vanished. They had found the river, though it was not the gentle river of their memories. This river rushed through a gorge that must have been fifteen to twenty feet deep and fifty feet across. Sharp rocks protruded from steep banks. Upstream, a large oak stretched from the edge of the opposite bank to the water below, its crown washed bare by the rushing water. This river looked as if it had been engineered by God to be an impassible boundary.

Squatting down and letting her head hang with dismay, Barb hung on her waking stick and asked, "What now?"

Matt heaved a huge sigh and took his pack off. Reaching into a pocket on the side, he removed his cell phone and turned it on. "Let's see if the GPS has any information we can use." Activating the app, he watched the screen. His heart wanted to see a full display of the area, a way out, but his mind reserved judgement until he saw the results. Within thirty seconds the map appeared, showing him exactly what he had seen before. That image held about twelve seconds before showing him standing at the Hemlock Gorge River. Matt thought the transition odd, but dismissed it when it showed their new location.

Seeing no signs of roads or civilization, Matt switched to terrain view. They were surrounded by hills and mountains. The river appeared to fall over a cliff a couple miles upstream and again a few miles downstream, rushing from one waterfall to the next. He then switched to satellite view. Nothing but forests. Expanding the view, the image continued to show nothing but forest.

"Well, which way do we go? Where is the store with the cold drinks?" Barb asked. Her voice betrayed a hopelessness because she knew the answer, but had to ask.

Turning the phone off and returning it to his pack, Matt leaned on his walking stick as he replied, "Let's see if we can find a nice camper in the middle of this nowhere." After securing his pack on his shoulders, he extended his hand to Barbara. "You know Toto, I sure wish we were back in Kansas."

"Are you calling me a dog?" Barb retorted, gently beating her husband on his chest.

Wrapping his arms around his wife, he explained. "Dog? No! Bestest and most favorite traveling companion? Yes."

She squeezed him back as they stared at the river blocking their return to civilization.

Their journey back to the campsite was much the same as their trek to the river. Matt tried to find the same landmarks he had used going east, but the west bound forest had a different appearance. The forest was the same, but many of his landmarks were on the wrong side of the hill and not visible on the return trip. Using fresh landmarks, Matt plotted their westbound course with the compass and a prayer that they stay on track.

The sun passed its peak and shadows were beginning to stretch as they began climbing a slope that was more than a rolling hill. Barb checked her watch and challenged her husband. "Hey 'eagle scout,' I think you missed our campsite."

Already trying to reconcile this truth in his mind, Matt tried to make light of their situation. "What do you mean? Are you saying I got us lost in this 'Garden of Eden'?"

"I don't know. It took us just over two hours to reach the river and I believe we've been walking a bit faster heading back, and a bit more than two hours. Besides the time, I could be mistaken, but I don't recall going down this mountain we are now going up."

Matt removed his pack as he strolled over to a fallen tree and sat. Frustration overtaking his senses, he pulled his water bottle from the pack and began to take a drink. Raising the bottle, he saw a flash of color. Lowering the bottle, he stood and stared down the hillside, nothing but trees. Squatting down, he looked again. This time, he saw a flash of deep burgundy red, the color of their Durango. Squinting his eyes so he could examine the area a bit better, he smiled then turned to Barb.

"Didn't miss it by much. About a hundred yards to the north."

Barb squatted down beside him and stared through the trees. "Damn but you're lucky!"

"No, I used up all my luck when I found you. My orienteering skills are a bit rusty, that's all."

Barb pushed him over, stood, and began tromping down the hill toward their camper.

Now mid-afternoon, Matt checked the status of the battery on the camper's control panel. *Half charged*, he thought. *I'll keep the solar panel connected a while longer.* He then set to collecting wood for a cooking fire. The ground was covered with fresh fall from hardwoods so this job was not difficult. Clearing leaves and debris in a large circle for the fire, he paused. *I wonder, if we were to set this forest on fire, would someone come put it out? . . . Probably not before we got burned alive!* He then made his fire circle larger and went in search of stones to contain the burning wood and coals. Stones were not as plentiful as wood, but an hour after he began his fire circle, he had a small blaze glowing.

"Any ideas?" Barb asked as she sat on a large oak limb her husband had brought to their circle.

Squatting next to the fire, Matt added a few larger sticks, watching as they quickly ignited. "Hamburgers cooked over fresh hickory, smoked to perfection." He looked to his wife with a meager smile, then stood and kissed her gently, sidestepping her question. "Now, I do have to get the axe out and cut the fresh hickory. Will you mind the fire?"

"I'm not talking about supper."

Matt sighed before responding. "I know, but the answer is no. I don't have any ideas, not really. I suppose tomorrow we can climb the mountain. See what's out there from a better vantage point. Maybe we'll spot a cabin with smoke curling from its chimney."

Barb raised one eyebrow and patted her husband on his rump.

"Okay, then. I'm going to get the axe and get us some smokey flavor for the burgers. If you don't want to sit while you watch the fire, you can get the grill out. I just need the grate, not the entire grill."

Barb sighed and looked into the growing blaze. Matt stepped to the front of their camper and unlocked a storage bin. Reaching inside, he removed a small charcoal grill and trail axe. Leaving the grill by the camper, he returned to the fire. "Don't worry about the grill, I got it. I'll be back in a bit, won't be too far away, just holler if you need me." He then bent down, kissed his wife, and tromped off into the woods toward a hickory tree with low branches.

"Green beans are hot and I fixed us a salad," Barb told Matt as she handed him a plate of buns.

Scooping burgers off the grill and into the buns, he asked, "Are we eatin' by the fire or inside?"

"Burgers," Barbara mused, "let's eat out here. I set the chairs up so we don't have to endure your not quite so comfortable log."

After dressing their burgers and fixing salads inside the camper, they returned to comfortable folding web chairs placed near the fire. Before sitting, Matt placed his plate on his chair and asked, "You want a beer?"

"You have beer? You're not supposed to bring alcohol into a federal forest."

"Who's going to arrest us?" Matt beamed, walking to the back of their car. A minute later he returned with two bottles of amber ale. Settling into his chair, he inhaled deeply, before lifting his burger.

"Good burger, lover," Barb smiled and tilted her beer to her lips.

Hours later, with a first quarter moon rising above the tree tops, its light filtering through the branches to the waning fire, Matt sipped a cup of hot coffee and stared into the embers. Seeing the stress of their situation building on his face, Barb reached over and touched his hand.

"Whether this is some strange and sick joke or just a bad dream, we'll get through it."

His eyes still focused on the fire, Matt turned his hand over and squeezed hers. His mind struggled to make sense of the day they had just experienced and feared what tomorrow might bring.

Four

Matt woke to sounds outside their camper. *What time is it? It's still dark. . . . How long have I been asleep? . . . What's that noise?*

Staring at the dark of the ceiling above him, he analyzed what he was hearing. It wasn't just one sound, but several. Listening intently, he identified one as rain, drops of water dancing on the roof of their camper. Listening to the gentle rainfall, he started to drift back to sleep. Suddenly, there was a snarl, a loud growling sound followed by a higher pitched growl, then a heavy thud into the camper on the side opposite the door.

"What was that?" Barb exhaled anxiously, sitting bolt upright.

Matt, re-awaking with the same reaction, wrapped one arm around her shoulder and a hand gently across her mouth, whispering, "I'm not sure, but be quiet."

Seconds later another heavy bump shook the trailer, followed by more growls. "Bears!" Matt whispered. He and Barb sat quietly, listening intently; muscles taught with fear. A larger bear grumbled as it worked its way around to the front of the camper. Then a smaller cub bleated and something metal banged against a tree.

Matt peered out a window. "Oou, ouch!" Still whispering, he gave commentary to Barb who was not sure she wanted to hear what was happening. "Coffee pot's a goner. Momma bear just smashed it. Grill might have survived . . . nope, baby bear got a claw stuck in it. Yep, it's a goner, as well. Good thing we doused the fire. . . . Uh oh, momma is heading toward the car." Unable to see either bear, both campers sat motionless, terrified they might hear bears rip into their car. Instead of sounds of ripping metal, they heard the younger bear bleating and the sound of crunching plastic. Seconds later the momma roared and Matt saw the younger bear run through the bushes with something tied to his paw. Momma crashed through the bushes in pursuit; small trees bent and swayed as they ran off through the brush.

"No more solar power," Matt moaned as he laid back on the bed.

"What? Why?"

"I forgot to put it away and baby bear just ran off with the controller. I'm afraid he smashed the panel."

Unable to do anything at this moment, both breathed deeply, then laid back into their bed. Holding each other's hand they listened to rainfall dancing on their roof and breathed heavily. Both wanted to talk but neither could summon words. Lying in uneasy silence, they finally drifted back to sleep.

Day Two

Barb emerged from their camper shortly after sunrise. Seeing Matt trying to reshape their coffee pot to something that might perk properly, she told him, "I do have instant and we have a kettle and other pots."

"Yeah, I know. It's just that I like perked coffee around the campfire in the evening." Matt was angry about the condition of his coffee pot, his voice was strained and his thoughts bordered on irrational. Continuing to speak, his voice slowly relaxed, easing its tension. "Listening to the pop of the perculating and that growing aroma. We don't do that at home and I enjoy it while camping."

"Well, I have the kettle on the stove. It should whistle soon, and I added extra water for grits." She then turned to their car. "At least they didn't damage the camper or car. What about the solar panel?"

Still holding his not quite round coffee pot, Matt sighed with frustration. "Yeah, it could've been a lot worse. I found the controller down the hill. It seems to be okay - a bit dinged up from bouncing around, but not so sure about the panel. I'll hook it up later and see what happens, not too hopeful. At least the battery is three-quarters charged. How about coffee and breakfast?"

Minutes later they were sipping instant coffee and stirring instant grits. After adding a shake of salt, Barb asked, "What are the plans for today?"

"I thought we were going up the mountain. Maybe get an eagle's eye view of this forest. See what there is to see."

Sighing as she rolled a spoonful of grits around her tongue, Barb replied, "Sounds good."

While Barb washed up the breakfast dishes, Matt stepped outside and fiddled with his phone. Finishing the dishes, she joined him, asking, "What're you doing?"

"Marking our location on my GPS app. There's something fishy with it, but maybe it'll help us find the camper if we get lost."

"What if we hang a flag in one of the trees? I have a red tablecloth."

"That, my dear, is a brilliant idea!"

An hour later, both stood back and admired the red tablecloth hanging twelve feet up a hickory tree next to their camper. Matt's hands suffered a few scrapes, which Barb soothed gently with tender loving care and a kiss.

"Let's go." Not wanting to get distracted by more intimate thoughts, Matt shook off Barb's playful attention as he pulled his hands back. Looking at her attempt to pout and frown, he leaned over and kissed her on the cheek, then lifted his pack up on his shoulders, retrieved his walking stick, and turned west, toward the mountain. Barb giggled behind him.

Wet leaves made the first part of the trek somewhat messy, requiring the assistance of their sticks. Twenty minutes into their journey, they got their footing and began to "instinctively" negotiate the slippery ground. Matt checked their compass periodically, but did not try to sight a westward line. Their goal was to get as high as possible, as quickly as possible, relying on Matt's GPS and the red tablecloth to guide them back to camp.

Forty-five minutes into their climb, they came across a well-defined deer trail running along the side of the mountain. Both hikers voted to follow the deer trail rather than continue to fight the mountain. Before changing their direction, Matt found a large branch and leaned it against a tree next to the deer trail. Seeing a puzzled look on Barb's face, he told her, "A marker to show us when we need to start sliding down the hill on the way back."

She grinned appreciatively.

The deer trail ran gently uphill until it came to a thick wall of rhododendron where the trail seemed to disappear. Stomping around, Barb found the trail continued back the way they came, after a four-foot climb up a sixty-degree slope. Matt climbed the hill first, using his walking stick and pulling on surrounding trees, then pulled Barbara up with her stick. After ninety minutes of following deer trails and three more vertical cutbacks, they stopped beneath a large rock overhang for a breather and lunch.

Barb had fixed sandwiches after cleaning up breakfast. Smelling the meat and bread as he unwrapped his lunch, Matt realized how hungry he was and chomped into his. Neither said much while they ate, however Matt did look at the rock above their heads and considered trying to climb up on it.

Standing, he took one more swig from his water bottle, pushed it into the pocket on his pack and smiled at Barb. "Wait here. I'll be right back." He then scrambled up a steep hill, pulling himself from tree to tree, until he reached the top of the overhang. The mountain continued to rise through more rhododendrons, but he was now standing on a large chunk of granite, the exposed area ten feet wide and stretching eight feet into the valley. One long side was blocked by the mountain and two ends dropped off into the forest. The fourth side, the longest edge, was open to the sky. Drawing a restorative breath, he looked out over the valley before him. Off in the distant east, possibly seven miles, was the river they had visited the day before. Matt could now see another mountain beyond the river. To the south was more forested mountain. To the north, the forest rolled gently until it came to a lake. A mile or so beyond the far side of the lake, the forest met a sheer cliff.

"Barbara, you need to come up here and see this," he called.

"What? How do I get up there?"

"It's not as hard as it looks. Just pull yourself up using the trees, like a ladder."

Matt reached out and helped his wife up the last of the climb, then held her arm as they walked out on the exposed rock. While she took in the view, he commented, "We are stuck in a bowl. No way we could have driven into this place and I have no idea how we got here. What's worse, I don't see any easy way out."

"I wonder if there are fish in that pond," she mused.

"Pond? That, my love, is a small lake. Near as I can figure, this bowl is about seven miles across and twelve miles or so long. That lake looks like a pond from here, but I'm willing to bet it covers several acres. I guess I'll have to make some kind of fishing rig."

Continuing to survey the land below them, she pointed. "Hey, there's our flag." Drawing a deep breath, she continued, "I believe there is some fishing gear under the bed."

Turning around, Matt surveyed the forest to his left and right and the mountain still rising behind them. The rock and mountain greeted one another at either end of the outcrop, making entry to the rock only moderately difficult. "I don't think we should climb any higher today. Save it for a day when there hasn't been rain."

"Beautiful sky. I wonder if that one small cloud feels as lost as we do?" she thought aloud. "You know, this could be quite a vacation if we had planned it. A beautiful valley."

"Yes, well this is NOT the one we planned. If it's somebody's idea of a joke, I'm not laughing. I am a bit concerned about how we are going to eat when our food runs out. When I get my hands on whoever did this to us . . ." Matt ground his teeth, staring across the valley for nearly a minute. "Ready to head back?"

Frustrated, she agreed.

Matt slid down the hill where they climbed onto the rock, then caught Barb as she came down. Situating their packs, Barb asked, "Matt. Do you think we could find that lake on the way home?"

"I suppose it's possible, why?"

"I'd like to wash my face with clean cold water and it didn't look to be that far from camp."

"Yes, I guess you're right. It's worth a try."

Maybe the cold water will wake us from this nightmare! Barb thought to herself.

Matt paused before bending over to pick up his walking stick. Looking at Barb, he sighed and wrapped his arms around her, holding her tight. She reciprocated. Squeezing a bit more, he whispered, "I have no idea where we are or how we got here, but we will find a way out."

Barb returned his squeeze, then pushed him away. Wiping a tear from the corner of her eye, she declared, "Come on, I want to wash my face."

Without another word, Matt picked up both walking sticks, handed one to Barb, turned toward the north and began walking. When they came to another wall of bushes, they began going down the hill along the wall. Twenty minutes later, the ground leveled out and the forest opened up providing a longer line of sight. Matt checked his compass and set a course going north-north-east.

An hour and a half after discovering the lake from the mountainside perch, Barb knelt down on a large rock and dipped both hands into the lake. Splashing the cool water on her face enlivened tired senses. Without looking up, she did it again, soaking in the freshness of the water as it wrapped around her face, replacing an aching weariness. Barb then drew a deep breath and looked up, across the shimmering lake. Tears immediately began to swell behind her eyes and she whimpered, "It's still here. We aren't where we're supposed to be. It's all real." Sighing, she put her wet hands on her knees and stood to face her unwelcome reality. Casting her eyes around the lake, once again, she whispered so softly that only the breeze, and one other might hear her. "God, what have we done to deserve this? Show us the way home, please." Shaking her head with frustration, she looked around the lake shore for her husband.

As Barb washed her face, Matt looked around the bank in the area where they stopped and found tracks of deer, racoon, and bear. Searching the forest, he breathed a sigh of relief that he did not see any bear. Feeling somewhat safe, he walked along the left, or westward, bank a hundred feet, or so, until his path was blocked by trees. He was searching for signs of man; a discarded fishing lure, a rusted beer can, a piece of string. Anything. He found nothing.

Returning to his wife, he knelt down on the rock she had used and refreshed himself as well. Before getting up, he looked out across the lake. Trees circled the entire body of water. Sometimes right to the water's edge, other times stopping ten to fifteen feet back. A movement in the water caught his eye. He smiled as a large trout swam past. Watching the fish swim away, Matt appreciated how round and healthy-looking it appeared. Then, looking more closely at the water's edge, he noticed several bugs scooting across the surface. *This lake is quite healthy*, he thought to himself.

When he stood, Barb asked, "Okay, eagle scout, which way back to camp?"

"I really have no idea, but south I think." He then pulled out his phone and powered up the GPS app. Once again, the screen lingered a few seconds on their campsite before showing their current location. "That's strange."

"What?" Barb asked as she stepped next to her husband.

"It shows us where we are but does not show the lake. We are standing beside the lake, but it isn't on the screen. There seems to be a lake several miles to the north, but not here."

"GPS must be wrong. Refresh it."

Matt tapped a refresh icon. "Nope, still not there." Shifting the screen slightly with his finger, he found the locator for their campsite. "Found the campsite, just over a mile, maybe two, due south." Before turning the phone off, Matt saved their current location, beside a lake that apparently wasn't there.

Their journey from the lake to their campsite was almost relaxing. The hills were gentle, the forest was not as dense as in other areas, and Barb spotted their red tablecloth long before they passed it. Once back in camp, Matt dropped his pack in a chair and entered the camper.

"What's the hurry?" Barb asked, following him.

Lifting the bed, Matt looked into the storage area beneath. "Looking for that fishing gear you said might be here. I saw a large trout when we were at the lake." Finding an old spinning rig, he retrieved it, along with a small tackle box.

"You aren't going back up there today, are you?" Barb challenged. "It's getting a bit late in the day."

"No. First thing in the morning, but I do need to make sure this rig is serviceable. What are our dinner choices?"

Returning to the folding chairs by the fire circle, Barb listed their options. "I believe we had planned to visit a local grocer for meats, so we don't have much. A package of dinner franks, really just big hot dogs, then there are the staple cans of Dinty Moore Beef Stew and I believe we also have Brunswick Stew as a reserve."

"The dogs, are they on ice?"

"Ice is giving out, but no, they are in the fridge. How long you think the gas will last?"

"The first tank was nearly full, but I filled the second tank last week. Just in case. We could be okay for a couple weeks."

"A couple weeks?!" Barb exclaimed. "I don't like that."

Matt took a deep breath and tested the fishing rig, casting a weight into the bushes. Trying to smile with hope, he responded, "Franks tonight, fresh fish tomorrow?"

Matt found a couple sticks they could use to cook the dogs over an open flame. Each cooked a second while eating their first frank. While they did have two cans of green beans, a household staple, they voted to not mess up a pot tonight, saving the beans for later. The hotdogs were barely satisfying but did fill the empty spot in their stomachs. For desert, Matt tested his misshapen coffee pot over a bed of glowing embers. He smiled when he heard the familiar percolating pops as water began to heat and transform into black deliciousness.

Half way through their coffee, Barb interrupted the silence. "Matt, do you see any way out of this place?"

"What, you want to leave already? I thought you liked it here."

"Funny. How the hell are we going to get out of here?"

"Based on what I saw up on the mountain, I'm not sure. Crossing the river isn't an option, so that leaves going over a mountain. My gut tells me we should follow the river, go south. The mountain to the south looked like a tough journey, passable and maybe not quite as bad as what we did today. I wish we had some decent binoculars."

"You mean Angela's bird binoculars won't work?"

"Only if my head was half the size it is and what I wanted to see was between twenty-five and thirty feet away. . . . No, thank you."

"So, what do we do?"

Matt paused in thought as he swallowed a large gulp of coffee. "While I would like to relax and do battle with a trout tomorrow, I think we should try the southern ridge. Pack enough sandwiches for two, maybe even three meals and go south. From what I could see, it might be tough but still the least severe climb. When we get to the top, maybe we'll see something that will spur us on."

"Spur us on?"

"You know what I mean. Something to encourage us to continue that direction. You want any more coffee?"

"No. I'll just have to get up in the middle of the night."

"Okay. I'll clean up and make sure we don't leave anything out for the bears. Join you inside, shortly."

"I'll help. Where's the solar panel?"

"I put it in the Durango this morning. I'll test it when we need power or have time to play with it."

Together, they stored the folding chairs beneath the camper. Matt hung the still misshapen grate on a nearby branch, which had been broken close to the tree trunk by the bears, and stirred the fire. Once the fire was down, he poured the remaining coffee onto the embers and dumped the grounds fifty feet behind their campsite; hoping that was far enough. He stored the coffee pot in the back seat of their SUV and took the cups into the camper with him.

Snuggled beneath a single blanket, Matthew and Barbara each said a silent prayer and listened to the quiet of the night.

Five

Day Three

Lying in bed, Matt looked out the window. Darkness was just beginning to fade. *Daylight's still an hour or so away*, he thought. Unable to go back to sleep, Matt quietly fixed a cup of instant coffee and took it outside. After setting up both chairs, he sat facing the east and waited for the sun to rise. The morning air was cool, but he didn't notice. Sipping his coffee, his mind replayed every event that had happened on this camping trip, from the delayed start to seeing the trout swimming in the lake. While events of Tuesday were unfortunate, there was nothing about them that signaled or warned him about this current situation. The only odd occurrence was the change in campsites. Looking down the hill to where site fifteen might have been, he dismissed the change in site as merely a favor on the part of the campground host.

He was halfway through his first cup of coffee when beams of sunlight began to shine through tree branches above his head. Taking another sip, he considered the view from the granite ledge on the mountainside. *Like Barb said, this would be an ideal vacation if it was voluntary and we could get out when we wanted to.* His mind raced between thoughts. *Still, how did we get here and how are we going to get out? Driving is out of the question and reaching the ridge to see what's beyond could be somewhat more of a challenge than we're ready for.* Preparing his mind for this very challenge, he studied his memory of the southern ridge, what he saw from the granite outcropping.

Wait a minute, let's look at this logically. Simple six point analysis. Who, what, when, why, where, how?

Who . . . no idea at this time, not enough information.

What . . . irrelevant, we are not where we are supposed to be.

When . . . there is a puzzle. Could this be a time warp of some kind? Haven't seen anything to indicate this. Still, not a pleasant thought.

Let's see, where . . . THAT is the million-dollar question. Where the hell are we and HOW did we get here.

Wait, I've missed one . . . who, what, when, where, why - WHY . . . why would someone do this to us?

"Good morning; pretty sunrise," Barb commented as she slipped her hands down Matt's chest from behind. "Thanks for letting me sleep, I needed it." Seeing Matt's mug was nearly empty, she offered, "You ready for another cup of coffee?"

"Yes, just about." He squeezed her left hand with his and drank the last of his coffee. Lowering the mug to his lap, he reconsidered. "No . . . I need something I can get a handle on, something to ease my mind. I think I'll fix us some pancakes. Maybe you can fix the coffee while I do the batter?"

"So, is that a yes or a no?"

Standing and wrapping his arms around his wife, Matt smiled. "Yes to a second cup and pancakes."

Pancakes were a camping tradition for Barbara and Matthew, though they usually had them on the first morning, not the third. They also enjoyed hiking and exploring the forest around their campground, but this was the first time they had been concerned with survival. Their schedule for this trip was to arrive Tuesday afternoon, enjoy the great outdoors for three relaxing days, then return home on Saturday. They brought enough food for six days, allowing for some choice of meals, and had planned on eating out while driving to local attractions. Steak from a local butcher was also anticipated, but that hadn't happened as yet. Today was Friday and neither had anything other than wishful dreams of returning home tomorrow. Barb always packed extra cans of soups and stew and such as rainy day reserves; these supplies would last only four more days.

Working side by side inside their camper, Matt and Barb cleaned up breakfast and fixed sandwiches for the day ahead. Each loaded their daypack with three sandwiches, several packs of snack crackers loaded with peanut butter, cookies, and three bottles of water. Matt made sure his phone was in the side pocket.

Stepping outside, Matt closed the camper door and patted his pocket, checking for the key so he could lock it. Reaching into his pocket, he realized the senselessness of his action and simply shook his head, inwardly hoping Barb had not seen. Raising his pack to his back, he wrapped a hand around his walking stick and took three steps to Barb's side.

"You ready?" Barb asked, then snickered, "Camper locked?"

Matt exhaled heavily, looked to the east, then toward the westward climb from yesterday. Squaring his shoulders, he stepped decisively between the two previous treks, starting today's southbound journey. Turning his head back toward Barb, he glared with embarrassment. "Let's go."

"We've put quite a dent in our bottled water," Barb commented after a few minutes.

"But we have the empties. If we don't get out today, we can refill them tomorrow at the lake."

"You certain the water is safe to drink?"

"As certain as I can be. We have searched for some sign of life and found nothing. Who or what is going to pollute the water, besides wild animals? What I could see of the lake tells me that it is healthy and not polluted. Besides, do you see an alternative?"

"Yeah. I'm still looking for that cold cola at the country store. Any chance we might get there today?"

"I saw a pig fly on the internet not long ago, so sure, there has got to be a chance. With an ounce of luck we'll see something of civilization when we reach the southern ridge of this beautiful resort valley."

"'Resort valley,' right." Barb snickered at Matt's sense of humor. "Any idea how long it'll take?"

"I'm hoping for about two hours, possibly three. Maybe eat lunch with a new view and improved sense of where we are." Cresting a hill, Matt paused to check his compass. Sighting a landmark on the next hill, he took Barb's hand and continued.

Landscape on this southern journey was more open, the forest less dense than either of the previous treks. The terrain was just as hilly as the eastward journey, but trees seemed to be somewhat more mature, with more space between them. As they continued further south, the ground had less undergrowth, making walking much easier.

Matt's estimate of reaching the ridge in two hours was much like a weatherman's forecast of when rain might start. Two and a half hours into their journey, Matt and Barb ran into a new obstacle. Emerging from the trees into what they thought would be a meadow, they found a ravine. Standing beside a great crevice spanning approximately twenty feet and appearing to be about thirty feet deep, both sighed with frustrated disappointment. Looking east and west, this jagged barrier continued out of sight in both directions.

Dropping his pack, Matt pulled out a pack of cheese crackers and a bottle of water. Munching on his snack, he walked up and down the crevice; peering down and left and right. After five minutes of pondering, he walked over to Barb, who was sitting on the ground, eating peanut butter crackers.

"What say we go west?" he offered.

"Why?"

"Well, we know the river is east, and we can't cross that. If we go west, I figure we'll either find the end of the hole or climb the mountain. I don't think this thing will split the mountain, do you?"

"I've given up thinking about this bizarre 'resort forest,' as you call it. If I had a bottle of whiskey, I might just sit here and drink it. I'm sure some sort of solution would come to mind."

Extending his hand, Matt smiled and helped his wife to her feet. "Yep, but where would that solution take us?"

Barb shook her head, took her husband's hand, and they headed westward, toward the mountain.

"What do you suppose caused this crevice?" Barb asked as they hiked along its northern edge.

"I have no idea, but if I were to guess, I'd say it's just like the river. A barrier put here by God to keep us from escaping this desolate forest," Matt replied. His voice betrayed a growing anger and frustration.

"Matthew, this forest is anything but 'desolate'."

"Okay, not desolate. Lush, yes. Green, yes. Full of life, yes. Friendly, enjoyable, welcoming? NO!"

Matt's pace became more forceful as he replied to Barb's jab about the forest being "desolate." He relaxed, however, after a quarter mile when he realized the crevice did not rise and fall. The terrain beside the terrestrial barrier was more flat and easier to walk. Trees grew up to the edge of the ravine in places and back about fifteen feet in others, similar to the surrounding forest. After a mile of weaving between widely spaced trees, they saw hope ahead. A tree lay across the ravine.

"You think we can use it as a bridge?" Barb asked cautiously.

Examining the tree from fifty yards away, Matt replied, "Possibly. Depends on how long it's been lying there. Could be weak or rotten on the other side. We'll look at it and see." He was extremely hopeful but tried to keep hope out of his voice. He wanted desperately to get out of this valley, but also wanted to do it alive.

Walking up to the large linear section of the trunk, Barb asked, "What do you suppose made it fall? I haven't seen any other damage around this area."

Looking at the trunk and the hole where the tree once grew, Matt chuckled. "Bear. Look at the tree, what would have been about six to eight feet up. Claw marks and not as though a bear was looking for bugs. I'm willing to bet a cub, or two, climbed up and couldn't get down. Thunder storm rolled in and momma bear wanted her babies on the ground with her."

"You're telling me a bear pushed this tree over?"

"Root base isn't that healthy, so sure, why not? You have a better theory?"

"No. Do you think we can cross on it?"

Matt was already trying to check out the top of the tree resting on the other side of the ravine. "Looks strong enough, maybe. How do you feel about walking on the log?"

"Scared as hell! But what choice do we have?"

"We could continue up the ravine, it can't go on forever."

"Have you seen anything that makes you think it ends anywhere soon?"

"Nope."

Without another word, Barb walked around the stump and climbed up on the fallen tree. At the base it was a good eighteen inches across and six feet from the edge of the crevice, which was at least thirty feet deep. Standing tall, she looked at the pathway ahead of her. Ten feet away, one limb jutted out to the right, then five feet beyond that another stood almost vertically in her way. The crevice was about twenty-five feet wide and roughly fifteen feet of the top of the tree rested on the other side.

"Here goes," she whispered, trying to take a deep breath for stability. Using her walking stick as a balance pole, she stepped slowly out across the ravine. Matt watched her every hesitant step, his heart pounding in his throat. She passed the first limb without difficulty but stopped to examine her options when she reached the second branch.

Ten feet from the far side, the trunk had shrunk to about twelve inches, and a branch tilted less than ten degrees off vertical, to the left. She would have to squeeze around it. Slipping the loop on her walking stick around her wrist, she grabbed the branch with both hands and moved her right leg around the obstruction. Straddling the limb, she paused and took a deep breath. When she finally shifted so she could pull her left leg around, the tree rocked. Instinctively, Barb wrapped her arms around the tree branch in front of her, closed her eyes, and held on.

"You're okay!" Matt called to her. "It was only a slight shift, you are okay. Relax so you can turn around and finish the crossing. You are okay!"

Barb opened her eyes and glared at her husband. "Easy for you to say, you're standing on firm ground." Slowly, she took another deep breath for stability, turned around without completely releasing the limb, and steadied herself once more. One more deep breath and she stepped forward. Without realizing it, Barb ran the last nine feet and lunged off the fallen tree. It rocked back as soon as she left it. Bending over with her hands on her knees, she looked back at Matt. "Your turn."

Learning from Barb's example, Matt hopped up on the tree, steadied himself and walked smoothly to the vertical limb. He, too, looped the strap on his walking stick around his wrist and stepped around the obstacle, one leg at a time. As before, the tree rocked when he pulled his left leg around, but he expected this and simply balanced himself on the branch when it happened. A few seconds later, he turned and walked down the top of the fallen tree, hopping off next to his wife.

"Show off!" Barb jabbed.

"Hey, you showed me how it was done," he chuckled. "You ready to climb a hill?"

"Can you hand me a water bottle?"

"Sure." Matt pulled a bottle from Barb's pack and handed it to her. She swallowed two large gulps and handed it back to her husband. He took one gulp and returned it to her pack. Before stepping off, Matt registered their location in his GPS.

Less than one hundred feet from the ravine, the terrain resumed its familiar rise. This time, however, it did not roll but continued upward at an increasing angle. A half hour into their climb the incline was so steep Matt pulled himself up using small trees, then assisted Barb by pulling her up with her walking stick.

Seeing no end to this ascent, Barb stopped and bent over, supporting herself on her knees. Out of breath from exertion, she stated unquestionably, "I can't keep this up. We've got to find another way to the top."

Leaning on his own walking stick and also out of breath, Matt looked left and right, east and west, before replying. "We know the river is a couple miles to the east. When we went west, we used deer trails until the climb got to be too steep. Which way you want to try?" He then took a bottle of water from his pack. After several short gulps, he offered it to his wife.

Barb slowly straightened up before accepting the water. She then took several short gulps and handed the bottle back to Matt. Looking straight at her husband, she pointed toward the river.

"Okay. East it is. May I ask why?"

"Cause that's the way I'm facing and I don't want to turn around."

Chuckling slightly, Matt leaned over and kissed his wife. He then turned around and assumed a gentler eastbound ascent. Walking on the side of a steep incline is not much easier than going straight up; harder on the ankles and legs. They made slow progress, turning every ten minutes, or so, and climbing the opposite direction. After two and a half hours their climb ended. Reaching the ridge did not give them any comfort, however, for all they could see were trees. Not off in the distance, but all around them.

"We need to find a clearing before we drop down the other side," Barb suggested.

"Why? What are you thinking?" Matt asked, thinking he might know the answer.

"I'm exhausted and it's getting late. I need to see something to go to, not just blunder around in this damnable forest forever."

"We never did stop for lunch and it seems to be about two o'clock. We've been pulling hard and I kind of agree." Pausing, he looked up and down the ridge. The slope on the far side of the mountain appeared to be similar to what they had just climbed and vegetation just as dense. Seeing what appeared to be more light about 100 yards toward the west, he suggested, "Let's see if that's your clearing just up there. Regardless, we will stop, eat, rest a bit, then make whatever decision there is to be made."

"Seems to be 'two o'clock'? More boy scout training?" Barb asked as she started trudging toward the brighter area.

"Sun is past its peak, just a bit, and my watch says ten past two." He then took her hand and they walked side by side.

Reaching an area of sunlight, both Matt and Barb drew a deep breath of awe. A rockslide, approximately thirty-five feet wide, had created an opening in the vegetation on the south side of the mountain. Forested hills and mountains extended all the way to the horizon. While the view was breathtaking, there were no signs of smoke or roads; absolutely no signs anywhere of civilization or even a hermit wanting to be alone. Dropping their packs, both plopped to the ground, pulled out sandwiches and water, and ate. Silently.

Finishing one sandwich, Barb looked out across the mountains then down to her second sandwich. "Well, do I save this one for a midnight snack or are we heading back to the camper?"

"I hate to be blunt, but I have no desire to die in the wilderness. I see no destination. Nothing. If we go back, we at least have water and a source of food until we can figure something out."

Opening her second sandwich and taking a bite, she responded, "Figure something out. Isn't that what we are doing on this expedition?"

"Well, yes. Actually we have discovered east and south are not the directions to go home. What say we do some fishing tomorrow; rest a day before we try the western ridge again?"

Chomping another bite laden with frustration, Barb challenged Matt's logic. "Why the western ridge? Why not follow the river? Don't rivers always go somewhere?"

"Usually. But if you will recall, my GPS showed this river takes several significant waterfalls. I'm not sure we're up to climbing down steep cliffs. We don't have the gear to do it safely."

"I don't care about 'SAFELY'! I want out of here!" Barb continued to stare across the forest, fuming with anger and frustration.

Matt stuffed the bag from his first sandwich back into his pack. After standing to stretch, he polished off the bottle of water he had been working on all morning and stuffed it back into his pack. "Whenever you are ready, we can begin our slide down the mountain."

"What?! You want to go straight down the mountain? Not back and forth the way we came up? Are you crazy?!"

"Yep, at least a little. I would like to get across that ravine and back to camp before dark. The thought of walking that tree in the dark scares crap outa me. . . . So, yes. I'm going DOWN the mountain. You coming?" He then extended his hand to help her up.

"We gotta be out of our minds to attempt this. Let's go," she muttered as she turned her back to the rockslide.

"It won't be so bad," Matt encouraged. "Just plant your heel firmly and grab a tree. Don't go too fast and we should make it down safely and in plenty of time for supper at camp."

"Whoopee, another sandwich."

"What, are we out of Dinty Moore?"

Barb just glared at her husband and walked down the ridge toward the first drop.

Neither Barb nor Matt ever thought about why they never encountered a deer trail on this slope, it was simply too steep for routine travel. They did, however, develop a quick and easy method of descending steep slopes. Drop to both heels and grab a tree. Matt dropped his walking stick four times, each time watching it slide down ahead of him. Barb dropped hers only three times. They stopped twice to catch their breath and empty dirt from their shoes. The sun was about to touch the western tree line when they reached the ravine.

"Okay, eagle scout, where is the bridge?" Barb asked, emptying dirt from her shoes.

Matt dumped his shoes, as well, before pulling out his phone. Finding their crossing, he saw the battery was now at 48%. Moaning, he turned it off. "West, about a half mile." He then reached out for her hand and they continued their adventure.

Reaching the fallen tree, Matt put his hand out to stop Barb from climbing into its branches. Looking around on the ground, he found a sizable limb which he jammed under the edge of the fallen giant. Pulling himself up on another branch, he verified that it shouldn't rock while they crossed. Matt went first to test his solution. He did feel a slight movement, but nothing like the threat they had experienced before. Barb paused after working her way around the limb, still expecting some significant movement. Leaning against the obstacle after a minor shift, she took a deep breath and tripped lightly toward her waiting husband.

Placing her hands on his shoulders and looking into his eyes, she asked, "What direction now?"

Not wanting to waste the battery on his phone, Matt used the compass and sighted a line of travel. "North by north east. If we miss camp, we'll probably find the lake or a stream leaving the lake."

Walking beside her husband, Barb took his hand. "I didn't see any stream leaving the lake."

"I didn't either, which makes me wonder about what feeds it. The water was fresh. Something to explore when we go fishing tomorrow."

At one point Matt tried to whistle a melody, but that lasted less than a minute. Both were too exhausted to spend any energy on anything not absolutely necessary to get them back to camp. Stopping at the top of a hill for a water break, Matt checked the compass to verify their direction. Barb looked around through the fading dusky light.

"That tree, I recognize it from our first day out," Barb commented, pointing toward a large oak which divided into two trunks about eight feet above the ground.

"It does look familiar," Matt agreed. "Let's turn west and see if we can stumble into camp."

Trudging through a darkening forest, both Matt and Barb caught scent of something that didn't belong. Looking at one another, both declared, "Coffee grounds!"

Ten minutes later they plopped into folding chairs beside their fire circle. Too weary to fix supper, they devoured what was left of their travel sandwiches and water. Exhaustion overwhelmed any desire to discuss revelations of their latest

adventure and bed was more inviting than a late night cup of
coffee.

Six

Day Four

Rolling over in her sleep, Barbara awakened to an empty bed. Matt was not there. Rising quickly, she pulled on her shoes and rushed out the camper door. She found Matt sitting in a chair, sipping on a cup of coffee, and staring out into the forest.

"Don't let the door slam. There are five or six deer down the hill," he told her in a voice just loud enough to reach her ears.

Looking in the direction Matt was staring, past large oak and hickory trees to the edge of a rhododendron thicket, she saw one large buck and one doe staring back at her. Another doe grazed while two spotted fawn wobbled between them. Barb closed the door carefully and stood behind her husband. "Wow."

"Couldn't be more than a day old."

"Wonder if that's one we saw the other day. She was about to pop."

"Don't know." He then sipped his coffee and continued to watch. "Water should still be hot if you want a cup of coffee."

"In a minute." She then opened a second chair and sat.

Seeing the humans watching, the buck casually corralled his small herd and they moseyed off toward a nearby hole in the rhododendron thicket.

"They don't seem to see us as a threat," Barb commented.

Matt took a sip of coffee before replying. "Makes you wonder. Deer are normally very self-protective and as you said, they don't see us as a threat. May be odd, but I don't feel any danger here, either. I'm not happy being imprisoned, but I don't sense any danger."

"Don't get too comfortable. I'm hungry and I want to go home. The sooner the better!"

Rising from his chair, Matt gave his wife a peck on her cheek. "Yes, ma'am! Message received. Bacon and eggs will be cooking momentarily." Stepping toward the camper, he paused. "I'm going to freshen my cup, you want some?"

"Sure. I'll be in in just a minute." Scanning the forest directly in front of her, Barb drew her arms in tight, hugging herself, as she felt a tear roll down her cheek.

"What are our plans for today?" Barb asked, crunching her last piece of bacon.

"I'd like to slow down just a bit. See if we can catch a few fish. Smoke 'em this afternoon so we have protein for a few more days. I'm tired of canned stew."

"Good thing. We don't have but two more meals in cans. Bacon's mostly gone. No more eggs. Four hotdogs and rolls left, and lunch will end our bread supply and sandwich meat. We're about done with food we brought for the weekend."

"How could we be out of food already? It's only Saturday? We planned to go home today."

"Cause we had planned on replenishing supplies at the store down the road. Add a couple steaks, maybe even some cold beer." She looked at him with wide eyes as she explained their situation.

"Right. Maybe I should see about some rabbit traps."

"Have you ever trapped a rabbit?"

"No. But I do know the basic principles." Matt smiled with artificial confidence.

"Let's go fishing. That you have experience with."

Standing beside the lake, Barbara watched Matthew tie a small spinning lure to the old fishing line. He had three choices: a silver spoon with green skirt, a red striped spoon, and a wounded minnow. Thinking the minnow would float and the spoons would snag on rocks, he picked the minnow. His first cast went a bit awry, landing barely twenty feet from shore. With Barbara laughing quietly, about twelve feet to his right, he reeled the lure in and tried again. His second cast sailed a beautiful sixty feet before splashing into the quiet lake. As he began retrieving his cast, working it slowly, Barb kissed him on the cheek and began strolling around the east side of the lake, to Matt's right.

"Hey, Barb, why don't you refill our water bottles?" Matt called as she walked away.

"Sure." Barb picked up Matt's rucksack and strolled over to where they had washed their faces two days before.

Positioned in a five-foot gap between two scrub bushes, Matt had easy access to the water. A tree stood a couple yards to his left, but his right was clear of obstacles, making right-hand casts easy. Each cast helped him recover forgotten talents and was now routinely landing his lure well into the lake. Feeling good about fishing, he worked the lure with growing confidence, which gave him a growing sense of calm. His calm was suddenly interrupted by a strike just fifteen feet from shore. A fish was investigating the bait and Matt had to be attentive if he was going to catch it. It was three more casts before he actually got a hit; a hungry fish was testing the lure. Working the lure in place he got a second hit and hooked the attacker. Not sure how strong the reel and line were, Matt worked the fish gently for five minutes, landing a large brown trout. With the fish safely on the bank, he pulled an old hook stringer from the tackle box, multiple diaper-pin style clips on a metal chain, and tried to rinse some of the rust off. Wanting to get back to fishing, he soon gave up on cleaning the stringer and secured his catch. After hooking the stringer to a bush to his left, he tossed the captive fish back into the water and prepared to catch another.

Once again his first cast fell short, however while retrieving it he looked around the lake for his wife. His first scan missed her and he started to panic. The pack of water bottles was on the bank where she had filled them, but where was she? Scanning the apron between the lake and trees more carefully, he spotted her squatting on the bank. Relieved, he released another long cast, this time squinting at sunlight reflecting off the water. The sun had risen well above the tree line and while it was not shining in his eyes, it was illuminating the entire surface of the lake. Reaching into his shirt pocket, he retrieved his sunglasses.

His eyes now protected from glare, he looked around the lake once more for his wife. To his utter surprise, she had taken her clothes off and was stepping into the water. Her dark hair lay gently on her bare white shoulders. Her shape was still enticing to Matt, and he couldn't take his eyes off her. Feeling a strong strike on his line, he instinctively jerked the pole, setting the lure hook securely. Matthew was now in trouble. He had a powerful fish on his line, yet he was completely distracted by his wife, who was now thigh deep in the lake and bending over to look at something in front of her. His heart beat fiercely as he wrenched his head back and forth between his catch and his wife. Leaning over, her image twisted Matt with desire. He wanted nothing more than to be beside her, wrapped around her, enjoying every sensual inch of her feminine form.

Fighting every urge to drop the fishing pole and dive into the water to be with Barbara, Matt landed the fish and hastily secured it to the stringer. After returning his catch to the water, he ran around the lake. By the time he had removed his clothes and stepped into the water, Barbara was in water just below her breasts and smiling appreciatively at his enlarged manly form. Seconds later he wrapped his arms around her and kissed her as if they were on their honeymoon, thirty years before.

"You do make it hard to fish for our supper," Matt breathed heavily when their lips separated.

Looking down in the clear water, Barb chuckled slightly. "Not so hard anymore . . . I didn't tell you to stop."

"Yes. Well. What are you doing in this freezing water?"

"I told you, I wanted a bath. Not really enough hot water in the camper, so this is what we get. Find us a way to get home and we can share a hot shower." Smiling seductively, she stepped back two paces and playfully splashed water on her husband.

Fifteen minutes later, Matt helped Barbara up what appeared to be stone steps at the side of the lake. Both stretched out in the soft grass, enjoying the drying warmth of direct sunlight. As Matt warmed, his appreciation of Barb once again began to rise. Rolling over to kiss his bride, she yielded to his touch and they made love with an intense passion, as though they were newlyweds.

While getting dressed, some forty-five minutes later, Matt noticed a rash-like mark on Barb's cheek and neck. As he stroked it gently, she chuckled. "You need a shave, young man."

"Oh, sorry."

"I'm not." Her eyes twinkled above a delighted smile.

They finished dressing and while Matt tied his shoes, he noticed something in the trees opposite where they had entered and left the lake. Thirty feet inside the tree line was what appeared to be an old log cabin.

Approaching the structure cautiously, they discovered it was indeed what it appeared to be. A log cabin. Boards on the front porch area, which was only inches above the ground, were decayed and gave way to their weight. Barb reached over and pushed on a rocking chair, which collapsed at her touch. Matt found the floor boards inside the structure were still sound, as were the walls. The roof, however, was collapsing in spots. Looking around the one room structure, measuring twenty feet square, they found a rickety table with two chairs, an old bed frame with remnants of a rope lattice, and a rusting two burner iron stove. An open cabinet, about four feet long, provided shelves and a work area. A rusted out pan, roughly twelve inches wide, six inches deep, and eighteen inches long, presumably used as a sink, sat on top.

"Well, somebody lived in this valley once upon a time," Matt sighed.

"Which explains the stone steps going into the lake," Barb agreed.

"Hey, this could be a real fixer-upper, if you're interested," Matt chuckled.

"No, thanks. I'll stay with our camper . . . or better yet, find out how whoever lived here got in and out, and go home!"

"You have a point. Whoever lived here had to have gone out for supplies and such. We know they didn't go over the mountain, so must be some way through it. A cave or tunnel somewhere."

Barb and Matt stared at each other, wheels spinning in both brains. Matt was the first one to speak. "Must be a tunnel somewhere at this end, else why would he settle here?"

"The lake provides water," Barb responded calmly, yet chewing slightly on her lip.

"Tell you what, I have two fish that need cooking. What say we smoke the fish this afternoon and begin a search of the base of the mountain tomorrow. Begin with whatever feeds this lake."

"Sounds like a plan," Barb agreed as she made her way out of the cabin. When they reached the lake, she poked Matt in the belly and laughed, "You don't suppose we made a baby this afternoon?"

Matt stared at her and smiling replied, "No can do. Took care of that after Bobby was born."

Hand in hand, they strolled to where Matt was fishing. As he retrieved his gear and two fish, Barb asked, "Don't you want to try for some more?"

"No. Sun's too high. I could come back this afternoon if you're interested in another bath." Looking to the sky, Matt shaded his eyes and commented, "Well, that rules out a time warp."

"What?"

"I had wondered if we were caught in some kind of a time warp. The answer is definitely no."

"Not sure I had thought about a 'time warp,' but how do you know?"

Matt pointed overhead. "See that contrail, the jet vapor trail? Appears to me to be four engines, possibly a 747. I could be wrong, but it is definitely a commercial sized jet airplane, so we haven't been mysteriously transported back in time."

"What if we jumped forward in time?" Barb asked, teasing Matt's sense of logic.

"You really think this valley will be here in this pristine condition one hundred years from now?"

Looking at the contrail, Barb replied, "I don't know about one hundred years, but maybe just thirty or forty?"

"You mean just long enough to miss our children having children? I don't want to miss that!"

Smiling at one another, they picked up the pack of water and began their trek back to camp.

Reaching their trailer, Matt instinctively began looking for a bucket he could use to ice the fish; keep them fresh until he could clean them. Standing dumbfounded beside their SUV, the pleasures of their visit to the lake vanished when he declared, "We don't have any ice!"

"And I'm not sure how much longer the fridge will last. How much gas do we have?" Barb replied. Her face showing a deep concern.

Reality had returned with a thunderous blow.

Taking a deep breath, Matt suggested, "I haven't switched tanks yet, so we still have a full can of gas waiting. You fix lunch with whatever we have and I'll get a fire going so we can smoke these fish. We can share one tonight and enjoy the other tomorrow."

"Sure, if the bears don't get them," Barb quipped.

"Right! I'd better get busy!" Matt dropped the fish on a rock in the fire ring and stomped into the woods to collect fresh hickory.

Barb delivered their last three sandwiches as Matt rocked back from a growing flame. They each ate ham and cheese, and split the third which was peanut butter and jelly. Washing the last of the peanut butter down his throat with air-temp water, Matt stood and looked to his wife.

"Sharp knife. I need a strong sharp knife to clean these fish."

"Second drawer, next to the stove. Help yourself." She smiled just a bit and stroked Matt's hand as he stepped past her. Looking down into the fire, she felt another tear roll down her face and thought to herself, *We will get out of here. No idea how, but we will get out of here. We won't die in this forest!*

Being mindful that fish remains can attract any number of wild beasts, from birds to bears, Matt took his fish beyond where the bathhouse should have been. Finding a large rock, he pushed leaves away from it and began scraping scales off the first trout, sunshine beaming down on his back through a small opening in the canopy. After gutting the first fish, he realized he had forgotten a few essentials. "Barb! Would you please bring me a plate and a bottle of water from the lake!"

Barb delivered the requested supplies and stood over Matt as he finished cleaning the first fish. When he dropped it on the plate and started to work on the second of his catch, she asked, "You aren't going to cut the head off?"

"Naw. I've always seen smoked fish with the heads on. Not sure why, but at least it's one less thing I have to clean up."

"What are you going to do with their insides?"

"Bury 'em. We do have a shovel, don't we?"

"Your dad's old army shovel."

"That'll do . . . If I can get it open. . . . Eh, we'll see in a bit. I need to get these beauties over the fire. How's it doing?"

Barb turned and looked at their fire circle. "Probably should add some more wood. I'll take care of that and you finish cleaning our supper. I just don't want it to be our last."

Without looking up, Matt felt Barb's despair. "Naw, we have two meals here . . . and tomorrow, I'll set some rabbit traps."

Barb responded with cold command. "No! Tomorrow we look for how the old hermit got in and out of this valley!" She then went to tend to the fire.

Returning to the fire with their fish, Matt found Barb sitting in a chair and one of two special sticks, which he had set aside, in the fire. "I was going to use those forked sticks to smoke the fish! I'll go get another. Meanwhile, please keep the fire growing, but DON'T use that forked stick!"

"Sorry, I didn't know."

Matt handed the plate of fish to his wife, kissed her on the forehead, and tromped off into the woods. He returned five minutes later with an armful of fresh wood. Dumping it beside the fire, he pulled one forked stick out and trimmed it with the axe. He then pushed both forked sticks into the ground inside the fire ring, on either side of the fire, and began to spread the fish on the prepared sticks. Barb couldn't help but chuckle when it was not as easy as Matt had anticipated. Eventually, with a bit of engineering and more small hickory sticks spreading their sides, he had both fish cooking over a fire that was rapidly changing to glowing embers.

Once he had the fish cooking, Matt went to work burying the scales and innards. The screw lock on his dad's old "Army" shovel took some persuasion, but with careful whacks of the axe and dousing with water, he got the shovel open and usable.

Over the next three hours, Matt repositioned the fish three times so they could take advantage of the heat and smoke. Realizing what he had done wasn't quite right, he longed for the Internet so he could look up how to smoke fish properly. As daylight began to fade, he and Barb sat beside the fire, each with half of one fish on their plate. They carefully picked tender meat off the bones and as the last pink of daylight disappeared, Barb announced, "Well, you better be good at trapping rabbit. That second fish was delicious, too good to save for tomorrow. But . . . now we don't have anything for supper tomorrow."

"What about hot dogs? Besides, daily trips to the lake don't sound so bad."

In the dim light of the dying fire, Barb could see the gleam in his eyes and the broad smile on his face. She could only lean over and kiss him. Then, after drawing a deep breath, she responded, "Dogs will be lunch. You clean up the fish and I'll start the coffee."

Standing, he returned her kiss. "Sounds good."

Matt collected all the fish bones, there was no meat left, and took them over to where he had cleaned the fish. After dumping them into the hole with the cleaning debris, he covered the hole and whistled as he returned to the camper. Checking the gauge on gas tank mounted on the trailer tongue, his smile increased. They had one full tank and the other was one-third full.

Sipping on fresh hot coffee, both Barbara and Matthew felt more hopeful about their tomorrow. Matt told her about the gas supply and they discussed how they might find the old hermit's exit, agreeing that since they did have two more meals in cans, the exit would be their focus for the next few days. When they finished their coffee, Matt used the last bit in the pot to extinguish the fire and both made sure there were no food remnants in their immediate camp area.

Snuggled into bed, spooning tightly together, Matt began teasing Barb about their swim. It wasn't long before their newlywed urges returned.

Seven

Day Five

Matt awoke the next morning more relaxed than he had been in many months. Still, something had pulled him from a deep sleep and he couldn't identify what it was; it was dark outside. Realizing neither he nor his bride had any clothes on, he snuggled back down under the covers. Barb intuitively rolled over, resting her head on his shoulder, her body aligned with his. Just as Matt closed his eyes for a few more minutes of contented sleep, he heard a strange noise. Slowly, his mind realized this was the same noise that had awakened him. Hundreds of bees! A swarm of bees! He suddenly realized there had been a hum of bees, so quiet it almost wasn't there, then the sound grew in a rush and quickly faded away into nothing.

Carefully sliding away from Barbara, he pulled on clothes and shoes. Opening the door, he looked cautiously into the dark, then slowly stepped outside. The strange noise, and whatever seemed to have created it, was gone. Wishing he had thought to grab a flashlight, he looked around their campsite in the dim light of predawn. All was quiet, nothing was out of place. Everything was as it had been the past four mornings of this unusual trip. Turning to go back into the camper, he caught a glimpse of a large shadow in the small clearing about fifty feet in front of his SUV, where the bathhouse was supposed to be.

His eyes growing accustomed to the darkness, he strolled carefully toward the shadow. As he drew closer, he realized the shadows were actually crates, plastic bins. Two plastic storage bins. The larger of the two bins was about two and a half feet long, a foot and a half wide, and just over a foot high. The second was only about two feet long and proportionally smaller. Looking to the sky and listening, he realized what he had heard were not bees but drones. *These crates were delivered by drones!*

Allowing his curiosity to overpower his caution, Matt opened the larger of the two bins. He found boxes of cereal, a box of instant grits, a jar of coffee (not his brand), bread, and cans of vegetables, soup, and stews. Ripping the top off the second bin, he found two reusable frozen ice blocks with ground beef, bacon, hot dogs, assorted lunch meats, a dozen eggs, and two half-gallons of milk. All total, it was enough food to keep him and

Barb fed for about seven days. Realizing what he had, Matt looked frantically for a note or letter or some explanation for their situation. Finding nothing, his emotions rocked between gratitude for the food and outrage for being held prisoner.

"AAAARRRRGGGGGGGHHHHHHH!!!!!! WHOEVER THE HELL YOU ARE, WE WILL GET OUT OF HERE! YOU CAN'T HOLD US HERE FOREVER!" As he screamed at the top of his voice, he slammed both bins with his feet, sending their contents sprawling across the ground.

Barb emerged from the camper a minute later, still trying to get her right shoe on. "Matt, what is going on?"

"The truth has been dumped on us! We are captives of some bizarre and sick mind!" he screamed. He was now picking the food up and putting it back into the bins.

"What's all this?" she asked when she reached her distraught husband.

"Food. Enough to keep us fed for about a week." He dropped a half-squished loaf of bread into the bin. "We are captives and this is our weekly ration."

"WHAT!?!"

"You heard me." Matt then picked up the bacon and dropped it back into the cold bin. "We've been wondering how and why we got to this place. We were kidnaped! Whoever did this must have figured we were running low on supplies and gave us a week's worth of groceries!" Matt was storming around picking up scattered supplies, still outraged by the situation. "We are nothing but hamsters in a great big cage!"

Barb remained silent, knowing her husband would have to calm down before he would talk sense. Matt took one more look around the area. Picking up one last can of Progresso soup, he dropped it into the larger bin, put the top on the bin, and picked it up. "Would you please get the smaller one. We will eat their food while we plan our escape!"

As they walked back to the camper, Barb called out, "Leave it outside. I'll put it away after we get coffee and breakfast. Anything that might attract bears will have to be stored in the car. I don't want them inside the camper. How would you like pancakes again?"

"Sounds fine. It's still some time till dawn, but I won't be able to sleep." Matt grumbled, dropping the bin at the camper door. His outrage subsiding, he calmed to a slow boil. "I need a cup of coffee."

Barb stayed out of the way while Matt fixed two cups of instant coffee; he took his outside to sulk and watch the sunrise. Barb went ahead and put the supplies in their small pantry and prepared to fix breakfast. Before mixing the batter, she took her coffee and went out to sit with Matt.

"No animals today," Matt grumbled as she sat beside him.

"Are you surprised?" she chuckled. "The way you exploded, I'll be surprised if we see any wildlife for days."

Matt gulped his coffee before continuing. "We've known this trip was screwed up! No way this is right! But to now be given a week's worth of groceries! It just turns that knife that's been in my side since we woke up Wednesday. . . . What day is it anyway? Sunday? Monday?"

"Sunday, I think. How did they deliver the stuff?"

"Near as I can figure, with drones. I thought I heard a swarm of bees this morning, which is the sound a pair of large drones would make. . . . I wonder how they'll drop a can of gas when we need that."

"Let's not wait around to find out."

Matt raised his mug in a toast to Barb's comment, "I'll drink to that!"

Seeing that Matt had calmed, somewhat, and sunlight was beginning to filter across the treetops, Barb went back into the camper to fix pancakes.

"Cakes are a bit richer than usual; what'd you do different?" Matt asked, finishing his stack of breakfast delights.

"I added two eggs that were cracked but still usable. Three didn't make it."

"Sorry."

Barb reached across the small table and placed her hand on Matt's. After a minute, she asked, "Plans for today?"

"Well, I don't have to figure out how to trap rabbits, so I think we should go explore the area around the lake. See if we can find the old hermit's way in and out."

"One more subject that I hate to bring up," Barb commented cautiously.

"What?" Matt looked at her with cold eyes.

"The toilet. How much longer before that holding tank is full?"

Chuckling slightly, Matt replied, "Good point. When we had all three kids camping with us, that tank lasted four days. It was near full when we dumped on the way out of the campground, but it was probably good for a couple more days, maybe. With just the two of us, we could get another four or five days before it tops out. I'll check the gauge." Opening the closet by the door, Matt pressed a few buttons, then turned to Barb. "Grey tank is half full. Black tank is three-quarters full. Guess I should start digging a pit for disposal. But more important, battery is about gone, again. If the solar panel doesn't work, no more fridge or hot water and we'll have to use the hand pump for water pressure."

"Better idea," Barb smiled. "Let's get out of here! Meanwhile, I'll clean the dishes and make us a couple sandwiches, I think I saw some sliced ham in that delivery."

"Great idea."

While Barb made sandwiches, Matt took a second look at the solar panel the baby bear had knocked around. Placing it in the best sunshine, which was filtered, he connected the controller and turned it on. This panel was supposed to produce one hundred watts, which was good enough to charge the battery; unfortunately the controller reported only forty-three watts. Chastising himself for not putting the panel away when he should have, he connected the wires to the battery and hoped for the best.

Walking toward the lake, Barb couldn't resist taking a verbal jab at her husband. "Just how many times did you kick that bucket of food?"

"What are you talking about?" Matt replied, returning from a journey through his own thoughts.

"That bin of food. How many times did you kick it? Eggs were broken. Bread was squashed. You really did a number on it."

"Yeah, well . . . sorry about that. I guess I lost it a bit."

"A bit?"

"It's just . . . well, we've known we didn't get here on our own, still no idea how we did get here, or even where 'here' is, but those rations just rubbed our noses in the fact that we have no say in our activities. We are prisoners!" His temper began to flare again.

"But we are going to find a way out, right?" Barb tried to soothe his anger. "I mean, I haven't seen any guards with rifles. We could always pack up all those supplies and go over the southern ridge. Can't we?"

"Yes, I suppose." Matt marched on, more determined than before to find a safe escape.

Reaching the lake, Matt stopped at the steps going into the water, his back to the log cabin, and looked around, studying the mountains and forest to the north and west. His eyes took in every foot of lake shoreline, the surrounding tree line, everything from water's edge to blue sky.

"What's that?" Barb asked, pointing toward the log structure.

"What?" Matt asked, turning to see what she was pointing toward. "We've already checked that building out."

"Yes, but there are two other buildings down there. One to the right and another to the left, behind the cabin."

Matt stared into the forest. Morning light filtered down through the trees revealing two structures they had not noticed before. Dropping his pack to the ground, Matt replied, "Let's go see. Maybe there is a hidden staircase to Narnia." He immediately started down toward the cabin.

"That was a wardrobe, not a staircase," Barb corrected as she followed.

Twenty yards to the right and ten yards down the hill behind the cabin they found a small wooden structure. Matt chuckled, "An outhouse." Looking inside, he continued, "Not bad shape, though it could use a new seat."

"Seat? What seat?" Barb laughed. When Matt pointed toward an oval hole in the wood, she exploded."That hole in the plank? Not me!" She then tapped the wood supporting the seat with her foot. It went through, creating a hole in the side.

Looking in a corner, beside the door, Matt found a book crumpled on a shelf, behind a decaying board. Lifting it, he laughed. "An old Sears catalog!" He put it back where he found it and suggested, "Let's go see what the other structure is."

To the left rear corner of the cabin was a small stone building, measuring about six feet by eight feet. Steps came down from the main building into this odd little building, as though it had once been connected. Pulling the decaying door open, they found a trough about thirty inches high, made of stone. A creek bubbled from the wall on the lake side and disappeared into the stone wall on the downhill side. The temperature was significantly cooler inside.

"It's a food locker!" Matt exclaimed. "The running water cools the building like a refrigerator. Ingenious!"

"Nice, but no door to Narnia?" Barb asked, not as impressed as Matt by this find.

"No, but it does tell us something about the old hermit. Let's get back up to the lake."

Returning to the sunshine, Barb turned to her husband. "Okay, Sherlock, what have you learned about our hermit?"

"That stone food locker kept food from spoiling. Cooler in the summer, kept it from freezing in the winter. He packed in enough supplies that he didn't have to go out very often. I'm willing to bet it wasn't an easy trip so he made it count. Probably only left his paradise two, maybe three times a year."

"Whenever he needed pipe tobacco," Barb quipped; her enthusiasm rapidly draining.

"Well, possibly. More likely flour, gun powder, and stuff he couldn't get from the land. I'll bet we'd find a nice garden plot around here, if we looked."

"I don't want to grow fresh veggies. I want to go home!" Barb exclaimed.

"Me, too, but let's look at this thing before we go off the wrong direction. We didn't find any personal belongings . . . nothing to suggest he went for supplies and couldn't get back. Either he left, intending to not return, or somebody else has cleaned up after him."

"Yes, so?" Barb responded, opening a bottle of water.

"We know it's no easy climb over the top of these mountains. More difficult if you were carrying six months of supplies. I said it yesterday, and now I'm more certain . . . there has got to be a tunnel through the mountain, or a low pass, somewhere."

"Let's go find it!" Barb replied, pushing her water bottle back into her pack and lifting it to her back.

Picking up his own pack, Matt suggested, "Let's find the creek feeding this lake, then follow that creek." He then leaned over and kissed his wife with a new enthusiasm.

Turning north, they walked along the edge of the lake, encountering two briar thickets and a rhododendron thicket, all of which they went around rather than through, before finding a creek at the northwestern corner. Matt stared at the tributary wondering aloud, "This isn't much of a creek to feed that lake. . . . Still, a bit more than what we saw in the food locker." Shrugging with resignation, he led Barbara upstream.

This delightful little stream flowed fairly straight toward the lake, with only a few bends. It measured only two to three feet wide and four to eight inches deep, rolling gently over stones that almost seemed to have been placed there to guide the water. A quarter mile from the lake they encountered a small pool created by a log lying across the stream. Water expanded to about ten feet before flowing over the log and continuing to the lake. Noticing deer prints around the edge of this anomaly, Matt looked around for signs of other wildlife. Finding only evidence of rabbits, he looked to the trees. This part of the forest was much like that around their camper, oak, hickory, a few scattered hemlocks, though none seemed to be as large. He did spot several squirrel nests in the higher branches.

Walking around the pool, Matt caught sight of a crawfish sitting next to a rock. Recalling how he caught these water critters as a boy, he dropped his pack and stealthily knelt by the water. Reaching into the pool with his left hand, he alarmed the crawfish which scooted backwards into his right hand. Examining the creature, Matt smiled and showed it to Barb. "See how clean his shell is? Another sign that the water is safe."

"So what are you going to do with it? Catch more for supper?"

"Naw, I'll put 'em back." Matt then leaned over the pool and carefully let the critter scoot away. Standing, he picked up his pack and declared, "Onward! Follow this creek!"

Matt and Barb chatted sporadically about the beauty of the forest and both wondered, aloud, who had put this stream there. While it had been flowing for decades, possibly longer, it just didn't seem to be natural. Did the hermit create this stream to fill the lake? And if he did, where did the fish come from?

Almost a mile beyond the pool, emerging from the forest, they found the source of the stream, and decided it was indeed not entirely natural, though it could have been created by an earthquake. Rising before them was a wall of stone with two waterfalls. To the right, or east, was the main river roaring over a cliff and tumbling one hundred feet, where it smashed into a bed of rock forty feet wide and eight to ten feet across, then tumbled over large stones another twenty feet before continuing southward.

Near the top, about ten feet below the fall, a boulder diverted water into a much smaller fall, only eight feet wide, which became the creek they had been following. Both curtains of water clung close to the stone wall behind them and were separated by a rock outcropping that began halfway up the cliff, jutting out nine or ten feet at the bottom.

"Well, is there a tunnel or cave behind the waterfall?" Barb asked, hopefully.

Matt studied the wall behind both falls. Red and white stone were apparent. There were no dark spots that might indicate a hollow space, the presence of a tunnel or cavern. He even poked the wall behind the smaller fall with his walking stick, confirming that what they saw was indeed solid rock.

"Doesn't look like it. . . . Pretty though, don't you think?"

Both Matthew and Barbara stared at the two waterfalls for nearly a minute. She reached out and took his hand as both sighed in dismay. Hopes of finding an easily accessible tunnel dashed onto the rocks, just as the water falling over the cliff above.

"How about we enjoy the peace of this wondrous spot with a sandwich?" Barb suggested, half-heartedly. "Then we can continue our search along the base of the mountain."

"Sure," Matt agreed. "There are miles and miles of mountain that can hide all sorts of secrets."

Both sat quietly enjoying the sound of the waterfall and the peace of the forest. Each had their own thoughts bouncing around. When she finished her sandwich and washed it down with half a bottle of water, Barb asked, "You said the food bins were delivered by drones. Where did they come from?"

Swallowing his last bite, Matt replied, "No idea. If there is a tunnel, they could have been launched from there. Or, they could have come over the mountain. I really don't know."

Barb considered this as she packed up her gear and made ready to move on. Matt did likewise. Lunch completed, they started heading south, keeping the base of the mountain to their immediate right. Matt examined the hillside, looking for some sign of a passageway. Barb did as well, but also watched the forest to the left and ahead of them.

The mountain side near the waterfalls was primarily rock, which slowly gave way to scrub then forest. After a hundred yards, the hillside was fully forested, covered with brush, hardwoods, and a few hemlock. Grasses were thicker toward the falls and thinned to nothing as the forest took over. The base of the mountain began to curve, creating coves and ridges. Looking toward the lake, the land was primarily flat and covered with a healthy stand of hickory, oak, poplar, dogwood, and occasional hemlock. Rhododendron thickets dotted the terrain, both lakeside and mountain, as though placed on a model train layout.

"So, how did they find our camp? If they came over the mountain, wasn't it dark when the packages arrived?" Barb asked after twenty minutes.

"I didn't see the drones, I just heard them. I can only imagine how large they were and what types of cameras they used for eyes. While it may have been a good payload for us, I'm sure they can handle much heavier and still deliver with expert precision. Modern drones are really something."

Several times during their walk, Matt climbed up the base of the mountain to examine a rock outcropping or a forest cove. Every search yielded only frustration and more anxiety. Progress was slow and conversation sparse. During a break, two hours into their search, Barb stood up straight and stared into the southern forest.

"What's wrong?" Matt asked, trying to see what had captured her attention.

"Not sure. I thought I heard something off in the forest. Something like a chainsaw, but it was real faint. I can't be sure."

Matt listened. "Sounds like it might be bees . . . or maybe just an old car rumbling down the highway."

Barb paused and grimacing at Matt's attempt at humour, drew in a deep breath, not sure whether to chuckle or cry. Letting her breath out slowly, she asked, "Any idea how close we are to camp?"

Dropping his pack so he could retrieve a bottle of water, Matt replied, "No. I was just asking myself that same question." He paused and drank nearly a quarter of the one-liter bottle. "I was thinking about going back the way we came, then back around the lake. Give this hillside a look from the opposite direction."

Still staring off into the distant forest, Barb responded. "You can if you want. I think I see our red flag. Not sure, but it could be."

"Where?"

Barb pointed toward the west-south-west. A hint of red shown through the trees.

"Your eyes are better than mine," Matt confessed. "I do believe you are right and I would never have seen it. Missed it completely." He then paused to wrap his arms around his wife and hug her hard. Both realized how hopeless their situation was and that they needed each other now more than they ever had. Each had clung to the other when Bobby was killed, relying on the other's strength to pull them through. They made it then, together. Both knew that together was the only way they were going to make it now. After a moment of silent contemplation, Matt sighed. "Let's go back to camp. Lead the way, Eagle-eyes."

Barb chuckled slightly and struck out toward the red flag hanging in the trees. Reaching a knoll, they found a tree with brilliant red spring foliage. A rhododendron thicket spread out to the southwest making further passage in that direction impossible.

"How's your phone doing?" Barb asked, her frustration showing in every syllable.

"Battery's going. How about we just follow the northern edge of this thicket and see where we end up?"

Stepping off without another word, they followed the edge of the bushes as though it were an improperly placed mountain lake. Nearly half an hour later, Barb stopped and pointed up the hill, ahead and to their left. A red tablecloth hung in a tree and their camper was visible below it.

Reaching camp, Matt dropped his pack by the fire circle, pulled out both folding chairs, then disappeared into the camper. Seconds later he emerged with two small bags from their morning delivery. Plopping down into the empty chair, he tossed one of the bags to Barb and ripped the second open.

Seeing Matt popping cheese-covered puffs into his mouth, Barb chuckled. "I thought you hated those things."

"I do, but right now I think I'd hate BBQ Chips even more."

"Well, thanks for the Salt & Vinegar. I like them."

"Now you know the three flavors available. No plain, just three flavors I can't stand. Eh."

Matt continued to pop the snacks into his mouth, one at a time, getting cheese powder all over his fingers and lips. Barb chuckled and enjoyed her selection.

Finishing his snack, Matt asked, "Supper?"

"We need to eat those hot dogs we opened a couple days ago. They'll go bad if we don't."

"Fine. I'll gather some wood for the fire." Matt then stood and tromped off into the woods to collect fire wood.

Holding her hotdog on a forked stick over the fire, Barb broke the silence that had deadened the past two hours. "What are our plans now?"

Twirling his stick so he could see how his dog was cooking, Matt replied, "We know the river blocks an eastern escape. We could go south, but how far before we find help? The deer have provided a relatively passable climb to the west, 'cept we haven't made it to the ridge yet. And the river and mountain form an effective barrier to the north. But somehow, I know that is the way to go. West. I still can't believe somebody lived in this valley and climbed over the ridge every time they needed supplies. There has got to be some passage through the mountain, somewhere in the lake area."

"How do we find it?" Barb asked, pulling her dog off the stick with a less-than-fresh roll.

"I don't know," Matt responded, pulling his somewhat burned dog off as well. "Right now, I have two thoughts. First, we go back along the base of the mountain back toward the lake. Same route as today, in the opposite direction. Keep an eye on the hillside for something we haven't seen down low. If we don't find anything tomorrow, then I suggest we try to make the western ridge the next day. Whoever delivered provisions can't be but so far away; we just need to find out where."

"I thought you said they could be on the other side of the mountain."

"Or on the other side of the river . . . I don't know. I don't know the range of the drones I heard."

The waning fire crackled just a bit as Matthew and Barbara sat close to it. Webbing wrapped around aluminum frames gave them comfortable support as each ate their dogs in silence. While cooking the second round, which emptied the pack of big dinner franks, Barb asked, "You going to fix coffee tonight?"

Matt thought for a moment, looking to the bed of coals and watching his dinner second-course blacken. "Yeah . . . sure. Might do us both a bit of good."

Minutes later, as Matt put the coffee pot over hot coals, Barb murmured, "Don't forget the solar panel."

"Thanks, I'll take care of it right now." He then walked to the far side of their SUV and picked up the panel and controller. After disconnecting the wires from the battery, he stored everything in the closet by the door, then checked the status of the battery on the control panel. Returning to the fire, he reported, "Battery is just over half-charged. I'll need to hook it up again tomorrow." Leaning back in his chair, he picked up on the aroma of perking coffee.

Stars were just beginning to twinkle in the night sky as the stranded couple finished their coffee that night. Exhausted from the day, the trip, their situation, neither made a move to get up and go to bed. Instead, they leaned back in their chairs and watched the stars arrive, recognizing them as the same stars that sparkled over their back yard at home.

Eight

Day Six

Matthew lay in bed and breathed in the fresh air. It had been warm enough the night before for them to open windows on either side of the bed. A gentle flow of fresh air helped both campers sleep more soundly. Lying on his back, head on the pillow, Matt stared at the ceiling and pondered what they might not have tried or done in their efforts to escape. Where had they not looked? Where had they not gone? Muddled answers caused him to give up on sleep and get out of bed.

Sitting on the side of the bed, looking out the window, he rubbed his face with dry hands then stretched. Feeling how rough his hands had become, he looked at them and sighed. Conceding that another day had started, their sixth on this bizarre trip, he stood and pulled on pants, shirt, socks, and shoes. Early morning's first light illuminating his efforts, he stepped to the sink and pumped water into the kettle; using the pump saved the battery and was less likely to wake Barb. He had enough for only one cup of coffee when the faucet sputtered. Heaving a sigh, he thought, *Out of water. Need to get some from the lake today.* Reaching into the pantry, he retrieved a bottle of drinking water and poured it into the kettle.

While the water heated on the gas stove, Matt stepped outside. Trudging thirty feet, more or less, behind the camper, he stopped and relieved himself. Returning, he setup two folding chairs. As he lifted the chairs from their resting place against the camper, he realized they had never set up the awning. Looking around, he thought, *Enough room . . . but naw, don't need it.* Morning chores done, he stepped back inside and added instant coffee granules to two cups and waited for the first whistle from the kettle.

"What's that?" Barbara asked.

"Sorry to wake you. Fixing coffee. Kettle just called. You want a cup now or later?"

"Now will be fine. I'll be out in just a minute. How's the day look?"

"Don't know really; haven't paid attention to it. When you come outside, we'll check it out together."

Barbara stretched and yawned in reply. "O-k-a-y."

When Barb settled into the chair beside Matt's, he told her a bit of bad news. "Last cup of coffee for a bit. Water tank gave out. We'll need to get some from the lake. Five gallons at a time."

"Don't we have two jugs? The big one and a three gallon collapsible thing?"

"Haven't used that collapsible in years. You think it might be safe?"

"We can rinse it with hot water."

"I suppose." Matt pondered the idea and drank from his coffee cup. "We can take both bottles with us this morning. The big jug is okay, but we can check the collapsible to see if it still holds without leaks. Then use a bit from the good jug to *sterilize* it."

"Sounds like a plan," Barb replied, yawning once again. "So, we're going to the lake today?"

"Indirectly. I thought we'd reverse our trek from yesterday. Get a different view of the base of the mountain. Start behind the camper and end up at the lake. Get water and return to camp. Need to take all the empty drinking bottles, too."

"Wasn't there water in the grocery supply?"

"Yes, I guess so. But don't throw any of these empty bottles away."

"I won't. Hey, two questions."

"What?" Matt asked, turning toward his wife.

"First, what are we going to do with that bag of trash we're collecting? I haven't seen any cans around." Her voice dripped with sarcasm.

"What's your second question?" Matt replied, not attempting to answer the first.

"What's for breakfast?"

"Not really very hungry. What do we have in cold cereal?"

"Oh, we are rich in cold cereal. They sent us a twelve pack assortment of sugary delights."

Matt looked to his wife and groaned.

Barb had a box of Frosted Flakes while Matt ate a box of Sugar Pops. Recalling that as a kid he just added milk to the box, Matt looked for the perforation on the side. Unable to find this critical line that converted the box to a bowl, he tore the top open. After pouring his cereal into a bowl he looked into the box. "No lining! What's the point of a personal sized box if you can't eat from it? It saved cleanup."

"Because most kids just eat this sugar coated nonsense as a snack, not a meal. You are showing your age, my dear."

"UGH!"

Finishing breakfast, Barb wiped both bowls and spoons off with a paper towel dampened from a water bottle. Matt was busy assembling sandwiches and stuffing them into plastic bags saved from previous lunches. He then dug into the camper's storage bin and pulled out both water jugs, though the collapsible container was more difficult to locate amid deflated floats, play equipment, ropes, and such.

His backpack with lunch and water on his back, walking stick in his right hand, and the big jug in his left hand, Matt looked to his wife. "Ready to go find our magical escape?"

"What about charging the battery?"

Matt looked up as he replied. "Won't do much good today. Too cloudy."

"Okay." Barb slung her pack on her back, grabbed her stick and the collapsed jug, and replied, "Lead on."

Heading due west, they turned to the north when the terrain changed from rolling to inclined. They had gone less than a hundred yards when they noticed a group of deer watching them. Matt and Barb smiled and continued their journey of the day. At one point, Matt stopped and stared at the hillside. He had spotted a dark area behind a young hickory tree. Dropping the water jug, he trudged up the hill, roughly fifteen yards. Filled with excitement and energy, he poked into the ground with his walking stick.

"What is it?" Barb asked, when she joined him.

"Just a wash. A shallow in the hillside. It looked dark and I hoped it was the portal to a tunnel. Sorry to get so excited." Turning back to their discarded jugs, he moaned, "Let's keep looking."

They found two more shallows in the hillside, however their excitement waned with each disappointing examination. Reaching the waterfalls, they stopped for lunch. Barb kept looking at the smaller waterfall as she ate, believing it might solve one of their problems. After stuffing her empty sandwich bag and half-empty water bottle back into her pack, she picked up the collapsible water jug and walked over to the smaller cascade. Standing just outside the splash zone, she removed the spigot and held it under a stream running just off the main flow. The jug filled quickly and with little splash.

"Well, it holds water," she announced.

"Very good. How about you empty it down to about half gallon and we boil that water to clean it," Matt suggested.

"Sure. I'm going to rinse it good first." Barb swished the water in the jug and poured it out. She repeated this several times, before doing as Matt had suggested, saving just over half a gallon for sterilization. She then turned to her husband, asking, "You going to fill the big jug while we're here? This little stream makes it real easy."

"Yes, but it also adds a mile to carrying it back. Forty pounds for an extra mile doesn't sound like much, but . . ."

"Maybe so, but there isn't any mud in this water. How are you going to get water from the lake without getting mud in it?"

"Those steps aren't muddy and there's lots of grass or weeds growing beside them. I should be able to draw water from there."

"It'll take you an hour to fill that jug."

Matt sighed and conceded. As he unscrewed the cap, he challenged his wife. "You going to help me carry this thing when my arm gives out?"

"Sure," she replied with a chipper smile. She felt she had won a contest without even trying.

Matt rinsed the big jug several times, as Barb had, then filled it just shy of full. Screwing the cap on he turned to Barb. "Let's head back. I have a feeling this will be a long, slow journey."

Barb chuckled as she lifted her relatively light collapsible jug and followed Matt along the creek. Matt stopped twice to shift his jug from one hand to the other before reaching the lake, and again upon arriving at the cabin. Each time he worked his fingers and rotated the arm that had been carrying the water.

Stopping beside the steps into the lake, he looked at his wife. "You said you were going to help. Give me your walking stick." He put his hand out expectantly. When she frowned and handed him her stick, he slid both sticks through the handle of the larger jug. Holding out his hand, he said, "Give me your jug." She complied and he slid the handle of this smaller jug down the two sticks. "Now, let's see if we can get back to the camper." He lifted both walking sticks in one hand and waited for his wife to do the same. Her hands were not as large as his and she fumbled a bit getting the sticks settled into a firm grip.

Seeing Barb was ready, Matt set an easy pace for this last leg of their morning travel. After half a mile, Barb stumbled as she shifted the weight and orientation of the sticks in her hands. Her shoulders feeling the weight, she tried to carry them with both hands, which made walking difficult.

Reaching their camper, Barb collapsed into a chair and heaved a sigh. "I never realized water could be so heavy."

Matt chuckled and proceeded to pour the contents of the larger jug into their fresh water tank. Returning to where Barb was sitting, he advised her, "We really need another jug. Get enough to keep us for a few days."

"Are you going back to the waterfall *now*?"

"No. Just back to the lake. Think I might do a bit of fishing, too. You coming?"

"I don't think so. You go have fun, I'm needing a bit more rest."

Kissing his bride on her forehead, Matt struck out for the lake with fishing gear in one hand and the practically weightless water jug in the other. Arriving at the lake, he strolled over to the spot where he fished successfully before, dropped the jug and fish stringer on the ground, and threw his first cast. Minutes later he slipped a fourteen-inch trout on the stringer and went after another. It took only five more casts before he landed a twelve-inch fish and decided to call it a day. He had two nice fish for dinner and proceeded to refill the jug at the steps.

Kneeling on the top step, which was above the water line, Matt leaned over and carefully dipped the jug into the water. With no effort at all, it began to draw water from the surface and was soon two-thirds full. "I knew I could fill this thing without getting any mud in it," he said to himself with satisfaction.

With fish and fishing rod in his right hand and a two-thirds-full jug of water in his left, Matt headed back for "home." The added weight of the water made the mile and a half journey seem like ten miles, but he pushed on until he found Barb sleeping in her chair outside their camper. Without waking her, he added the water to their tank and proceeded to build a fire to cook their fish.

Barb woke while Matt was building the fire and took over fire duties so he could clean his catch. Recalling that he had seen some heavy duty aluminum foil in the camper, he wrapped the fish in foil and dropped them directly into the hot embers. After fifteen minutes, more or less, he turned them over using two sticks. Clumsy but effective. Ten minutes later he heard a change in the sizzling sound coming from the fish and decided to remove them from the fire. This time he used the sticks to simply drag them away from the embers where he could more easily grab them. Burning his fingers a bit in the process, he dropped them on plates. One for each of them.

Curling the foil back, Barb marveled at how good hers looked. Then she tasted it; the meat flaking off the bone. "Could use a bit of spice, next time."

"I agree. I'll see what we have in the camper and put an order in to the grocer for what we need," Matt chuckled sarcastically.

Finishing his fish, Matt was about to start a pot of coffee for their evening repose when it started to rain. Not a heavy rain, but just enough to drive them inside. Barb collected their dishes while Matt knocked the fire down so it would not burn into the night, or burn their forest down. By the time he had finished his work, the rainfall was increasing.

Matthew and Barbara turned in early that night, listening to rain beat on their camper roof.

Nine

Barbara and Matthew lay in bed together, their bodies aligned, holding hands, and listening to the rain beating rhythmically on the roof of their camper. This gentle sound lulled them into an easy and peaceful sleep. Their sleep was abruptly shattered sometime during the night when a clap of thunder shook their small home.

Seconds later, before the shock of thunder had completely faded, they felt a heavy slam against their camper. Then another at the end opposite their bed, then another near the door. Fear escalated to panic when they felt their bed rocking. In the dark of night, with rain pouring outside, they could not see anything, but they felt as though they were caught in a major earthquake. That is until they heard the source of their rocking. A deep guttural snarling.

A large male bear had discovered their camp site and was not happy with their presence. Shining a flashlight out the window on Barb's side, all they could see was what appeared to be a furry belly. The bear was on his hind legs, his front paws above the window, pushing against the trailer. Neither Barb nor Matt could move as drool and slobber dripped across the glass of the window. Then, with a fierce growl, the creature pushed off the camper and smashed one of the chairs left beside the fire circle. A second chair sailed off into the forest.

Their eyes now adjusted to the dark, Matt and Barb watched as the bear moved to their car, snarling with discontent and bumping against the side of the Durango as he passed. Reaching the front of the vehicle he reared onto his hind legs and slammed both front paws down onto the hood with a bone chilling roar. As his roar faded, he sniffed the air. Dropping back to the ground, the beast ambled over to where Matt had cleaned fish for supper.

"I forgot to bury the fish guts!" Matt whispered with regret.

"What?!" Barb challenged, her voice barely loud enough for Matt to hear.

"I was going to bury them after dinner, while the coffee perked. Then it began to rain and well . . . I forgot."

After slurping up the rain soaked fish remains, the bear looked back at the campsite and roared belligerently once more.

Rain pouring around him, he sniffed the air. A bolt of lightening highlighted his silhouette as he ambled down the hill.

"Don't have to bury them now," Matt chuckled, trying to ease his own fear after the clap of thunder faded.

"Next time you clean fish you bury the remains RIGHT THEN!!!" Barb chastised, still in a hushed, yet angry voice.

Hearts pounding, they both laid back on the bed, not quite as close as they had been minutes before. Rain pounding on their roof did nothing to relax either one. Barb heard Matt's breathing relax some time later as he slid into a deep sleep. She stewed and said multiple prayers; thanks for staying alive, a prayer for release from their nightmare, and for patience until they got home. Her heart more calm, she too eased back into a deep sleep.

Day Seven

Morning arrived without sunshine. The sky grew somewhat lighter, however rain continued to fall. Not wanting to get soaked, Matt used the toilet in their miniature bathroom. Flushing it, he noticed that there was a "ripe" aroma coming up from the holding tank. Shining a flashlight down the utility, he could see the tank was essentially full. Refuse was within inches of the connecting collar below the toilet. "One more day," he moaned to himself. "Please, Lord, one more day. I don't want to dump this thing in the rain."

Pumping the water handle below the kitchen sink, Matt listened to sputter, sputter, sputter, then flow as air pushed water through the line. Putting just enough water into the kettle for two cups of coffee, he carefully placed the pot on the stove and lit the burner beneath it. Placing one hand on either side of the stove, he leaned forward and breathed deeply, desperately seeking a more comfortable peace.

"Is it still raining?" Barb asked as she stretched in bed.

"Not as hard as last night, but yes."

"I had the strangest dream last night," Barb continued, with a yawn. "We were attacked by a humongous bear."

"That was NOT a dream. I'm a bit scared to see what it did to the car, not that it matters."

"So you *really* forgot to bury the fish and we *really* did have a huge bear rock this camper?"

"Yep."

"Why can't I dream about going home?"

Matt smiled at his wife. "Grits for breakfast?"

"Sure, why not."

Just then the kettle whistled and Matt finished making their first cup of coffee to start the day. He then refilled the kettle with water for instant grits. Barb climbed from the bed and squeezed past Matt so she could reach the bathroom. Closing the door, she exclaimed, "UGH! We've got to do something about the tank!"

Matt remained quiet.

Scraping the last bite of country bacon flavored instant grits from her bowl, Barb asked, "Plans for today?"

Matt looked out the window. Rain was now falling with an increased intensity. "Sit inside, where it's dry . . . read a good book. I think I brought one."

"We haven't had much time for reading this trip, have we?"

"Oh, we've had the time but my mind has been rather full trying to plan a trip back home." His voice betrayed his ever growing anxiety.

"How's that going?" Barb grinned at her husband, trying to help him relax just a bit.

"Maybe a good novel will inspire me to see things I've missed."

Matt found his travel bag, stuffed in the wardrobe beside the bed, and dug out two books he had brought for reading. Deciding on mystery over fantasy, he tossed "Treasured Adversaries" onto the shelf over the bed and carried a Dan Brown novel, "Digital Fortress," over to the sofa. Without a second thought, he moved jackets and walking sticks from the sofa to the bed and plopped down to read. Barb wiped out their bowls with a wet paper towel, then picked a book she had been reading, from the shelf over their bed, and settled at the other end of the sofa.

This camper had been purchased slightly used from an engineer who upgraded to a full size motor home. Twenty-four feet long, it provided a queen bed at one end with a *full* bath at the other end. The bed had a narrow isle and wardrobe on either side with a shelf and reading lights over the pillows and ample storage beneath the mattress, which was also accessible through two small doors on the outside. Along one side of the camper were a sofa, which converted into a double bed, and kitchenette featuring a three burner stove, small microwave oven over the stove, two way refrigerator under the stove (gas / electric), a one basin sink, and pantry cabinet from floor to ceiling beside the sink. On the back wall was a corner bath and another closet, where the jackets were normally hung, then the entry door on the side. A large u-shaped dinette filled the space opposite the kitchenette. The dinette also converted into a full size bed. Next to the dinette was a low shelf with cabinets below. Situated opposite the sofa, this shelf was good for a small television, but Matt had refused to have one in *his camper*. This trailer was advertised to sleep six, however their boys would not sleep together, so one slept in a tent outside. The previous owner had added several improvements; including a pump to pressurize the water tank for when there was no water service or power and a removable black-water tank so they could dump sewage without having to move the trailer. Matt asked the previous owner why he didn't just use a portable dump tank. The engineer replied, "Tried that once. You'll appreciate this design if you ever have to use it." While it was a good camper for a family with three children, it was a better camper for a couple of empty-nesters.

Barb looked up from her romance novel and realized what Matt was reading. "You trying to escape our bizarre mystery by digging into another?"

Matt looked at the cover of his book and smiled. "Well, at least I know this one will end, in another two hundred pages or so."

"Hey, we could write this story of our vacation. It might become a best seller and make us rich!" Barb chuckled.

Matt scrunched up his face. "Naw, no way to make this adventure believable. Nobody'd buy it. Pure fabrication."

Barb chuckled slightly and returned to her romance. Rain continued to pound the camper; so heavy at times the occupants became concerned for their safety. The downpour subsided around midday, giving Matt a chance to go outside and stretch his legs. Walking around the camper, he found little damage from the bear attack the previous night. Only a few scratches. Their SUV, however, was not so lucky. The hood was smashed in and had scratches down to the metal from where the beast had drug his claws across it as he dropped back to the ground.

"It's going to cost a fortune to repair this. That is if the engine runs," Matt mumbled to himself. Suddenly he realized where he was. "What am I thinking? We'll probably never get this car out of these woods!"

He then looked at the forest that surrounded them, holding them hostage. Sighing, he felt the rain begin to fall again and returned to the camper, where Barb was fixing lunch.

"What'd you find out?" she asked, handing him a sandwich.

"Camper's fine. Bear left his signature on the car. Forest is still out there laughing at us." Matt tore a bite from his ham and cheese delight. Swallowing hard, he moaned, "I know there has got to be a way out of here, but I just can't find it. I don't even know which way to run anymore. I don't even think I'm angry any more . . . just lost. I can't think of a time when I had so little control over my situation."

"I can. When I was in labor," Barb reminded him, popping BBQ flavored chips into her mouth. "You wanted to move things along and not one of those kids listened. Everyone took their time and kept us in painful waiting for hours."

"Yeah, you're right." Matt grinned with memories of their children filling his mind. "Never listened to me later, either. Still, they are good kids." He then finished his sandwich with a smile on his face.

Finishing her lunch, Barb asked, "So, what are your thoughts for our next grande attempt to leave this woodland paradise?"

Matt swallowed the last of his lunch and thought. "To be honest, I really don't know. I need to dump the holding tank. That'll probably take most of tomorrow morning. Need to read the instructions again, so I don't screw it up. Then . . . I just don't know right now. You have any ideas?"

"Well, we will definitely need to go for a walk. This rain is really killing our step count. I mean, look how well we have been doing with all the exercise every single day!" At this point her voice changed from humorous to very sarcastic. "But I do agree that the waterfalls are hiding a secret . . . and we haven't been back to that overlook."

"Overlook?" Matt asked, puzzled by this suggestion.

"That big rock on the what . . . western ridge?"

"That slope above the rock was way too steep to try, especially with all this rain. It could be deadly!"

"Still, we haven't made it to the top, so we don't know what's on the other side. Could be Las Vegas is just over that ridge."

Matt took a deep breath and sighed. "Right. I think I'll take a nap. Wake me if anything important happens." He then moved to the bed. Finding coats and walking sticks in the way, he hung the coats up and put the sticks by the door, then returned to the bed and stretched out. Try as he might, he could not relax enough to fall asleep. His mind replayed their attempts to escape over and over again, each time looking for that one small detail they might have missed. After an hour, he returned to the sofa and "Digital Fortress."

Rain continued throughout the afternoon, bringing on an early dusk. Supper consisted of Dinty Moore stew, cold buttered bread, and water.

Looking at her water bottle, Barb asked, "I wonder if we could get some of that powdered drink mix, you know like peach tea or lemon-lime? I'm getting a bit weary of water."

"I'll ask the maitre d," Matt replied with a grin. "Would be nice though, a bit of variety."

Darkness filling the forest, the campers went to bed a bit earlier than usual. Rain fell steadily all night, with an even tempo, lulling both into deep sleeps.

Day Eight

Day eight began as day seven had ended, with rain. Resolved to make something of the new day, Matt prepared bacon and eggs with hot coffee for breakfast. His resolve faded somewhat when Barb called his attention to the rising volume in the black-water tank. Fortunately, the rain faded to a drizzle as morning progressed.

Reaching to the shelf in the closet by the door, Matt pulled down a notebook on trailer utilities. Flipping the plastic sleeved pages, he found handwritten instructions about removing the black water holding tank. Not wanting to get the notebook wet, he sat to the table and studied these pages, reading them in great detail, twice.

"Okay, first we have to release the tank by rotating a ring around the base of the toilet." He stepped into the bath and knelt next to the toilet. Finding a ring, as described, he tried to turn it, as instructed. Nothing happened. After a second attempt, he looked back at the instructions then knelt by the toilet again. This time he ran his fingers around the entire circumference of the ring. Feeling a clip on the back, he pressed on it and then tried turning the ring. It slid one quarter turn, counterclockwise, with no difficulty.

"He must have added the lock after he wrote the instructions," Matt told his wife. "Now, we drop the tank."

After putting on a jacket to provide some protection from the misty drizzle, Matt retrieved the stabilizer crank from the front storage bin. Moving to the rear of the camper, he told Barb, who was following him, "It says to first to remove the tank connector used to dump the black and grey water tanks."

Matt Looked at the dump valves, recalling how he would pull up to a dump station before heading home and use these valves to empty the tanks one at a time. Knowing this was not an option, he looked again and saw a ring, similar to the one below the toilet, on the black water tank below the release valve. Finding the lock tab, he pressed it and turned the ring. The U-shaped connecting pipe slipped away from the tank. Standing, he recited the next steps from memory. "Okay, now unplug sensor cable, release two holding straps, crank the tank down a few inches, slide a lock across the toilet connection, then crank it to the ground."

Looking under the camper, he found the sensor cable, a simple electrical wire with a four-wire lead and connector, like on a utility trailer. Unplugging it, he next found the straps as described and popped the latch on each one. He then inserted the crank, which was used to raise and lower feet which stabilized the camper, onto a rod above the holding tank. As he turned the crank, the tank began to drop. Stopping after a few inches, he found a cover on the toilet connection which swung around over the hole. Contents secured, he lowered the huge plastic container to the ground, just like a spare tire on some trucks. Once the tank rested on the ground, Matt slipped the lift cable from its slot and rolled the tank out from under the camper. It actually had two large wheels on one end and a smaller wheel near the other.

"That guy was a genius!" Matt exclaimed. "Now, where is the handle for this thing?"

"What does it look like?" Barb asked.

"Not sure. According to the drawing in the book, it slips over this handle on the tank and makes it easier to tow."

"Could it be about a foot and a half long and curved?"

"I guess, why?"

"Well, on a trip a few years back, Bobby was using it do dig up a rock. The rock was stronger than the handle and broke it. We didn't know what it was so I told him to throw it away."

"Okay. Let's see if we can get this tank moving." Matt paused before lifting the handle. His mind replayed antics of their youngest son, not only while camping but at home as well. Memories of the daredevil made him smile while tugging at his heart. Sighing, he reached down and lifted the handle of the septic tank, putting it down right away. "Ugh. Too heavy to lug all the way to the lake."

"YOU AREN'T GOING TO DUMP THIS IN THE LAKE?!"

"No, in the outhouse by the cabin. Either that or we dig a pit near here. The outhouse hole is already quite deep and smell won't bother us that far away."

"Okay," Barb agreed with little certainty.

"Let me get some rope. You get a towel I can put on my shoulder."

Matt went back to the storage compartment at the front of the camper and dug out a piece of old rope, as big around as his finger. After looping it twice through the handle of the tank, he wrapped the rope in the towel Barb provided and hoisted the tow rope to his shoulder.

The wheels on the tank were not designed for the terrain they had to travel, but with a bit of care and fortitude, they made it to the cabin in just under an hour. When they reached the outhouse, Matt pushed the tank in front of the hole in the seat cabinet, which he had made a few days before by kicking the wood to see how sound it was. Lying parallel to the ground, the tank stretched across the outhouse with the handle in the doorway. Squatting down he inspected the spout now resting next to the hole. Standing, he slid the tank back and made the hole a bit larger by kicking the top of it with his foot. "That should work," he mumbled and pushed the tank as close to the hole in the outhouse cabinet as possible before pulling the dump handle. Sewerage slowly gurgled from the tank.

"Press that orange button on the handle," he told Barb. When she did as asked, the sewerage flowed smoothly, almost gushing through the hole into the pit below. When Barb released the button, the flow stopped. "You have to hold it," Matt instructed.

"This thing is hard to push!"

"I'll do it," Matt conceded and moved to the other end of the tank, where he could hold the button. "You're right. This is a tough knocker."

Once the tank emptied, Matt raised the handle to encourage the last bit to leave, then closed the valve, commenting, "Should have brought those water battles. We could flush it out and add a bit of fresh water to help the chemicals work better."

"Just a minute," Barb responded and ran up to the cabin. She returned a moment later with a large pot. "Will this help?"

Matt smiled. "Yep." He took the pot from Barb and started toward the lake. "I'll be right back." Returning moments later, he set the pot filled with water next to the holding tank. After removing the seal over the toilet connection, he poured the water into the tank. Bending over he told Barb, "Help me shake this thing a bit."

Together, they lifted the tank and rocked it, swishing water around inside. He then emptied the rinse water. Grabbing the handle, he pulled the tank up the hill to the lake, where he added two pots of fresh water. Handing the pot back to Barb, he asked, "Why don't you store this in the outhouse. We might need it again."

Taking the pot by the handle, she moaned, "Hope not!"

While Barb took the pot to the outhouse, Matt closed the seal over the toilet connector. He had the rope over his shoulder and was ready for the trek back to camp when she returned.

"That wasn't so bad," Barb chirped as they walked.

"You weren't lugging the tank!" Matt retorted.

"So, it isn't even lunchtime. You think we can look for a way out this afternoon?"

"We'll see. First, we need to get this tank back where it belongs. Which way do you want to go?"

"I vote for going south. Look for smoke over the forest. See if somebody, anybody, lit a fire to dry out." Barb sighed, but her voice carried little hope.

"We don't have time to make the ridge before dark. If I were to try, I'd go west, back up on lookout rock and see if there is a deer trail that will take us over the ridge."

"You'd never be able to make the climb after all that rain the last two days. I think south is a better option. Maybe first thing tomorrow morning?"

"We'll see. First, finish the job at hand." Matt's tone was harsh. He was exhausted from lugging the full tank, frustrated by not knowing how to get out, angry about the damage to their car. At that moment he wanted out far more than Barbara, but he knew he couldn't say anything or her pent up anxieties would explode as well.

Seeing that the rope allowed the tank to bounce too much, Matt used the handle. It wasn't difficult, but the angle of the tow kept bumping the tank into the ground. He compromised and used a shorter length of rope. By the time they got back to camp, the rope had caused considerable irritation and Matt's hand glowed red. He didn't say anything, thinking he might find some lotion after the tank was reinstalled.

Lying down at the end of the camper, Matt tried to orient the tank to crank it back up into position. First he forgot to remove the rope, then it faced the wrong way. Oriented correctly, he had trouble getting the lift disc inserted correctly. It came out easily enough, but was not cooperative about slipping back into the engineered holder. Once he began cranking it back into position, it swung around. Anticipating another problem, Matt slid the cover seal away from the connecting ring then tried to position the tank for a smooth connection. Positioning was important for a leak-proof seal with the toilet. Just as with the lift disc, getting it to slip back onto the toilet flange was not easy as removing it. Once he did get it correctly positioned, he then lifted it and called out, "BARB! Rotate the ring at the base of the toilet!"

"I don't see what you are talking about," Barb called while Matt held the tank in place. "What ring?"

"Look to the bottom of the toilet, at the floor. There is a ring about one inch high, it needs to slide clockwise one-quarter turn. It will click in place."

"I don't see a ring! You'll have to come show me."

When Matt released the tank to instruct Barb, it dropped just enough that he could not lock it in place. Sliding out on the wet ground his back struck a large root or rock. Holding his side, he pushed into the bathroom with Barb, which was an incredibly tight fit, and bent down.

"This ring, RIGHT HERE!"

"I can't see with you in the way."

Matt took a deep breath and let it out slowly as he moved out of the bathroom. "You get down on your knees and put your hand on the bottom of the toilet . . . at the floor." When Barb had done as he said, he continued. "Do you feel that ring move?"

"Yes, I do. I didn't see it as a movable ring before. Sorry. How far do I turn it?"

"One quarter turn. It will click in place."

Barb tested the ring and it did click. "You're right. It does."

"Good, now release it so I can reconnect the tank."

"How do I release it? I'm pushing on the tab at the back but it doesn't move."

Sighing once more, Matt gently pulled his wife from the toilet and got down on his knees. Using his hand that had been irritated by the rope, he pressed hard on the tab until he felt it release, then turned it back one-quarter turn. Standing, he told Barb, "Okay, it is ready. I'm going to raise the tank again. When I tell you to lock it, please turn the ring until it clicks."

Without waiting for a reply, he exited the camper and dropped to his back on the ground behind the camper. Once again something jabbed his side. Feeling for the source of the pain, he found it was a rock that had come loose. With no loss of aggression, he sent the rock sailing and moved back under the tank. Once more he lifted the tank, jiggling it until it slipped into position. "Okay, turn that ring!" he called.

Barb tried to turn the ring, without success. "It won't turn."

"Are you turning it clockwise?"

"Yes, but it won't budge."

"Okay, just a minute." Matt then jiggled the tank some more, nudging it with his knee. As he was about to drop the tank and rest his arms, it slipped upward, just slightly. "TRY NOW!"

"Just a second, I thought you were coming back up here!" Barb's voice came from the middle of the camper, not from the bathroom above Matt.

"TURN THE DAMN RING!"

Seconds later he heard a click. Sliding out from under the tank, he grabbed the first strap. Before he could connect it, he heard water running into the tank and it began to sway slightly.

"DON'T USE IT YET! IT ISN'T SECURE!"

"Sorry! I had to go."

Mumbling to himself, Matt steadied the tank and pulled the first strap into place. When he flipped the latch, it caught his finger. Blood trickled from his thumb as he secured the second strap, this time being careful to keep his fingers clear. Seeing the sensor connector, he plugged it in, smearing the trickle of blood all over it. Sliding out from under the camper, he restored the U-shaped drain pipe and grabbed the crank, which he returned to the storage bin with significant force. Stepping back into the camper he opened the door to the bathroom and reached into a cabinet for a bottle of deodorizing chemical. Not finding the bottle he expected, he moved toilet paper rolls aside and back, then hand towels aside and back. All the stress of the past week suddenly wrapped around him and squeezed him as though a snake about to enjoy a fresh kill.

"Where is the bottle of sanitizer?" he asked, turning to Barb who was sitting on the sofa.

Barb looked horror stricken.

"Barbara, we bought a new supply of the stuff. Where is it?"

"Your thumb is bleeding."

"Don't worry about my thumb! Where is the sanitizer? We bought a box last week."

"I don't know. I put it on your workbench in the garage. Didn't you put it in here?"

Matt glared at his wife. Doing all he could to control his anger, he scowled, "That's just great! Now, every time we use the toilet it's going to stink up the camper!"

"Not if we could get out of this place!" Barb retorted without thinking.

Drawing a deep breath, Matt grabbed his daypack, checked it for water, then grabbed his walking stick and left.

"Where are you going?" Barb called after him.

"I'm going to find a way out of this God forsaken prison!"

Barbara sulked for a minute. She could not believe her husband had just blamed her because he hadn't put the deodorizing chemical into the camper. He bought it, why was SHE supposed to put it into the camper? Not hearing him moving about outside, she went out to find him. He was nowhere to be seen.

"MATTHEW! MATTHEW WHERE ARE YOU?" Barb screamed at the top of her lungs. Listening to the quiet of the forest respond to her plea, she thought aloud. "That fool wouldn't go off without me." Again, the quiet of the forest assaulted her ears. "Fine. He's gone up to the rock. I won't be taken in by his stupidity. I'll prove him wrong. I can make the south ridge without his help."

Ten

Her own anger rising, Barb collected her daypack, three bottles of water, and her walking stick. Slamming the door to the camper, she turned toward their SUV and stomped away. Leaving the campsite, she turned slightly right and headed south, mumbling to herself.

"He thinks he can get over that west ridge. He's a fool. Maybe there isn't anyone south of here, but at least it's a direction we can travel. He'll never make that ridge the way he's going."

Matt and Barb had spent all morning servicing the waste water tank, dumping it at the cabin and reattaching the empty tank to the camper. It had been a difficult task which triggered his anger and sudden departure up the western slope. The sun now just past its peak, Barb's stomping soon gave way to a dedicated march through the forest. Without a compass or anything to guide her, she continued from one hill to the next. Every time she saw something she thought she recognized, a tree or clearing or rock outcrop, her fervor gained strength and she quickened her step.

Two hours into her mission, she arrived at the ravine. Looking east and west, she asked herself, "Where is that tree we crossed on?" Looking both directions again, she thought aloud. "Matt would say the river is east and the west ridge is impassable. So which way do I go?" Looking both up and down the ravine, once more, Barb noticed a pile of debris fifty yards, or so, to the west. Curiosity set her feet in motion.

Reaching the debris, she found it to be limbs from a tree. Looking to the ground, she saw chips from a chainsaw. Walking closer to the edge of the ravine, she looked down. The tree she and Matt had used as a bridge lay at the bottom. All but a few branches had been cut, with chainsaws, and tossed into the ravine, where they couldn't be used as a bridge.

"AARRRGGGHHH! DAMN! DAMN! DAMN! DAMN! DAMN! DAMN! DAMN!" Barb screamed and stomped in a circle where the tree once rested. Her arms flailing at the sky, she quickly exhausted herself and fell to the ground, where she sat and cried. Staring at the empty space which had once held hope for freedom, she sobbed. "Those weren't bees I heard the other day, they were chain saws! They've cut off our southern escape." Drawing a deep breath, she calmed, somewhat, and her mind grabbed a single thought. "I've got to tell Matt! I hope he's back at camp when I get there."

Wiping tears from her face, Barb scrambled to her feet and turned in the direction of camp. She had reached the ravine in less time than their first trek south. Driving herself hard to get back to Matt, using her frustration and anger as fuel, her pace would have returned her to the campsite in even less time, had she been on track. Every time she reached the top of a hill, Barb looked for something familiar, anything that might keep her direction true. Just over two hours into her race back to the camper, she arrived at the lake.

"Noooooo, how did I miss the camper? I followed familiar landmarks all the way." Taking a bottle of water from her pack, she guzzled nearly a third of it before stopping. This was the first water she had drunk since leaving the camper. Sighing, she stuffed the bottle back into her pack and turned down the now familiar path to their campsite. Sunshine was being filtered by the tops of the trees as the sun slid down the sky. Fatigued and disheartened, her current pace was significantly slower than it had been all day.

Seeing the camper, her pace quickened and Barb began calling to Matt. Only silence replied. Finding the campsite empty with no sign of her husband, she opened the door calling, "Matt! Matt are you here?" The camper was empty. Dropping her backpack on the ground, she plopped into a chair.

"Now . . . Matt would tell me to wait here so he wouldn't have to go looking for me. But, he hasn't been back . . . not that I can see." Barb paused her one-sided conversation and thought. *Has he come back and gone looking for me or is he still trying to reach the west ridge?* Taking the two-thirds full bottle of water from her pack, she sipped as she continued to reason aloud. "I'll give him an hour or so. If he's not back by then, I'll leave a note on the table inside and go after him. Yes, that will give me some time to rest, then I'll be able to go find him." Taking another sip, she assured herself, "Yep. Rest a bit then go after him. That damn fool." Realizing she had not eaten lunch, Barb went into the camper, retrieved a pack of peanut butter crackers, and returned to her seat outside.

Enraged by problems with dumping the waste water and then problems getting the tank reset, Matt did all he could to not blow up at his wife when he discovered they had no deodorizer for the waste tank. Small problems, but he was like a pressure cooker ready to explode, Barb's last comment about escaping was more than he could handle. It was either get away from the immediate troubles, including Barbara, or erupt. Grabbing the barest of essentials, water and walking stick, he struck out in search of a way home.

Slipping only once as he climbed the slope behind their camper, Matt quickly reached the deer trails running along the hillside. Looking at the trail marker he left on the previous trip, he said to himself, "Good. I may need that to know where to turn down to the camper. Now, to the ridge."

Zig-zagging back and forth, following deer trails, Matt had gradually ascended the steep slope. At each cutback, he struggled to reach the next trail, but pure determination drove him onward and upward without rest or distracting thoughts. When he reached the rock outlook, he stood beneath it and pondered. *I could continue to follow the deer trails as far as they take me, then go straight up, or I could take another look at this valley. Maybe now that I've been there, I might see something I missed last time.*

Taking a bottle of water from his pack, he drank sparingly as he pondered. Returning the bottle, he pulled the pack back onto his shoulders, grabbed his walking stick firmly, and looked up the rise beside the overlook. Looking down at his stick, he looped the leather strap around his wrist, something he had never done before but considered essential for the climb ahead of him. Then, reaching forward, he pulled himself from one tree to the next, just as he had the last time he visited this spot.

Out of breath and having been slapped in the mouth by a leafy twig, Matt dropped his walking stick and backpack at the edge of the trees. Retrieving his water, he rinsed the leaves and bark from his mouth before stepping out on the stone overlook. Dark clouds gathering to the north gave him some concern, until he saw that they were drifting to the east. Looking south, he noticed a break in the tree line. *The ravine,* he thought to himself. Nothing else in the southern or eastern views gave him hope or second thought. Sipping from the bottle of water he still held, Matt looked back to the north, studying what he could see of the lake region. Knowing where the waterfalls were, he scoured the tree lines even though he could not actually see them. All he could see was the unending forest of the western slope. He then turned his attention to the hillside below where he was standing. Deer trails made for easier travel, but they were essentially invisible from above. Chuckling slightly, he said aloud, "You can only see them when you are on them."

Turning around, Matt looked to the hillside behind him. All he could see was dense forest, trees and bushes, primarily rhododendron, and a steep slope covered with leaves. Briefly considering going back down and following deer trails or going straight up, he decided. "Well, I guess I've got to try."

Taking one last sip of water, he returned the near empty bottle to his pack then wearily hefted it onto his back. Reaching down for his walking stick and hearing a growl too close for comfort, he froze. Heart pounding in his ears, Matt wrapped his hand around the walking stick and turned his head to the left as he slowly rose to upright position.

Standing on all four feet at the opposite end of the stone overlook, barely ten feet away, was a large bear. Head lowered slightly, it stared at Matt for several seconds before snarling possessively. As Matt stood, his head rose above the bear's head. Now threatened by an intruder, the bear quickly rose on its hind legs. Standing over eight feet tall, it growled from deep within its chest. Instinctively, Matt lifted his walking stick so he was now holding it across his own chest with both hands. Unable to breathe, Matt stared at the bear. Sensing Matt's fear, the bear stepped forward, falling back to all four feet and coming to rest fewer than four feet from Matt.

Matt stepped backward and grabbed frantically for something to break his fall. All he found was air, until his back hit a tree, which spun him around into another tree and then another, until he crashed into the hillside below the overlook. Unconscious, Matt lay mangled between trees he had used to pull himself up only minutes before.

Sitting in their campsite and slowly drinking water from the bottle in her hands, Barb thought about how someone had cut that tree at the ravine. Then she wondered how she had missed the camper completely and ended up at the lake. Finishing the last of her water, she stepped into the camper. Finding paper and pens in a drawer, she wrote, "Going up the west slope to find you. Been a long day, sun is beginning to set in the trees. Maybe an hour or two of daylight left. I still love you."

Traipsing up the hill behind the camper, just as she and Matt had done days before, Barb thought only about catching up with her husband. "Going off separately was silly and stupid," she muttered to herself. "We've got to stick together if we're going to get out of here."

Reaching the first deer trail, Barb looked to the sky above and then through a narrow break in the trees east of her. Distant trees were still in full sunlight, however where she stood was now in shade. Shaking her head, she followed the deer trail as it zig-zagged up the mountain. Not as adept at climbing as Matt, she fell several times at cutbacks, once cutting her hand. Wiping the trickle of blood on her pants, she continued.

Nearly two hours into her search, Barb stood beneath the rock overlook and dropped her backpack and walking stick onto the ground. After pulling a bottle of water from her pack, she took a sip and looked toward the sky. Only the tops of the trees were in sunlight, the rest of the valley was fading into dusk. Looking down at her hand, she saw that the bleeding had stopped, but it was a bit of a mess. Dribbling water over the injury, most of the blood and dirt washed away.

Worry about Matt filling her, she closed her bottle and bent over to put it back into her pack and gasped with fear. Three yards ahead of her, lying on the trail, was what appeared to be Matt's walking stick. Dropping her bottle, she ran to the stick. It was Matt's. Looking around, her eyes going up the steep slope beside the overlook, she saw Matt halfway up the hill and four feet into the bushes, twisted around and between trees.

Scrambling up the hill, her feet refusing to gain traction, Barb pulled herself from one tree to another until she reached Matt. When she touched him, to see if he was alive, he moaned. A quick scan of his situation convinced her that she was not going to extract Matt without some help from him. Using her hands and the limited light, she checked for bleeding injuries and broken bones, but found none.

Taking a deep breath, Barb tried to recall essentials from a first aid course she and Matt had taken three years before. Speaking softly, more to calm herself and collect her thoughts, she recited memories. "Trauma victim will likely be in shock. Need to keep them still and warm." Barb paused and reviewed their situation. "Well, *still* isn't a problem but no way I can keep him warm on this hillside. I need to get him below the rock. Then I can build a fire. Now, how do I . . ."

"What?" Matt moaned feebly.

Angry with Matt for his stupidity and unbelievably relieved that he was indeed still alive, Barb was somewhat sarcastic in her tone. "Oh, good. You're alive. Now you can help me."

"What?" Matt moaned feebly, again.

"Can you move at all?" Barb asked, hopefully.

Matt attempted to straighten out his legs, but trees blocked any movement. "What the?"

"Matt, you are twisted among trees. Let me help you get out of the tangle. I'll lift one leg at a time. You help me by moving just that leg as I lift. Are you ready?"

"I think so, which leg?" Matt was now gaining some sense of his predicament but was still too feeble in mind to fully comprehend what Barb was doing.

Barb climbed the hill a bit and carefully lifted Matt's left foot and leg. He assisted by straightening it out as she lifted. Setting his left leg down, stretched out up the hill, above his torso, Barb moved over to his right leg.

"OUWWW!" Matt cried out.

Barb reexamined his right leg, foot, and ankle. "Matt. Your right ankle is badly twisted. It may actually be broken, I don't know." *Don't say that, stupid,* she chastised herself. "Matt, I'm going to lift your right leg and foot, it may hurt, but we've got to get you out of these trees."

Matt squelched a scream and straightened his leg out with his wife's help. He was now lying on his left side, his back and pack pushing against one tree and his waist pushing into another. His left arm was pinned beneath him and behind the tree pushing against his back.

Reaching into the air with his right arm, Matt asked, "Help me up. I can't roll over."

"You can't roll over because you are twisted between the trees. I need to roll you over on your stomach so I can remove your backpack and free your left arm." Seeing the position of his legs would prevent Matt from rolling over, Barb shifted gears. "First, I need to move your legs again."

One by one, Barb lifted Matt's legs to the other side of a small tree, then gently pushed him to his stomach. Now able to reach his backpack, she disconnected the straps and removed the pack, tossing it down to the trail. Looking back, she saw Matt trying to rise into a crawl position.

"AGHHH!" he screamed. Dropping to his right side, he grabbed his left arm.

"What's wrong? How does it hurt? Is it broken?" Barb called out excitedly.

"Not broken . . . don't think so, anyway. More like a really bad bruise."

Barb took a deep breath and reconsidered Matt's situation. "Okay, Matthew. You can't stand on your right leg and your left arm is useless for now. I need you to roll back onto your back and then sit forward. You'll be trying to sit uphill, so it may be difficult. Are you ready to try?"

"Is there anything behind me?"

"Yes, a tree. Let me help you." Barb then scooched behind Matt and lifted his shoulders so he could lie flat in her lap. She then pushed him into a sitting position.

Sitting upright, more or less, for the first time, Matt looked around. Shadows were fading into dusky light and he was surrounded by trees. His feet were up the slope from his seat. "Boy, I'm in a bit of a pickle. Where's the bear?"

"Bear?" Barb asked, becoming excited.

"Oh, don't worry. I must have chased him off." . . . "Can you help me up so we can go home now?"

Taking another deep breath and preparing herself for the next struggle, Barb replied, "Right now I just want to get you down to the trail without doing more damage. Remember to not put any weight or pressure on your right foot. I'll lift you under your right shoulder. Ready? One, two, . . ."

Not waiting for affirmation nor reaching the proverbial "three," Barb lifted Matt's right shoulder. He responded by lifting himself on his left leg and falling into the tree beside him. Wincing as his left arm wrapped tightly around this same tree, he began to shift his weight until he stood on his own.

Looking down toward the deer trail, he suggested, "How about I sit and slide down the hill?"

Chuckling with a bit of relief, Barb responded, "Good idea, but you'll mess up your pants."

Glaring at his wife through a smile, Matt said, "Help me sit. Please."

Moments later, Barb helped Matt hop to the trail beneath the rock outcrop and lowered him into a sitting position. Relieved that they were both alive, she pronounced, "I'll make a fire. We'll sleep here tonight and work our way back to the camper tomorrow. No arguments. Do you have matches in your backpack?"

Looking sheepishly at his wife, Matt replied, "I think so. What'd you do with it?"

Barb looked around and found the pack where she had tossed it after removing it from Matt's back. Rummaging inside she did find matches in a waterproof container. "Okay, I'll get some wood. Sorry I didn't bring us a steak to cook for supper, but I do have some peanut butter crackers."

"No idea what I have in the way of food in my pack," Matt replied. "But a fire would be nice, I'm beginning to get cold."

Realizing that cold was one of the signs of advancing shock, Barb went to work collecting wood and building a fire. Working hastily, she piled the wood randomly and burned six of their ten matches without achieving a fire. Seeing Matt's face appear more pale and sickly, she stopped rushing and restructured the fire into a small teepee. One match and moments later, they had flame and a growing heat source. Using her coat as a pillow, she helped Matt lie next to the fire. She tried to get him to drink some water, but he was not interested or cooperative.

Resigned to stay awake, in case her husband needed her and to feed the fire, Barb sat next to her husband and stared into the flames.

Day Nine

Feeling something tickling her face, every muscle in Barb's body tightened and froze. Her natural instinct would have been to jump back, but her mind was still watching the fire that had gone out hours before. Opening her eyes slowly, she found herself staring into another pair of eyes. Large, dark, round eyes. Looking beyond the eyes, she realized they belonged to a small deer. Not a fawn but a young doe.

Seeing this odd creature's eyes staring back at hers, the doe lifted her head and tilted it to the side. She then sniffed the air, snorted, and leapt down the trail.

Barb drew a breath slowly and did her best to appreciate what had just happened. Realizing she had been asleep and her husband was supposed to be sleeping beside her, she sat up quickly. The fire had gone out, however Matt was indeed still lying next to her. Relieved, she reached over and felt his face. It was warm and looked almost rosy in the first light of day filtering through the trees. Rising to her knees, Barb put a hand on either side of Matt's head and held him gently.

Several seconds passed before Matt responded to the caress. Fluttering his eyes as he opened them, he then tried to reach his arms into a stretch. Feeling pain shoot through his left arm, he pulled it in and looked at his wife.

"Good morning. Where are we and what happened?"

Smiling with relief, Barb began with what she knew. "We are on the deer trail below the lookout rock, on the western mountain. I found you wrapped around several trees and you said something about tangling with a bear. . . ." Realizing her husband was more okay than not, Barb felt a rage growing within her and she blew up at her husband. "Coming up here alone was stupid, and you know it! You were damn near killed, then how would I get out of here? No way I could do it alone; NEITHER of us can! We have got to stick together or we'll be stuck here forever!"

Matt did not respond. He simply looked at his wife, knowing she was right.

Rage subsiding, Barb's voice filled with loving concern. "Now, how do you feel?"

"I'm not too sure," Matt moaned as he tried to sit up. "I must be alive or I wouldn't hurt this bad. Can you help me sit up?"

Barb carefully rolled her husband to a sitting position, using the opportunity to check him once again for injuries. "Where do you hurt the worst?"

"Left arm aches and my right ankle is pounding. Other than that, I just feel like I've been run over by tractor-trailer."

"Not a truck, but what do you remember about a bear?"

"Bear?" Matt pondered briefly. "Oh, yeah. Up on the rock. I was looking around the valley, wondering if I might see something we missed before. As I was about to climb to the ridge, a big bear showed up. Seems he didn't like me on his rock."

"Did he knock you off?"

"I don't think so. I seem to remember he rose up then dropped back down to all four. I must have stepped backwards and fell off." Matt grew quiet, considering his memories of the event.

While listening to Matt's story, Barb checked out his ankle, rolling his sock down. "Well, your ankle is a size ten-x and not very pretty; a bit purplish. Doesn't appear to be broken."

Drawing a deep breath, Matt shifted as though he were going to stand. "How about we get off this mountain and see to my ankle when we get home."

"Home? You must have damaged your head as well. But, no, not going back to camp. I want to get your ankle in cold water at the waterfall."

"Don't we have one of those instant ice packs in the camper?"

"We did. As I recall, you used four of them when Bobby hurt himself on that cross-country bicycle."

"Yeah, but it was a six pack. What about the other two?"

"Look, that was years ago and if we do have them I doubt they would still work. I vote for the waterfall. We can look for the cold-pack when we get to the camper."

Matt rolled his jaw as he considered their situation. "Okay. Help me up, please."

Barb did as requested; lifting Matt by his right shoulder and holding him as he hopped into a sense of balance.

"My walking stick," Matt requested.

Barb left him standing unsteadily and retrieved his stick and backpack. He balanced with the stick while she hooked the pack over his shoulders. She then retrieved her own pack and walking stick. Putting her hand out in invitation to begin, she commented, "Okay, let's see what you can do."

Using his stick for support, Matt tried to begin walking. His right leg collapsed when he put it forward, causing him to thrust all his weight on the stick. Catching his breath, he confessed, "Nope. Need some kind of crutch."

"Okay, you sit and I'll see what I can find." Without giving Matt a chance to argue, Barb gently pushed him back to the ground and went in search of a crutch. She returned five minutes later with a fallen tree limb that was not quite straight but was as big around as his wrist and had a forked branch he could rest under his arm.

Once more, Barb helped her husband to his feet and placed the crutch under his right arm. The length was a little short and it took both hands to keep his balance with it, but it seemed to work.

"Not very solid," Matt complained as a clump of bark fell off the limb.

"No, but it is the best we have for now. When we get back to camp, I'll see about cutting you a proper crutch. Till then, make do." She then collected both walking sticks and looking to her husband, took a deep breath and directed, "Lead the way to the waterfall."

Heaving a sigh of determination, Matt did as commanded. "Aye, Madam."

The sun had nearly reached its peak by the time they reached the waterfalls. Sitting on a rock at the base of the smaller section, Matt removed his right shoe and sock and plunged his throbbing foot into a pool of icy water, taking his breath away.

"It's cold, I'll give you that!" he told Barb once he regained his ability to speak.

"Good. I'm glad I was right about something." Straightening after helping Matt get into the water, Barb moved a few yards away, where it was dry. Leaning on both walking sticks, one in each hand, she looked around. "Do you recall hearing chainsaws a couple days ago? You said it sounded like bees."

"Not really, why?"

"I went to the ravine yesterday. I still think going south makes more sense than trying to get over the western ridge. Anyway, when I got to the tree we used as a bridge, it was gone. Somebody had cut it up and dropped it into the ravine. Chainsaw debris all over the place and not a single usable branch was left where we could get it."

"So they're watching us and know what we're doing. . . . How long do I have to freeze my foot?"

"I don't know, maybe till it falls off?"

"Don't you think that's a bit extreme!"

"I don't know. You think sumo wrestling a grown bear isn't a bit extreme?"

"I didn't wrestle the bear!"

"Bet you tell your grandchildren you wrestled with it. Grabbed it around the belly and tried to drag it down."

Matt looked at his wife with wonder. "What do suppose the kids are doing about us being missing?"

"Well, we haven't been gone two weeks yet, so I doubt either has even considered us missing. Angela might have left a couple messages, but she won't get really upset until two or three days after I don't answer the first one. She has a busy life, you know. Then, Steven, well, we hear from him once a month, maybe. We raised independent kids. Now, I wish we hadn't."

"I wonder what they told people at work."

"Who?"

"Whoever it is that kidnaped us. They wouldn't just let us go missing, they'd have to tell our employers something. I was supposed to meet with the Safety Commission right after we got back. That was two or three days ago. For that matter, they might have told the kids something."

Barb wiped a tear from her eye and stepped over next to Matt. "Let me see your foot."

Matt raised his foot from the icy pool. The swelling had subsided somewhat and the color had toned down to look more like a bad bruise.

Barb examined the injury. "Okay, I'm going to say it isn't even sprained but just twisted and badly bruised. I hope we do have those ice packs in the camper. But, for now, we need to bandage it with something. Any chance we have an ace wrap in our packs?"

"I doubt it, but look." Matt replied, examining his ankle with growing frustration.

Barb rifled through both packs. She found remnants of one first aid kit but nothing that would serve to wrap Matt's ankle. "What happened to all our preparedness? We never went out without supplies when the kids were young."

"I'd say Bobby used up our supplies and we never replaced them, but I think Steven was the one who used the ace bandage we did carry," Matt responded. Remembering outings, even those with injuries, brought a smile to his face.

"That's right. His last trip with us he wrenched his wrist on a makeshift zip line." Barb smiled, as well. Then, as though a light had switched on, she turned to Matt. "Take off your shirts. We've got to wrap that ankle with something."

"My shirt?"

"Your t-shirt. I can rip it into strips and bind your ankle."

"It's soft cotton, love. Won't bind anything and won't stay tied."

"It's all we have and we've got to try. Now, strip!"

Matt did not argue and doing his best to be seductive, stripped down to his waist. This could have been fun, however when he removed his t-shirt, with flair, he revealed a very irritated underarm.

"What happened there?" Barb asked, her laughter changing to concern. "Don't tell me; the crutch is tearing up your arm."

"I don't know. Too many problems. Too stupid. Take your pick. . . . Hey, at least it's not falling apart like I thought it would."

"You should have told me," Barb scolded and began tearing Matt's shirt into strips which she used to wrap his ankle, pulling it as tightly as she could. Wrapping completed, she fixed the end with a large safety pin she had found in the first aid kit.

"Don't put the jacket on, we need it for the crutch," she warned him as Matt put his shirt back on.

The crutch now padded, Barb got their packs on their backs, took a quick drink of water from the small falls, and prodded Matt. "Let's try to get moving."

She watched as Matt started down the trail toward the lake, stopping him after a couple steps. Seeing that the crutch was again scratching his arm, she rewrapped it, running the sleeve of the jacket over the branch then folding the bulk of the jacket over the fork under his arm.

"Much better, thank you," Matt complimented as he started to hobble away.

"Wait, you forgot something." Undoing his backpack, Barb stuffed his shoe and sock inside. "Now, let's head back to camp. Don't stub your toe."

Eleven

The sun journeyed quickly across the afternoon sky as Barbara and Matthew slowly made their way back to camp. Blue skies and billowy white clouds would normally lift their spirits, however today they only reminded the couple how slowly they were moving. Barb commented, "I wish I was a cloud . . . I could simply float out of this nightmare."

Walking around the lake, without shade, Matt began sweating profusely, which added to his painful discomfort. He refrained from saying "I told you so," when they stopped to retie the makeshift bandage, three times, each time noting that the cotton was stretching and providing less and less of the needed compression.

Sunshine had abandoned the campsite for the day, yielding to evening shade by the time the weary and wounded travelers returned, where further disaster greeted their eyes. Taking a deep breath, Matt asked, "Who do you reckon, our host or that bear?"

Rocks in the fire ring were scattered about the site. One mangled chair hung from a tree limb; they didn't see the other. Their once damaged and repaired coffee pot was now flat. In the middle of all the mess, the ground was dug and scuffed as though a tribe of indians had done an enraged war dance. Stepping to the side of the carnage, Matt stooped down and put his hand flat on the ground.

"Bear. By the size of his paw, it could have been that one that chased me off the lookout rock. He sure has an attitude."

"Do you think there is only the one?" Barb asked, retrieving the chair from the tree.

"We know there are a momma and cub and at least one mean male. Do we need more?"

Pushing himself vertical with his crutch, Matt spied their second chair in the bushes. "There's the other chair. Can you get it?"

Barb retrieved the seat, opened it, and placed it next to the remains of the fire circle. "It seems to be usable. Sit and I'll see what we have in the camper to wrap your ankle. Also, get you some pain killers. You haven't complained, but I know you have got to be hurting." She then disappeared into the camper, returning after only a few minutes. Handing a bottle of ibuprofen to Matt, she advised him, "Okay, here are pills. Not one but two ice packs, not sure they are any good, and an equally promising bandage." She then unrolled an old elastic bandage that had lost most of its stretch. "We really do need to restock our emergency supplies."

"You mean you're willing to go camping again after this adventure?"

Barb crinkled her face as she considered her response. "Probably not. No way we are getting our camper out of here."

Matt unwrapped the cotton bandage from his ankle, moaning at the deepening of the purple color. He then smacked one of the ice packs, activating the cold. Placing it on his ankle, he felt a cooling sensation; not cold, just cool. Not wanting to worry Barb any more, he shifted it around his ankle as though it were working.

"You should tie it in place with the shirt," she advised him and took the dysfunctional pack from him. "This isn't going to help! Try the other one."

Matt quietly smashed the second, and final, ice pack. It immediately produced significant cold, which Barb tied to his ankle. She then quietly stepped into the camper again, emerging seconds later with two bottles of cold water.

Handing one bottle to Matt, she commented, "Fridge still works." She then twisted the cap off and took several gulps of refreshing cold water. Matt did the same. Lowering her bottle and twisting the cap back on, she glanced around their campsite. "Well, where should I start? Chair or coffee pot?"

"Last time I fixed that coffee pot, you told me we had other pots inside. Why don't you bring me the chair and I'll see what magic I can work on it." Matt's voice was soft and not very convincing.

Barb looked at his face and for the first time saw it totally void of inspiration, drive, enthusiasm, or resolve. For the first time since they met, thirty-two years before, he seemed to be beaten by circumstance. Feeling his loss as her own, Barb retrieved the battered chair and grill from behind the camper and brought them back to Matt. Heaving a sigh of uncertainty, Matt took the chair and turned it around a few times before trying to open it. This was an inexpensive aluminum tube frame chair with a nylon web seat. The rear support had a major bend toward the seat, one hand rest was broken and the tube beneath suffered a major dent, and the front rail had a bit of an "S" curve to it across the front and going up one side. The back support was misshapen, but not badly.

"If I had a tube bender from work, I could fix this thing nearly as good as new."

"Can you do anything with it here in 'Never Never Land'?" Barb asked, dropping the grill beside the remains of the fire ring.

"I'll need to be gentle. This aluminum won't take but so much abuse." He then tried to open the chair, with no success. Pointing to a small log just out of his reach, he asked, "Hand me that log, please."

Barb handed him the log, which he placed along the top of his right leg with the widest part facing up. He then placed the worst bend, in the rear support, on the log and began rolling it back and forth while applying pressure about twelve inches either side of the bend. With each roll, the bend relaxed just a bit. After ten minutes, or so, the bend was almost removed. He repeated this process with each of the other bends, often smacking himself about the head as he manipulated the chair.

An hour into the repair process, Barb interrupted his work. "How's your ankle, Mister Wizard?"

Looking down at his injury, he smiled. "Much better, thank you. Maybe we should dispose of the ice pack and see about wrapping it."

"Not sure how much compression we'll get from this old elastic, but it will definitely be better than nothing." Barb removed the t-shirt bandage and ice pack. Swelling in Matt's ankle had gone down, but the discoloration was still bad. Wrapping the old elastic, she chuckled. "Sure wish we could send out for more ice packs and a couple ACE bandages."

"I'll contact the concierge and see what can be arranged," Matt replied with a wry smile.

Matt resumed working on the chair after Barb finished wrapping his ankle. After thirty minutes, he stood, opened the chair, and carefully lowered himself into it. "Not too bad. We just need to be careful of this broken plastic arm rest." Feeling good about his work, his face lit up with challenge as he called out, "Now, let me see my coffee pot!"

Shaking her head with disbelief, Barb picked up the twice-flattened pot and handed it to Matt. After turning it over in his hands several times, examining both sides closely, there were only two now, Matt held it above his head and called, "Concierge, a new coffee pot, please."

Sitting down in the chair Matt had been using, Barb brought up a new subject she had been avoiding. "Matthew, we have a growing problem."

Afraid of what was coming, Matt sniffed the air. "We're getting a bit ripe? Need another bath in the lake?"

"Not just us, but our laundry. We packed for five days and it's been what, nine or ten?"

"Yeah, I've been recycling my underwear. Maybe we should make a date to bathe us and wash some clothes tomorrow."

"You've been 'recycling' your underwear?"

"Well, not recycling so much as not changing as often as I should. I was alright up till a couple days ago, when it rained. I was going to talk with you about it, but since then we've been dealing with one problem after another. What I was wearing didn't seem so important the last couple days."

"Laundry! Tomorrow!"

Both sat silently looking into the forest for several minutes, each lost in their own thoughts. Matt was the first to speak. "That's going to be a lot of laundry to carry and I'm not sure how much good I'll be."

"I need to find you a better crutch," Barb responded, still looking into the trees.

"I guess so, but what I was just thinking was about that cabin. It has water, an outhouse, even a cooling room. Everything we need to keep going is more convenient there."

"Are you saying you want to move to the cabin? I'd rather spend our energy getting out of here. The only change I'm interested in is going home."

"Yes, I want to get out of here, too. I'm just saying it might be easier to continue from the cabin than to keep hiking back and forth to the lake. We could take the mattress up there and we have that portable gas stove."

"We don't have enough gas for that small stove."

"We could take the bottle off the camper, but I'm not saying we do it. Just think about it."

Barb turned her head and glared at her husband. She didn't want to admit it, but he had made several good points. Rather than argue, she opened her water and took a gulp. It wasn't as cold as when she took it from the fridge, but it was still cool and refreshing.

"Matthew, how are you feeling?" Barb asked, cracking the silence surrounding them.

"Fair. Ankle's hurting again. Why?"

"I just realized part of our problem is we haven't eaten anything all day. How would you like a peanut butter and jelly sandwich, oozing both?"

Matt looked to his wife, seeing her right eye raised and a hint of a smile on her lips, he nodded. "Can I help?"

"Yes. Don't get up. If you fall over again, we'll never get anything to eat."

"I haven't fallen over!" Matt objected forcefully.

"Not yet, but you can't stand steady either. Sit still while I fix us something to eat."

The couple enjoyed their sandwiches, even licking jelly from the paper towels holding them. As the evening wore on, neither was motivated to move, however when Matt got up to relieve himself, Barb remembered he needed a new crutch. She wandered the woods near their camp for fifteen minutes before returning for their axe to cut a small tree that would provide a much better walking support. After wrapping the t-shirt bandage around the fork of its branches, she gave it to Matt. Testing the new crutch, Matt approved and hugged his wife with growing gratitude. Not wanting instant coffee, they turned in shortly after sunset.

Day Ten

Matt had taken a couple pain killers to help him sleep, but a not-so-gentle throbbing in his ankle robbed him of peaceful slumber. He checked his wristwatch multiple times throughout the night, at 10:30, 11:44, 1:05, 3:22, 5:10. At 6:44, he gave up and quietly slipped out of the bed, dressed, took a bottle of water from the fridge, and hobbled outside. Shortly after setting up a folding chair, he returned to the camper for a jacket and his bottle of pain meds.

Settling into his seat, he watched the forest slowly awaken. Five deer, including two spotted fawns, passed by. A chipmunk was offended by his early presence and fussed each time it stopped while crossing the campsite. Resting his foot on the largest stone in the remains of the fire ring, pain in Matt's ankle subsided as meds took effect and he soaked up the quiet and fading morning mist.

His mind was more relaxed than it had been in days, or simply numb from the previous forty hours. Matthew sipped his water as he wondered why they had been kidnaped and brought to this inescapable location. He thought about his job and some of the sensitive experiments he was exposed to; dismissing this as a reason since he had no critical knowledge of anything secret. He considered Barbara's work at the college. She was an administrator working with students, mostly graduate students, and didn't have contact with any sensitive information. Maybe a foreign student with influential ties, but nothing to warrant this kind of isolation. Unable to find anything in their work lives to blame, he looked at their private lives. They did not take part in any civil actions that ever gained notoriety. They had graduated out of the PTA and attended church only casually. Walmart was their store of choice, simply because it was convenient, and they rarely went to any theater. They did, however, enjoy eating out at various restaurants. There was nothing remarkable about their life; why were they so important to be pulled away from it?

Heaving a sigh of frustration, Matt finished his bottle of water and stared into the now familiar forest. Moments later, as his mind began to float toward the cabin, he felt a pair of hands slide down his shoulder and across his chest.

"How long have you been out here?" Barb asked softly, nuzzling into his neck.

Reaching up and tenderly squeezing her hands, he replied, "I have no idea. Couldn't sleep. Ankle gave me a fit all night."

"How's it doing now?"

"Actually, not that bad. Resting it on the rock seems to have helped."

"You haven't fixed any coffee?"

"Naw, I didn't want to wake you."

"Okay. How's about I fix some coffee, then French toast for breakfast? We need to eat that bread before it starts to grow penicillin."

Matt kissed her hand and nodded. She leaned over and kissed him, then returned to the camper. A few moments later, she delivered his cup of coffee.

"Toast is cooking. You want it out here or inside?"

"Let's eat at the table. Will you take my coffee back inside?"

Barb took the coffee she had just delivered and put a hand out to help Matt stand. She followed as he limped to the camper and settled at the table with his coffee. Moments later, she slid a plate laden with three slices of hot French toast in front of Matt. He added a bit of syrup and began picking at it, eating only small bites. He ate better when Barb turned off the stove and joined him with her plate of tasty toast grilled with cinnamon and egg.

Finishing her breakfast, Barb asked about their plans for the day. "You think you could make it back to the lake this morning? We need to wash our bodies and clothes."

Managing a smile, he replied, "Sure. How are we going to manage everything we need to take? I won't be able to carry but so much."

"Good point. How about we empty our day packs and fill them with dirty laundry. If we cram tightly, we should be able to get all of it. What about water?"

"I think we're okay on water for another day or two. Give my ankle time to heal so I can carry my share of the load. Do I get another cup of coffee and a pain pill before we go?"

"Do you really need one?"

"Coffee, ABSOLUTELY! . . . Guess I could skip the pain pill, for now."

It only took a minute for the kettle to whistle, so Matt stayed at the table while Barb did a quick cleanup of the breakfast dishes. After donning their laundry filled backpacks, they added a bag of garbage to the growing collection stored in their SUV and headed for the lake.

Matt stopped after just a few steps and called, "Solar Panel! Battery is about gone."

"Good idea, it's a pretty day. I'll get the stuff and you tell me how to hook it up."

Barb trekked back to the camper and retrieved the equipment from the closet. Matt met her at the front of the camper, waiting to connect the wires. "First, connect the controller to the back of the panel." As he talked, he pointed to parts and connections. "Good, now give me the ends of the long wire . . . yep, the clips. Now, go put the panel and controller toward the front of the car, in the sunlight." As Barb placed the gear, Matt connected the wires to the battery.

"Okay to turn it on?" Barb asked after placing the panel and controller on the ground.

"Go for it."

Seconds later the controller came to life, showing forty-three watts from the panel. "That's not a lot of power, is it?"

Collecting his backpack, Matt replied, "Nope, but better than nothing. It will take a lot of sunshine to restore full power to the battery at that trickle rate."

Direct sunlight had just begun to cross the lake, from the far side, as they disrobed and slipped into the water together. Sharing an old soap-on-a-rope Matt had used a few times over the years in showers at public campgrounds, they took turns scrubbing the past week from each other, having a bit of fun as they rubbed. Bodies cleaned, they turned to cleaning their clothes on the steps. Matt dropped the soap once, but found the rope by swishing his hand around beside the steps. In his enthusiasm to get the laundry clean, Matt also washed one of their towels set aside for drying after the bathing. Barb insisted on drying herself first, then handed the not-so-dry towel to Matt.

"Hey, at least we have one clean towel," Matt defended himself.

"You aren't really into laundry, are you?" Barb taunted. "I mean you lose the soap in the weeds then wash the towel we, you, need to dry with."

"Hey. I found the soap, and your lost underwear in the process, and we had two towels. No harm done. As soon as I get my shoes on, I'd like to check out that cabin again."

Hoisting himself up with his crutch, Matt hobbled down to the cabin, while Barb finished wringing their clothes out and stuffing them into the backpacks. When she joined him, he was standing in the middle of the cabin, holding what was once a broom. Using his crutch for support under his right arm, he swung the broom with his left. Each sweep left broom straw amidst the barely disturbed dirt.

"That'll never work," Barb chuckled. "But you do have the right idea. We need to clean this place out before we can even consider moving in here."

"But why go to the trouble of cleaning it up if we aren't going to move in?"

"In its present state, I would not consider it. If we can get some of the dirt out of here, I might consider it," she replied with conviction. "Let's get back to camp. We need to string a clothesline and get stuff drying out."

Matt didn't mention it, but being in the cold lake water significantly eased the swelling and pain in his ankle. By the time they got back to camp, the swelling had begun to return, yet he was almost able to put weight on it without screaming out in pain. Working together, they strung a clothesline. Matt then pulled clothes from the packs and unrolled them as he handed them to Barb to hang. Direct sunlight would not reach this wet laundry, but a gentle breeze could speed up drying time.

That afternoon, Barb insisted that Matt stay off his ankle. He tried to bury himself in a book but found he spent most of his time simply staring out into the forest. After supper, Barb got the laundry in. Finding a few pieces were still dampish, she hung these in the shower. Matt collected the solar panel. The battery was now back up to fifty percent. When they got ready for bed, Matt retrieved the broom from the bathroom. This device had a four foot long handle, but the broom was only eight inches wide, if that. The nylon bristles were designed for sweeping smooth vinyl floors, not rough hewn wood.

Holding it up, Matt asked, "What do you think?"

Barb chuckled slightly and shook her head. "Good for the camper. No way it will sweep out that cabin."

Twelve

Day Eleven

Taking care of dirty laundry seemed an easy task, however Matt's ankle was seriously swollen again when he awoke the next morning. Getting out of the trailer for morning coffee proved to be more difficult than the day before.

"I'm not going to lift you back into the camper just for breakfast. We can sit out here and have cereal," Barb declared, not happy with the situation.

Matt didn't like the overly sweet selection of sugary treats on the breakfast list, yet reluctantly accepted a box of Fruit Loops. Their milk, having lost its sweetness and on the edge of beginning to sour, did nothing to enhance the flavor. Every bite increased his frustration and desire to escape, yet did nothing to provide a solution. Without thinking, he tossed the last bit into the bushes then begged Barb for a second cup of coffee.

Equally distressed by their situation, Barb also disposed of the last of her cereal by tossing it into the forest, albeit somewhat more distant from the camper. Returning with Matt's coffee a few minutes later, she also delivered two bottles of water from the fridge. "Strap these to your ankle, they might help." She then returned to the camper for her own second cup of coffee.

Matt groaned while using the old elastic bandage to secure the bottles of water to either side of his ankle, then settled back to drink his coffee. Lowering the cup after his first sip, he watched rain drops create circles in the black liquid.

Sighing, Barb stood and took Matt's cup. Seeing that he could reach his crutch, she headed for the camper. After putting their coffee on the table, she held the door as Matt hobbled toward her. Once he was inside, she folded the chairs and leaned them against the trailer before joining Matt at the inside table.

"Well, I guess we read or sleep this morning," he moaned.

"It will be good for your ankle to stay put," Barb replied, opening a book.

They talked little, read little, yet stared out the window at a gentle rain quite a bit throughout the morning. After three mindless hours, Barb got up and started to go out into the drizzle.

"Where you going?" Matt asked, genuinely concerned.

"I'm going to put the awning up. That way we can sit outside."

"Awning is motorized. Do you know where the crank is?"

"Should be in the storage well. I guess you haven't looked." Her tone was short and put-out.

"I was going to, but somehow just didn't see the point." Matt tried to defend himself, knowing defense was pointless.

Without another word, Barb retrieved a ring of keys from a drawer and went outside. Minutes later the awning began to extend and then stopped.

"AGGHHH!" Barb screamed as Matt hobbled out, water bottles falling from his ankle as he stepped down.

Without a word, he went to the awning arm on the side opposite where Barb stood with the crank and shook it. "Try now."

Barb resumed cranking, stopping two more times as the awning jammed. Each time, she and Matt jiggled the arm closest to them, and the process resumed.

"Why does it do that?" Barb asked after finally getting the awning fully extended.

"Jerking. The motor operates smoothly so the arms slide smoothly. We ain't smooth enough." Matt raised his eyebrows and smiled, trying to diffuse his wife's anxiety.

Barb chuckled at his humor and stored the crank. Matt retrieved the bottles of water, which were no longer cold, and opened both chairs. Sitting, he opened one bottle and offered the second to Barb.

"No, thanks. I prefer mine cooler than ankle temperature."

Matt chuckled, took a sip, and stared out into the rain. Neither had any interest in lunch and both continued to look at their books occasionally while spending the majority of their time looking into the forest and dreaming of other times.

Drizzling rain stopped in early afternoon with clouds parting and sunshine pouring down from a blue sky. Not having any motivation, neither Matthew nor Barbara made any attempt to do anything the rest of the day, beyond sitting and gazing into the forest. A squirrel provided some entertainment when it found the fruit loops Matt had discarded. Feeling the temperature rise, Barb did remember they had damp laundry and hung it back out on the line, then returned to her chair under the awning.

When afternoon faded into evening, Barb made ham and turkey sandwiches, using the last of the bread and sliced meat provided by their hosts. Unable to perk coffee, they settled for instant before retiring.

"The end of another exciting day in paradise," Matt mumbled as he tried to find sleep.

"Do you suppose this is what we will get to enjoy when we retire?"

"God, please NO! This isn't retirement; it's hell in its worst manifestation."

Lying side by side, but not touching, each eventually found sleep.

Day Twelve

Hearing the sound of a swarm of bees outside the camper, Matt fluttered his eyes. Listening, he lay still until the sound faded away, then checked his vitals. He could see the roof of the camper, so his eyes worked. He heard the delivery bees, so his ears worked. His left shoulder ached only a bit; it was better. His right ankle seemed to not hurt as badly as the day before; that was good. Rolling his shoulders, he stretched out as best he could, then looked over at his wife. Her eyes were open and looking at his.

"Well, should we go see what the grocer brought?" Matt asked.

"Are you up to it? How's your ankle?"

"Okay, I guess. It's not throbbing."

"Good. Wrap it before you put your shoes on. I'm going to the bathroom."

Barb then rolled out of bed and stumbled into the loo. Matt sat up, rubbed his eyes, then fumbled around in the stack of laundry on the sofa until he found clean underwear.

"I forgot to get the clothes from the line last night," Barb moaned, seeing Matt looking through the laundry after pulling on socks. "Your jeans are on the line."

"I'll just wear what I had on yesterday. No problem."

Having little difficulty getting his right foot through the soft jeans, Matt stood and finished pulling them up. Smiling at his wife, who was now looking for her own clothes, he reported, "Better. Ankle's much better."

"Good. Now, step outside, please, so I can have room to dress."

Matt kissed his wife on her forehead and complied with her wish, grabbing the crutch as he stepped out the door. His feet firmly on the ground, Matt took the crutch in his left hand and stretched out with both arms as far as he could, calling out in a loud yawn, "AAAAHHHHH." Taking a deep breath and letting it out in a humpf, he finally turned his head toward their delivery and called to his wife. "Barb, would you please hand me my jacket. It's cold out here."

Not quite finished dressing, her pants not closed, Barb stepped out of the camper and handed Matt's jacket to him. "Egad, you're right. That bit of rain yesterday must have been a cold front. I need my coat, too." She then turned back into their camper. After Matt got his coat on, he tucked the crutch back under his arm and slowly hobbled over to the bins.

"What'd we get this time?" Barb asked, coming up behind him, still adjusting her own jacket.

"Haven't opened them yet. They gave us a bottle of gas, which was nice; keep the fridge chilling." Squatting down next to one of the bins, he paused. "Did it rain last night?"

"I don't think so, why?"

"This bin is wet." Looking at the gas bottles, he added, "So is the gas." Considering a small puddle of water on the plastic bin, he pried the lid off. "Ha! We need to be careful what we ask the forest for."

"What do you mean?" Barb asked, coming to look over his shoulder.

"Instant ice packs, ace bandages, a new first aid kit, even a coffee pot and our brand of instant coffee. They are listening to everything we say! . . . Wow! A bottle of sanitizer for the toilet! A refreshing surprise."

Barb discounted Matt's concern over the wet lid and opened the second bin. "You're right. Peach tea, plain potato chips; let's see what else . . . eggs, more lunch meat, bacon, bread. Looks like they expect us to stay another week in paradise."

Each closed the bin they were examining and stood. Matt tried to lift his and immediately dropped it. "Well, doing better but ankle says to not carry the bin. Guess I should just grab an armload and shuttle back and forth."

"Let's take one load over, then I want to see your ankle," Barb responded. She then popped the lid from Matt's bin and pulled out the first aid supplies. Handing them to Matt, she said, "Take this and sit down." She then grabbed an armful of groceries and followed him back to the camper. After storing her carry, Barb checked Matt's ankle. "It's better. Don't think you need to ice it, but you should use one of those new bandages and wrap it up." She then returned to the bins.

Lifting out regular size boxes of cereal, this time plain corn flakes and Cheerios, she found a note. Reading the message, she chuckled and called to Matt. "Hey, get this, they want their bins back. Note in the bottom of the bin says, 'Please leave empty bins in the clearing.' "

"Can we fill them with rocks?" Matt replied.

"Remember, they can hear you."

Matt then got a twinkle in his eye but said nothing. Barb continued to ferry groceries from the clearing to the camper. Matt wrapped his ankle with a new bandage. When Barb finished emptying the bins, Matt waved to her and catching her attention, put a finger to his lips. He then hobbled over to their SUV and quietly opened the back door. Without a word, Barb understood his intent. Together they removed all the collected garbage from the vehicle and stored it in the empty bins. Neither bin was full when they completed their silent task, however Matt did retrieve the two bins from the first delivery and set them beside the new delivery. Smiling at one another, they returned to their camper for a breakfast of bacon and eggs.

After breakfast, they enjoyed a second cup of coffee inside the warmth of their camper. Whispering, Matt asked, "Did you hear the drones at all this morning?"

"No. Why?" Barb replied, also whispering.

"I didn't hear them arrive, but I'm certain they left in the direction of the lake. That with the water on the one bin and the gas tank . . . I want to go back to the waterfalls."

"Can you walk that far?"

"Will have to. It may take a bit longer than usual, but I have to."

Looking at her husband with understanding and admiration, Barb agreed. "Let me clean the dishes and we'll go. Do you need any pain meds?"

"Probably wouldn't hurt, no pun intended. I'll hook up the solar panel while you clean up."

Matt had to stop halfway to the lake. Sitting together on a fallen tree, Barb asked, "So, what's so important that you need to abuse your ankle today?"

Replying in his normal speaking voice but with a bit of urgency in his tone, Matt replied, "I'm certain the drones left in this direction. On top of that, the water on the bins. It hasn't rained since noon yesterday, where did the water come from?"

"The falls," Barb acknowledged. "You're thinking there is a tunnel or something behind one of the falls."

"Bingo."

"But didn't you look for a tunnel or a cave?"

"I did, but just because I didn't find it the first time doesn't mean it isn't there. I've missed things on the first pass before." Another moment slipped by in silence before Matt announced, "Time to go!" He then stood, positioned his crutch, and put a hand out to his wife.

Barb accepted his hand and held onto it as they slowly made their way toward the waterfalls. Resting beside the lake, sitting in grass warmed by sunshine, a movement at the western tree line caught Barb's eye.

"What's that?" she asked, pointing toward the forest across the lake.

Matt didn't have to ask where; a line of rhododendron trees was shaking, as though a beast of some kind was tromping down the hillside. When the disturbance reached the lower bushes, closest to the lake, the shaking stopped and a snarling noise began. As the noise grew louder one bush shook violently for several seconds, then all was quiet for nearly half a minute, when it shook again, more violently but only briefly.

Barb and Matt looked at one another. Each had an expression of wonder and fear. "Wait here," Matt said softly, as he stood and walked cautiously toward the bush.

"MATTHEW! What if it's a bear?" Barb called in a loud whisper.

Matt shrugged his shoulders and continued toward the bush. Stepping over a heavy stick, he picked it up and approached the bush. It was now snarling, softly. Crouching down, he crept past the outermost bush and pushed branches away with the stick. A great golden beast, ensnared by the bush, whined, pleading for help.

Relieved he was not facing a bear, Matt stood and pushed past the bush in front of him. Caught between branches, the beast held perfectly still as Matt assessed the situation. Coming down the hill, this dog had become captured when an open steel hook on its collar, which might have once held tags, locked onto a lower rhododendron branch. In an attempt to break free, it had become turned around, twisting the branch and collar together. Matt could see the dog was having trouble breathing. He carefully reached over its back and around its neck to unbuckle the collar. Tension from the branch held the buckle tight, so Matt turned the offending branch to release the pressure. Feeling the collar snap free and fall off, the dog whipped around to the right and exploded out of the bushes, racing toward Barbara.

Stretched out in a full run, this blonde bombshell appeared to reach six feet in length and weigh at least one hundred pounds.

"BARB! Protect yourself!" Matt called out.

Immediately the dog stopped, turned around, and raced back toward Matt. Not stopping until he had knocked Matt to the ground, he bathed his rescuer with a grateful tongue; tail wagging nonstop.

"You found a friend!" Barb laughed out loud as she walked up.

Now rubbing the dog's head and neck, Matt appreciated the animal more fully. Standing about twenty inches tall, it was a healthy adult male Labrador Retriever, actually weighing more in the range of 60 - 75 pounds. Realizing that he was getting love from only one person, the dog moved over to Barb, bathing her with slobbery affection.

Examining the dog's neck, Matt said, "His collar got snagged on a bush, but he doesn't seem to be hurt in anyway."

"Can we keep him?" Barb asked as though a little girl falling in love with a new puppy.

Looking at the collar, which he had retrieved from the bush, Matt saw no signs of any identifying tags. "Ask him. I don't think we have much of a say in that matter. But, time to move on. We'll see if he follows us to the waterfalls."

When they first resumed their journey, the dog bounced around them, taunting them to play with him. Reaching the end of the lake, he gave up on play and proceeded to patiently lead them through the forest in the direction of the waterfalls. Watching the forest on both sides of the stream they were following, the dog would pause frequently to allow Matt time to catch up. Arriving at the waterfall, he took a drink and sat, as though waiting for a new adventure.

Unable to safely negotiate the rocks to look behind the larger falls, Matt trusted Barb to do this and describe everything she saw. Frustrated with finding nothing new or of value, Matt hobbled to the edge of the smaller fall. While Matt stood, staring at the falling water and rocks, the dog casually got up from where he was watching, walked around Matt, and disappeared.

Barb and Matt stared at one another until they heard barking from behind the small fall. Eager to see what the dog was trying to show them, Matt picked his way along the rock wall to the left of the fall. The space was just over a foot wide and he got only a sprinkle of water on his back. Arriving at the back side of the water he looked around and seeing nothing, whistled for the dog. Seconds later, the dog appeared from behind the rock beside the fall. Walking toward the animal, Matt found a four foot wide entrance to a tunnel concealed by the wall itself. He actually had to go behind the small fall, turn around, and step to the side away from the main fall, before he saw it.

Stepping only a few feet into the tunnel, or cave, both Barb and Matt stopped. It was pitch dark. Looking around, Matt spotted three tiny red lights farther in, just above head height. "Back up," he whispered. When he and Barb were back to the opening, he knelt down and rubbed the dog's neck. "Go inside, show me what's in there."

Immediately the dog turned and trotted into the darkness. As he progressed, lights came on, triggered by motion sensors. Peeking around the corner, Matt could see the tiny red lights were now brighter. "Cameras," he thought out loud in a soft whisper. He then motioned for Barb to leave.

Once outside, Matt put a finger to his lips and pointed toward the lake. About fifty yards from the waterfalls, he stopped and talked to Barb in a whisper.

"That tunnel is wide enough to get our supplies in and out, and they have motion sensors and cameras watching it. I'm not sure, but they may know we've found it."

"Wouldn't they just think the dog stumbled into it?"

"I hope so. . . . He seemed to know it was there. Went right in as though he had done it a hundred times before."

"That's one smart dog. Where is he?"

Matt whistled as loudly as he could in the direction of the waterfalls. Seconds later the golden rocket bounded through the forest toward them.

"Matt. If they already know that we've found their tunnel, why don't we check it out? It could tell us something."

Matt thought for a minute, scratching the dog's head. "Okay. I wasn't sure, but don't really have a reason not to. They've got to know we're here. Let's go back."

As Barb and Matt walked back toward the waterfalls, the dog sensed where they were going and took the lead. As soon as he stepped into the tunnel, lights came on, illuminating the way for Matt and Barb. Beyond the entrance, the tunnel was ten feet wide and a little taller. After forty feet, or so, it opened into a much larger tunnel, nearly twenty feet across and fifteen feet high, all lit by lights activated by motion sensors and monitored by cameras, just like the entrance. The floor and walls, throughout, were relatively smooth and there were no shadows, other than their own. Fifty yards into the mountain, it all came to an end. The tunnel resumed the size of the entrance, just over four feet wide, but was blocked by an iron gate; not bars but a solid sheet of metal. Multiple cameras recorded the entire space, lit by an array of spotlights.

After checking out a modern electronic security lock securing the barrier, Matt yielded. "I've seen enough."

"Let's head back to camp. You need to get off that ankle," Barb suggested.

Petting the dog vigorously, Matt agreed. "Yes, but I want to make a stop on the way."

"O k a y," Barb acknowledged slowly, wondering what her husband was up to now, and where they were heading this time.

Matt noticed that as they left each section of the tunnel, lights behind them went out.

Arriving at the lake, the dog turned to the left and went down to the cabin. "He's reading my mind," Matt chuckled.

"You still thinking about moving in here?" Barb challenged.

"Thinking about it."

The dog bounded ahead of them, bursting through the door as if he owned the place. Matt stopped at the step to the porch and stared. Beside the door was a new straw broom, sturdy enough to clean the dirtiest and roughest of floors. Anger began to rage inside him as he turned and stormed past Barb, back toward the lake. Barb looked at him in wonder, then she, too, saw the broom and understood.

Had Matt not been hampered by a bad ankle and crutch, Barb would not have caught him before reaching their camper. Slowed by his temporary disability, she caught him lakeside. When she touched his shoulder, he turned on her like a madman.

"THAT is outright manipulation! THEY want us in the cabin so they can keep tabs on us better! Maybe nicer for us, but a whole lot easier for THEM! It'll have to be a whole lot colder than this before I move up here!"

Hearing Matt yelling, the dog crept out of the woods and sat about twelve feet away. His head down and his eyes locked on Matt, the dog waited to see what would happen next.

"Back to camp," Barb directed.

Matt complied without argument. The dog followed cautiously, ten to twelve feet behind. Half way back to camp, sensing that the man's anger had subsided, somewhat, the dog trotted beside them.

Barb fixed three ham sandwiches for lunch. The dog enjoyed his and waited for more, which did not happen. Matt wrapped cold water bottles from the fridge to his ankle to reduce swelling from the morning hike. While Matt recovered, Barb and the dog gathered firewood. The retriever was actually quite helpful, carrying small branches while Barb picked up limbs too large for his mouth. All settled around a warming fire for the afternoon.

Barb idly read her book. Matt mentally conjured multiple schemes involving the tunnel. The dog slept, becoming alert every time one of the people got up for anything.

Supper featured quarter pound frankfurters, delivered that morning. Once again, the dog was not truly satisfied with just one, even though it was in a roll.

"Should we name this beast?" Matt asked as the dog devoured the hot dog and roll separately.

"If you name him, you've got to take care of him," Barb replied.

"He has a family somewhere. He was wearing a collar," Matt explained, rubbing the dog's neck with both hands.

"I knew a family once who called their dog 'Dee-O-Gee'."

"Dee-O-Gee?"

"Yes, as in D O G, dog."

"Why not?" Matt chuckled. "Welcome to paradise, Dee-O-Gee."

Dee-O-Gee whoofed and stole what was left of Matt's potato chips. Chuckling, Matt retrieved the new coffee pot and proceeded to perk a pot over the glowing embers. Drinking their hot evening delight, Barb asked Matt what he had been thinking about all afternoon.

"Do you have a plan yet? I know you've been working on something around that tunnel."

"Actually yes, but I'm not so happy with it."

"Care to share?"

"Sure. Wait until time for the next delivery. Should be in five or six days, before sunrise. Then, we greet our grocery men, or women, outside the tunnel. I'm thinking that the gate will be unlocked then and we can somehow get past it. If we have to, force one of the grocery men to open it for us."

"You and me overpower how many military type people?" Barb responded skeptically.

"Who said they were military? Besides, we might have Dee-O-Gee on our side, if we treat him nicely."

"I'm getting cold. You ready for bed?"

"Yeah, I guess so," Matt groaned as he stood. "Do I have to keep my ankle wrapped overnight?"

"Naw. We'll give you a break." Barb then stood, folded her chair and leaned it against the camper. After pouring the last of the coffee onto the fading embers, she put the grounds into a bag, which she added to the bins waiting for pickup. Matt put his chair with Barb's and stirred the fire a bit, making sure there was nothing left to flame up overnight.

Dee-O-Gee watched what they were doing with interest, until they opened the door to the camper. Watching Matt climb the steps, Dee-O-Gee squeezed in ahead of Barb. Feeling the warmth of the camper, he curled up under the table and waited for the people to settle into bed. Everything quiet, the newest member of the team put his head down and was soon sound asleep.

Thirteen

Day Thirteen

Matt awoke to the sound of whimpering. Opening his eyes and seeing only faint shadows, he listened more intently, then sat up. Dee-O-Gee was sitting beside the bed, whimpering.

"I guess you want to get out of the camper?" Matt asked, smiling inside and out. "Move back so I can get out of bed."

As Matt began to swing his legs out of the bed, Dee-O-Gee moved to the door and sat, waiting. Matt slipped around the bed and shuffled across the camper. Opening the door, he looked outside for the first time that day. It was not yet daylight, actually predawn. Darkness was lingering in the trees as Dee-O-Gee leapt to the ground and ran around the rear of the camper. Feeling his own call of nature, Matt closed the door and stepped into the bathroom.

Several minutes later, Matt's movement in the bathroom awakened Barb. Rising to her elbows, she saw Matt standing in front of the sink. Puzzled, she asked, "What's the matter?"

"I was just wondering if washing my hands was a wise use of water."

Somewhat alarmed by the statement, Barb challenged Matt. "Excuse me?"

Turning toward his wife, Matt replied, "We can get more water; it is a bit of bother, but we can get more water. However, my real concern is the battery. This battery takes forever to charge and I'm not sure how long it will keep operating the pump. Sounds ridiculous when I say it out loud. I guess when it stops, it stops." He then turned back to the sink and quickly washed his hands.

When he returned to bed, Barb looked around the camper. "Where's Dee-O-Gee?"

Matt thought for a mere second before recalling. "Oh, he asked to go outside. I'll see if he's ready to come back in." He then climbed out of bed, again, and walked over to the door, which he opened and looked out. Not seeing the dog, he gave a quick whistle and waited. Dee-O-Gee did not appear and feeling the cool air, Matt shrugged his shoulders and closed the door. He was just about to climb back across the bed when he heard a bark. Once again he crossed the small camper and opened the door. There sat Dee-O-Gee, patiently waiting to invited back in.

"Well, are you coming in or do you just like to see me holding the door open?"

Dee-O-Gee responded with a soft "whoof" and squeezed past Matt. By the time Matt had closed the door, the dog was curled comfortably under the table. As Matt climbed back into bed, Barb chuckled. "He sure has you well trained." Matt flopped onto his back and pulled the covers over his chest.

An hour or so later, when daylight was beginning to filter through the window, Dee-O-Gee sat at the foot of the bed and barked once, softly. Barb was the first to sit up and acknowledge his presence. "Yes?"

"Aargh." It was a soft comment, followed by a tongue licking his lips.

"Matt," Barb called, pushing on her husband. "Dee-O-Gee wants breakfast. Come to think of it, I'm a bit hungry, too. You up to fixing pancakes for all of us?"

"Sure." Matt then stretched in all directions possible, sat up on the side of the bed, and stretched his arms again. "Let me wash my face, start the coffee, then pancakes. Will that do, dog?"

Dee-O-Gee looked at the man for a few short seconds then replied, "Aargh." He then circled around, sat under the table, and waited.

Matt did fix coffee for himself and Barb, then pancakes for all. Dee-O-Gee politely waited his turn then gentlemanly devoured three cakes before moving toward the door. With one more batch of cakes in the griddle, Matt reached over and let him out. Matt and Barb both chuckled about Dee-O-Gee's presence and manner; a welcome break from their constant struggle. After finishing their breakfast and starting a second cup of coffee, Matt and Barb cleaned the dishes. When they took the remains of their coffee outside, Dee-O-Gee was nowhere to be seen.

"By the way, how's your ankle?" Barb asked as they sat under the awning, books in hand.

"Okay, I guess. It's a bit sore."

"How's about we take the day off and let your ankle recover?"

"Does that mean I don't have to mow the grass today?"

"Hmm, I'm not sure. If I let you skip it today, it'll still have to get done." Barb smiled and they leaned into one another for a quick kiss.

Believing Matt had developed a plan to get through the tunnel and then home, Barb settled back and read. After about an hour, she paused. Closing her book, marking her place with a finger, she stared out into the forest for several minutes before glancing over at Matt and returning to her book. She maintained this routine throughout the morning. She did, however, have to wipe tears from her eyes during multiple pauses.

Matt, however, would read a page or two then gaze out into the forest, contemplating his idea of snaring the grocers. He was known, at work, for his calm in difficult situations. He had often been quoted as saying, "The only thing that keeps an incident from becoming a disaster is how you handle it. Be calm and think it through." While others thought he was "calmly" thinking it through, his mind was more often racing to figure out how to handle whatever gosh awful mess he was facing at the moment.

While reading, Barb thought he was calmly analyzing their situation. She struggled desperately with how she might help Matt without causing him greater concern. In reality, Matt was near panic as he mentally reviewed different scenarios. Repeatedly, he would replay the tunnel in his mind and then what he would have to do to gain passage through the gate. Each time he played the scenario in his mind, he would find a new obstacle, which he would consider until he devised a solution. Comfortable with his plan, for the moment, he would return to reading, for another page or two, whereupon he would repeat the exercise; often revising his plan. He did his best to smile whenever he caught Barb's eyes looking at him. He couldn't let her know that none of his plans worked for more than a few seconds.

"I'm getting a bit peckish," Barb announced following a reading pause that was filled with tears. "You interested in lunch?"

Looking to the sky and determining that the sun had indeed passed its peak, Matt replied, "Sure, why not." His tone betrayed his frustration. Looking at his wife and seeing that she had been crying, he tried to smile. "Tough book?"

"Not the book. Our current story. Nobody would believe this if we could tell them." She reached over and squeezed his outstretched hand. "I'll get sandwiches, you get us some tea. Have you seen Dee-O-Gee?"

Standing and testing his ankle, Matt replied, "Not since breakfast."

"How's it doing? Think you'll be up to a short walk after lunch?"

Matt smiled without overt commitment and began to move toward the door.

Lunch consisted of deli meat sandwiches, chips (Matt had plain and Barb had sour cream with onion), and peach tea. Hoping Dee-O-Gee might return, Barb saved a quarter of her sandwich. When he didn't show, she slowly finished it.

After lunch, they bandaged Matt's ankle and started toward the river. Matt stopped abruptly at the front of their SUV. "We forgot to get the solar panel in last night!"

Barb went over and checked the controller. "Seems to be working. Lucked out this time; apparently no bears came to play. Let's go."

Sighing with relief, Matt joined his wife as they walked past the grocery bins and resumed their adventure, stopping at the first meadow. Sitting and thinking, they enjoyed the change in scenery. As they were about to return to camp, Barb asked, "So, do you have a plan yet?"

Feeling they were far enough away from camp and electronic ears, Matt shared his thoughts. "Sort of. Get up early the day before we expect the next delivery and make our way to the waterfall. Then, wait until they come out, and ask for release."

"That's it, just 'ask for release'?"

"Well, yes actually. You said they might be military types and most possibly in some number for safety and efficiency. We have no idea what we will encounter until we actually encounter them."

"Okay. Why the day before?"

"Hunch. We got groceries first time on the fifth day, then the second delivery was yesterday . . . day twelve, I believe. So that's four days, a delivery, then seven days before the next delivery. Not sure there is any logic there, except the groceries

should last about a week. By going up a day early, we will learn
how long it will take and how to make the trek in the dark."

"Wait! In the DARK?"

"Yes, in the dark. Both deliveries have arrived just before
dawn. If we are going to catch these guys, we need to be at the
waterfall at least an hour before dawn."

"And just how do you plan to awaken in time to do this?"

"Two alarm clocks. I'll have to burn a bit of the battery on
the phone and employ the ole injun trick - drink water before
going to bed."

"'Ole injun trick'? Another of your scout skills?"

"No. I learned it from my dad. Drink enough water so that
you have to wake up at a certain time to go to the bathroom."

"How much water do you need to wake up at four in the
morning?"

"Don't know. Guess I'll have to start testing my aging
bladder."

Barb stared at her husband as though he had lost his last
ounce of sense. "How's your ankle?"

"Okay for the most part. Only hurts now when I walk on it."

"Alright injun scout, let's get you back to camp."

As soon as Matt tucked the crutch under his right arm, Barb
took his left hand and they strolled back to camp. Reaching their
trailer, Matt settled into a chair and rested his foot on a
comfortable log. Barb retrieved two glasses of peach tea from a
pitcher in the refrigerator and they sat peacefully enjoying the
quiet of the forest.

"I hate to admit it," Barb commented after a couple minutes,
"but I miss the noise of kids and other campers. I like the quiet,
but somehow it is becoming depressing."

"I know what you mean," Matt agreed. "The noise of other
campers yelling at one another always annoyed me, but like you,
I miss it."

"Should I scream out into the forest?"

"Naw, it would only come out as anger and frustration.
Besides, we always trained our kids to be respectful of the forest
and all the critters living here. I don't think they appreciate our
outbursts. . . . What are you thinking about for supper?"

"I'm not really in the mood to fix anything but we have
ground beef we could turn into burgers, trusty and reliable

dinner franks, and always satisfying Dinty Moore or Brunswick stew."

"Oh, my, such variety. I thought we got skinny franks this time."

"We did. Sorry. I guess I was just recalling our good ole days. You know, the previous delivery."

"Let's splurge and do burgers. Do we have cheese and buns?"

"Cheese, no buns."

"Okay," Matt decided, "Texas Burgers . . . big, fat, and juicy with cheese melting from the inside."

Reacting to Matt's suggestion, Barb added, "I believe we have barbeque sauce and steak seasoning to zing them up a bit."

"Good. You start the burgers, I'll get some wood and build the fire."

"No, not with your ankle. I don't want you traipsing all around the forest. I'll get the wood, you fix the burgers. Be sure to dig out some beans. Make them green and baked."

"What, we have a new delicacy? Baked green beans?"

"Two cans, different types, smarty." Barb then stood and ventured into the forest for more firewood.

Matt limped into the camper and began preparing oversized burgers, flavoring the meat with steak seasoning and stuffing them with cheese. He also pulled out two cans of beans; cut green beans and traditional baked beans. Leaving the meat under an aluminum foil cover, he joined Barb by the fire. Seeing several larger logs, he retrieved their trail axe from the storage compartment and began splitting fire wood. Working together, they had a blazing fire going less than half-hour after deciding on their menu.

As the fire began to collapse into hot coals, Matt retrieved the grill from its nearby limb. Barb brought the meat out and returned to the camper to heat two cans of beans.

Seeing only two burgers nearing perfection, Barb asked, "Nothing for Dee-O-Gee?"

"Do you see him anywhere? If he was in this part of the forest, I imagine the aroma of cooking beef would have brought him running. He knows where we are if he wants to return."

The burgers were filling, the green beans savory, and the baked beans a perfect complement to the evening meal. As Matt put the coffee pot over the coals, Barb asked, "So, plans for tomorrow?"

"How about fishing? Then we can wander up to the water fall and fill our bottles." After Matt made his suggestion, he silently mouthed, "Check out the area around the falls."

Barb looked at him curiously at first, then understood. "Sounds like a plan. So, maybe fresh fish tomorrow night?"

After enjoying their evening coffee, Matt collected trash and carried it over to add to the delivery bins. Walking into the clearing, he stopped and looked around. The bins were gone. Shrugging his shoulders, he turned around and went to pick up the solar panel, only to find it had been knocked over. Examining the panel in the dim light, he found a new scratch mark on the back. Shaking his head, he put the panel and controller back in their Durango, along with the bag of trash.

Closing the door to their trailer, Matt updated Barb. "Our hosts have picked up the garbage and may have tried to hijack the solar panel."

"What?"

"The bins are gone, apparently picked up while we were on our outing. The solar panel was knocked over. A fresh scratch on the back appears to have been made by a claw trying to lift it." He then went to the camper's control panel and pressed a button. "Battery is up to 80%."

"You don't think they would try to steal the battery, do you?" Barb asked with genuine concern.

"They can't do it with a drone. Would have to come in with a real live person to unstrap it, disconnect the wires, and lift it out. That thing is heavy."

"But you have the cover off to connect the solar panel, don't you?"

"Yes, but it's still wired in and quite heavy. Not the job for a drone. I'd set up some kind of warning system in case they came at night but it would be easier for them to come while we're off exploring. They know when we're here and when we're not. No way to really stop them if they want to steal it." He then filled a ten-ounce glass with water and drank it down.

"You're going to have to get up in the middle of the night."

"Precisely, my love, precisely. Let's see when the one glass alarm sounds."

Barb sighed, a tear forming at her eye and a grin on her lips. "Come to bed."

Matt climbed into bed and snuggled down next to his wife. Together they listened to the quiet of the night and slipped into a deep, exhausted sleep.

Fourteen

Day Fourteen
Matthew and Barbara woke when sunlight began to warm their camper. A bird chirped outside the window on Matt's side. The birdsong was not pleasant, more like a call to get up and get the day started. Rolling over and sitting on the foot of the bed, Matt growled, "I hear you!"

After a breakfast of cold cereal and milk, they loaded empty water bottles into their day packs, added towels, and struck out for the lake shortly before 9:00 a.m. beneath a partly cloudy sky. Matt stopped halfway to their destination and rubbed his ankle.

"How bad does it hurt?" Barb asked with sincere concern. "Will you be able to get to the falls and back?"

"My ankle's fine. A bit sore, that's all."

"Why did we stop?"

"I don't think there are any microphones in this area. We should be able to talk without being overheard."

"Okay." Barbara looked somewhat impressed and curious about what Matt wanted to discuss.

"Next break will be at the lake. I'm certain they have devices monitoring that area, as well as at the waterfalls, so this is our only chance to talk about what we're after."

"Which is . . ." Barb interrupted with a smile.

"I want you to fill the bottles with water from the falls. I'm going to study the wall and area where they might be releasing the drones. The more familiar we are with the area, the better prepared we'll be to achieve escape."

"Are you thinking about confronting the grocers or sneaking into the tunnel?"

"I don't think sneaking into the tunnel will do us any good. I'm certain that door will lock behind them. That's the way I would design it."

"What's your best and worse case scenario?"

"No idea at this time, however the worst case would be they are big, burly, heavily-armed military men with a single purpose and that would not be to take us inside. The best case is they are mousey high schoolers who have no loyalty and would be happy to take us inside."

"So, you are actually expecting something in between muscle-men and kids and not really cooperative. Right?"

"Pretty much. Let's get going."

Matt adjusted the pack on his back and reached his hand out to Barb. Together they hiked as though they didn't have a care in the world. Reaching the lake, they stopped at the steps near the deserted cabin and refreshed themselves with a handful of water. Before continuing toward the waterfall, Matt looked across the lake and saw a huge black bear watching them.

"Was that bear here when we arrived?" Matt asked Barb.

"What bear?" Her heart immediately began to race.

"Across the lake."

Barb looked out and gasped. "Is that your friend from the overlook?" Her voice was strained and excited.

"And probably the one who smashed in the hood of our Durango. But I didn't see him when we stopped for water, did you?"

"No. I would have said something. Probably screamed." Her voice more normal now, her heart also slowed to a rapid beat.

"Well, don't. He seems to be content with watching us for now. Let's move slowly toward the falls. I'll keep an eye on him and we can run to the cabin if we need to." Matt carefully nudged Barb forward.

"You really think that cabin will provide protection from that brute?"

"Only because I don't think he'd fit through the door."

Chuckling at Matt's comment, Barb tried to walk casually around the lake, constantly looking back toward the bear. Matt did the same. When they reached the creek that fed the lake from the falls, both looked back; the bear was nowhere to be seen. Both hearts continued to beat somewhat faster than normal as they followed the stream toward their destination.

Matt stumbled twice as he tried to keep an eye out for the big black lord-of-the-forest. Seeing no sign of the beast did not give him comfort; rather, it kept him on edge. When they reached the waterfall, Barb took a deep breath and tried to convince herself and Matt that they were safe.

"He probably stopped by the lake for a drink of water, just like we did, and is now gone back to wherever it is he goes," Barb mused, trying to restore her own confidence. "You didn't leave the solar panel out did you?"

"No, I figured it was too cloudy to mess with today. Why?"

"I was just thinking that bears seem to like our gadgets."

"Baby bears, anyway. Let's fill the bottles." Matt then dropped his pack and strolled along the wall of the mountain, exploring the area in detail as he walked.

Barb picked up his pack and dumped the empty bottles on the ground. She quickly established a pattern of filling two bottles at a time in a pool at the base of the fall, capping them, and putting them back in the pack, then repeating with the next two bottles. When she finished filling all the empties in both packs, she joined her husband. He put his finger to his lips when she walked up and began to speak. After surveying the immediate area once more, some twenty feet from the waterfall, he nudged Barb back to the packs.

"Okay, fresh water for another week. You ready to head back to the lake?" Matt asked openly in a normal speaking voice.

"Any sign or sound from our big furry friend?" Barb replied with a smile.

Lifting one pack to his back and holding the second for Barb, Matt continued. "Not since we saw him at the lake. I'll bet he's munching in a berry patch about now."

"Fresh berries, that does sound nice."

Chuckling with one another, the now hopeful couple strolled toward the lake. Reaching the area near the cabin, they dropped their packs and began to undress. Splashing into the water, Barb stopped when the water was shoulder deep and turned to Matt. "I thought you were going to fish today. Fresh fish for supper tonight?"

"Yep, I was. I guess I was distracted by the thought of swimming with you again. Guess I'll have to come back after lunch . . . maybe."

Clouds slid from the sky as the campers frolicked in the water. Sunshine bouncing off the water's surface became blinding and they retreated. Using the towels they had brought, just for this purpose, they dried and dressed.

"What would our kids say if they could see us?" Matt asked, chuckling as he pulled his pants on.

"Yes, I'm worried about what they must be thinking or doing. It's been two weeks and we have never been out of communication with both of them this long."

"I've wondered several times if anyone has reported us as missing or have we simply ceased to exist?" Matt replied, his face now drawn with a deep concern. "Folks at work know I'm not there and you're obviously not back at the college. How far have our kidnappers gone to cover up our abduction?"

Barb pulled her shirt on and stared at her husband. Her face had gone cold and tears began creeping from her eyes. "I've done my best to not think about that and pray that our kids are looking for us."

Both went completely silent as they continued dressing. Matt finished first and after slinging his pack over one shoulder, stared down at the log cabin until Barb was ready. She was delayed, stopping to dry her eyes several times. He then picked up her pack and held it while she slipped into the shoulder straps. Their trek back to camp would have been silent as well, save for the reappearance of their golden friend.

Dee-O-Gee bounded around the lake as the couple reached the trail to their camper. His energetic return, wagging tail, and bouncing from one person to the other, restored their smiles and hopes for escape.

"Well, it is indeed good to see you again Dee-O-Gee. I trust you didn't have a run-in with that bear this morning," Matt laughed as he patted the dog.

Dee-O-Gee whoofed gleefully and collected all the love he could before heading back to camp, ahead of his people.

"How'd your injun clock do last night?" Barb asked as they passed the halfway point between the lake and camp.

"Not as good as I'd hoped. Woke up about 2:30; shooting for 4:00. Rest assured, if I get it right tonight, we'll be taking a midnight stroll."

"You sure we need to do a 'midnight stroll'?"

"More than ever. While at the waterfall I did see a motion-activated camera. They're not only listening to our conversations, at some points they're watching us."

"Are they watching at the lake?" Barb asked, blushing.

"Haven't seen any cameras in that area," Matt assured her. Seeing her breathe a sigh of relief, he added, "But then I haven't specifically looked for them either."

"How are you going to look for them at night?" Barb challenged, slapping her not-so-modest husband across the shoulder.

"Red lights. The detectors in the tunnel have small red lights that go bright when activated. We can go back to the lake this evening if you would like to see if we can find any up there." Matt grinned but neglected to tell his wife about the camera he spotted watching him stare at the log cabin.

Lunch was deli meat sandwiches and assorted chips. Like Matt, Dee-O-Gee preferred plain chips to sour cream and onion. He also found he was not fond of peach tea. When he kept nosing around Matt's glass of tea, Matt poured some into a bowl. Dee-O-Gee sniffed it then lapped a couple tongue fulls. With this new taste in his mouth, he raised his head, flapped his tongue several times, then took another taste. This time he sneezed, as though trying to spit the tea out, and grabbed a potato chip from Matt's hand.

Laughing at Dee-O-Gee's antics, Matt dumped the tea from the bowl and filled it with fresh water. Dee-O-Gee lapped it up, cleaning the bowl before sitting contentedly and staring at this man who had tried to 'poison' him.

A half-hour later, Barb noticed that Matt was sitting under the awning and staring into the trees. She tried to follow his line of sight but could see nothing so intriguing. "Okay, lover; questions. First, shouldn't you put the solar panel out now that the clouds have cleared away? Second, are you going to catch dinner for tonight? And third, WHAT are you staring at?"

"No to fishing, my ankle is growling a bit. Maybe tomorrow. I'll set the solar panel up in just a minute because right now I'm trying to decide just what is up in that tree."

"Where? What tree?" Barb asked, trying to see whatever had Matt's attention.

"I was thinking about the camera I saw at the waterfall and noticed a tiny red blink up that tree." Matt pointed to a tree some twenty feet away.

"I don't see anything," Barb replied, looking up and down several trees.

"That's the point. You have to know it's there to see it. Causes quite a few questions to come to mind." Matt stared at the cloaked device, resting in the crook of a branch about twelve or thirteen feet up the trunk.

"I saw it! What is it?" Barb exclaimed, seeing it as it happened to blink.

"I'm not sure . . . but I think it's a camera." Matt was getting irritated at the presence of a spy device invading their privacy. Contemplating what he could do about it, he felt his anger rising and knew he had to distract himself if he was to come up with an answer. "Well, as you said, I should hook up the solar panel and grab as much of this wondrous sunshine as I can."

Running wires from the battery to the controller, then from the controller to the panel should have been a simple operation. Dee-O-Gee thought this was a curious job and kept tripping Matt as he moved from point to point. Despite the dog's help, Matt did think more about the device in the tree. His mind searched for alternatives as he turned the controller on then verified the panel was collecting power and sending it to the battery. Rubbing Dee-O-Gee's neck, one option stuck in his mind. With the panel now working, Matt calmly walked over to their wood pile and picked up the trail axe.

"Dee-O-Gee and I are going to collect some wood for later," he called to his bride who was inside the camper, fixing two tumblers of tea. By the time she poked her head out to respond, they had disappeared.

Matt traipsed around the forest over the hill beyond the clearing that would be a nice place for a bathhouse. Not seeing what he wanted on the ground, he started looking at small trees. Despite distractions of Dee-O-Gee chasing a pair of squirrels, Matt found a tree that met his needs; bending it over he swung the axe once. The base of the tree splintered, which was corrected with a second, more aggressive, blow. Holding the tree, Matt looked at it from end to end; about an inch and a half in diameter and eight feet long. *Need to clean it up*, he thought and began looking for a more solid tree he could use as a block. Not finding anything on the ground, he stepped over to a grown hickory tree and placed his thin tree against it. With only a few well-placed strikes, he cleaned the top and bottom such that he had a pole, not quite seven feet long, with a short branch sticking out near the top.

Dee-O-Gee grabbed the trimmed branches and proudly carried them back to camp. Matt, however, returned so that he came up behind the camera. Placing his axe against the tree serving as the camera stand, he raised his new pole. Setting his strike behind the camera, as a golfer sets a swing against his ball, Matt reared back and slammed the protruding branch into the back of the camera. There was a loud crack and the camera pushed forward around the limb, but did not fall. Shaking his head, Matt saw the device was attached with a velcro strip. Without hesitation, he began using the branch on his pole to manipulate the strip. Several minutes later it opened and the camera fell to the ground. Dee-O-Gee whoofed and retrieved the fallen object.

Once again, Dee-O-Gee held his head high and walked beside Matt as they returned to the camper. As soon as Matt put his hand out, Dee-O-Gee gently gave the camera to him. Impressed with Dee-O-Gee's manner, Matt rubbed the dog's neck. Sitting in his chair beside Barb, he reached over to a fresh tumbler of tea Barb had provided. The intrusion now removed, he was still irritated that this device had even existed in their private campsite.

"So what is it?" Barb asked as Matt examined the small black box.

"It appears to be a wireless camera. No control switches on it so it must be controlled remotely." Running his finger across a smooth panel that spanned the front, he added, "This must be a motion sensor."

"What are you going to do with it?" Barb asked, her voice now betraying her own growing anger.

"I want to smash it, but it seems to still be working."

"So . . ." Barb involuntarily reached out and patted Dee-O-Gee who was now sitting such that he leaned into her leg.

"I remember Bob, our network specialist, explaining how these things worked when he installed them in some of the labs. Definitely not my field of expertise, but I seem to recall that there is signal light that changes with network access. Thing is, I only see the one light that keeps flashing red. Does that mean it is transmitting or trying to connect to a network? . . . I don't know."

"How do you figure it out?"

"Not sure, but my ankle is fussing at me right now, so what I think I'll do is put it in the car for now. Play with it more later." Matt stood and turned toward the Durango.

"What's the range for a device that small?"

Stopping, Matt looked at his wife. "A brilliant question, my love. I don't know but it does raise a question I hadn't considered." Tossing the camera to Barb, he moved toward the camper. "Hold this while I get my phone."

Matt retrieved his phone and turned it on as he sat down next to Barb. "Down to 38%, I need to plug it into the camper and recharge it now that we have some power. But, where are wifi networks?" Matt flipped through a couple screens until he found "Available Networks." Tapping the screen several times, he exclaimed, "Drat! I was hoping this thing was a simple wifi device and I might be able to attach to their network. Should have known better; must be military grade using a more powerful transmission system. Guess that's why there are no setup buttons or controls on it."

"So, you going to hang onto it?"

Matt thought for a moment. "I think so, but I'm going to wrap it up in something so it can't hear or see anything. AND, I think we should keep our eyes open for blinks of red, wherever we go."

As Matt took the camera to the SUV, Barb turned her attention to Dee-O-Gee. Rubbing his neck with both hands, she called to Matt. "So, since you aren't going fishing, should I send Dee-O-Gee out for fresh rabbit or do you have an idea for supper?"

"Yeah, actually. Didn't we get some apples in the last delivery?"

"Yes, why?"

"Well, we have bacon and ground beef, what about adding apples and making 'slurp'?"

"Not a bad idea, except slurp doesn't use apples. It calls for peppers, onions, and tomatoes. We do have the peppers, if they're still good, and onions."

Matt smiled with an impish grin. "Well, if the peppers have gone bad, use the apples."

Shaking her head, Barb replied, "I'll see what I can come up with."

Dee-O-Gee raised his nose, sniffing the air with interest, as Barb placed two bowls of 'slurp' on the camper dining table. Matt chuckled and looked Dee-O-Gee in the eye, telling him, "I'll let you try this after I've had a taste. May be great or . . ."

"Or what?" Barb challenged. "And don't fret, I've already dished some out for him. It's cooling."

Matt spread butter on a piece of bread and raised one eyebrow toward his wife. "Let's see." He then lifted a spoon and dipped it into the slurp. Slowly placing it into his mouth, he pulled out the empty spoon and let the contents roll around his tongue. The corners of his mouth rising, he said, "Woman, you are a magician! Absolutely delightful!"

Dee-O-Gee grew impatient with Matt's proclamation and started patting his feet with his head almost resting on the table. "Okay," Barb conceded, getting up and putting Dee-O-Gee's bowl on the floor. "But don't blame me if it's too hot."

Dee-O-Gee sniffed the bowl once, then gingerly tasted its contents. After considering the flavor, he devoured the remainder without pause. Matthew and Barbara were halfway through their dinner when the dog's presence almost got to be a nuisance.

"Is there any more?" Matt asked.

"Only a smidge. Guess I should let him have it." She then stood and scraped the remainder of the slurp into Dee-O-Gee's bowl. The dog waited for Barb to sit before cleaning his bowl a second time.

Sipping coffee next to an evening fire, Barb asked, "So, tomorrow morning, are you going fishing?"

"I believe so. Also need to consider dumping the waste tank again. Maybe do both in one trip?"

"I checked the gauge on the waste tank this afternoon. You have a couple more days if you want to wait. Maybe let your ankle get back to full strength?"

Matt reached out and took Barb's hand, silently nodding agreement. For the next half-hour, they sat quietly watching stars appear, and listening to Dee-O-Gee snoring.

Fifteen

Day Fifteen

Matt woke in the middle of the night, courtesy of his "injun" alarm clock. Scooting down the bed, he swung his feet to the floor and sat up. Rubbing his eyes then dropping his hands to his lap, he realized the camper was well lit by moonlight streaming through the windows. Raising his arm, he looked at his watch. 4:15. Drawing a deep breath, he stood in the narrow space beside the bed and slipped around to the foot. His first real step toward the bath was nearly his last. Feeling a large furry body as he put his foot down, he thrust his leg forward, throwing himself off balance. Grabbing the table and counter simultaneously, he caught himself and looked down. Dee-O-Gee looked up briefly, then put his head back down, only slightly offended by the interruption to his sleep. Matt rubbed the dog's neck and made his way into the bathroom, limping slightly from a bit of pain in his ankle.

Moments later, while still taking care of business, Matt heard Dee-O-Gee growling. A deep full-chested growl that served as an intense warning. Seconds later, Matt heard their chairs, fire stones, and anything else not part of the earth being bounced around. The bleat of a baby bear was followed by the low short chastising roar of momma bear. Dee-O-Gee barked once in response, a deep throaty bark which seemed to say, "Move on intruder!" Momma bear responded with a long, low, defiant roar, then herded her youngster out of the campsite with motherly snarls.

Finishing his business, Matt cleaned himself up and stepped over the alert, but still prone, Dee-O-Gee. Reaching the bed, he shook Barb, whispering, "It's time."

"What? What time is it?"

"About four-thirty. Come on. Put your dark jeans and jacket on, nothing bright or light. Don't know that we'll need flashlights, good moon, but grab them anyway."

Dee-O-Gee looked at these two people as though they had lost their minds. It was still dark outside, but he joined them as they slipped out of the camper. Matt held his finger to his lips, indicating they should not make any noise. A hundred yards up the trail toward the lake, Matt teased Barb.

"You slept through a bear visit, but Dee-O-Gee protected us."

"What are you talking about and why did we have to be quiet?"

"We had a visit from momma bear and her cub. Dee-O-Gee told them to move on so they did. As for why the quiet, two reasons. First, I didn't want to draw the bears back, and second, I'm not one-hundred-percent sure we got all the surveillance devices out of the campsite. Don't want to alert our host to our midnight stroll."

"Okay. Now, did the bears wake you or was it your alarm clock?"

Matt chuckled, "Bladder. Worked like a charm."

Hearing the banter between the people, Dee-O-Gee added his own comment, "Whoof." His head down slightly, he continued plodding begrudgingly beside them.

"I don't think Dee-O-Gee is a night owl," Barb chuckled.

Bending down to rub the dog's ruff, Matt replied, "No, but he is good to have around."

Reaching the lake, Matt slowed his pace and walked as close to the water's edge as possible. Seeing the puzzled look on his wife's face, he pointed to the cabin. A faint red dot blinked beside a tree halfway between the edge of the trees and the cabin. Putting a finger to his lips, he mouthed, "Move slowly."

Dee-O-Gee picked up on their slowed pace and also slowed his steps to stay beside them. Reaching the stream feeding the lake, Barb asked, "So we don't trigger the motion sensor?"

Matt nodded and whispered, "We should probably be quiet from here on. Don't know what else they have in these trees."

Barb nodded and Dee-O-Gee whoofed softly. Now believing they were just out for a late night stroll, he swished his tail and trotted casually ahead of his rather strange people. Searching the woods for danger, he kept an eye on both Matt and Barb. Arriving at the waterfalls, his mood became more playful.

Crouching down at the edge of the tree line, Matt ruffled Dee-O-Gee's neck then threw an imaginary stick into the area to the left of the falls. Dee-O-Gee looked at him as if to say, "You didn't throw anything," however when Matt threw his arm in the direction he wanted the dog to go, Dee-O-Gee took off running. As he ran in between the mountain and the trees, two bright red dots appeared on the rock walls. The first was only a few feet from the smaller falls and the second was about twenty-five feet further down the wall.

Matt nodded and signaled Barb to head back to the lake. Dee-O-Gee circled around through the trees beyond the second camera and met up with his people as they hiked along the creek. Matt paused and silently praised their companion, ruffling his neck with both hands. Reaching the lake, they quietly and slowly slipped past the cabin. The eastern sky was showing signs of dawn's arrival.

"Two cameras with motion sensors," Matt announced as they entered the forest beyond the lake. "And this golden fur beast is a natural, worth his weight in gold."

"Well, he is golden, in daylight," Barb agreed, squatting down to lavish a bit of attention on their companion.

Daylight had made its arrival by the time they returned to camp and Matt was too charged to even consider going back to bed. Seeing her husband's excited energy level, Barb asked, "Bacon and eggs?"

"Sounds great. You cooking or am I?"

"Why don't you fix us some coffee then get out of the way and I'll do the honors."

Barb fixed extra bacon and an extra egg for Dee-O-Gee, who made them disappear, along with a piece of bread torn into the mix. Sitting under their awning with a second cup of coffee, Barb asked the question of the day. "So, now what?"

Matt thought for a moment, looked around the campsite, then announced boldly, "We found that camera yesterday, but I'm not sure that's all there is. I think I'll spend the morning looking for other devices. Hidden microphones, maybe another camera. I'm really ticked with their spying on us."

"Hey, they do provide a nice concierge service through their spying," Barb taunted.

"Yeah, but I think I'd rather take what comes than have them monitoring our conversations."

"Okay. First, finish our coffee, then I'll do the dishes. I need you to see about our sewage situation."

Matt took another gulp of coffee and lowered the cup to his lap. "Ten-four." After drawing a deep breath and letting it out slowly, he downed the last of his coffee and got up. Stepping into the camper, he first put his cup by the sink, then went to the coat closet. Opening the door he started pushing buttons.

"Fresh water is down to one-quarter, might need to get some today. Black water is showing three-quarters, okay there. Grey is only half . . . which is odd, but okay. Battery is seventy-five percent; need to connect the solar panel." Matt reported to his wife, who was waiting to come inside. "Also, do we have a USB cable for the phones?"

"Cables are in the car. What's odd about the grey water tank?"

"It's been reading half-full for days. All the water from the sink should have near filled it by now."

"What do we have to do to empty it?" Barb asked, squeezing past her husband who barely made room for her to enter.

"We usually empty it at a dump station, which we don't have and I don't have any good ideas, right now. It isn't removable and is larger, which may be why it's only half full. The black water tank is smaller, so it can be removed, but needs to be dumped more often. I'll look into that later, right now I'm going to hook up the solar panel."

Stepping out of the camper, Matt was greeted by Dee-O-Gee who was waiting for a new excursion. Head held high and tail wagging, he bounced around trying to get Matt to play. Matt did give in, somewhat. Leaning over, he petted the dog with affection before stepping around him. After retrieving the solar panel and connecting it to the battery, Matt checked the front seat of the Durango for USB cables. Finding what he needed, he connected his phone to the panel controller. The charging symbol immediately appeared on the phone. Seconds later it showed "37%" and a charging bar slowly circled the current level. Satisfied, Matt laid the phone next to the controller and stepped over to the clearing where there was no bath house and stared out at the forest.

Feeling a nudge at his leg, Matt looked down. Dee-O-Gee was wagging his tail and offering Matt's phone to him, USB cable still attached. Sighing with frustration, Matt moaned, "Dee-O-Gee, no. I left that there to charge." Seeing the dog's ears go back and his tail stop, Matt took the phone and petted the retriever.

"Thank you for finding my phone, but I need to charge it. Now, let's go plug it in again and this time, leave it there."

Walking back to the solar panel, Dee-O-Gee was happy again and wagging his tail. Matt plugged the cable back into controller and laid the phone down. Looking at Dee-O-Gee, he told the dog, "It's okay. Leave it here, please." Satisfied that the dog understood, Matt turned away and took one step. Hearing a scraping sound, he turned around and caught Dee-O-Gee trying to pick up the phone once again. "Dee-O-Gee NO!" Matt returned and put his hand out, instructing the dog, "NO. Leave it here! It's okay. I know where it is."

Dee-O-Gee sat back and whoofed politely, tail swishing unabated. When Matt stood and started to back away, Dee-O-Gee looked down at the phone, up at Matt, back to the phone then trotted back to the camper. Matt followed, shaking his head from side to side with disbelief.

Standing at the rear of his SUV, Matt studied the campsite, searching, examining every tree for something that didn't belong there. Not sure what he was looking for, Matt moved his search into the camper. Barb was still working at the sink so he began his search around the bed. Methodically, he searched every nook, cranny, crevice, cabinet, alcove, and light fixture from one end of the camper to the other; bumping Barb and interrupting her cleaning multiple times. Finding nothing after the first search, yet convinced there had to be at least one listening device somewhere in the camper, he began again. This time he ran his fingers inside the valance covering the window shades. Feeling something small inside the end of the valance next to the bed, he looked again. Unable to see anything, he retrieved a flashlight. The light revealed a disc about the size of a quarter and twice as thick; he pried it loose with his pocket knife.

"What'd you find?"

Examining the device, Matt replied, "I believe we have a microphone." Holding it so Barb could see, he pointed to an area of mesh about the size of a pencil. "This must be the microphone itself, the rest is transmitter." With little effort, he broke the device in two, showing a circuit board inside. "But it ain't transmitting any more." He then resumed searching the camper.

Convinced there was more than one audio device spying on them, Matt took his search back outside. When he began examining the SUV, Dee-O-Gee helped. Together they searched the engine compartment, bumpers, lower body, door frames, and fenders. Matt was relieved and irritated when he discovered another bug inside the front wheel well. Two devices found and destroyed, he wondered how far they might transmit and was there a relay somewhere nearby.

"Let me think," he mused aloud. "It's got to have a clear line to receive and transmit, not blocked by metal, so it wouldn't be in the car . . . or maybe around the window?" Considering the possibility, he ran his eyes and fingers around the perimeter of the front window. Finding nothing, he sat back in the passenger seat and searched the car with his eyes. "Can't be a strong signal so needs to be outside the interference of metal," he repeated to himself. About to give up on any more devices being hidden in the car, he started to get out when his eyes saw the sunroof cover. "Why not?" he thought. Sliding the sun shield back, his search was rewarded. Stuck to the glass above was a box, slightly smaller than a box of playing cards.

"Hey Barb, you asked how far that camera might transmit?" he called as he carried the device over to their seats, where Barb had just settled with a book.

"Yes?"

"About this far." Matt held the box up. "Found it in the sunroof of the Durango. I believe we can now cut them off." Matt turned the box over, looking for a switch. Finding only one blinking LED, he looked for a way to open the box. After rotating it several times he found a removable panel. Inside was an unbranded black lithium battery. Popping the battery out, he smiled when the LED went dark.

"So, can we talk freely now?" Barb asked, her face bright with anticipation.

"Not sure," Matt replied, bursting Barb's bubble of delight. "Trying to think like our kidnappers, would you put all your eggs in one basket?"

Drawing a deep breath, Barb fussed, "Well, get back to looking. I'm tired of this game!"

Matt did continue looking, for over an hour. He searched the outside of the camper, the Durango, inside and out again, even scoured the trees with his eyes. Yielding, he suggested a new activity to his wife.

"How about we make a couple sandwiches and go to the lake. Fish, swim, whatever comes naturally . . ."

"There will be no more 'naturally' as long as that camera is watching." Seeing Matt staring at a tree, she asked, "What are you looking at?"

"Not sure." Matt stepped over to a tree that had just come into full sunlight, near the corner of their awning. Standing on his tiptoes and reaching up, he plucked another microphone from a fork in the branches. "That makes three plus one camera and transmitter. I don't think there are more, but let's not talk about it. Care to go to the lake?"

"I'll do sandwiches, you get the fishing gear."

Matt simplified his grilling technique that evening, beheading and splitting two trout such that they lay flat on the metal grill, which had to be repaired again from the latest bear visit. Turning the fish over, he realized Dee-O-Gee didn't have his nose in the way.

"Barb, have you seen Dee-O-Gee?"

"No, he was at the lake with us, didn't he come back? . . . You know, come to think about it, I did see him trotting toward the mountain while you were fishing."

"Humph, have you noticed that he always comes from the west and disappears to the west? I wonder if he knows a path over the mountain?" Matt replied, pondering his new realization.

"Why don't you ask him, next time he comes to visit?"

Fish that night was great, green beans were green beans, and bread was cold but smeared with butter. All in all, not a bad dinner. While returning from the lake, Matthew and Barbara decided there was no chance of a grocery delivery the next day so they would sleep in, which made watching the stars appear just a bit more delightful. A plan for escape was slowly coming together.

Sixteen

Day Sixteen

Barb sat up, wide awake and looked around. Listening intently, only the quiet of the forest met her ears. Sniffing the air, she sensed a bit of rainfall, not much, just a drizzle sometime during the night. Looking out the window she saw dawn creeping into the trees. Looking down at her husband, she wondered how he could be sleeping so soundly when she was wide awake. Unable to decipher what had awakened her, Barb got up, took care of personal business, then got dressed and went outside to welcome the new day. Matt never stirred.

Sitting outside, she found a bit of peace by watching the day arrive. A wisp of mist from the overnight drizzle lifted like smoke in the sunshine, brushed away by a pleasant breeze coming from the lake direction. Watching the forest, she witnessed the now familiar herd of deer passing through. One buck, three does, and two spotted fawn quietly stepped through the forest. The buck and one doe pausing to look back at her. Then they were gone and a chipmunk appeared near the fire circle. Not finding anything to eat, the chipmunk quickly searched elsewhere.

"How long have you been awake?" Matt asked as he opened his chair and plopped down beside her.

"No idea. Don't wear a watch nor carry a phone. I guess I've been awake long enough to watch the night evaporate, the deer pass by, and a new friend decide we don't feed well enough."

"A new friend?"

"Chipmunk came looking for something to eat. Didn't find anything so he moved on."

Yawning with a giant stretch, Matt replied, "Okay. Good morning. . . . Plans?"

"None that I'm aware of. You said something about fishing today."

Yawning once again, Matt replied, "Yeah . . . no, we had fish last night. We'll do something else for supper tonight. What about breakfast?"

"You feel like fixing anything? I don't."

"No, not really."

"Cereal. You know where it is."

Leaning forward in his chair and rubbing his head, Matt sighed. "Okay. You want coffee with your cereal?"

"That would be nice. You get started; I'll join you in a minute."

Matt stood and stretched once more, raising his elbows as he pulled his arms behind his head. He then stole a peck of a kiss and returned to the camper. Barb listened as he started water for coffee and banged around in the cabinets getting bowls and cereal out. Hearing the kettle whistle, she stood and returned to the camper for an elegant breakfast, a choice of corn flakes or Cheerios.

After pouring hot water into two cups for instant coffee, Matt filled the kettle and put it back on the stove for a second round. Conversation over their cereal was sparse, almost nonexistent as each pondered their own thoughts. The kettle whistled before either was ready for their second cup, so Barb turned the burner off and continued absent-mindedly dipping her spoon into her cereal until it was all gone. Done with his cereal, Matt downed the last of his first cup of coffee and stood to make his second. Refilled cup in hand, he stepped outside and sat to consider wonders of this new day, including where Dee-O-Gee might live when not visiting with them.

"MATT! WE HAVE A PROBLEM!" Barb yelled.

"What?" Matt asked, slowly rising from the comfort of his chair.

"Sink won't drain."

Matt opened the closet and checked the gauges. "Says the tank is only half-full. Anything blocking the drain?"

"I checked and no."

"Hmpf." Matt pulled the camper notebook and started flipping pages. The previous owner had done marvelous documentation on this camper, primarily for his brother who liked to borrow it for beach weekends. "Okay, grey water tank. Here's what we have. *Thirty gallon capacity. Not removable. Best solution is to empty at dump station. Alternate solution is to use the portable black water tank. Dump sewage then use that tank as transport. Note: sewage tank is only twenty gallons.* Sounds like a lot of work. *Solution number three, least desirable, is to drain onto the ground.* Uh, oh, we have a note in the margin. *See note below. If the grey water tank gauge continuously reads half-full, check the sensor connectors. A heavy jolt to the carriage, i.e. hitting speed bump too fast, can dislodge connectors to the three-quarters and full sensors."* Matt paused for a moment. "Barb, we've not had this problem before, but did we hit a speed bump on the way in?"

"There was that speed bump near the entrance to the campground but you rolled over that. Barely bumped at all."

"That's what I thought. . . . Well, doesn't matter now. The tank appears to be full and needs emptying. Should we transport to the outhouse or just drain onto the ground?"

"You can't drain that dirty water onto the ground!" Barb exclaimed, glaring at her husband as though he had lost his mind.

"Actually, you can. It is nothing but soapy water and the only contaminant, soap, will not hurt the environment. The larger problem, I believe and I'll verify, is that there is no way to drain the tank that won't flood our living area. I do NOT relish the idea of stomping around in mud for one day or ever how long we are stuck here."

"We need to empty the sewage anyway, let's just do that and get it done."

Heaving a huge sigh, Matt agreed. "Okay, if you need to use the toilet, now's the time. It will be out of commission for most of the day."

"Most of the day?!" Barb challenged, with total disbelief.

"Yep. I figure we'll dump the black water, that'll take a couple hours up and back. Then drain twenty gallons from the grey water, another couple hours all total just getting back to the lake. Stop for a bit of swimming, whatever, then come back and reinstall the sewage tank. That's pretty much all day. We should probably get some fresh water and refill that tank as well."

"Fine. Get out and give me a few minutes. I'll let you know when it's time to drop the tank."

Downing the last gulp of his second cup of coffee, Matt retreated to the great outdoors. While he waited for Barb to take care of her business, he connected the solar panel, placing it where the sun would be shining on it in a couple hours. The battery had charged very little the day before, though his phone was now fully charged.

Having removed the black water tank a week before, this process was much easier the second time. Less than thirty minutes after making their plans, the couple was dragging the three-quarters full tank toward the cottage by the lake.

Once Matt got the tank situated in the outhouse for discharge, Barb retrieved the pot they had stored there for rinsing the tank. She went to the lake for rinse water while Matt emptied the tank. After her second trip, she asked, "Where are you going to fill the water jugs?"

A twinkle in his eye, Matt replied, "I've been thinking about that. What I came up with is to submerge this twenty-gallon tank into the lake. Let it fill with clean water, and pump it somehow into the fresh water tank in the trailer. That way we don't have to mess with those small jugs we hate carrying."

Barb stared at her husband with total disbelief for the second time in this one day. "You are completely and totally out of your ever-loving mind!"

Smiling ear-to-ear, Matt chuckled, "Eh, just a thought."

"Okay, mister comedian, how do you plan to fill the jugs?"

"Don't want to go all the way to the falls this morning, so I thought we could either fill them in the stream where it fills the lake or simply fill them from the lake. Whatcha think?"

"If you can fill them without getting a lot of mud in them, fill them at the steps. Otherwise, up to the stream."

Dragging the empty black water tank to the lake's edge, Matt took the larger of their two jugs to the steps and dipped it into the water. With the air lock open, the jug slurped water and a bit of plant life and dirt into the spout. Seeing what was drawing, he stopped and poured the water onto the bank and tried again, not to the side of the steps but directly in front. Same result.

"Okay, we're getting too much debris. Let's go to the spring." Reaching the spring, the engineer in Matt examined the area. Unable to find a spot where water was deep enough to reach the spout, he began taking his clothes off.

"What are you doing?" Barb asked.

"Going out into the lake where there is no floating debris." Completely naked, Matt lifted both jugs and strolled into the lake. Stopping about twenty feet from shore, with water just over his knees, he looked down at his feet. Having a reasonably clear view of his toes and seeing virtually no debris, he carefully dipped the first jug. It filled quickly. Holding it between his knees, he opened the collapsible jug and dipped it into the water. Nothing happened. Reaching around the jug, he pulled a tab on the bottom, extending the jug from flat to cubicle. The jug now filled quickly. Satisfied with his harvest, Matt turned and lugged both jugs back to shore. Barb installed the caps while Matt got dressed. Slipping both walking sticks through the handles on both jugs, the couple began their journey back to camp, picking up the sewage tank on the way.

Weary from carrying the weight of the full water jugs, Matt collapsed into his chair upon returning to camp. Barb sat next to him, fanning her face with her hand, declaring, "That was work!"

"Yes. You want a cold water?"

"I'll just share yours, if you don't mind. Thanks."

Matt got up and retrieved a bottle of water from the fridge. After downing almost half the contents, he handed the bottle to Barb. She took a couple gulps and kept the bottle.

"Okay, first we fill the fresh water tank." Matt then went around the camper and proceeded to empty the two jugs into the fresh water fill tube. Before dealing with the grey water, he checked the fresh water gauge, thinking aloud. "Only half, hmm. We just added eight gallons, which is less than half a tank, so we could have about fourteen gallons. That's close to three quarters, but not quite. I bet it's really three-quarters. Close enough for now."

Positioning the portable sewage tank next to the trailer such that the dump pipe was higher than the tank itself, Matt pulled the hose from the rear bumper. Connecting it from the dump valve to the tank, he was delighted to see how cleanly it attached, saying, "This guy was really thinking." He then pulled the valve stem and listened as grey water dumped from one tank to the other. When it suddenly stopped, Matt closed the valve and disconnected the hose. Soapy, grey water flowed from the hose for a few seconds then stopped. Satisfied that the portable tank was now full, he capped it and prepared to return to the outhouse by the cabin.

Seeing Matt drag the tank to the front of the SUV, Barb called, "You want sandwiches this trip?"

Standing erect after placing the end of the tank to the ground, Matt replied, "Sure. Maybe grab a couple towels."

A half-hour later, Barb carried a bag of sandwiches and two towels, while Matt lugged the portable tank toward the outhouse. Arriving at their destination, both immediately set to their separate tasks. When Matt finished dumping the tank, Barb handed him a pot of rinse water.

"Thanks, but we don't need to rinse it. That was all soapy water. I will use it to add to the tank as 'starter,' though." He then added the water to the tank and placed the pot on its shelf in the outhouse. Returning to the lake, they sat and enjoyed sandwiches. Both kept looking across the lake, hoping Dee-O-Gee would return.

Washing the last of his sandwich down with a half bottle of water, Matt looked to his wife. "How about a swim?"

Capping her own bottle of water, Barb agreed. "Why not."

Seconds later Matt was stripping down and dove into the lake. Coming up a few yards from shore, he turned and saw Barb entering the water by the steps. She was wearing a t-shirt.

"I'm not putting this gorgeous body on display for a bunch of snoopers I don't know!" she exclaimed, sweeping her hands down her sides with flair, then dove into the water from the bottom step. She came up next to her husband.

"So, you would put yourself on display for a bunch of busybodies you DO know?"

"Don't push it buster, this could be a l-o-n-g camping trip, if you know what I mean."

Chuckling, Matt lifted her from the water, cradling her in both arms, and dropped her. She came up sputtering and splashing, making sure most of her airborne water went toward Matt's face. They continued to splash and swim for nearly thirty minutes before Matt pulled the plug on their frivolity.

"Okay. I still have to get that tank back in place and check the wiring on the grey tank. Time to head home."

"Camp!" Barb reminded him with more than a little force.

Sighing, Matt complied. "Right. Camp. Time to return to camp and rigors of our survival."

While Matt dried himself and dressed without any concern, Barb turned her back to the cottage and the hidden camera before removing her shirt, drying with a towel, and dressing in dry clothes.

"Rigors of survival?" Barb asked as they walked back to their camper.

"Well, kind of," Matt defended. "We've done true 'rustic' camping, but not for a while. Before the kids came along we went backpacking all the time."

"Yes, and that was over thirty years ago."

"No, we took Steven with us on the Appalachian Trail. He was a year or so old."

"Yep, and that was over thirty years ago, and our last trek on the AT if you will recall."

"That was kind of a rough trip. Good experience though, look at him now. He caught the bug early and still has it. Moved to the west coast just to play in the forest. What ever happened with that young gal he met on one of his outings?"

"Susan or Rachel?"

"How many have there been?" Matt asked with alarm.

"As I understand it, he hiked with a group of people mostly his age. He met a lot of young women on those outings, but none really caught his eye. Not until Rachel. She seemed to be special and I thought, from what Steven said, they might have a future. He talked about bringing her home for a visit."

"So what happened and how do I not know this?"

"You don't know this because you are always more in tune to your work than your kids. She married someone else. About four months ago, he met Susan on a winter survival trip."

"She's the one who didn't need any help and challenged Steven every time they turned around."

"That's the one. And yes, they are still challenging one another, last I heard. As I recall, they were going on a high-country survival skills week about the same time we came on this trip."

"Good for him," Matt laughed. "Bet our bed is more comfortable than his."

"The only thing 'rough' about this trip, Mister Harper, is the fact that we can't get out of here."

"Not yet, but we're working on it." Matt tried to smile at his wife but his face wouldn't cooperate.

Approaching camp they recognized a golden beast sitting in front of their SUV. Dee-O-Gee whoofed and raced up to meet them, tail wagging his entire body as both people patted him.

Dee-O-Gee tried to be helpful as Matt reinstalled the black water tank and checked the wiring on the grey tank. Wherever Matt's hands went, Dee-O-Gee put his nose, often lifting and pushing Matt's hands out of the way. When Matt laid on his back to inspect the wiring, the dog laid next to him, resting his head on Matt's chest. Two sensor wires were dangling next to the tank. When Matt tried to reconnect one to the three-quarter full sensor, lower of the two connectors, it was too short. Snapping that wire to the full sensor, he pulled the second wire down to the three-quarter sensor and it snapped on easily.

Matt's work done, he looked to his assistant. "Dee-O-Gee, let's go." The dog rolled his eyes at Matt but did not move. Putting a hand on either side of the dog, Matt patted firmly, "Let's go! Back out of here!" Dee-O-Gee immediately scooted back and waited while Matt rolled out from under the camper.

"I need to lock the ring inside," Matt told the dog and went to the camper door. Dee-O-Gee scooted inside and sat in front of the stove before Matt could get through the door. Fortunately, the stove was beyond Matt's path but when he squatted down by the toilet to twist the lock ring, Dee-O-Gee was there to help.

After adding a deodorizer provided by their host, Matt grabbed a bottle of water from the fridge and took a seat under the awning next to his wife. Opening the water, he asked, "Supper?"

"Well, we have those skinny hot dogs you don't like and a pound of ground beef."

"Any rolls?"

"Long skinny ones and round ones; which is your pleasure?"

"Let's do burgers and trimmings."

"You mean green beans?"

"Green beans, brown beans, whatever we have."

"I'll see what's in the pantry . . . in a bit." She then took a swig of water and returned to the book in her lap.

Supper was what had become a staple; hamburgers, buns, green beans, and baked beans. There was plenty of cold water for the two people and an extra beef patty grilled for Dee-O-Gee. While finishing their evening coffee, Matt surprised Barb with an announcement.

"Well, time to turn in. Early call for the grocery run."

"What? Are you going out again already?"

"Look, I'm having trouble keeping up with the days. I do know we are running low on supplies so we must be getting a delivery soon. Maybe tomorrow, maybe not, but I don't want to miss the next one and have to wait another week before taking some sort of action."

Barb looked at her husband with a mixture of surprise, relief, and admiration.

Seventeen

Day Seventeen

Matt's injun alarm clock woke him. Struggling to see his watch by light of a full moon, he smiled and scooted out of bed. Dee-O-Gee lifted his head and moaned a bit as Matt stepped over him, both times.

Shaking Barb gently, he told her, "Come on sleepyhead, it's quarter past four. Time to go to the grocery store."

Reluctantly pushing the covers off, Barb commented, "You are out of your everlovin' mind!" She then stood and made her way to the bathroom, carefully stepping over the dog who dominated the center of the camper.

Matt dressed while Barb took care of business, then asked her to wait a minute while he ushered the dog outside. Glad of the extra room, Barb dressed and joined the crew in short order. Cloaked in dark pants and jackets, walking sticks in hand, Matt and Barb stepped off toward the lake. Dee-O-Gee sat by the camper step and looked at the two people as though they were undoubtedly insane. Watching them pass the Durango, he stood, shook a bit from head to tail, looked at his people again, and ambled after them.

All three were wide awake by the time they reached the lake and Matt silently signaled to go around the west side rather than pass the cabin. Barb did not question this move and enjoyed the scenery in moonlight. They had been walking a brisk pace till now, however being less familiar with this route, Matt traveled more cautiously. They reached the waterfall area at a quarter till six. Matt perched on the rocks near the falls while Barbara slipped into the trees where she had a clear line of sight to the falls. Dee-O-Gee looked from one to the other then went with Barb.

Dawn began shortly after their arrival, but that is all that arrived. Matt kept his vigil until first rays of daylight had begun to push night aside. Satisfied that there would be no delivery this day, he hopped off his perch. Seeing Matt approach, Barb emerged from the trees and they began their return back the way they had come, along the base of the mountain. Walking along the edge of the lake, Dee-O-Gee stopped and began growling softly.

"What is it boy?" Matt asked, squatting down and rubbing the dog's neck.

"Look ahead, down at the water's edge," Barb whispered, a bit of terror in her voice.

Looking through the trees, Matt made out the shape of the large bear bending over the water. After a slurp and brief survey of the lake's calm surface, the bear turned toward the trio and began lumbering in their direction. Dee-O-Gee growled a low soft warning.

"Let's go around by the cottage," Barb suggested.

"Good idea," Matt agreed, gently turning with his hand on her shoulder.

When they reached the area of the cabin, they moved slowly, creeping along the water line in hopes they did not set off the motion sensors on the camera. Dee-O-Gee followed suit, walking slowly between the two. As soon as they passed the lake, Matt and Barb both breathed an audible sigh of relief. Dee-O-Gee looked at the two people then turned and raced past the end of the lake and into the woods on the western slope.

"Well, I guess he doesn't like our grocery trips," Matt chuckled.

Barb and Matt chatted aimlessly as they continued. Reaching their camper shortly after eight o'clock, Matt suggested they have pancakes for breakfast. Hoping Dee-O-Gee would show up he fixed a couple extra cakes, but the dog did not return. Matt set the extras aside while Barb cleaned up. Later, close to noon, they took the cakes down the hill and scattered them around the edge of a rhododendron thicket. Sitting under the awning, they saw a multitude of birds and two chipmunks enjoying the unexpected treat.

Not having any specific tasks on his mind for the day, Matt explored the area around their campsite, looking for more surveillance devices. Not finding any, he plopped down into his chair next to Barbara, who was about to finish her third book.

"What are you going to read when you finish that one?" Matt asked, his voice carrying a hint of teasing.

"I was hoping to pick something off my shelf in the study. You going to do anything to make that possible?"

Feeling the sting in Barbara's tone, Matt softly replied, "I'll see what I can get at the store tomorrow morning." Getting up, he checked on the solar panel, then the gauges in the closet. Finding all was as good as it could be, he went to the refrigerator for a bottle of water. Reaching for the handle, he stopped and looked at the top of the refrigerator. An orange warning light was on. After pressing all the buttons and seeing that the light went out only when he turned the unit off, he realized the problem. Without a second thought, he exited the camper and went around to the front, where the gas bottles were connected.

"First tank of gas is gone," he called to Barb and switched the valve to the second tank. After turning the gas on, he went inside and lit the stove. It took several seconds for gas to reach the burner. Seeing the gas was now flowing, he turned the stove off and returned to the refrigerator. Looking at the buttons, he made sure it was set to gas and then pressed the on button. Seconds later he heard a clicking sound as the pilot tried to ignite. Seeing the warning light come on again, he repeated the process of turning the unit off, then on again. Third time, he heard only one click, then silence and the warning light stayed off.

Reaching into the ice box for a bottle of water, he noticed that they were indeed low on lunch meat. Looking deeper he did find a pitcher of peach tea but not much for supper, half a pack of skinny hot dogs. Disgusted with his options, he called to his wife. "You ready for a sandwich for lunch?"

Sticking her head inside before answering, she replied, "Sure. Do we have enough meat for two or will one of us have peanut butter & jelly?"

"We have meat and cheese for a couple, maybe even tomorrow, but no more."

"Let's have meat then and hope we get to the store tomorrow."

Sitting under the awning with peach tea and ham and cheese sandwiches, they discussed ways to make the skinny hot dogs more palatable. Suggestions from both became a bit silly, such as boiling them in beer, which they did not have, or wrapping them in biscuit dough or pancake batter, or heating in a can of baked beans, which they did have. They settled on the easy way, skewered over the fire. Matt spent the afternoon collecting and splitting firewood.

Neither wanted to mess with a pot of beans, any color, so supper consisted of skinny dogs in buns adorned with mustard and ketchup. They each had two, which exhausted their supply of rolls and hot dogs.

"How much weight you reckon we are losing on this adventure?" Barb asked, after swallowing her last bite.

Looking at his wife, Matt smiled. "Don't know that we're losing any, but I did enjoy watching you in the lake. Even in the wet t-shirt."

Barb blushed. Feeling her embarrassment subsiding, she asked, "Coffee tonight?"

Matt nodded, smiled, and licked his lips as he stood. Before retrieving coffee supplies, he stopped and kissed his bride with tender passion. That evening, he drank a bit of extra coffee and increased his water intake, just a little, at bedtime.

Day Eighteen

Matt squinted at his watch when his bladder woke him. *Quarter to four; it worked,* he thought. Rolling over, he stroked Barb's bare body, whispering, "Time to rise and shine, lover. Got to get to the grocery store before it opens."

Barb was putting her shoes on by the time Matt returned from the bathroom. "You always that full with this injun trick?" Just like the day before, she was dressed in all dark clothing.

"No, not quite. I drank more last night to get up a bit earlier. We called it close yesterday." He then began to dress as Barb took her turn in the bathroom.

"What time is it?" she called.

Looking at his watch again, Matt replied, "Not quite four. Need to get a move on."

Reaching the lake, Matt kept their pace up as he turned west toward the mountains, actively watching for the bear. Reaching the waterfalls at five thirty-four, Matt kissed Barb, telling her, "I feel like today's the day. Let's catch us some grocery boys." He then climbed to his perch outside the range of the first camera. In his dark clothes, he resembled a rock on the hillside. Barb disappeared as she took her position in shadows of the trees and they began their wait.

Twenty minutes, more or less, after Matt and Barb set up their watch, Barb heard voices. Looking toward the falls, she saw five people emerge from behind the water. All were dressed in

Army fatigues. One carried the small bin, two carried the larger bin, and two more each carried a drone. Each of the drone carriers also carried rifles on their shoulders and two others had pistols on waist belts. Seeing the guns, Barb waved her hands in an attempt to tell Matt to stop.

Matt heard the voices and watched silently as the two drone carriers put their loads on the ground. One pulled his rifle to ready position while the other worked with the team connecting drones to the bins. In the dusky predawn, lit only by fading light of a setting moon, the gun bearer appeared to be young, about twenty-four, and quite nervous.

"Jeff, put that gun down and give us a hand," one of the men called. His voice was youthful and carried no authority.

"That bear hangs around the lake, he doesn't come up here," a woman's voice called. Her voice was more assertive.

"Yeah, well why are we carrying two guns if he doesn't come up here?" Jeff challenged. His voice and the way he constantly shifted the rifle in his hands betrayed that he was uneasy. "Some animal's been settin' off the cameras."

Matt chuckled a bit then leapt to the ground, landing in a crouched position and calling loudly, "I don't suppose we could get some rib eye steak and German beer . . ."

Matt barely had time to stand upright and did not finish his request before a rifle shot rang out, then a second.

Eighteen

"JEFF! PAUL! What the hell are you two doing?" the woman's voice screamed.

"Bear!" Jeff screamed back.

Turning around the woman saw Matthew crumpled on the ground and Barbara rushing toward him. The two men, without rifles, turned and reacted. One tried to restrain Barb while the other pulled a flashlight and began examining Matt's face and eyes.

"What's the verdict, Tom?" the woman asked.

"He's out. Going to need medical attention."

Barb fought her way loose from the much larger man and dropped to the ground next to her husband, crying, "What have you done?"

The woman pulled a radio from her waist-belt. "HQ we have a situation at the launch site."

"The bear?" the radio crackled in reply.

"No sir, the camper has been shot with tranquilizer. Twice."

"Med team is on the way."

The woman then knelt down next to Barb and tried to console her. "Ma'am, medics are on the way. Your husband will be okay."

"What do you mean okay? You shot him! I heard the gunshots!"

"Powder load tranquilizer ma'am, they are meant to stop the bear when he gets too close." Standing, the woman turned on the two holding rifles. "Paul, why did you shoot? I know Jeff's an idiot, but you have better sense!"

"Yes, ma'am. When I saw the man jump from the wall, he did look like a bear and the way he reared up . . . well, I honestly thought he was going to attack. I wasn't sure Jeff hit the target. He was wild, ma'am."

"Let's hope he did miss."

Minutes later two men rushed up, one carrying a medical case the other a collapsible stretcher. A third man came up behind them, at a less urgent pace. He stood over six feet tall with a blockish head adorned with heavy black hair, round wire-rimmed glasses, and was dressed in khaki slacks and stripped sport shirt. He was athletic in build and walked with confidence.

While the two medics examined Matt, the dark-haired man turned to the woman. "Corporal, what the hell happened?" His voice was strong, baritone, and carried great authority.

"He jumped off the wall and reared up, sir. The guys thought he was the bear."

Shaking his head, the man stepped next to his medics. "Well?"

The man who had not been able to hold Barb stood next to her, preparing to restrain her should this be needed. As soon as the dark-haired man started talking, Barb's disbelief raged. When he came within reach, she exploded, reaching out for him, screaming, "Who are you and what is going on here? You've killed my husband!" Moving as quickly as she did, she was able to get a solid blow into the man's head and scratched his neck.

Grabbing her arms and trying to push her away, the man yelled at his men, "Get her under control! My god, you're twice her size." Seeing Barbara subdued, he pulled a white handkerchief from his back pocket and placed it on his neck. Seeing only a spot of red, he turned his attention to the medic, asking abruptly, "How is he?" He continued to press the handkerchief to his neck, checking it occasionally for more blood.

"One dart appears to have fully deployed, not sure about the second. It appears to still have half a load."

"Thank heavens for small mishaps. Get 'em inside. Hood the woman."

"What about him, sir? Don't know how, but he's fighting it," one of the medics reported.

"He's taken enough sedative to knock out an eight hundred pound bear; he'll be out before you get him inside. Come on, let's go."

One of the medics pulled a large black cloth from his kit and reached up to tie it around Barb's head. Before he could get the hood on her, she began kicking both the medic and the man holding her, screaming hysterically.

"Please ma'am," the medic responded. "Your husband will be okay, but we need to take him inside to keep an eye on him till the tranquilizer wears off. If you don't cooperate, I'm afraid the Commander will leave you outside, on your own. . . . Do you want to go inside with your husband or stay out here?"

Seeing the dark-haired man already returning to the waterfall, Barb glared at the medic and relaxed. Another medic opened the stretcher and with the help of one of the "grocery boys" locked the poles and spreader bars into carry position. They then lifted Matt onto the stretcher's tight mesh cover.

"What about the supply delivery, sir?" the corporal called out to their commander.

"Send it on," he replied, without turning back. "Someone let me know when they're confined."

Ten minutes after leaping from the rock cliff, Matt was being carried through the tunnel behind the waterfall. Hooded and restrained by a soldier on each arm, Barb walked behind him. When they reached the iron gate, everyone stopped while Matt was transferred from the stretcher to a gurney. Groggy to the point of nausea and unable to focus or understand what was happening, Matt tried to lash out at his capturers. A soldier grabbed his flailing arms and respectfully held him down while a medic secured him with belts.

Hearing the metal door clang shut, Matt tried again to fight back; his head rolled from side to side as he was wheeled through another tunnel. Struggling to keep his eyes open, he watched lights pass by on the walls, then overhead as the tunnel became a corridor. Matt saw an observation room of some kind when the entourage stopped briefly. Through large windows, he saw people at terminals and a wall of screens, much like a NASA Launch Control room. Fighting the belts and doing his best to understand, he could see multiple images containing cabins, campers, houses, and screen after screen of numbers. Doing his best to focus on just one image, he vomited and passed out.

Hearing Matt retch, Barb exploded again. "WHAT'S GOING ON? MY HUSBAND IS SICK! I NEED TO TAKE CARE OF HIM! WHAT'S GOING ON?"

"Get these people to sick bay, and clean up the mess," a voice exclaimed with displeasure.

"Yes, sir. We are trying, sir," the corporal replied hastily.

Barb felt one of the men holding her tug on her arm and they were moving again. After taking ten or twelve steps, she was turned right and they continued for another twenty seconds before stopping again. Hearing the gurney being maneuvered through a doorway, Barb relaxed a bit. Seconds later she was tugged forward then pushed into a chair. As the man who led her through the tunnels held her, another ripped velcro restraints open and applied them to her arms and legs. Feeling the straps, Barb started to wriggle, but quickly realized fighting was useless. Once fully restrained, her hood was removed.

Barb's first vision was her captors leaving the room. Once the door closed, she looked around. The room measured about ten feet square and appeared to be a standard examining room, like you would find in a doctor's office. Matt laid, restrained, on a gurney beside her. A single unit of built-in cabinets had shelves behind glass doors above, wooden doors below, and a small hand sink. There was a towel dispenser, trash can, disposal bin for used medical supplies, and a rack for boxes of disposable gloves. Walls were painted white and the floor was light speckled concrete. Overhead were two banks of florescent lights. There was no clock nor any windows and only one door, directly across from where she sat.

By accident or design, Matt's head was next to Barb's chair. She looked at him, wanting nothing more than to get up and caress him, care for him, see that he was all right. Unfortunately, she could do nothing but sit. She tried to loosen her restraints, but surrendered that effort quickly. Looking back at her husband, she saw where they had done a poor job of cleaning up his vomit from the side of the gurney. Her own stomach wretched slightly, then settled. She was a mother, this was nothing new to her. Sitting in the silence, she focused on Matt's breathing, which was slow but steady. Exhausted, her own head began to bob and she slowly fell asleep.

Hearing the door open and voices entering the room, Barb snapped awake. She recognized one of the two people as a medic who had attended to Matt at the waterfall. In the lighted room Barb could see he wore desert fatigues. The other was a woman, red hair tied into a bun, standing about five feet nine inches, of medium build, also wearing desert fatigues. Barb recognized the uniform as military and was surprised to see a medical corps patch on the woman's right arm. Seeing two metal bars on her collar, Barb realized this woman was an officer and most likely a doctor. Barb watched and listened.

"You say he was shot with two darts?" the doctor asked, examining Matt's eyes.

"Yes ma'am. Though we believe one did not fully deploy."

Checking her watch, the doctor asked, "What time was this?"

"0550, approximately."

"I see he vomited, did anyone check his mouth?"

"Yes ma'am, immediately. Sorry we didn't get all the gurney clean."

Turning to Barbara, the doctor reached out and lifted Barb's chin, turning Barb's head from side to side as she examined her eyes. "How are you doing, ma'am?"

"Not very well, as you might imagine. I'm thirsty, hungry, and worried as hell about my husband."

"Your husband will be out for another two to three hours, and he'll feel pretty bad when he wakes. We'll give him something for that." The doctor looked around the room. "Corpsman, set up a basic heart and stress monitor, feed it to my office, then get someone to help you clean out these cabinets. When everything is clear, remove the restraints and bring our guest some breakfast. Would you care for something to read while you wait, ma'am?"

"Sure, how about a map back home."

The doctor smiled and turned back to the medic. "Bring her an assortment of books from the commander's library." Looking at Barb, she asked, "Do you prefer mystery or romance?"

"Mystery . . . no, I've had enough mystery for a while . . . what other choices do you have? Anything on survival skills?"

Looking toward her medical corpsman, she said, "Tell you what . . . Randy, look in my office and get the copy of *Vrenessbith* on my desk. That's a good survival story." Heading for the door, she stopped. "I'll check back in an hour or so."

Both the medic and doctor left, closing the door behind them. Moments later, the door opened and the medic returned with a friend, who carried two large bins, similar to what they used to deliver groceries. The medic unbuttoned Matt's shirt and connected seven medical leads to Matt's chest before plugging the cable into a port on the wall beside the bed. The other man removed a book from one of the bins and put it on the counter next to the sink; he then began removing supplies from the cabinet. In less than a minute, all cabinets were cleaned out and both men left. After setting his bin on the floor outside the door, the medic returned and removed Barb's restraints. "Breakfast will be here in a few minutes." He then left and Barb heard the door being locked from the other side. The examining room had been transformed into a holding cell.

Barb immediately stood and checked on her husband. His breathing was still steady but shallow, his skin slightly cool to touch. She kissed him on his cheek and whispered, "You stupid fool." Satisfied that Matt was as good as could be at this point, Barb looked around her cell. Four cinder block walls capped with an acoustic drop ceiling. After stretching and embracing a yawn, she plopped back down into her chair and stared at the door. Weary of watching her sterile and unchanging environment, Barb lifted the book and stared at its cover.

Puzzled by the title, "Vrenessbith - Catharrachd," she opened to the title page and read aloud to herself. "Ca hair zah. To fight bravely or resolutely. Hmm, I wonder if this doctor is trying to tell me something."

She was becoming involved in the second chapter when the door opened and a young lady, dressed in fatigues, entered. While an armed guard stood in the doorway, she placed a tray of food on the counter. "Bacon, scrambled eggs, English muffin, butter, and coffee. Will there be anything else, ma'am?"

Seeing the armed guard and this female soldier standing calmly before her, Barb exploded with pent-up emotion. "YES! I need an explanation of what the hell is going on here and why we are being held hostage!"

The female soldier who delivered the food snapped to attention and replied very formally, "I'm sorry, ma'am. I do not have that information."

Staring at her coldly, Barb responded, "Fine. I would love a Diet Coke. The colder the better, please."

"Yes, ma'am. I'll see what I can do for you." She then turned and left.

Hearing the door lock engage as soon as the door closed, Barb sighed and slowly nibbled at her food. She was hungry and the food was good, but she was not in the mood to eat. Not as long as Matt was in a zombie state next to her. While pushing her breakfast around the tray, Barb wondered how they had arrived at this wholly bizarre situation. Try as she might, she could not assemble any events in a logical order that revealed their current position, yet here they were. Locked up in a military compound inside a mountain in God only knows where. Consuming half her food while pondering, she continued to twiddle the fork with her fingers and returned to the book, *Vrenessbith.*

While Barb considered a scene in the book, the door opened and the doctor entered. After putting a not-so-cold bottle of off-brand diet soda on the counter, she turned her attention to Matt.

"Has he made any sounds or movements of any sort?"

"What? You're supposed to be monitoring his vitals and don't you have cameras and microphones monitoring this room?"

The doctor stared at Barb for several seconds before speaking. "Ma'am. I understand that you are upset, but I am not in security. I am a doctor and my only concern at this moment is that while your husband's vitals are all steady, he is not showing signs of regaining consciousness."

Swallowing hard, Barb replied, "No. No sounds or movements. I'm also concerned that his skin is so clammy."

The doctor pressed her stethoscope to Matt's chest and listened to his heart once again. She then pressed her hands against his arms, and paused to scratch above her right eyebrow. "His heartbeat is strong and while his skin is, as you said, clammy, I believe he is okay. Apparently he took more sedative than we thought. I'm going to give him another hour or so before we take corrective action. I don't like mixing drug cocktails, rarely works out well."

As the doctor looped her stethoscope around her neck, Barb lifted the bottle of soda. "Is this really the best you have? This stuff tastes like crap when it IS cold."

"What did you ask for, ma'am?"

"A COLD Diet Coke. Is that possible?"

Turning to the armed guard standing in the doorway, the doctor responded. "Corporal, see that our guest gets a cold coke right away."

"DIET coke!" Barb emphasized.

"Yes, ma'am. Corporal, please see to it." Stepping toward the door, the doctor stopped and turned toward Barbara. "How's the book?"

"Interesting. A lot better than these bare walls."

Chuckling, the doctor replied, "Wait till you get to the memories." She then stepped through the door, which was closed and locked.

Barb went back to reading, however was interrupted before completing the next page when the female soldier who had delivered breakfast returned with a cold 20oz bottle of Diet Coke. Placing it on the counter, she apologized, "Sorry, ma'am," and quickly retreated.

Barb immediately opened the drink and savored several gulps before returning to her reading. Pausing at the end of a chapter, she enjoyed another gulp of Diet Coke, now half gone, and looked to her husband. Seeing him stir ever so slightly, she jumped up and placed a hand on each side of his head. "Matt! Matt! Wake UP!"

Matt's movements, if there were any, stopped and the door slammed open. Bursting through, the doctor pushed Barb aside. "How much movement was there? Did he make any verbal sounds?"

Struggling to maintain her position by Matt's head, Barb replied. "I didn't hear him say anything. His hand shifted, that's all."

Turning toward a corpsman standing at the foot of Matt's bead, the doctor ordered, "Get the adrenaline kit."

The medical corpsman stepped outside the room and returned within seconds with a small pouch, which he handed to the doctor. Carefully considering her actions, she drew a significant dose of epinephrin from a vial and prepared to inject Matt. Turning to Barb, she warned, "He may have a sudden reaction to this injection, but it won't last long. This is merely an attempt to jump-start waking him up; it is not going to counteract the tranquilizer. For that we need him responsive so he can eat and drink."

"What do you mean?" Barb asked, her face taut with concern.

Sighing slightly, the doctor shifted personalities from military personnel to a person. "If we were a full hospital, I would have IV solutions that we would have used when he came in. But we are merely a glorified first aid clinic and I am the only doctor. I am not an anaesthesiologist so I have to tread carefully.

Your husband could wake up on his own in four or five hours, or we can jump start the process. The Commander wants you out of here, so . . ."

Turning back to Matt, the doctor jammed the needle into Matt's arm and slowly pushed the plunger. Seconds later, Matt's eyes opened and he tried to sit up. Prepared for this response, the corpsman stepped in and assisted Matt, removing the restraints and helping him sit upright. Turning on the gurney, Matt dragged the medical leads with him. Looking around the room, he stared at the doctor, the corpsman, then finally at his wife. Recognizing his wife, Matt collapsed into the corpsman's arms, who laid him back on the gurney.

"I'm going to be sick," Matt moaned.

The corpsman took a plastic trash can from the doctor and held it while Matt vomited into it. A moment later, Matt rolled his head to the side and reached his hand up toward Barb. "Where are we and what happened?"

The doctor stepped forward and taking Matt's wrist, checked his heart rate. "Sir, where you are is not important at this time. Right now, I need you to drink cool water slowly. When you feel up to it, I need you to eat something. If you will do that, you can return to the outside in an hour or so." Stepping back and turning toward the door, she instructed the corpsman, "Remove the leads and help him get dressed." She then left.

By the time Matt was dressed, a bottle of water arrived. A corpsman helped Matt sit up, opened the water, and stood to his side as Matt sipped the bottle. The entire time, Matt looked around the room, trying to focus his mind on where they were. Barb reached out and held his hand, which provided comfort but no answers. A third the way through the bottle of water, Matt vomited again; the corpsman was ready.

A half-hour after Matt woke, he could sit without assistance and began conversing with Barb, who stopped his queries. "We will talk when we get out of here. Too many eyes and ears on us at this moment."

Matt looked to the corpsman, who feigned a smile, then ran his eyes around the room. He could not see any obvious surveillance devices, but was not about to challenge his wife. He did ask, in a clear tone, "What the hell happened?"

Barb smiled at his improvement and replied, "They thought you were a bear and shot you with tranquilizers."

"Tranquilizers? You mean more than one?"

"Two."

"Only one fully deployed, sir," the corpsman quickly interjected. Seeing Matt react to his comment, the medic smiled. "Sir, I believe you are about ready for lunch. One moment." He then stepped to the door and knocked three times. When the door opened, he told the guard, "Don, he's ready for lunch." The door closed and locked again as the corpsman returned to Matt's bedside and again took his pulse.

"Are you going to babysit me, now?" Matt challenged, wanting to be alone with Barb.

"Sorry, sir. You aren't out of the woods just yet and I need to get you there."

"Speaking of woods," Barb asked. "Where are these beautiful woods?"

"Just outside our facility, ma'am."

"And where is this facility?" Matt asked, feigning innocence.

The corpsman smiled silently as he recorded Matt's pulse on a chart.

"Why have we been kidnaped and imprisoned in your lovely woods?" Barb asked. Her tone and expression were ice cold.

"I can't answer that ma'am. I'm just here to see that your husband recovers from the incident."

"An 'incident' that wouldn't have happened if you had not kidnaped us!" Matt challenged forcefully, wheezing as he finished speaking.

The corpsman started to check on Matt but was distracted by the door opening. The doctor entered carrying a sandwich on a plate. Rather than crowd the room, she handed the plate to the corpsman, who handed it to Matt. "Eat this in small bites, sir."

"What the hell is going on here? Why is this door open?" a baritone voice bellowed from the hall outside the examination room.

"Trying to give our guests some breathing room, sir," the doctor responded.

The Commander pushed the doctor into the room as he took over the doorway. "He looks fit. Hood them and get 'em back outside. Now!"

"He's still somewhat weak, sir," the doctor challenged.

"He looks fine. Get them outside!"

"Can we at least ferry them back to their campsite?" the doctor pleaded.

"No, doctor. Get them outside now or you will find yourself in a less desirable post."

"Yes, sir," the doctor replied with less than eager obedience. Turning to the guard at the door, she said, "Corporal, gather the team. Tell them to bring two hoods." Turning back to Matt, she sighed, "Finish your sandwich, sir. Time to go."

<h1 style="text-align:center">Nineteen</h1>

Blinking their eyes to adjust to the sudden appearance of midmorning sunlight, Matt and Barb watched as four soldiers disappeared behind the waterfall. The campers had been hooded and led out of the mountain facility with a soldier on each arm. Hoods were not removed until they were outside in the area where Matt had been shot earlier that day.

"What do you have there?" Matt asked, seeing Barb was holding a book.

"A book the doctor suggested I read. It's about surviving in the Scottish Highlands." Seeing that her husband was pale and appeared unsteady, she asked, "You up to hiking back to camp or should we sit by the waterfall?"

"Let's get a move on. Slowly," Matt replied with hesitation in his voice. "What happened to our walking sticks?"

Barb pulled her head back suddenly with surprise. "You know, I don't have a clue. We had them when we left camp, but I never thought about them after you got shot."

"Let's look around. They should be around here somewhere."

Matt stumbled a few feet, over to where he had been sitting on the rock wall, and found his stick was lying in the bushes where he left it. Barb trotted over to where she had been hiding, but her stick was not waiting for her. Thinking back to the early morning event, which occurred a long four hours before, Barb retraced her movements.

Leaning on his own stick, Matt stood to the side. Watching Barb leap from the bushes as she had when he was shot, he turned his head behind where she had been hiding. "Found it!"

Barb froze in her tracks and looked to where Matt was pushing through bushes. Seconds later he leaned over, using his own walking stick for support, and lifted Barb's. "You gave it a pretty good heave when you took off," he chuckled.

Handing the stick back to Barb, Matt suggested, "Let's go to the waterfall. I want to rinse my face before we head back."

Matt moved slowly across the very long twenty feet, relying on his walking stick for balance. Once he got to the fall, he stretched his hand out and grabbed some cold water, wiping it across his face. Dissatisfied with the result, he handed his stick to

Barb and reached into the waterfall with both hands cupped together. This time he splashed his face with chilling refreshment. Taking a deep breath, he repeated the exercise then stood tall, stretching as best he could. Now ready to move on, he reached out for his walking stick. Stabilizer in hand, he carefully stepped off the rocks and reached out again, this time wrapping his arms around his wife. She reciprocated without hesitation. They stood, wrapped around one another, for more than a minute before Barb relaxed.

"Come on, we're supposed to have groceries that need to be put away before the bear finds them." Barb then looked up and kissed her husband smartly.

Walking was slow. Matt had to stop several times due to dizziness and a touch of nausea. Reaching the lake, he knelt down and rinsed his face again in the creek where it emptied into the larger body of water. Standing tall, he smiled. "Okay, let's keep going."

The second leg of the journey progressed much more smoothly. Walking down the trail, below the lake, Matt asked, "Did you see anything odd inside the mountain?"

"What do you mean? A military installation seems pretty 'odd' to me, but all I saw was one room. I was hooded whenever we moved. Why?"

"I was pretty groggy when we went in, but I do recall seeing lights change from wall to ceiling, then a room filled with tv screens."

"What kind of tv screens?" Barb looked across at her husband with concern and curiosity.

"Not sure. I seem to recall something like a NASA Control Room. Lots of people at terminals and a wall of television screens."

"Noooo, I was hooded and didn't see anything. Anything worth watching?"

"Had a lot of trouble focusing, so none of this might be real. I think there was an image of the lake area, and a house. A small house on an empty street. Then there were screens full of numbers, kind of like stock market reports. Must have been a dozen or more, all with different images, but one. One was blank."

"You saw all this in your drugged out mind?"

"I don't know. I couldn't focus on anything, but I am certain I saw something like that. Would have looked again on the way out, 'cept then I was hooded."

"Well, I didn't see anything coming or going. Hooded both times with a pair of gorillas holding my arms."

"Okay."

They walked quietly for the remaining journey back to camp where they found two bins of groceries at their usual delivery point. Looking at her husband, Barb suggested, "Your color is still a bit washed out. Why don't you sit down while I put this mess away. Then I'll fix you a proper sandwich, if you're up to it."

Matt nodded and proceeded over to the camper, where he opened both chairs and plopped down into one. Barb carried the two bins to the camper without opening either one, doing her best to hide the strain of their awkward weight. She had not been shot, but she was exhausted from the morning activity. Once she put the groceries away, she stepped out to see what kind of sandwich Matt was in the mood for. He was sound asleep, his walking stick still resting in one hand, across his lap, and going down beside his leg.

Barb fixed herself a ham and cheese sandwich and settled into the second chair, next to her husband. Finishing lunch, she resumed reading the book the doctor had given her, *Vrenessbith*. Learning that "hags" in this story shared memories, she recalled what the doctor had told her but found the concept nothing more than curious.

Feeling the afternoon sun stream through an opening in the canopy and shining on his shoulder, Matt felt like he was a burrito at a gas station food service, being cooked under heat lamps. After stretching, he looked around. The first thing his eyes locked onto was a blinking red light in a tree thirty feet in front of him.

"Morning, 'Sunshine'," Barb chirped, closing her book onto her lap.

"Morning? What time is it?"

"Oh, I'd say somewhere around four o'clock. Check your watch."

Matt raised his wrist, looking at his watch. "Pretty good. Quarter past."

"How do you feel?"

"Hungry. Weren't you going to fix lunch?"

"I did, hours ago. But you were asleep so I didn't bother you. What do you want for supper?"

"What do we have? We got groceries, didn't we?"

"Yep. Usual fare."

"Burgers? I'll get a fire started."

Barb looked at her husband with disbelief. "How about I get you something to drink and take care of the fire. I'm not sure you're quite up to collecting firewood, just yet."

"Yeah, sure." Matt blinked his eyes a couple times. "They're back."

"Who's back?"

"Our host. Their surveillance is back." Pointing toward the blinking red light, he continued. "Camera up in that tree is watching us. Probably put microphones in the camper, too."

"I've told you we shouldn't leave camp without locking the camper," Barb chuckled. "I guess we shouldn't talk about our hosts anymore."

Matt looked toward his wife and nodded with a smirk. She retrieved a bottle of water and a packet of peach tea granules he could add to it for flavor. Delivering the water, she kissed him on the forehead and traipsed off into the near woods for firewood.

Dinner featured freshly grilled hamburgers with cheese, and both baked and green beans. This had become a staple meal, which they were growing weary of. Throughout dinner, Matt glared at the blinking red light in the tree. After starting their evening coffee pot, he considered the surveillance devices he had previously removed. As the pot started to perk, Matt got up and walked over to their SUV. Opening the door, he saw the moon roof was still open and there were no devices hidden there. Thinking dusk would make the red lights easier to spot, he climbed up on the hood of the car and looked around. A small plastic bin sitting on top of the camper caught his eye. Frosty white with a blue top, it measured about nine inches square and three or four inches high.

"I need a ladder," he thought aloud.

"What are you doing?" Barb asked, curious but not chastising.

"I found their new transmitter, but no way I can reach it."

"Where?"

"On top of the camper." Matt looked down from his perch on the hood of the SUV and smiled at his wife. "I've got a job for you!" He then jumped down and circled the camper, looking for the stick he had used to remove the first camera from the tree, long with a short branch sticking out near the end. Finding the desired device under the tongue of the trailer, he took his wife by the hand. "Come with me, little one."

"I'm not sure I like this. Are you feeling okay?"

"Not great, but I'll soon be better." Matt led his wife around the back of the camper where he handed the stick to her. "Climb up on my shoulders, then use this stick to knock the box off the top of the camper."

"What box?"

"You'll see it." He then put his back against the camper and made a step with his knee.

Barb understood and reluctantly climbed from Matt's knee, to his hand, to his shoulder. Matt then stood as tall as he could, one hand on each of her ankles. Barb looked around the roof of the camper. Spotting the plastic bin, she reached out with the hooked end of the stick Stretching as far as she could, she used the branch to cradle the bin and pulled it toward her. Bin in hand, she dropped the stick to the ground and handed the box to Matt.

"Just drop it or I might drop you!" he called out.

Once she dropped the box, Matt slid his back down the side of the camper, recreating the step with his knee and guided her first foot from his shoulder to his hands. She carefully lowered herself to his grip then to his knee and the ground.

"Who needs a ladder?" Matt chuckled and kissed his wife lovingly. He then picked up the box and returned to their coffee pot.

While enjoying their evening respite, Matt examined the contents of the plastic bin. A small wireless transmitter. Unlike the previous model, which had only one light, this one had three lights: a red power light and two blue lights, one for reception, the other for transmission. Turning the box over in his hands,

Matt discovered another difference; this one did not have an accessible battery compartment. Thinking for a moment, Matt then closed the box and walked over to the car, where he pitched it up on the roof. Returning to his seat, he took a long gulp of coffee and smiled at Barbara. His eyes sparkled with mischief.

"They know we've found it. Now, let them wonder what I'm going to do with it."

Twenty

Day Nineteen

"You know where we haven't been since our first day?" Matt asked as he drank the last of his first cup of morning coffee. Sitting back in the dinette, he grinned at his wife, an empty plate with only a swath of unsalvageable remnants of fried egg and bacon in front of him.

Barb popped the last of her buttered bread into her mouth and leaned back as well. "No."

"The river. We haven't been to the river since we first arrived. How about we trek that way today?" Matt raised both eyebrows expectantly. When Barb did not respond, he made them dance.

Barb silently raised one eyebrow before replying, "Sure. Why not. You set out the solar panel while I clean up. Be ready to go in a few minutes." She then downed the last of her coffee and stared at her husband, thinking, *You're up to something.*

Matt whistled as they began their eastward journey from camp. Taking Barb's hand, he winked at her and led her forward. She looked at him questioningly, but played along. Thirty minutes and just over a mile later, Matt stopped at a fallen tree and sat on nature's bench.

"We need to agree on a plan. Something we can do right under their noses." Matt declared in a dead serious tone.

Chuckling at Matt's change in attitude, Barb confirmed, "So we aren't really going to the river. Just needed to get a safe distance away from camp."

"Precisely. Now, I'm open to suggestion, though I have a feeling the only way out of here is over the western ridge. How do we get there without tipping them off?"

"Unfortunately, I agree that we are going to have to go west. For some reason I prefer the southern reach, but they cut that off when they removed our bridge over the ravine."

"Were you able to get any information from them while I was knocked out?"

Barb chuckled as she replied, "They were very good about saying absolutely nothing. You'd think they might suffer castration if we learned anything from any one of them."

Matt scrunched his face with disappointment, shifting his posture with discomfort. "Okay, west it is then. Start with the lookout rock? Tomorrow? Tonight?"

"Let's see what we can find tomorrow. I'm not tackling that mountain in the dark again."

"What do you mean 'again'?"

"You don't remember dancing with the bear and falling off the rock? It was nearly dark when I found you. Only the tops of the trees had sunlight on them; these woods get dark fast. But you wouldn't remember that because you were messed up then, too."

"Sorry, seems it's becoming a habit. I'll try to stop." Matt paused and looked at Barb with an apologetic plea for forgiveness. "Tomorrow, after breakfast, we fix sandwiches and head for the lookout rock. Agreed?"

"What do we do once we get there?"

"Not sure. Deer trail runs through there, so we can follow the deer or climb the mountain. THAT decision will be made once we get there."

"Sounds good. One more question. What are you going to do with their transmitter?"

"Can't take batteries out of this one; it's sealed shut. I had thought about leaving it in the woods somewhere. Open the protective bin and hope it fills with rain."

"I could use that container. Good size for luncheon meat. Why don't you just toss it in the lake?"

Matt pondered a few seconds. "Not a bad idea. Tomorrow, we can hike to the lake, like we're going for a swim, and head west from there."

"Won't they see us from the camera at the cabin?"

"Possibly. You have a better idea?"

"Let's go to the lake this afternoon. Our laundry is getting a bit ripe. Then, when we get back to camp, you can find and disable all their little toys."

"Sure. I was trying to give them a false feeling that they were beating us, but that works. You do realize that as soon as we're gone for a while they're going to put them back."

"Probably. I just want to be the cat rather than the mouse for a few minutes."

Smiling from ear to ear, Matt stood and kissed his wife with love and passion. "Let's head back. It looks like we're going to have a long day."

Matt was pleased to find an adequate supply of plain and ripple style chips in this week's groceries. Finding a pound of butter, he fixed a lunch of two peanut butter, butter, and jam sandwiches to go with their chips. Today's feast was topped with bottles of cold water, which were finished as they walked to the lake.

Before starting their afternoon excursion, while Barb gathered their laundry in a pillowcase, Matt stood between the camera in the tree and the Durango. His actions shielded from view, he lifted the transmitter from its protective container and wrapped it in his towel, leaving the container on the SUV. Reaching the lake, he stopped and dropped the bag of laundry. Grabbing his towel by the ends with the transmitter tucked into the fold, he swung it in a circle several times. Feeling it had built up enough velocity, he smashed it into the trunk of a hickory tree.

"You didn't hurt the tree did you?" Barb chuckled.

Matt looked at the tree, rubbing the strike zone with his hand, then removed the transmitter from his towel. "Tree's okay. Can't say the same for their transmitter. Case is cracked and in rather sad shape." He then reared back and with all his might flung the box skyward across the lake. It splashed fifty feet from shore. Satisfied with himself, he smiled. "Let's do laundry."

Doing laundry involved sitting on the steps near the log cabin and scrubbing their clothes with a bar of bath soap. Barb did the smaller items, like t-shirts and underwear, while Matt waded out a few feet and did the jeans. They tossed the bar of soap back and forth, dropping it more than once, which resulted in Matt fishing around the bottom of the lake with his hands for the lost bar.

"I hope this soap doesn't bother the fish," Barb commented as she rinsed their clothes.

"You and me both. I'd hate to taste soap next time we have grilled trout."

Barb stared at her husband. "You are hopeless." Realizing she was holding a pair of his soapy and wet underwear, she threw it at him smacking him squarely on the side of his head. "I don't want to damage this lake!"

Removing the underwear and rinsing his face, he replied, "Nice! . . . I don't either, but what choice do we have at the moment? Besides, it's a good size body of water, which changes regularly. Yes, we will impact this immediate area, but while unfortunate, I don't think it will be permanent. Let's finish up and get back. I have some hunting to do." He then tossed his underwear back at her. Being alert, she caught them in her hand.

On the return trip, Barb told Matt that she found spaghetti in this week's grocery delivery. "Noodles and chunky style sauce, roast garlic I believe. So, you okay with spaghetti for supper?"

"Sure. Nice change. We have garlic for untoasted garlic bread, don't we?"

"I believe so."

"Good. You work on supper, when you're ready. I'll be hunting invasive devices."

Reaching the campsite, Matt stretched a rope behind their camper, where the sun would shine for another couple of hours. He and Barb then hung out the laundry. After hanging up two pair of jeans, Matt stepped over to the SUV and looked around. He already knew about one camera, but pondered where other devices might be hidden. Unable to see anything obvious, he began by investigating the Durango. Finding nothing in or around the vehicle he stepped toward the camper, noticing a "clean" spot on the side of the trailer tongue. Reaching down to rub this odd spot, he discovered a microphone similar to what had previously been in the Durango wheel well. One. He then casually, retrieved his long stick and removed a camera from the tree opposite the camper. Two. Thinking about where he and Barb most often talked, Matt moved inside and searched the camper interior from one end to the other. He found one under a shelf inside the bathroom cabinet and another in the lowest inside corner of Barb's wardrobe. "They must like to listen to you snoring," he laughed. Four. Unable to find any more, he took them to a log behind the camper and smashed them with his trail axe. Satisfied with his work, he stood and looked to the forest just in time to see a red dot blink ten feet in front of him, another camera. Five. Returning to his smashing location, he spied a black spot on the end of the awning rail. Six. Done.

Going inside for a cold bottle of water, he discovered a six pack of beer. "We really shouldn't be wasting valuable refrigerator space on beer. I'll take care of one right now." He took one bottle outside and settled under the awning to watch the eastern sky reflect a brilliant sunset.

"I thought I'd help with the space problem in the fridge," Barb announced as she sat next to him. Opening her bottle of beer, she commented, "Beautiful sky. Did you get all of them?"

"Found six. Two cameras and four microphones. Almost wish I hadn't destroyed the transmitter. I might have been able to tell if it was picking up any more signals."

"Remember that for next time." Barb took a gulp of beer and winked at her husband.

"Yeah, right." Matt replied with a chuckle and a glug.

Day Twenty

Awaking with a new sense of purpose, Matt fixed breakfast and Barb prepared lunch, two sandwiches each. She then packed the sandwiches into their haversacks with crackers and three bottles of water, each. Breakfast ready, she set the packs by the door with their walking sticks. Both enjoyed a hearty breakfast of bacon, eggs, and grits, smiling at one another as they chatted about prospects and hopes for this day.

Finishing breakfast, Barb rinsed their plates before joining Matt outside. Expecting to find him eagerly looking westward, she was alarmed when she found him glaring toward the north.

"What's wrong, Matt?"

Matt lifted his hand holding the broken transmitter they had thrown in the lake the previous afternoon. "I think they are sending us a message."

"What message?" Barb asked, choking on a mixture of anger, frustration, and fear.

"Play by their rules or else. Those bastards seem to always know where we are and what we are doing!" Looking at the cracked box, he turned and threw it toward the east with all his might. He felt little relief when it smashed into an oak tree and scattered in pieces. Turning back to Barbara his face was a portrait of revolt, anger, and determination. Picking up his pack and walking stick, he growled, "Let's go."

Two hours into their journey, they arrived at the exposed granite boulder. "Short break," Matt said, dropping his pack to the ground. Still boiling inside, he inhaled deeply as he retrieved a pack of cheese crackers and a bottle of water.

Barb put a hand on his arm. "Sweetheart, you need to be careful when we start this climb. We want to escape, not kill ourselves."

Still standing, Matt dropped his head, took another deep breath and let it out slowly. Reaching down, he took Barb's hand and looked into her eyes. "I know and I'm sorry. I'll do my best to focus on just one thing from here on. Climb this damn mountain and get us home!"

"Matt. Let it go, at least for now."

Sighing, Matt nodded his head and ate a cracker. Barb tugged on his arm and made him sit with her.

Finishing their crackers and half a bottle of water each, both silently stood and turned toward the climbing path beside the rock. They then donned their packs and looked at one another, asking simultaneously, "Ready?" Chuckling, Matt delivered a quick peck to Barb's cheek and turned to the climb.

Reaching the lookout rock was relatively easy, except for the awkwardness of their backpacks. Standing on the rock, Matt examined the hillside on each end, deciding to ascend where the bear had appeared previously, at the southern or left side.

Using his walking stick to push rhododendron branches back, Matt stepped off the big rock and looked up the hillside. Seeing a steep but passable climb, he held the branches for his wife, telling her, "Let's go." Over the next ten minutes they managed to go fewer than fifty yards. The slope of the hillside went from thirty degrees at the rock to nearly seventy degrees. Every inch gained was acquired by pulling on small trees he could grab firmly with his hand. Whenever Matt could get a strong footing, he reached back and pulled Barb up by her walking stick. The crest of the hill, the end of their climb, was not yet in sight; just more bushes, trees, and climb.

Reaching for and grabbing the next rhododendron, Matt realized he had made a mistake. The entire branch he was pulling on broke, sending him sliding, falling, and rolling down into and past Barbara.

"Are you okay?" Barb asked, watching him trying to right himself ten feet below herself. "That wasn't as bad as when the bear pushed you off the lookout."

Pulling himself upright, Matt groaned and looked up the hill to and past Barb. He then looked to his left, southward. Seeing the hillside was essentially the same as what they were attempting to climb, Matt sighed and shook his head. "I don't think this is our way over the mountain."

Grimacing at her husband's realization, Barb replied, "I think you're right. Let's go down and see where the southern deer path takes us."

Matt nodded and proceeded to slip down the hill, passing from one tree or bush to the next. Barbara did likewise.

"Shame we're not built like bears," Matt moaned once they again stood beneath the lookout rock. Seeing the puzzled look on Barb's face, he explained. "They apparently climb these hills without difficulty."

"I wouldn't bet on it. That bear could have just come up from the deer trail. Either he smelled you or wanted to take in the view."

"Eh. Let's see what the deer do." Matt then turned south and started walking. After fifteen minutes of relatively easy walk, they ran into another rhododendron thicket. Neither could see any trail going up nor above them. Looking down, they recognized the trail they had used the first time they found the lookout rock. Looking at the hill, the climb, above them, Matt yielded without contest. "I see no way to make the ridge from here. Let's see what's at the northern end of this run."

Turning and starting ahead of Matt, Barb responded, "I know what's at the other end. More of this blasted rhododendron thicket."

"Well, let's see if there is any possible climbing room there. If not, we'll drop down to the lake and rethink this thing, again."

Reaching the northern barrier, Matt and Barb studied the hill above the deer trail. A steep, inhospitable, climb. Barb then studied the thicket in front of them. "Where do the deer go when they get here? I've seen deer on this trail; where do they go?"

"What do you mean 'you've seen deer on this trail'?"

"When you danced with the bear, the next morning I awoke to a deer right up in my face. She ran this way, but where did she go?"

"You never told me that, but as for where she went . . . I have no idea. I do know deer can travel through these thickets, don't know how but I know they do. I tracked one on a hunting trip a few years back. Tracks just continued into the thicket like it wasn't there. Magic, I guess."

"God's way of protecting critters from idiots like us. Let's head for the lake. I'm hungry."

An hour later, Barbara and Matthew dropped their knapsacks to the ground, across the lake from the cabin and plopped down beside one another. After a couple bites of ham and cheese sandwich, Barb asked, "Do you think they can hear us this far away?"

"I don't know, does it matter? Isn't it our duty to try to escape? . . . As I recall it was the duty of every prisoner of war to try to escape."

"Prisoner of . . ."

Before Barb could finish her thought, they were bowled over by a golden beast.

"Dee-O-Gee! Where did you come from?" Matt yelled with delight.

The frisky golden retriever stole what was left of Matt's sandwich from his hand, then turned on Barb, bathing her with his tongue. While this was a delightful and unexpected reunion, it got Matt thinking.

"Dee-O-Gee, where did you come from? Do you know a way over the mountain?"

Dee-O-Gee looked at Matt and looked up the mountain responding, "Whoof." He then turned and bounced down the lake shore, encouraging his people to follow him back to camp.

Twenty-One

Matthew and Barbara held hands, their arms swinging together, slightly. Both were exhausted, frustrated, bone weary, and in deep need of a solution, but Dee-O-Gee danced his way down the path causing them to laugh. Talking about their attempt to scale the mountain above the lookout rock, they laughed painfully at themselves.

"You're lucky you didn't kill yourself when you rolled down that hill," Barb jabbed amidst their light-hearted banter. "My heart literally stopped!"

"Well, it wasn't intentional, believe me. I might have some bruising and it will take a bit to clean the crushed crackers from my pack."

"Dee-O-Gee didn't mind the smashed condition of your sandwich."

"Dee-O-Gee appreciates anything edible." Matt watched the light hearted furry spirit lead them into their campsite, just as rain began to fall.

Dee-O-Gee wasted no time waiting to see how heavy the rain would be. Feeling the first drops, he darted under the awning and sat beside the two folded chairs. When Barb opened the door to put her haversack inside, he squeezed through and spread out in the middle of the floor.

Matt dropped his pack by the camper step and opened both chairs under the awning. He then retrieved a bottle of water from his pack and flopped down into his chair. Putting his hand on the bottle, preparing to twist the top off, he stopped and looked toward Barb. "You going inside?"

"No room, why?"

"Instead of water, I thought I'd have another of those beers."

"I'll get you one." Barb then stepped inside, but did not return immediately. She did return, however, after three or four minutes, delivering Matt's beer and carrying a cold bottle of water and a peach tea packet. Handing the beer to her husband, she asked, "How certain are you about that lake water?"

Twisting the top off the beer, he replied casually, "As certain as I can be, why?"

"I was just making a pitcher of peach tea and the water from the spigot was a tad off color. Wasn't brown, but wasn't as clear as it could be, either." Barb opened her bottle of water, drank a gulp and added the tea mix. Putting the top back on, she shook the bottle while waiting for Matt to respond about the water tank.

Matt thought silently for a moment, then stood and looked around their campsite. Without a word, he climbed up on the dented and scratched hood of their Durango, in the rain, and looked across the top of their camper. Returning to his seat under the awning, he looked around their campsite once again. Sitting, he looked to Barbara. "I'm assuming it's safe to talk, doesn't look like they have replaced the surveillance gizmos again. First, use bottled water from the grocery delivery for cooking and such. Use the water tank to flush the toilet, but that's all. I do admit that my stomach has been just a tad queezy since we filled the tank last time. Maybe the lake water, maybe not, but if we don't get out tomorrow, I'll drain the tank and get fresh water from the falls."

"Tomorrow?" Barb asked, staring at her husband and waiting for further explanation.

"I'm convinced that Dee-O-Gee is coming and going from this valley whenever he pleases. We're going to follow him out next time he leaves. Hopefully, tomorrow."

"What makes you so sure?"

"It struck me today when he bowled us over at the lake. Look at him. He is well fed, reasonably well groomed. He has a home somewhere besides the middle of our camper and it isn't in this valley. He knows a way over the western ridge and I bet he'll show us if we just follow him."

"So, you are just going to ask him to lead us to his other home?"

"Sure. . . . Maybe. . . . Haven't quite figured that out. I do know we need to be ready to travel whenever he decides it's time to move. Could be first thing in the morning, lunch, tonight, I don't know."

"Not tonight," Barb chuckled. "He's snoring in the middle of our kitchen. I don't think he likes to travel in the rain. What do you want for supper?"

"Don't really want to build a fire in the rain, what do we have in the soup realm?"

"I believe we have some chunky type soup."

"Sounds good, maybe two cans so we can all have our fill?"

"I'll see what I can do." Barb then took a glug of tea and settled back into her chair, watching rain fall into the forest in front of them.

Barb found a small box of instant rice with the groceries and used that to stretch their one can of chunky beef vegetable soup. The box of rice was supposed to provide four servings and the soup three, however Dee-O-Gee made sure there were no leftovers.

Matt fixed their evening coffee on the stove. He and Barb settled into their chairs under the awning and watched daylight disappear with a very gentle rain. Dee-O-Gee settled down between them and appeared to go to sleep, however as soon as Matt started folding their chairs, Dee-O-Gee disappeared into the forest.

"Oh great, he's just taken off. In the dark! In the rain!" Matt moaned.

"No way we could follow him over the mountain tonight. He'll be back, soon," Barb replied, folding her own chair and stacking it against Matt's.

Matt and Barb had just settled into bed when they heard what sounded like a soft bark. Matt got up and opened the door. Dee-O-Gee scooted in, tracking muddy paw prints across the floor. Without hesitation, he laid down in the middle of the camper and looked up at Matt as though questioning why he wasn't already in bed.

Matt shook his head and patted Dee-O-Gee's head as he stepped over him.

Rain continued off and on throughout the night. This peaceful lullaby was interrupted at one point by a snarling outside and a bumping against the camper. "The big bear has come to visit," Matt whispered to Barb. At one point the bear seemed to become more agitated and his snarling became more intentional, with threatening growls. Dee-O-Gee responded with a deep throated growl of his own. The bear immediately reacted by raising up and slamming his paws against the side of the camper, similar to previous attacks against the SUV. Dee-O-Gee stood, hackles raised, and let out a deep, more threatening growl of his own. Chairs were heard being knocked over as the bear snarled several more times, each time somewhat more distant from the camper.

As soon as the only sound outside was falling rain, Barb got out of bed and loved on Dee-O-Gee, praising him for his heroics. She then continued to the bathroom.

Day Twenty-One

Sitting beneath the awning outside their camper early the next morning, Matt breathed in the fresh smells of a forest just washed with rain. Drops of water fell on the awning as he sipped from his cup of coffee. Dee-O-Gee returned from his first morning walk and seeing that Matt was not yet working on breakfast, the dog spread out at Matt's feet and sighed.

Matt looked down at his friend and pondered how to get him to lead them out of the valley. His thoughts were interrupted when Barb stepped from the camper, yawning as she walked toward the chairs. Having just climbed out of bed, she was still wearing shorts and a t-shirt, though she had put on sneakers.

"Did the bear do any damage to the camper?" Barb asked, stopping to look at the side of their tiny home, wondering if the incident last night were real or another dream.

"Only a few scratches. Surprised his claws didn't tear through the side."

Plopping down into her chair, she yawned once more. "T h a n k h e a v ens for small favors."

Leaning over for a morning kiss, Matt put his hand on her leg and could not resist teasing his wife. "Another week in this wilderness and you'll be competition for Dee-O-Gee."

Puzzled, she replied, "What are you talking about?"

Stroking her leg, Matt chuckled, "Your legs. Almost as much fur as our friend."

Barb smacked his hand away and glared at him. "I notice you haven't shaved your face since we arrived, and your beard scratches my face at night."

Matt put his hand back on her leg. "I'm not complaining. Just happened to notice."

Pushing his hand off her leg once more, she growled, "You can keep your 'noticing' to yourself. Is the water still hot?"

"Should be. Bacon and eggs for breakfast?"

Rising to get her coffee, Barb asked coldly, "Who's cooking, you or me?"

"I will." Matt then swallowed the last gulp of his coffee and stood. Grabbing Barb's arm before she got away, he kissed her lovingly. Barb returned the kiss but continued to glare at her husband.

Seeing both people moving toward the door of the camper, Dee-O-Gee rose and scooted inside behind Barb, pushing Matt off the step.

"I guess he's hungry, too." Matt chuckled.

While Matt fried up bacon, Barb changed into more suitable attire for the day, still glaring at her husband as he smiled at her. Dee-O-Gee focused on the frying pan.

Each of the three enjoyed two eggs and two strips of crispy bacon. Barb and Matt each had two pieces of buttered bread while Dee-O-Gee made one piece of plain bread disappear with his eggs and bacon. As Matt worked on his second cup of coffee, Barb finished her first and asked, "What are the plans for today?"

"I was thinking we would prep both day packs and make them ready to go. Then I'd start to work on Dee-O-Gee; convince him to lead us outta here."

"That could be today or three days from now; what do we put in the packs?"

"Same as always, a couple sandwiches, crackers, water, flashlights. Oh, we might add a change of underwear. Don't want to offend anyone."

"Some of the clothes were still a bit damp when I took them down last night. I was going to hang them again today, but I'll see if we have dry underwear."

"Okay, but can we spread the damp laundry out in the Durango? I don't want to delay when Dee-O-Gee is ready to go. He tends to disappear rather quickly."

"I'll see what I can do," Barb sighed. "You start on the dishes, then we'll prepare our packs."

Opening the SUV, Barb found the laundry on the front seat where she had put it the night before. Underwear and t-shirts were dry, but a separate pile of jeans were still a bit damp. While spreading these out, she got a whiff of garbage stored in the back seat. Without hesitation, she packaged all the trash in one of the grocery bins and put it over on the drop site. She then left the doors open on the Durango and carried the dry laundry back to the camper.

Matt was just finishing the breakfast dishes when Barb returned. Hearing him talking, she paused outside the door.

"So, Mister Dee-O-Gee, we know you have another home and there must be folks there who love you. It would be very nice if you would take us to meet these fine folks who have done such a great job raising and caring for you. You think you could take us to your home today?"

Entering with an armful of clean laundry, Barb looked across the camper. Dee-O-Gee sat in front of the sofa, listening attentively. "Do you think he got the message?"

"Don't know, but I'll try again after we get packed. How do we stand on clean underwear?"

" 'Clean' is a relative word, but I think we're okay. You want me to get started on sandwiches?"

"That would be nice, thank you."

"Woof!" Dee-O-Gee added, and laid down with his head erect.

"Somehow, I do think he understands what I asked and is willing to help," Matt chuckled. He then finished rinsing the frying pan and laid it on the counter to dry.

"I'm glad you think so," Barb responded, laying bread out for sandwich prep.

Morning duties completed, Matt went outside. Dee-O-Gee followed. Matt stood at the edge of the awning and stared out into the forest. Dee-O-Gee shot past him, returning seconds later with a stick in his mouth.

"Sure, I'll play. As long as you take us to your home." Matt looked intently at the dog for a few seconds. Seeing him pat his feet impatiently, Matt threw the stick; Dee-O-Gee took off at a dead run, leaping over small bushes and sticks. Reaching the area where the stick landed, he sniffed briefly, then finding his prize, picked it up and pranced back to Matt. This routine was repeated five times before Barb joined them, setting both packs and walking sticks next to the camper wheel.

"Are you throwing it in the same direction every time?" she asked.

"Nope. Different direction each time. Are we ready to escape?"

"Guess so, just need our guide to cooperate. What about your phone?"

Taking the stick from Dee-O-Gee, Matt paused. "You know, I haven't turned it on for nearly a week. Got it charged up and forgot about it. I guess we should take it." Heaving the stick behind over the grocery zone, he added, "Yes. Definitely need to take the phone."

"Thought so, it's in your pack. Side pocket."

Dee-O-Gee returned with his stick, however instead of holding it for Matt, he dropped it to the side and stared up at Matt and Barb. "Are you ready to take us home?" Matt asked hopefully. Dee-O-Gee moaned slightly and meandered over to the camper where he stretched out behind the chairs.

"Guess not," Barb chirped. "I'm going to follow his lead and read for a bit. That book the doctor gave me is getting quite intriguing. You want a book?"

"Sure. Mine is on the bench at the table. No, I'll get them. I need to check our battery."

"My book is by my side of the bed," Barb called out as Matt approached the camper door.

Seeing the battery was at three-quarters charge, Matt picked up the two books and returned to their outside reading room. Handing Barb's book to her he looked at the cover. "Vrenessbith Cath-ar-ak?"

Barb took the book and opened it to the first page, showing Matt how to pronounce the title.

"Ca-hair-ZHA," Matt pronounced. "Hmm. Resolution and bravery. Any good?"

"I'm enjoying it, or would if I could get back to it."

"Sorry." Matt then settled into his chair and opened "Digital Fortress."

The remainder of the morning passed without event. Barb and Matt read; actually, Barb read and Matt looked into the forest with heavy sighs. When Matt got thirsty, he retrieved water for himself and Barb. Seeing Dee-O-Gee's expectant expression, Matt poured water into a bowl Barb had set out for him.

Barb fixed sandwiches around noon, replacing the morning sandwiches in their backpacks, which they ate for lunch. Dee-O-Gee ate more of Matt's chips than he did, but showed no desire to eat Barb's salt & vinegar variety. After lunch, Dee-O-Gee wandered off toward the river. Matt watched him carefully. Realizing why the dog had wandered off, Matt sighed and reopened his book. Dee-O-Gee returned a few minutes later and resumed his resting position behind the chairs.

When the sun began to slip toward the tree tops, Barb asked, "Thoughts about supper?"

"We have some ground beef and canned stew."

"I don't know that I can face Dinty Moore again, not right now."

Just then, Dee-O-Gee got up and walked to the front of the Durango where he stopped and looked back at Barb and Matt. Seeing that they were not moving, he barked once, sharply.

"I think he's telling us it's time to go," Matt said excitedly. "Grab our gear."

Barb barely had time to stand before Matt grabbed both packs. Handing one to Barb he slipped the other across one shoulder and grabbed the walking sticks. Barb slipped her book inside her pack, threw it over a shoulder, and accepted her walking stick.

Stepping next to Dee-O-Gee, Matt said, "Home!"

Dee-O-Gee barked once more, softly, and headed toward the lake, his two companions following closely behind. When they reached the lake, Dee-O-Gee turned left, continued around the lake, and up the western slope.

The pace was comfortable for all three travelers but as they began their climb, Barb called out, "Hey guys. I need a break. Just a short one."

Dee-O-Gee looked at Barb and sat, staring at her. Amazed and pleased by the dog's apparent understanding, Barb pulled a bottle of water from her pack. After a quick gulp, she returned the bottle. Seeing Dee-O-Gee had not shifted his position nor his gaze, she said, "Okay, sorry for the delay. Let's go."

The climb up the hill was difficult for both Barb and Matt. Dee-O-Gee patiently waited as they slipped and helped one another and continued. Reaching a wall of rhododendron, the guide stopped and sniffed the ground. Approaching a hole in the wall of bushes, he sniffed again, more intently. Apparently satisfied with conditions, Dee-O-Gee looked at both people, then disappeared into the hole.

Matt dropped to his hands and knees and looked into a hole not quite three feet around and not quite round, either. A tunnel appeared to have been created by animals pushing through the thicket. Branches and twigs stuck out at irregular intervals, but this hidden passageway went up the mountain more than thirty feet before turning to the right. Taking a deep breath, Matt started crawling into the thicket but stopped after just a couple yards. Feeling his backpack grab on a branch, he called, "Dee-O-Gee! Wait!" He then backed out of the thicket and removed his pack. "Guess we'll have to carry them."

Barb looked at the tunnel and removed her back pack. "I've a better idea." She then slipped the pack on in front of her, like a baby carrier, and dropped to her hands and knees. Entering the tunnel, she stopped and called softly, "Matt, I'm not sure we should go in there."

"Why? What's the problem? Dee-O-Gee seems to think it's safe."

Barb picked something off a branch and handed it to Matt. "Looks to me like bear fur."

"Look, Dee-O-Gee checked it out and thinks it's safe." Matt implored, eager to get out of their prison.

"What do you mean, he 'checked it out'?" Barb charged, questioning Matt's thinking.

"Didn't you see how he sniffed everywhere? He even checked for the bear's scent on the air. Evidently the beast is somewhere else. Now, PLEASE. Let's get out of here!"

Looking into the tunnel and seeing their guide waiting for them, Barb conceded and crawled forward. Matt followed closely behind, his pack slung in front of him as Barb had suggested.

The climb inside the thicket grew steeper but being in close quarters with the bushes and on hands and knees, both people continued. Sliding their walking sticks beside them, both humans had to frequently adjust their packs which kept slipping off their shoulders. Dee-O-Gee proceeded cautiously, stopping frequently to sniff the ground and the air. When the climb leveled out, they passed a second tunnel off to the left. Sniffing the air, which was rather foul, Dee-O-Gee moaned, presumably at the slow pace, and pranced a bit trying to encourage his people to move faster. The tunnel grew somewhat tighter after this point, but with more greenery and fewer broken limbs. The incline returned but was less severe.

Twenty long minutes after entering the tunnel through the rhododendron thicket, they emerged safely on the other side, approximately twelve yards from the mountain ridge. Dee-O-Gee was ready to run, but seeing that his companions needed time to straighten out kinks in their arms and legs, he waited impatiently.

Rising above them, the forest on this side of the rhododendron thicket was more open and primarily poplar and maple, with scattered oak. The ground had a gentle rise and was more open with trees separated twelve to twenty feet, though the canopy was nearly solid. Standing in shadow, and seeing rays of sunlight streaming across the ridge above them, Matt and Barb trudged their last twenty yards to freedom.

Reaching the crest of the mountain, Barb stopped and drew a deep breath of fresh air, then she looked down the other side. Ahead of them the hill was nearly as steep as what they had struggled with in the thicket, yet was open and forested the same as what they discovered coming out of the rhododendron. The sun had already reached a distant ridge further to the west and the day's last rays lit only the top of the mountain.

Dee-O-Gee barked politely, encouraging his guests to keep going. Recalling how they descended the southern slope, Matt stepped out and began the descent. Barb followed suit. Hopping down the hill hit a snag only once, when Barb tripped and fell into Matt, who grabbed her with one arm and a tree with his free hand. Both walking sticks flew down the hill ahead of them. Dee-O-Gee checked on his people, looking at them as though they were the clumsiest beings he had ever encountered. Two hundred feet down the mountain, the terrain changed. Hickory trees were replaced by hemlock with branches interlocking from one tree to another. Unlike the sparse hemlock around the campsite, which were four to six inches in diameter, many of these trees exceeded nine inches.

Daylight was fading fast as Matt and Barb used their walking sticks to push branches aside in an effort to keep up with their guide who trotted beneath the dense growth without difficulty. Problems with the hemlock were short lived, for they soon found a trail beside a briskly flowing creek. Dee-O-Gee turned right, north, on the trail and increased his pace. Matt and Barb did the same.

A quarter mile after finding the trail, they came upon a dirt and gravel road, which intersected the path then splashed across the creek. Matt and Barb looked up and down the road. Realizing that this road showed signs of frequent travel, they both turned to one another. Before either could ask about following the road, Dee-O-Gee barked and continued down the trail. The couple followed their guide, continuing down the path which paralleled the stream.

Dusk was filling this new valley as Dee-O-Gee ran up on the porch of a log cabin and barked. They were now at the end, or beginning, of the trail they had been following. A small light flickered through a window of this cabin surrounded by magnificent hemlock and now being swallowed by darkness. Matt and Barb soaked in the beauty and serenity of this unexpected treasure, their reverie interrupted when the door opened and an old woman let the dog inside. Seeing Matthew and Barbara, she retrieved a double barrel shotgun from inside the door and pointed it at her unexpected guests.

"Prince Albert don't normally bring home strays, who are ye and what are YEU doin' on MY mountain?"

Twenty-Two

Barbara and Matthew stared at the old woman. She had to be in her 70s or 80s, possibly older. Dressed in coveralls, a not-so-clean t-shirt, leather boots, and her silver hair pulled back into a bun. Wisps of hair floated around her round face as she wrinkled her diminutive nose. Cold dark eyes glared at her uninvited guests.

Hearts racing, their minds struggled with what to say. Both started to speak at the same time, but Barb prevailed. "Your Prince Albert just led us over the mountain and brought us here. I like that name, but we've been calling him 'Dee-O-Gee'."

" 'Dee-O-Gee?' What kind of fool name is dat?" Despite her age, her voice was not weak or crackling, rather it was full and powerful.

"We didn't know what to call him so we simply spelled out dog, D O G," Matt replied, almost laughing.

Lowering her shotgun, the old woman responded, "Hmpf. Round these parts he's a dawg. Dat's spelled D A W G, and dat makes even less sense. Still, he's adopted ye' so I guess ye is all right. Come inside." She then set the shotgun back inside the door and turned into her cabin, leaving the door open for her guests.

After dropping their packs and walking sticks on the porch, Matt closed the door behind them as Barb proceeded with introductions. "My name is Barbara, or Barb for short. My husband is Matt."

Warming her hands by the fireplace, the old woman looked over her shoulder toward the couple. After several seconds, she replied, "Folks hereabouts call me 'Gram', but don't try to spell it out and call me G R A M! I can still use dat shotgun. What was ye doin' on the mountain? Get lost?"

"Not exactly," Matt replied. "We've been sort of camping on the other side. Dee-O-Gee, excuse me, Prince Albert found us and has been taking care of us."

"I figered he'd found another home somewhere. Didn't ever think he'd bring 'em here, though. Ye the ones what took his collar off?"

"Yes, ma'am," Matt replied. "That's how we met. He got it snagged on a bush and couldn't get loose."

"Shouldn't be wearing dang collar no way. County officers say he's supposed to have tags on so he has to wear dat collar. Dangerous for a dog what roams the thickets de way he does. Everbody round here knows where his home is, anyway. . . . How'd you get over the mountain? Dem idiots has closed de tunnel."

"Prince Albert led us through a tunnel in the rhododendron thicket," Barb replied.

The old woman turned toward Prince Albert, who was stretched out by the fire. "I told ye to stay outa Grumpy's tunnel! He's gonna have ye fer breakfast one day!"

"Grumpy?" Barb and Matt asked, simultaneously.

"Dat bad attitude tub o lard dressed up as a bear."

"Yes, we've met," Matt sighed.

Gram looked at Barb for a few seconds, mostly staring into her eyes, then briefly at Matt. "I s'pose two of ye is hungry, but here's de deal. I'll share my pot o stew tonight, but you folks needs to be gone at first light. I want nothin' ta do wit dem idiots what took over the mountain and de oder valley and if'n ye was campin' there, as ye said, dey'll be comin' here lookin'. Dey don't like trespassers."

"Trespassers?" Barb asked. "There have been others?"

"Let's get a bowl of stew fers ye'." Gram proceeded to pull three bowls from an open shelf cabinet and filled them from an iron pot hanging over the fire. After adding two full ladles to another bowl for Prince Albert, she added a loaf of bread to the table and the three sat. "Bunch o kids went explorin in de tunnel right after dey got here, six or seven months back. Wasn't nothin' wrong wit dat, kids used de tunnel to git to de lake all de time. Somebody shot at de boys an dey came here to hide out. Closest place to de tunnel. Wasn't here but an hour or less when a bunch o goons in army suits came and hauled 'em away. Saw de boys in town a couple days later; dey was okay so I didn't worry 'bout it no more." She spooned stew from the bowl to her mouth, then staring at her guests added, "Till you two showed up."

The dog, Prince Albert, watched the people from a prone position. As soon as they began to eat, he stood, walked over to his bowl, and cleaned it. Looking back at the people, he returned to the other side of the fireplace, where he had been keeping watch, and flopped out again.

Barb took another spoon of stew, then asked, "What's in this, it's quite good."

"Hmm, let me see. Squirrel, rabbit, onion, a can of corn, a few mushrooms I found back a ways, dash of red pepper, and salt. Hope you ain't llergic to none of dat."

"No, I think we're good." Barb then smiled at Matt, who was finishing his bowl of stew and bread.

"That was indeed delicious, Gram. Thank you," Matt complimented and looked around the cabin, with more than a cursory glance.

It was a one room log cabin, approximately twenty feet square, very much like the one next to the lake. A large stone fireplace was centered on one wall with an iron stove and cabinets to the left and a worn out arm chair to the right. Across the room, toward the back, was a single bed, then a wardrobe, and a work table filling the front corner on that side. The table, where they sat, was off center toward the fireplace. There were two doors, opposite one another, and three windows - two on the front and one behind the arm chair. The floor was bare wood, which showed decades of foot traffic in the flickering firelight. Overhead, open rafters held drying herbs, blankets, and other articles not identifiable in the shadow.

"Maybe we should just move on, now," Barb suggested, not seeing a place for them to sleep. "I don't want to cause you any trouble."

"Trouble is eider already on de way or not. Eider way, won't arrive till after dawn. Dem folks don't git up dat early," Gram replied. "Mark can help me move de table so ye two can stretch out here by the fire. I'll give ye directions ta town in de mornin'."

With that said, Gram stood, collected the bowls, and deposited them in a wash tub on the cabinet by the stove. She then poured water from a pitcher over them and set the pitcher down. Turning back to her guests, she informed them, "If ye needs to take care of business, out de back door to de right. Foller de trail, only twenty yards or so. Make sure ye latches de door when ye' leaves or ole Grumpy might show up and mess things. He's done it afore."

Gram stepped over to the table and stood, waiting for Matt to lift his side. When the table was moved, giving Barb and Matt room to sleep, Gram disappeared out the back door.

"Well *Mark*, what are you thinking?" Barb asked Matt once they were alone, teasing him about Gram's mistake.

"I don't know what to think. Gram has been here for quite a while and doesn't care for the folks who kidnaped us. Not even sure she knows. I guess we should rest here tonight, then find our way to town in the morning. She did say there was a town nearby." Pondering for a few seconds, he got up and retrieved their knapsacks from the porch. He was waiting for his phone to finish coming on when Gram returned.

"Dat ting won't work up here. Does okay in town, I guess. See folks with 'em all over, but when de boys came here, one of em 'ad one and it didn't work."

Matt immediately powered the phone off and put it back into his backpack. "I guess it's my turn." Stepping across the cabin, he looked at Gram, who was sitting on her bed. "To the right, then twenty yards."

"An don't fergit to latch de door when yer done."

Returning five minutes later, Matt told Barb, "Far nicer than the one by the lake. Take your flashlight."

Barb retrieved a light from her pack and took her turn with the facility. When she returned, she looked to Gram. "Yes, I latched the door back. Thank you for your hospitality."

Glowing embers of the fire provided the only light in the cabin, which now filled with shadows and quiet. Following Gram's lead, Barb and Matt stretched out by the fire and were soon fast asleep.

Day Twenty-two

Matt was awakened the next morning by a cold nose pushing against his own. Opening his eyes, Matt found Prince Albert intentionally trying to awaken him. Pushing the dog away, he heard Barb chuckling behind him.

"Time to wake up, sleepy head," Barb whispered into his ear. She then patted his leg and informed him, "Daylight will be here soon and we need to hit the trail." Rising to her feet, she stretched, then patted Prince Albert. "Care to go out back with me?"

"Whoof!"

Barb and Prince Albert disappeared out the back door while Matt sat up and rubbed his eyes. Suddenly, all his senses awoke. He heard a coffee pot popping. In addition to the coffee, he smelled ham, country ham frying.

"Eggs'll be cookin in a bit. Coffee's black."

Looking around he saw Gram standing at the stove with a cast iron skillet spewing forth enticing aromas. She stepped back and opened the oven door, removing a pan of fresh biscuits.

"How long have you been up?" Matt asked, pulling his shoes on.

"Oh, bout an hour or so. Don't need so much sleep when you gits old. Never did sleep dat much no ways."

Pouring himself a cup of coffee, Matt asked, "How long you lived here, Gram?"

"I was born in dat bed dere, just like my momma afore me. Is dat long 'nuff?"

"You've lived in this cabin your entire life?" Barb asked, joining the conversation. "Matt, pour me a coffee, too, please."

"No. I got married as a young gal and lived with him fer a while. Came back here when my ma passed on. Took care of Pa till he passed, then just never left again."

"Any children?" Barb asked, pausing before her first sip of coffee. "Of your own, I mean." She then sipped the coffee and looked at Matt. His eyes were wide open. Looking back at her cup she realized the coffee was the blackest beverage she had ever tasted, on the extreme side of extra-bold.

Seeing the looks on her guests' faces, Gram told them, "I don't put notin in my coffee, but dere's a bit of milk in de cold house and some sugar on de counter dere." She pointed toward several canisters.

"Where is the 'cold house'?" Matt asked sheepishly.

"Back door den left, about twelve feet, corner o' cabin. If yer goin', take de pitcher and fill it."

Matt grabbed a pitcher from the table and disappeared out the back door. Turning left, he followed a stone pathway to the corner of the cabin, where he found a small stone building. Pushing the door inward, he discovered a fully stocked pantry cooled by a spring bubbling up on one side and disappearing on the other, about eight feet away. Dipping the pitcher into the spring, he looked around and saw a quart glass bottle of milk, about one third full. Picking up the milk, he marveled at meats, vegetables, a few eggs, and dairy products stored in this small stone cold house. Tucking the milk under his arm, he stepped out and closed the door behind him.

"How often do you go to town?" Matt asked as he placed the pitcher of water on the table then added milk to his and Barb's coffee.

"Not very. My grandson drops off supplies on his way ta work. Eggs is ready. You two sit and eat up now. Ye needs ta be past de road afore daylight gets ere."

All three sat to a hearty breakfast of country ham, scrambled eggs, fresh hot biscuits, and coffee. Between bites, Barb asked, "So we just follow the trail to the road?"

"Nope. Beyond. Best way ta town is ta jus follow der trail. Yer libel to git hit if ye' takes da road. Kinda narrow and twisty."

"So they use the road to get inside the mountain; any idea what they are doing in there?" Matt asked.

"Don't know and don't care. Ye' want ta know stuff like dat, talk to folks in town."

"And to get to town, we follow the trail, not the road," Barb repeated. "How far?"

"Jes go down de pat ye came ere on, den keep going till ye gits dere. Takes me a while now dat I'm gettin old. Can't say how many minutes, just a while. Maybe not quite dree miles."

Finishing their breakfast, Gram stood and cleared the table; adding these dishes to those in the basin she had used last night. She then put a pot of water on the stove while her guests collected themselves to leave.

"How can we repay your hospitality?" Barb asked, ready to leave.

"Well, 'cording ta Prince Albert ye fed 'im well 'nuff and took care of 'im. I can't ask fer no more den dat. Now be gone, de bot' of ye'." Gram opened the door so her guests could leave. When Prince Albert started to follow, she grabbed his neck. "Not you Prince Albert. You is staying ere wit me." Watching Matt and Barb descend her steps, she closed the door.

Dawn was still approaching as Barbara and Matthew made their way down the trail away from Gram's cottage. Fortunately the trail was well defined by shadows of bushes and trees. They had no difficulty reaching the road and had just rounded a bend in the trail beyond when they heard a vehicle approaching. Protected by rhododendron, they watched the lights pass.

"What time is it?" Barb asked.

"Can't see my watch, but it was about ten til six when we left Gram's," Matt replied. "She's quite a character."

"That she is," Barb agreed.

The trail paralleled a stream, for the most part, but was just wide enough for one person. At times they could see the road they had crossed, off to their right, but saw only the one vehicle going up the mountain. Matt and Barb chatted occasionally as Matt led a brisk pace for just over an hour. Some thirty-five yards after the stream took a sharp bend to the right they emerged from the forest. Stepping into daylight, they found themselves in a rather narrow valley. Sunshine streamed over the eastern ridge, behind them, reaching only the top quarter of the western slope, less than a mile away. In front of them, the trail crossed a grassy meadow, slightly smaller than half a football field, before reaching the first building of a town that was small yet filled this valley.

"Civilization at last!" Barb sighed.

"Don't count your chickens before they hatch," Matt warned. "Let's continue with caution." As they set out across the meadow, Matt checked his watch, 7:14.

Continuing, Matt noticed a small brick building surrounded by a high chain link fence, to the west just beyond the meadow. Looking to the mountain in front of them, they could see a row of nine small Craftsman homes resting a quarter way to the top. Their rich natural colors seemed to be just waking as morning sunlight fell across their front porches. A road ran in front of them then at the far right, west, cut back sharply and disappeared as it descended behind trees. Three Victorian homes stood proudly below the line of homes perched on the mountain. Walking across the meadow, Matt smiled as his line of sight made it look like the weather vane on top of the Victorian Widow's Watch closest to the base of the mountain seemed to reach the front door of the left most home above.

Coming to the end of their trail, Matt and Barb found themselves in a cul-de-sac, surrounded by the three stately Victorian homes. Each of these homes was well maintained with wide manicured lawns. Matt couldn't help but look to the homes above, chuckling to himself when he saw that none were endangered by Victorian spires below. Continuing down the street they passed six brick single story houses, three on either side, before coming to an intersection.

Standing in the center of the intersection, Matt looked right, to the north, where the road passed the fenced brick building on its way into the forest they had just left. Going left, the road passed a pharmacy / post office before turning right and climbing the hill. Matt checked the pharmacy door; posted hours stated they did not open until nine o'clock. Across from the pharmacy was a bakery. Workers were busy inside but this business also did not open until nine o'clock. Next to the pharmacy was a general merchandise store. Beside the bakery was a yard goods shoppe, then a hardware store. Continuing down the street, they passed two service stations facing one another. One to the left had locks on its pumps and looked like they only did mechanical repairs, while the other, on the right, appeared to have replaced its repair bays with snacks and drinks. There was no sign of life at either business. A vacant brick building and open lot used for parking filled the right side of the street before a T-intersection, the second road going north and south.

Looking beyond this intersection, Barb and Matt found the only visible activity in this sleepy town at a feed store. Excited by the prospect of talking with a "real" person, Barb and Matt headed that direction, but stopped before getting there when another Victorian home grabbed their attention. Sitting opposite the parking lot and wrapped by a wide green lawn and spreading oak trees, this grandest of homes sat nestled inside the intersection of the roads.

Larger than the other Victorians at the opposite end of the street, this home had a sign out front boasting that it served as a coffee shop, diner, public library, and had rooms to rent. They opened at 6:30 a.m.

"Coffee!" Barb exclaimed.

"Internet!" Matt replied.

Entering the home, both were overwhelmed by the dancing aromas of fresh cinnamon rolls, fresh coffee, sausage, bacon, and biscuits. "Take a seat, I'll be with you in a jiff," a pleasant female voice called out.

Looking around the dining room, they found twelve tables, of various sizes; four were empty. Barb strolled over to a table for two nestled in a bay window. They each dropped their walking sticks on the floor by the window and their knapsacks beside their chairs. A young woman in her late twenties, dressed in slacks and a blue striped blouse, stepped next to their table. "What can I get for you folks?"

Barb wasted no time thinking about what to order. "Cinnamon rolls and coffee please. Two orders."

"They'll be right up."

Before the waitress could turn away, Matt asked, "Do you have internet service?"

"Yes, sir. Across the foyer, in the library, but Missus Barker does NOT approve of food or drinks in the library. Coffee and pastry will be right up, if you can wait, which I would recommend." Seeing Matt's puzzled face, she continued. "A couple of high school seniors are in there trying to finish a big project that's due today. We only have two computers and they're keeping both of them real busy." Checking her watch, she finished, "And they need to be out of here in about fifteen minutes or the principal will cook their behinds. I better go give them a nudge . . . be right back with your order."

While they waited, Matt pulled his phone from his backpack and turned it on. A moment later the screen went dark and reported, "Service Has Been Terminated." Controlling his anger, Matt brought up his mapping app. Seconds later, just as the waitress delivered coffee and two steaming cinnamon rolls, either of which would have been enough for both Matt and Barb, the app pinpointed their location in roughly the center of West Virginia, a town labeled as Benmill, in the mountains close to absolutely nowhere.

"Excuse me Miss, where is this town, Benmill?" Matt asked before the waitress could leave.

"Well, sir, first we aren't officially a town, just a community. As for where we are, well it's a two and a half hour drive to get to any major city. But I wouldn't worry abut it, because you did find your way here, didn't you?"

Turning to return to the counter she was nearly bowled over by two teenage boys who ran up to her. "Thanks, Ronnie, we're gone." Turning toward the door, one of the boys stopped suddenly and looked back at Barbara. "Hey, it's YOU!" He then called to his friend who was nearly out the door. "THAD! STOP! IT'S THAT GAL IN THE LAKE I TOLD YOU ABOUT!" Turning back to Barbara, he blushed slightly. "Ma'am."

"What are you talking about?" Matt demanded.

The boy started to speak then stopped and turned toward his friend. "Thad, get to school and turn our project in. Tell Mister Blair that I won't be in today, something real important just came up."

Thad took a folder from his friend and ran out the door. The young man then turned toward Matt and Barb. "You guys shouldn't be here and the old man is going to blow the top of the mountain off when he finds out you escaped!"

"What?" Barb asked, her face awash with panic.

"Come in here. I'll show you."

Matt took a big bite from his cinnamon roll and left it on the table as the young man led them into the library where he sat to one of two computers and started typing. In less than a minute the screen showed a grainy image of Matthew and Barbara swimming at the lake, naked. Images of the two of them going down to the cabin and at the campsite were more clear and made it easy to identify them.

"You got these pictures off the internet?!" Matt exclaimed.

"Quiet! I'm about to be in enough trouble. But, no. NOT off the internet. My dad works in the mountain and I kind of used his computer and found this stuff. He's really mad about the way they grabbed you guys. I think you better talk with him before you get caught."

"Before we get caught?" Barb asked, her panic growing.

"Yeah. I'm betting that they know you're gone and this is the only place you could escape to. THE ONLY PLACE." He then pulled out a cell phone and dialed. "Dad, have you gone to work yet?" . . . "Good, turn around and come home. I think you need to talk with somebody." . . . "Yes, sir, it's VERY important." . . . "I can't. Thad's already left. He took our report in." . . . "Yes, sir, I know I'm in trouble for skipping again, but you really need to meet these people. A S A P." . . . "Yes, sir. We're on the way. Ten minutes."

Looking to Matt and Barb, the boy realized Matt's phone was still on. "Sir, you might want to turn your phone off. I'm willing to bet they put a tracker in it, and you need to come home with me."

"What?!" Matt asked, astonished by the boy's demeanor. Looking down he saw his phone was indeed still on and immediately turned it off.

"Folks," Ronnie, the waitress interrupted, "Walt doesn't normally stick his neck out. It has had his ears boxed too many times, if you know what I mean. But if he thinks you're in trouble, trust him."

Flustered, Matt's brain tried to process events of the past five minutes and couldn't make any sense of them. But then, he couldn't make sense of the past three weeks either. Looking to Barb, he hoped for some sign of how to continue. Seeing her eyebrows raised, as though saying "what have we got to lose?", he reached for his wallet. "How much do we owe you?"

"On the house. Now, get out of here!" Looking out the windows, she added, "Walt, back door."

Matt ran over to their table and grabbed their backpacks and walking sticks, pausing to take one more chomp from his cinnamon roll before racing to catch up with his wife and Walt.

Twenty-Three

Walt, the young man, led Barb and Matt through the Victorian house, out a back door, and to a service road that ran behind the inn and other businesses on that block. Walking quickly, they paused behind the pharmacy before crossing the road that ran to homes on the hillside. Continuing, they swept secretively behind the houses Matt and Barb had passed on the way into town. Reaching the Victorian homes, they cut between two and crossed the cul-de-sac to the third, which backed up on the meadow. Walt did not go up to the front door, but scooted down the driveway around to the back, where he was caught.

"WALTER! Why aren't you in school?"

"Hi Mom, I have a really good reason this time! Honest!"

"And I suppose these people with you are your good reason?"

"Yes, Ma'am. Dad's on his way back."

Looking again and more closely at Barbara and Matthew, the mother asked, "You two look vaguely familiar. Have we met?"

"Not exactly, Mom. They're from Dad's project."

"You mean . . . ?"

"Yes, ma'am."

"I knew it would happen sooner or later. Come on folks, inside." The woman then unlocked the back door of her home and ushered everyone inside. "Wait here, please," she instructed as she left Matt and Barb in the kitchen and rushed to the front, checking windows on the side as she went. Returning to the kitchen she took a deep breath and sighed. "Well. Would you folks like some coffee, soda, anything while we wait for my husband?"

Barb whispered to her husband, "Matthew, this is either very very good or very very bad."

Chuckling, Walt's mother responded, "Ma'am, I'm not sure it's either. You're in a pickle and it will be up to my husband to figure out what to do. My name is Linda, by the way."

"I'm Barbara. This is my husband Matthew."

"Yes, I'm aware of who you are. You have been a topic of conversation in this house for the past three weeks, since you arrived. Now, can I get you anything?"

"A cold Diet Coke would be nice," Barb requested. "Thank you."

Walt quickly jumped to the refrigerator and grabbed a cold Diet Coke, which he delivered with a smile. Barb and Matt looked around the large open kitchen. The wall behind them, between the two doors, was lined with cabinets, floor to ceiling. To their right, was a similar wall which had a long counter separating upper and lower cabinets. A third wall, which they faced, featured a large gas stove and side by side refrigerator. On the outside wall was a sink and a row of windows above a prep counter with open cabinets below. An old farm table, large enough to seat eight comfortably, sat in the middle of the floor.

"Walt! Linda! What's going . . ."

"Jerry, I would like you to meet your guests. This is Matthew and Barbara. I believe you are familiar with their story." Linda interrupted her husband who had just come in the back door and stood stunned. He was dressed in creased casual slacks and long sleeve sport shirt.

Jerry walked across the kitchen and stood in front of Matt and Barb. "Mister and Missus Harper, I am indeed very sorry for everything you have been through. I know you have a million and one questions. My name is Jerry Tanner. We should go to my study and talk."

Jerry led Matt and Barb down a hall wide enough for the couple to walk side by side, then into a room on the right. This room was comfortably setup as a study / office, with a large wooden desk, a leather sofa and matching reading chair, floor to ceiling windows on either side of a stone fireplace, and shelves of books lining two walls. A low-profile computer sat on the desk with two printers on the credenza behind.

Jerry looked at his son as he entered the room. "Walt, if you're going to join us, you'll need to get a chair from the dining room." Turning to his guests, he put a hand toward the sofa. "Linda, are you staying?"

"I wouldn't miss this for the world!" Her voice was quite chipper as she sat on the sofa next to Barb.

Jerry popped his phone from his belt and set it on the coffee table as he sat in the reading chair. He then took a deep breath and waiting for Walt to return, explained, "It may seem odd that my family is included in our conversation, but they have been my only support since you were abducted."

Before Walt got seated, however, Matt shot his first volley, with controlled but unmistakable force. "That's real nice. Now, where are we and what the hell is going on?!"

"Mister Harper, may I call you Matt?" seeing Matt nod, Jerry continued. "I am an economist and data analyst, currently on sabbatical from Virginia Tech. For the past five years, I have studied economic and spending trends around the world. Three years ago I met with some friends at a conference who are doing similar work. Together, we identified certain characteristics in people that affected various economies."

Matt shifted in his seat, like a wild tiger ready to spring.

"Please be patient, sir. I'm trying to explain why you are here." Seeing Matt shift and ease back a bit, Jerry took another deep breath and resumed his explanation. "The three of us developed a complex matrix of data collection, largely theoretical at the time, however we identified profiles for a number of people, or families, whose behavior could have a significant impact on our nation's economic well-being. Playing with our crude models, we learned more about what we were doing and observing. Ultimately, we refined that list to eight distinct profiles who could potentially crash the world economy."

"You're saying my wife and I are threats to the world economy?" Matt blurted out.

"Please be patient, sir. But to answer your question, no, not exactly. May I continue?" Jerry waited for nods of affirmation from both Matt and Barbara. "This entire line of exploration was done more as a lark, more recreation than an investigation into reality. You might say, a game 'economy geeks' would play. Word got out about our 'little game' and just over a year ago a colleague of mine who was serving as director for an economic conference asked us to present our work. It was meant to be a bit of comic relief at an otherwise very serious conference. What our audience, other economists, found intriguing was our theoretical data collection techniques. We actually got them to work in a crude fashion. We also learned to trace and forecast trends in Internet usage. Any way, attending this conference was a man who recruited us to refine our data collection techniques and analysis. He didn't seem to care that these tricks were all just that, hypothetical wizardry, and he got funding to refine our data collection and explore our economic theories. Our peers liked the data collection but nobody supported our theories, or even believed them plausible.

"Each of the three of us was offered a one year contract to further develop our data mining system. The other two declined but as the university was singing budget woes and this man was offering twice my salary to work from home, I said 'why not.' Good news for the university and me. I had to have help from my friends, who thought I was a bit crazy, but together we brought our theories and crude mechanics into a reasonably smooth reality."

"I still don't see what this has to do with us," Matt interrupted, growing more exasperated.

"I'm getting to that. Once the data retrieval worked, our *benefactor* talked me into testing the system against the economic nonsense that started it all. Once again, I analyzed the eight key theoretical families who might cause *world economic collapse*. We had no names, nor real people in mind, only characteristics. Profiles. I did not know that the man who funded this idiotic study had made provisions to identify four families who most closely met our characteristics and remove them from . . . how do I say this? Get them off the Internet and otherwise prevent them from potentially doing any damage to the world. He took a theoretical 'what if' game and turned it into reality."

"WHOA! Wait just a minute! You're telling me that my wife and I have been tagged as using the Internet for world economy terrorism in some reality game?!"

"A blunt but accurate way to phrase it." Jerry shifted in his seat, moving closer to the edge. "May I explain a bit more?"

"By all means, please!" Matt threw up his hands and surrendered, for now, to the absolute lunacy of what he was hearing.

" 'Terrorism' is not accurate, because none of our profiles included any *intentional* acts. Your spending patterns, that is those of the eight profiles, included a high likelihood that you either have already or would in the near future execute a purchase, or act on a decision, possibly utilizing the Internet, that would cause some facet of the world economy to spiral downward out of control."

"Stop there a minute!" Matt interrupted. "I'm having more than a bit of trouble wrapping my head around this. Let's go back to the beginning. You said this whole nonsensical whimsy started with a 'matrix of data collection.' Please explain."

"Yes, sir. What is real and people don't realize it, is the Internet has made our economy very fragile. Too much happens too fast with absolutely no regulators. Anywhere. Our model is constantly running complex simulations which look for and theoretically, I have to use that word, but theoretically predict potential economic disasters. Most of the events, not necessarily all but most, utilize the Internet in some way. We then do what we can to avert them. This was the original 'game play' and was never meant to be 'real world.' However, simulations are being run on a massive parallel processing system comprised of computers around the world. Data is collected 24/7 from websites, each based on one of three models: gaming, shopping, and research, such as Google. We also draw information from state DMV records. Thus far the IRS has been inaccessible and most uncooperative.

"Our data collection model is powerful and unique, powering simulations that have tracked back to eight different profiles. You and Missus Harper present a 99.94% match to one of these profiles and our simulations predict that one, or both, of you will likely trigger a catastrophic economic event within the next ninety days . . . well sixty-six now."

Matt drew a long slow breath and looked at Barb. She was pale and just as befuddled as he was. Matt let his breath out slowly and repeated what he understood. "Okay, what you are saying, Mister Tanner, if I heard you right, is in your game world you believe we might have done or are going to do something, you do not know which, that triggers a great catastrophic event, but you do not know what it is nor when it occurs?"

"Simply put, yes. As you said, in a 'game world.' It was never supposed to reflect on real people. On you." Jerry's voice now revealed that he was exhausted and not at all on board with what had happened to Barb and Matt.

"You are DEAD WRONG! Neither of us shops online. The only thing I do online is email and verify my bank balance once or twice a week. I pay our bills through the mail with checks. We rarely go out to eat or go to the movies. We shop at the same grocery and other stores we have used for nearly fifteen years. How the hell are we a threat?" Matt challenged, his voice filled with disbelief and anger.

"Sir, in defense of the theory, the world is changing at an incredible rate - primarily due to the power of the Internet. Your profile says you will begin, or have begun to use the Internet for purchases or financial transactions, possibly a stock purchase, I don't know, but one of these transactions will trigger the catastrophe we are trying to avoid. A combination of 'The Butterfly Effect,' where some insignificant event affects the entire world, and 'The Domino Effect', where that one insignificant event triggers another event then another, ultimately it is not insignificant but a disaster."

Matt stared at Jerry. "I'm sorry, sir. I don't want to insult your work, your theory, but this all sounds like a total crock of bull! I would love to dispute it, but what you are saying has absolutely NO credibility. I don't even know how to dispute something so totally ludicrous!"

Barb jumped in, asking timidly, "Are there others?"

Jerry was now visibly tense and growing defensive with Matt's verbal assaults. Moving his eyes from Matt to Barb, he drew a deep breath, attempting to restore his own self-control and credibility. "Yes, ma'am, we have identified two other possibilities."

"You have them locked up somewhere as well?" Matt challenged, recharging his energy.

"Yes, sir, but I cannot tell you where, because I don't know where they are."

Heaving a sigh, Matt started to speak but Barb cut him off, her voice now exerting some authority. "How long will we be kept locked up?"

Looking down at the table and fiddling with his phone, Jerry replied with reservation. "Until the simulation says you are no longer a threat."

"And what if what we do has already been done or, heaven forbid, your locking us up in this forest is what causes this catastrophe?" Barb challenged.

"Ma'am, when you were kidnaped, I stopped playing theoretical games and am dealing with a new reality, considering all possible events and outcomes. I even tried to contact the FBI to stop this thing . . . the Army locked me up and threatened my family!"

"Wow, Dad," Walt interrupted. "I didn't know they actually locked you up!"

Jerry glared at his son. Seconds later his face softened and he continued. "Linda convinced me it was better to cooperate and keep us all safe, the two of you and my family, so please . . . be patient! You should not be here but powers greater than me are in control."

"GREAT! Who IS in control?! I want one minute with them!" Matt exploded.

"This part I do not fully understand." Jerry took a deep breath and considered how much he could tell. Looking to his wife, he gathered courage from her and told everything. "Somehow we have the U. S. Government backing this project and it's being supported and enforced by the U. S. Army. Brian Bard, our 'Commander,' as he likes to be called, has some very powerful friends somewhere." Barely louder than a whisper he added, "Wouldn't be surprised if somebody isn't making a lot of money off this somehow."

Matt looked down, rubbing his head with both hands. Looking up and grinding his teeth, he challenged, "What about OUR families and OUR jobs? What have you told them?"

Seeing her husband was exhausted, Linda explained. "Everyone outside the project has been told that you suffered a fatal crash on the way to the campground."

"WHAT!?" Barb and Matt exploded in unison.

"WOW!" Matt continued, "We thought we had been drugged or were on a bad LSD trip. Glad to hear we are only DEAD!"

Shaking his head, Jerry started to explain, but was interrupted by his phone, which he picked up and reluctantly answered. "Yes sir?" . . . "I know. They are here with me. Have your men stand down and I'll try to bring them . . ." . . . "BRIAN! They are not going to contaminate anyone or anything in Benmill! They are presently in my house under MY supervision. If I need help, I'll call. Till then, stand down!" . . . "Fine!" He then ended the call and carelessly dropped the phone on the table. Looking at his guests, he chuckled slightly. "They know you've flown the coop. . . . Where were we?"

"You were about to tell them how they were killed," Walt chirped in reply.

Jerry rolled his eyes at his son's response and looked back to his guests. Barb's face was now red with anger and she was near tears. Matt was coming dangerously close to taking all his pent up anger on him personally, vigorously rubbing his hands together, grinding his teeth, and staring at Jerry with burning eyes.

Drawing a deep breath, Jerry tried to calm them down. "Please, Mister Harper, I am NOT the enemy here. I am doing everything I can to end this nightmare we are all caught in." Turning to his wife, Jerry said, "Linda, would you please get me something cold to drink. I'm afraid we've still a long way to go." As Linda left the room, Jerry returned his gaze to his guests, who were still on the edge of launching at him, and resumed. "First, please understand that NONE of this was my idea. I fought against it but our 'Commander' has more clout than I ever imagined. Should have never agreed to work with him."

Linda returned with a large glass of ice water and handed it to Jerry who continued. "Thank you. My apologies for that." He paused to draw a long drink of restoring water. "Your death. Yes. You had a flat tire on the way to the campground." Seeing both Matt and Barb nod with astonishment, he continued. "As you pulled back onto the highway, an eighteen-wheeler came over the hill and smashed into your camper and car. Both exploded in flame. Your bodies were incinerated. You were identified by DMV records using the license plate on your camper. The plate on your SUV was unreadable."

"Okay, what happens when we are exonerated of all wrong doing?" Barb asked, coldly.

"Witness protection. You won't be able to return to your old lives. I'm sorry," Jerry apologized.

"Hey," Walt interjected, "at least you get an all expense paid vacation in the most beautiful valley in West Virginia."

"Walt!" Jerry chastised. Walt shrugged his shoulders and feigned remorse.

"Speaking of which, how did we get to this 'vacation paradise'?" Matt asked. His voice was now softer and heavier than it had been the past several days. Barb reached over and squeezed his hand.

"Army Corps of Engineers. Took them the better part of two days to airlift you out of your campsite and get you settled into our forest. They worked extra hard to get you between the trees. I thought they would locate you closer to the lake."

Shaking his head, Matt conceded, "Beautiful site except for the bears who think it's theirs. We have a bear beating on us every four or five nights."

"Can I explain that Dad? Please," Walt begged.

"Go ahead," Jerry agreed.

"They put you right on top of Ole Grumpy's scratching site. There are rocks under your camper that he likes to use to scratch his back on. Only place in the entire valley he likes to roll around." Walt smiled, well pleased with himself.

"All the locals know the spot," Jerry explained. "Brian, our 'Commander' picked that location based on a review of topographical maps. He liked the proximity and fact that it was similar to the site where we picked you up. Had I known where he was thinking, I would have stopped him. Idiot."

"You don't like this 'Commander'," Barb observed.

"No. He's not military, yet commands an Army troop. He's not scientific, and bends our theories and observations to suit his mood of the moment. HE is the source of all your problems and mine."

Matt and Barb looked at one another, wanting more than ever to simply sit in their own living room and resume their quiet, boring, uneventful life. "So what do we do now?" Barb asked, trying to show some acceptance.

Drawing a deep breath, Jerry replied, "Go back. Maybe settle into the log cabin. I'll do everything I can to get you out as soon as possible. Even if I have to fiddle with the data."

"Can we stop the invasive surveillance?" Matt asked. "I'll keep destroying any that I find."

"That would be a problem, you see Brian also signed on to test new communications equipment. You recall how you got a map of the area on your cell phone?"

"Yes, but I won't ask how you know that."

"Four towers were erected around the valley to intercept and control any communications within the valley. They also act as long range receivers for those transmitters you keep destroying."

Matt thought for a moment, then looked to both Jerry and Linda. "The way you were talking about 'Ole Grumpy,' you seem to be familiar with this area and the valley."

Linda responded first. "Yes. We both grew up in the area. This house is my family home. Jerry's grandmother still lives in a log cabin on the mountain."

"Gram?" Barb asked excitedly.

"You met her?" Jerry asked. "I need to drop in on her."

"Yes. She was delightful. Even warned us about 'the idiots in the mountain'. I take it Walt was one of the young men they chased out at the beginning of the project?"

"Guilty as charged," Walt acknowledged.

"That log cabin by the lake isn't in near as good shape as your grandmother's," Matt challenged.

"I know," Jerry agreed. "Needs a lot of work but it has quite a history." Seeing he had touched his guest's curiosity, he continued.

"My great-grandfather came to this area when he was seventeen, that was about 1912. While hunting, he stumbled onto the tunnel and discovered the valley at the other end. He explored the valley and met an old hermit, who was building the cabin you found. This old man took my grandfather in, providing he worked, hunted, basically earned his way. They got along. Old hermit died shortly after they completed the spring house. Legend has it that they hid something secret in the stone trough of the spring house, but nobody alive today knows what that secret is."

Seeing Barb getting a bit uneasy, Linda whispered to her, "Come to the kitchen with me." She then smiled at her husband. "We need to take care of something, continue."

Barb followed Linda into the kitchen, where Linda stopped and turned around. "I could tell you were not into Jerry's story about the cabin. How would you like a hot shower?"

"That would be heaven! I have clean clothes in my pack," Barb replied with appreciative delight.

When they reached the master bathroom, upstairs, Linda offered, "I can put all your clothes through a quick wash and dry, if you'd like."

"Linda, you are a heaven-sent angel." Barb then stepped
into the bathroom and disrobed in private, handing her clothes to
Linda around the edge of the door.

Linda put Barb's clothes into wash, retrieved a soft drink for
herself from the refrigerator, then returned to the study, where
Jerry was continuing his story.

Jerry paused as Linda and Barbara left the room. Looking back at
his son and Matt, he resumed. "Okay, so Grandfather went to
town only three times a year. The valley provided for most of his
needs. On one of his trips, he met a young lady in transit from
Louisiana to Pennsylvania. She was to be married in
Philadelphia. They immediately fell in love and she ran away
with him into the valley. Common law marriage. She got
pregnant and was visited frequently by the 'old witch' who lived
just the other side of the tunnel; really about four miles the other
side."

"That would be Gram's cottage. She's no witch!" Matt
interrupted.

"No, though some folks in this area would argue the point.
Anyway, the 'witch' told her that she carried more than one child
in her belly. When it came time to deliver, her pain was intense
and she sent her husband, my great-grandfather, to get the witch.
One baby was born by the time they returned, two more
followed. A month after the births, weather started to turn cold,
so they agreed to all move into town where she could get help
with their babies. All three were boys. They had planned to
return to their private valley when the weather improved, but
never did."

Seeing Linda return without Barbara, Jerry asked, "Is
Missus Harper okay?"

Linda nodded and resumed her seat on the sofa. Seeing
Matt growing concerned, she whispered, "She's getting a hot
shower." Matt nodded acceptance and looked back to Jerry.

Jerry shifted his jaw for a second, then continued.
"Grandfather, great-grandfather that is, worked odd jobs around
the community while the family stayed with the 'witch.'
Whenever he needed money, he would journey to the cabin;
always returning with ample coin. Folks in town figured he must
have a buried treasure, but nobody could uncover his secret.

Ne'er do wells ransacked the cabin, with no result. Years later, when WWII broke out, the three boys went to enlist, together. Their recruiting officer would not allow all three to enlist, so they drew straws. My grandfather drew the short straw and had to stay home. One of the brothers came home, the other did not. Buried in France. Grandfather stayed in the Benmill community, working at the old lumber mill, but his brother went off to college on the GI Bill and Granddad assisted by them through the secret in the cabin."

Jerry paused to see that Matt was still following his story of the mysterious cabin in the inescapable valley. "Jump ahead a few years. My grandfather had two boys. One, my uncle, married the 'witch's' granddaughter; the other, my father, moved to another community not far from here. As a teenager, my father often spent summers at the cabin. Well, Dad went to college, where he met my mother. His job was accounting and they settled about forty miles from here, in a larger community. He made good money and never had to go to the cabin for funds; thus, the secret was lost. I would spend summers at the cabin until the year I was sixteen, when a ferocious black bear scared the bejeebers out of us during a violent thunder storm."

"I remember that storm," Linda smiled, a twinkle in her eye.

"Must be the same bear that's there now. He doesn't like thunder storms either," Matt chuckled.

"Grumpy's old, but I don't think he's *that* old," Walt interjected.

"Don't know, could be," Jerry considered. "But I didn't go back to the cabin after that. As I recall, my dad bought some cedar shingles to repair the roof. Left overs from when a friend of his did his roof. Dad never got around to fixing the roof, so they should be stored at the end of the cabin, next to the spring house."

"WHOA, Dad! You're asking them to repair the roof on YOUR cabin?" Walt challenged.

"No. I just remembered they might be there, that's all. Should get the Corps of Engineers to repair the roof. Anyway, while I didn't go back to the cabin, I did visit Benmill frequently, or more specifically, Linda. We married, and I eventually got a job teaching Econ at Virginia Tech, in Blacksburg, Virginia. I've already told you how I was recruited to work on the Gumdrop project . . ."

"The 'Gumdrop Project'?" Matt asked, interrupting Jerry's story.

"Yeah, stupid name but it's just a label. You are part of the 'Gumdrop Project.' Anyway, several of us were sharing childhood stories over lunch, about nine months ago. I was talking about our private valley when Brian Bard, the project manager overheard us and explored my valley as a solution for his outrageous scheme. He literally stole the valley; executed 'Power of Eminent Domain.' "

"So that old cabin is yours but really isn't. Who holds title to the land?" Matt asked, his curiosity peaked.

"There is no written deed, per se. I do hold a common law deed that says my family owns the valley, me, my brother, and cousins. If anyone, other than the government, were to try to take it, I would win in court."

Matt sat silently for a moment, carefully considering everything Jerry had told him. Shifting forward on the sofa, so he now sat on its edge, he challenged his host. "Fascinating story; cabin needs a lot of work. However, I still have two questions, if I may." Seeing Jerry shrug acceptance, Matt continued. "First, you said it took two days to move us here. By my calculations, we got to the campground late Tuesday and woke to this nightmare on Wednesday. Today is day twenty-two, but you are saying it is really twenty-four, so today is NOT Wednesday, but Friday?"

"Correct. You've done well to keep up with the days," Jerry affirmed. "Your second question?"

"Yes, my second question isn't so easy. You said you ran simulations of our life and determined that we are a threat to the stability of world economy. What possible event did you insert into your simulation that caused a catastrophe?"

"It's not as easy as just inserting a single event, but testing impacts of multiple events and their eventual outcomes."

Barb returned, wrapped in a plush dandelion yellow robe. As Barb sat, Linda jumped up, "I need to put your clothes in the dryer. I'll be right back."

"Feeling better?" Matt asked, smiling when he saw an exposed lower leg was freshly shaven.

"Much. What is this about simulations of our life?" Barb replied, sweeping the robe back over her legs.

Matt turned back to Jerry, "You mentioned a stock purchase earlier."

"Yes, that is the one key factor that seemed to be a lynch pin in your entire simulation. The online purchase of some stock."

"THAT is where your simulation fails. COMPLETELY! I do own stock, however I do NOT trade online. I don't even have an online account. I have a stock broker who is a trusted friend. It is HIS job to keep up with fluctuations in the market. Not mine! I have no desire to get into that nightmare!"

"Mister Harper, Matt, I believe I told you there are three personality profiles that could cause the disaster our simulations have predicted. Keep in mind that the disaster is not a direct result of a single action but a domino effect, possibly even the simple flutter of a butterfly. . . . The first profile is the *devil-may-care, act now and think later* trader. This person could easily dump a large volume of stock without thinking beyond his mouse click, thus causing a disaster. The second is the active trader who likes to do his homework and trade for sport. Misinterpreting market trends is common among these traders and, again, a single ill-informed trade of some volume could easily cause a shift in the market. Then there is you, or your profile. May not currently own stock, or as you said, uses a licensed broker. You, however, could respond to an invitation to a 'free trade' from an online company and do something really stupid. There are dozens of online trading companies who prey on people like you."

"Jerry, I did get an email invitation not long ago with an opportunity to 'get in on the ground floor' of new companies. 'Three days of free trading from their reserved list of selected promising opportunities.' Some such nonsense. Thing is, as I said, I have a broker I TRUST and I immediately deleted that invitation."

"I know," Jerry murmured.

"WHAT? HOW do you know?" Jerry exploded.

"When you were identified as a potential candidate, our project director sent that invitation. It was sent to a half-dozen maybes and contained a worm that enabled us to monitor your computer. Yours failed miserably."

"Yes, my anti-virus caught your worm. So WHY then are we still suspect?"

"As I said before you are a 99.94% match to a specific profile. Nobody in America was a closer match to any profile. And it isn't just stock purchases. It could be online real estate transactions, intercepted money transfers, almost anything. Maybe even something so simple as inadvertently making a movie reservation at a wrong theater. Remember, it is not necessarily the event itself, but the fall of dominos it will trigger.

"One more thing I need you to remember, Mister Harper. Missus Harper. Even when I saw your personal profile, I never imagined anyone would take action against you. This was all theoretical and I was led to believe we would be watching you, not kidnaping you!" Jerry's face enforced this belief.

Standing in the office door, Linda informed everyone, "Two Humvees just pulled up out front,"

"I guess we aren't out of this yet," Barb sighed.

"No, ma'am. The best solution, right now, is to return to the valley and give me a chance to prove you are no longer a threat."

"Then witness protection?" Matt challenged.

"I don't see any other way," Jerry replied, somewhat apologetically.

Sighing, Barb asked, "Can we at least send a message to our kids?"

"Not sure it would get through. The project controls Internet access and all phone service from Benmill, land line and cellular. I'll bet there are even filters preventing communications with your known family," Jerry responded.

"Okay, we go back. What's going to keep us from escaping again?" Matt challenged.

"Army Corps of Engineers. They have a lot of fencing on hand and are probably already closing the western ridge. I'm assuming you went over the western ridge because you met Gram and are here."

Sighing, Linda leaned over and whispered to Barbara, "Your clothes should be dry. Join me in the laundry off the kitchen." Once in the privacy of the laundry room, she softly told Barb, "I'll get a message to your kids."

"Thank You," Barb replied, expressing absolute gratitude. "I'll give you their email and social media accounts."

While Barbara swapped her robe for clothes, Linda went back to the study and offered everyone lunch, also telling them, "Two more Humvees in the back. Old Man Bard must really be upset."

Matt stood and looked to his host. His voice heavy with frustration, he half jokingly asked, "Last meal for the condemned?"

Jerry didn't reply, he simply put his hand on Matt's shoulder. Matt shook it off.

Twenty-Four

After a lunch of sandwiches loaded with meat, cheese, pickles and other condiments, iced tea and home made brownies, all of which far surpassed anything Barb and Matt had had in recent weeks, Jerry took the couple out the front door. Armed soldiers quickly restrained both escapees. Matt knocked one large soldier down the steps when the soldier roughly grabbed Barb. Other soldiers quickly strapped their wrists, hooded them, and forcibly put them in separate vehicles. Matt continued to fight all the way, refusing to walk and screaming about the safety and care of Barbara. Not knowing they were in separate vehicles, he became more agitated when she did not respond to his calls.

Jerry shook his head and sighed as four Army Humvees left his cul-de-sac then turned up the mountain road to the right. Standing in his driveway, he pondered what he had done and what his next move should be. Seeing all four vehicles disappear into the forest, he went back inside.

"I guess there's no point in Walt going to school this late," he said to Linda, who was putting the last of lunch away. "But I do have to go in and face the 'Commander.' Wish me luck." He leaned over and kissed his wife on her cheek, then ambled out the door.

As soon as Linda heard Jerry's car door close, she called, "Walt! Get your father's computer on!"

Walt knew all his father's passwords and had the computer humming when Linda arrived. Sitting to her husband's desk, she cranked up Firefox and logged into her Facebook account. Using the notes from Barbara, she found accounts for both children, Steven and Angela. Without hesitation, she sent each the same message: *Your parents are alive and well.* Both messages appeared to have been sent, then disappeared from the screen. Linda checked her sent log and found nothing. When she tried to connect to Angela's account and send her a friend request, she could not find the account. Steven's disappeared as well.

"Okay, let's try another way." Linda then logged into her personal online email account. Ignoring the inbox, she opened a new message and entered the email addresses Barb had given her. Once again, she entered the simple message: "Your parents are alive and well." She then hit send and sat back, thinking aloud, "I can check the status when I get to work." Leaning forward to log out of her account, she got a message in her inbox, "Message Failed. Addressee Not Found."

"That was way too fast," Walt commented from behind her. "Message failures take hours to be returned. Something's fishy."

"Yes, I know, but I have to get to work," Linda agreed.

Jerry arrived at the mountain facility in time to see Matthew and Barbara being walked into the tunnel, still hooded. Matt was walking, now, but yanked his shoulders away every time a soldier tried to use force. Being treated with a bit of respect, Barbara was more compliant.

Four Humvees passed Jerry on their way back to the US Army Corps service garage as he forced himself toward the entrance. Taking a deep breath, he trudged into the tunnel, through security, down three hallways, and into his office. Touching his mouse to wake his computer from dormancy, he moved to sit but was stopped.

"Sir, you are wanted in the Commander's Office, immediately."

"Thank you. I was expecting as much." Jerry sighed.

"Immediately, sir. I am to escort you."

Looking up, Jerry recognized the corporal waiting for him; Brian's personal "assistant." Without further delay, Jerry exited his office and walked to Brian's. The corporal was with him, maintaining a distance of precisely three and one half feet behind. Close enough to apprehend but not stumble on one another's feet. Another soldier opened a door labeled, Chief Administrator, allowing Jerry to enter unabated.

"He's expecting you. Go on in," the escort said as he stopped by his own desk in an outer office.

Jerry continued to a door marked "Private" and opened it.

"TANNER! WHAT THE HELL DO YOU THINK YOU ARE DOING?" a powerful baritone voice yelled.

Expecting this explosion, Jerry responded in a calm, almost exasperated voice. "Look, we got them back and no harm done."

"You couldn't wait to contact their kids, could you!?" Brian Bard, Project Manager, bellowed.

"What are you talking about? I have not made any attempt to locate or contact any family members."

"Don't lie to me. I'll have you kicked off this project in a heartbeat. Two attempts to contact the Harper's kids from YOUR house. That damned Facebook and by email."

"Look, Brian, my wife or son may have attempted the contact, but I have NOT."

"Your WIFE and SON shouldn't know anything about this project!"

"Well, it's a good thing they do. It was my son who recognized the Harpers at the inn, where you were very likely eating breakfast at the time!" Jerry glared at Brian, debating whether this was over or not. "You may like keeping your family in the dark about your work, but I talk with mine. You ought to try it sometime."

Once more, Jerry waited to see what else, if anything, was about to fly his way. Hearing nothing, he excused himself. "Since you don't seem to have anything further to say, I do have work to do. I need to prove the Harpers are NOT a threat to world economic stability."

Without waiting for any response, Jerry turned and left the Project Manager's office. Passing the secretary's desk he mumbled, "He's all yours! Shoot 'im if you have half a chance."

The secretary smirked, then closed the door to the inner office without looking inside.

Matt and Barb experienced deja vu as their hoods were yanked off and they stood in a drizzling rain near the waterfalls. Both sighed, but Barbara was the first to speak.

"Nice walk out in the 'real' world."

Matt rotated his left shoulder where a soldier had used excessive force. Exasperated and frustrated, he moaned, "At least we now know that 'real' people still exist. Guess we should get back to camp; get out of this rain." Sighing and accepting their plight, for the moment, he asked, "Ideas for supper?"

Looking around them, they found their walking sticks and knapsacks dropped not far away. Retrieving their gear, they set off toward the lake. Walking past the cabin, Matt couldn't resist teasing his wife, "You missed the story about how magical that cabin is."

"Magical?" Barb replied, her face filled with disbelief.

"Yep. Seems that cabin produces coins, money, gold, something like that. Jerry's grandfather knew the secret but it was lost through the generations."

"Right," Barb replied, shaking her head.

Both were disappointed when Prince Albert didn't join them, but they continued with little conversation. Matt's last comment, just before reaching their campsite, was, "Home sweet home. I'm ready to just sit back and stare at the forest for a minute or two. What about you?"

Turning into their campsite, both stopped and stared. Their camper was lying on its side.

Linda Tanner served as Senior Planner in the Mountain Products division of SWI Cooperative, helping small business startups find their foothold in today's fast changing marketplace. It was her job to coordinate financial, marketing, information technology, and production planning for fledgling businesses who specialized in products native to the West Virginia mountains. When Linda arrived at her desk six hours late, the CEO popped into her office.

"Linda, everything okay?"

"Yes, sir. We had a bit of an emergency at home this morning."

"Okay, as long as you are all right. We have three new applications today. Being Friday, it would be nice if you could acknowledge them before you leave."

"Sure." Linda smiled and looked at her computer screen, which now displayed her desktop.

Without hesitation, Linda called up Facebook and did a search for Steven Harper. She smiled when she saw a recent picture of him with Susan. While reviewing his details, her screen flashed and she was returned to her own home page. Without hesitation, she reached down and unplugged her computer. Her IT specialist, at SWI, had once warned her, "If your computer ever does anything odd or unexpected, pull the plug. Don't hesitate. Don't use the power button. Just pull the plug. You might prevent anything in memory from being written to disc and coming back to haunt you."

Trying to hold the image of Steven's information in her mind, she wrote a name on a notepad. Susan Scott, Trinidad, CA. After reading the name two times, trying to make sure she had it right, Linda plugged her computer in once more and rebooted. Bypassing warnings about "abnormal shutdown" she watched as her desktop reappeared. Clicking on her list of clients, she scrolled through the names. Finding one she thought might help her, she smiled, lifted the receiver from her desk phone, and punched in the client's number.

"Heather, this is Linda with SWI, how are you today?" . . . "Great, and that burp last month, you have overcome those issues?" . . . "Good. Heather, I need an odd bit of a favor and it needs to be kept confidential. . . . I need the contact information for Susan Scott in Trinidad, California." . . . "Yes, I will definitely wait." . . . Seconds later, Linda wrote down Susan's information. "Heather, one more big favor, and please don't ask me about it." . . . "Thank you. I need you to send her a text message. *Tell Steven his parents are alive. Project Gumdrop.*" . . . "That's right. It does sound like a bizarre candy company. Please send that as soon as we get off." . . . "Already sent? Thanks. Call me if you need anything. I owe you a big one. Bye."

Hanging up the phone, Linda leaned back in her chair and smiled. "Stop that one Brian Bard!" Taking a deep breath of satisfaction, she leaned forward and opened her company email, looking for three new applications for assistance.

"WHAT THE HELL HAS HAPPENED?" Barbara exploded with disbelief. "Excuse my 'French'."

"My thoughts exactly," Matt replied, walking briskly over to their camper. As he approached, he noticed that stones of their fire circle were scattered about and their chairs were missing. A quick look around found one chair in nearby bushes. Unable to see the door or side of the camper, he looked at the ground. "A lot of scuff marks and here is what appears to be a bear paw . . . and another here. My first guess is Grumpy needed his back scratched." Shaking his head and grinning slightly as he drew a

breath, he ran a foot over several large rocks sticking up from the
ground that had been covered by their camper.

"What are you grinning at?" Barb asked, bewildered.

"I was just remembering what Walt told us about this
campsite. Ole Grumpy's scratching spot." Looking around the
underside of the camper, Matt noticed water leaking from a crack
in the fresh water tank. Shaking his head, he tried to figure out
how to climb up to the side, now facing the sky. Walking to the
tongue of the camper, he coughed. "Gas is leaking." Checking the
gauge as he closed the gas valve he added, "Should've turned it
off before we left. About gone. Barely enough to register on the
gauge." Sighing, he climbed up the tongue and onto the side.

"What are you doing?" Barb called out in a panic.

"Need to see how much damage has been done. Maybe we
can right this thing and be okay."

"You are out of your mind!"

"Maybe, but I'm not in the mood to go to the cabin right
now and I don't see any other alternatives. I'd like to stay here, if
we can." Squatting on the front edge and looking across the side
of the camper, he reported, "Several scratches and a few gouges,
look like claw marks. Door is half ripped off. Awning appears to
be okay." Feeling the wall give under his weight when he stood,
Matt crawled to the door and laid down, hanging his head inside.
"Well that seals it, window is busted in and a tree branch has
punctured the side over the sofa." As he crawled back to the
front, Matt looked more carefully at the gouges and scratches.

Climbing down from the camper, Matt's eye caught the red
light of a camera watching them. Taking a deep breath, he
clinched his teeth and looked at the paw prints in the dirt. The
rain had stopped, but had been just enough to soak the ground
without washing it. Taking a deep breath and holding it a few
seconds, he restrained an angry explosion. "They want us to
think this was done by Grumpy, the bear . . ." Turning toward
the camera he exclaimed, "BUT IT WASN'T!"

Barb followed Matt's line of sight. Seeing the red light, her
own anger rose. "How can you tell?"

"A list of mistakes. The gouges in the side, supposedly done
by bear claw, pull down. Grumpy would have to push at the top,
but the awning isn't damaged. I also don't think the bear would
tear the door off, no reason there." Running his foot along the

line where the camper wheel had been resting, he pointed with his toes. "Boot marks. Brushed away, but still boot marks. Our home away from home was lifted, not pushed." Walking over to the water tank, he pointed to the crack. "It was hit, with something like a hammer."

"Why would they do this to us?!" Barb cried.

"That S-O-B project manager of theirs, he doesn't like the way we play his game. HE wants us at the cabin. Probably easier to keep tabs on us up there."

"But WHAT does it matter WHERE we are? We are trapped in this valley!"

Wrapping his arms around his bride, Matt tried to console her and himself. "I don't know, sweetheart. I just don't know anymore."

Standing together, sheltered in one another's arms, they felt more drops of rain as a dark cloud passed overhead, crying with them.

"What do we do now?" Barb asked, after several minutes of trying to accept this new development.

Releasing his wife, Matt located both chairs and set them next to the scattered fire circle. When both sat, he began. "Well, we can sleep here, or somewhere else, under the stars as it were, but I don't like that idea. I love the stars, but I don't like wet and not sure Ole Grumpy would understand."

"Maybe move up to the lookout rock? I woke with deer up there," Barb suggested, a bit of lightness in her voice.

"Naw, I like a hot breakfast. It'd be a lot of work to move our camp up the mountain."

"It's going to be a lot of work moving to the cabin!" Barb retorted.

"Yes, but at least it is shelter and some protection from critters."

Barbara looked at her husband as though he had lost his mind. "That cabin offers NO protection from weather or critters!"

"Actually, it does. The walls are solid and Grumpy won't fit through the door." Matt cocked his head with a bit of whimsical smile.

Still staring at her husband, Barb stated the obvious. "So, you're saying we need to move to the cabin and play by their rules."

"I didn't say anything about 'playing by their rules.' Remember, the first duty of a prisoner of war is to escape." Matt then put a finger to his lips signaling his wife to be quiet. Walking to the rear of the camper, he retrieved his camera dislocation stick and with one blow knocked the first camera from its perch. Quickly surveying the area, he located the transmitter in a tree near the Durango. After smashing the transmitter and hurling the pieces into the forest, he resumed his discussion. "As I was saying, the first duty of a prisoner of war is to escape. We now know of a town and we have friends there."

"Have you forgotten that the U.S. Army is putting a fence across the ridge?"

"*May* be putting up a fence. Besides, if they do, you think Grumpy will let it stand? I believe he likes his freedom more than we do, and this is HIS territory! We may have to make a few trips up the mountain . . . maybe cut a few wires on each trip."

"Oh, you have a fence cutter in the car?"

"No, but I do have some tools. Vice-grips might do it, not sure. I feel certain it would be difficult and I doubt I could cut enough to get us through in one night."

"So, you're suggesting we move to the cabin and look like we are playing nice, but in reality we 'tunnel' out after dark, one snip at a time." Seeing Matt nod, she continued. "Why only one snip at a time?"

"Not sure my vice-grips have cutters on them. Even if they do, or don't, it takes a lot of force to cut through chain link fence. Not sure how much abuse my hands, or yours, will take at one time. Maybe cut three or four in an evening, rest a night, then return." Matt grew quiet with pondering. "You know, a second thought. If we can find where they join sections of fence, we can remove the joiner wire. THAT might be easier."

"Does it matter which wire is removed?"

"Some might be welded, but maybe we could cut the top and bottom then just undo the wire."

"Sounds too easy," Barb replied, somewhat skeptical.

"Cut, disassemble, does it matter? Just figure it will likely take more than one night. In the meantime, what say we collect some food and supplies and go to the cabin?"

Twenty-Five

Friday noon, actually 12:05 PST, Steven Harper turned his Jeep Wrangler east off US-101 into remote Humboldt County, California. Roads grew narrower and narrower until he carefully steered his four wheel drive vehicle up a demanding path defined only by a shear drop to the right and a sharp rise to the left. An hour after leaving pavement and civilization, he turned the engine off and stared at a log cabin sitting in a clearing on the side of a mountain. Susan Scott hopped from the Jeep and spun around with her arms spread out, then turned to Steven. "Welcome to Scott Mountain."

"Your family has their own mountain?" Steven asked as he grabbed two bags from the back seat.

"Yep. My granddaddy claimed this mountain and built this cabin."

"I thought your dad bought this place to escape civilization," Steven challenged.

"He did, but the man he bought it from was named Scott, just like us, and whomever built this cabin must have been somebody's grandad, why not mine?" She raced over to Steven and wrapped her arms around his neck. "Nice place to escape to, don't you think?"

After a quick kiss, Susan released Steven so he could put their bags on the porch. Looking around, all he could see was unspoiled forest, a deep valley, and another mountain.

Taking a deep breath, Susan chirped, "Wait until tonight. The night sky is unbelievable. No light pollution whatsoever." Seeing Steven looking at his phone, she added, "And you might as well turn that thing off, because there is no reception and no power to recharge the battery. Water comes from a well and it is cooooold and sweeeeet, like you won't believe until you get some. Toilet is the little square building out back." Watching Steven turn his phone off and shake his head just slightly, she asked, "Still glad you came?"

Wrapping his arms around her, he replied, "Absolutely!" They then shared a passionate embrace. As their lips separated, he asked, "So, why did you drag me all the way out here? Why not the forest campground?"

"Because our last three or four trips have been to the redwood forests. I love those trees as much as the next guy, probably more, but I thought you needed a change. Someplace you've never been before."

"I've been that stressed out?" Steven thought for a moment, then added. "I actually thought I had everything under control until this week."

Steven Harper, eldest son of Barbara and Matt Harper, worked as an electronics engineer, designing microchips. Steven could work from anywhere in the world but he liked the relaxed, free-flowing environment of his employer's primary corporate headquarters and manufacturing facility in northwest California. More importantly, he liked the offerings of the forests in northern California. Hiking, boating, fishing, and Susan. He met Susan on a group survival outing and while their first meeting was contentious, they had become inseparable, constantly challenging one another. This was their first outing since receiving the news about his parent's fatal accident.

"Well, you can bring me up to date while we relax and explore this beautiful mountain. Right now, let's see what we can put together for supper. I'll open the cabin, you bring in the groceries."

Dropping a box of food on a table in the kitchen area, Seven looked around. The kitchen was equipped with an old iron wood stove, an authentic butcher's block, a sink and hand pump, and a table with four chairs. The only cabinets were below the counter on either side of the sink. Susan's father had installed open shelves above these counters, either side of a window at the sink. Across the cabin was a sitting area with a fireplace. Two closed bedrooms filled the rear wall and were separated by a narrow hallway which led out back, to an outhouse.

"I guess I should fetch the firewood your dad told me to bring up here."

"Only if you want your meals cooked," Susan replied.

Steven had been handling the death of his parents with grace. Angela, his sister, had become hysterical. Having just learned that she was pregnant, she had been planning how to break the news to her parents when she got the call about the accident on the highway. That was just over three weeks ago.

When Steven inquired about obtaining death certificates and retrieving special items from his parents' house and disposal of their property, he was stonewalled. Explaining that he lived 2,500 miles away didn't help. Somebody from the government had taken control of his parent's estate and was not sharing any information. Suspecting something was amiss, Steven had contacted James Thompson, who was a police detective and close personal friend of his father, Matt Harper.

Thompson made several inquiries in an official capacity; he too was stonewalled. He did, however, obtain a copy of the official accident report. After studying this report, Thompson's detective instinct told him something was wrong. A close family friend, the kids called him "Uncle Jim," he had even borrowed that camper several times and something about the pictures in the report didn't add up. The camper, or what was left of it, pictured in the report was the correct brand and model, but there was something that wasn't right and he couldn't put his finger on it. To satisfy his curiosity, he made plans to personally view the remains of the Durango and camper. The North Carolina Highway Patrol granted permission after his third request. Thompson told Steven that he planned to drive across North Carolina this Friday, twenty-four days after the accident. He thought he might make a weekend of the trip, thinking if he wasn't satisfied with the wreckage, he could go all the way to the campground where Matt and Barb were planning to stay. His departure was delayed by an investigation of multiple homicides that required his attention and then heavy rains across the state.

Day Twenty-Three, now Twenty-Five
Feeling an excruciating pain in his shoulder as he rolled over, Matt exclaimed, "We have GOT to get that mattress up here TODAY!"

Not wanting to get their mattress wet, Matt and Barb spent their first night in the cabin on the floor, which to Barb's surprise was mostly dry.

Lying on her back, Barb stared at the ceiling above her. Heavy log rafters supported planks laid side by side. Scattered about were small holes with roots hanging down. Feeling as though nothing were right in her world, she sighed and announced, "I am going to visit the facility and then wash off in the lake."

Matt pondered a few seconds. "Good idea." He then clambered to his feet and offered a hand to his wife who accepted the assist.

While Barb visited the outhouse, Matt went up to the lake. He chuckled when Barb removed her shirt and, using a stick, hung it over the camera facing the lake area. Reaching the stone steps, she disrobed and stepped comfortably into the water. After rubbing her hand over most of her body, she said bluntly, "Need to remember to get soap from the camper."

"What, you would contaminate this pristine body of water?" Matt teased.

"You don't know how good that shower felt yesterday. Then waking up on that floor this morning . . . I can't tell you, well the effects of that shower were all washed away. I need soap, at the very least."

"What did we bring for breakfast?" Matt asked as he rubbed his own body with fresh water.

"Not a matter of what we brought, but what can we easily fix? Cereal. Milk is in the cold room." Seeing Matt's surprise, she added, "I put it there myself." Stepping to the stones leading out of the lake, Barb paused. "We didn't bring any towels, did we?"

"Couldn't bring everything in one trip," Matt chuckled. "Guess we'll have to air dry."

"At least it's not raining," Barb replied. Stepping out of the lake she shook her hands and arms, bent over to pick up her clothes, then plodded barefooted and bare-bodied down to the cabin. Matt smiled and followed her example.

Both campers had the change of clothes they had stuffed into their packs before following Prince Albert over the mountain. Barb's were fresh, thanks to Linda. Once dressed, over dampish bodies, they sat down on the floor with bowls of cereal. Corn flakes and Cheerios.

"Plans for today?" Barb asked, putting her empty bowl down beside her.

"Well, we thought to bring some stuff last night, but today I want to focus on getting that old gas stove and mattress out of

the camper. We should have one full bottle of gas, which will be
heavy, and it will be tough to get the mattress out. That makes
two trips, there and back. I'd like to make a third to retrieve other
things we'll need to cook and generally survive as long as we
have to. We can load linens and light stuff into the food bins and
carry them between us." Looking at the pained expression on
Barb's face, he concluded, "It is going to be a lloonngg day."

It was close to 9:30, midmorning, when Matt climbed into their
camper. Walking across cabinets, which were now the floor, he
made his way to their bed. Staring at the mattress and the way it
lay across the space, he heard Barb call, "Take the sheets off
first!"

"What?" he called back, looking around to see where his
wife was.

Still standing outside the camper, she replied, "I know you
are trying to figure out where to start. You have no room to
maneuver, so do something easy first. Take the sheets off and
toss them out. That will at least get you started."

Shaking his head with amazement, he did as Barb had
suggested. Pulling the sheets off was easier said than done. The
top sheet came off easy, but the bottom sheet did not want to let
go of the mattress. Tugging on the sheet to free it, however, also
freed up the mattress and got it moving toward the door. Matt
didn't toss the sheet out, as suggested; he simply tossed it toward
the door and began tugging on the mattress. It took him fifteen
minutes to move the bulk from the bed area to the door, keeping
it flat between the floor and ceiling, which were now two walls.
He cringed every time he heard a cabinet door crack under his
weight.

Reaching the door, Matt got under the mattress and pushed
it up. It fit nicely through the door, sideways, but wouldn't bend.
Trying to stand the eighty-inch semi-rigid box vertical between
the dinette and closet proved to be a problem of geometry. Matt
climbed out from under / behind the mattress, where he had
been pinned against the closet and bathroom doors, until he
stood at the end. Pushing it didn't work, it simply pushed against
the closet. Climbing back under to the closet, he pushed only the
end up with one extended arm, curling the mattress just a little,

then pushed the bulk with his shoulder. The end slipped painfully out the door; like birthing a baby. He repeated this process until the mattress flipped vertical, again pinning him against the bathroom door. Taking a deep breath, the weary obstetrician squatted down and lifted with all the strength he had left. The mattress rose and hung on the door as it tried to fall over. "One more push," he said to himself and spread his feet across the pantry cabinet. Putting both hands up, he shoved. The mattress flopped outside the camper shell as the pantry door cracked.

Barbara, who had been cheering him on with advice from outside, applauded his accomplishment of the seventy-five-pound delivery. Grabbing the sheets from the dinette, Matt climbed out and stood victorious on the side of their home-away-from-home. Tossing the linen to his wife, he advised her. "Now your turn. You need to catch this thing when I try to lower it. I'll turn it and push it off slowly, but you need to stop it from getting too dirty. My wife doesn't like to sleep on dirty."

Barb smirked and replied, "I'll do my best. Send it down."

Barb was not able to catch the delivery but did keep it from falling into the dirt by intercepting it with her body as it landed on end in front of her. Leaning it against the bottom of the trailer, she looked up. "Before you come down, grab the rest of the linens, towels, and stuff, and our clothes. We can stuff them in our backpacks."

"10-4," Matt acknowledged. "Toss me the packs and I'll stuff them with what I can."

Filling the second knapsack, Matt realized how hungry he was becoming and grabbed luncheon meats and fixins from the fridge, which he stuffed into one of the packs. After hoisting both knapsacks out the door, he found their loaf of bread and tossed it up as well.

Back on the ground, Matt and Barb negotiated how to carry the mattress the mile or so back to the cabin. Packs on their backs and ready to move on, they decided to hoist it to their heads, which proved to be more difficult than anticipated. The mattress was not cooperative and kept giving way where not supported. Barb suggested they carry it to the Durango and lift it on the roof then slide it to their heads.

"It'll get dirty," Matt replied.

"But we'll get it to the cabin. We can clean it off before we put the sheets back on it," Barb conceded.

Lifting the mattress up to the roof of the SUV was also a trial; the middle wanted to sag. Not bend, just sag enough to make handling it difficult. Matt got his end up then moved toward Barb, lifting the sag as he went. Successfully raised, Matt took a lesson from the effort and suggested they use the walking sticks to hold up the middle; spanning between them, each could hold one end of each stick in either hand. This worked, sort of. The mattress resting on their heads, Matt in front and Barb toward the back, each held their end of the sticks up, one end in each hand about two feet apart. They set out for the cabin.

A third the way back, Barb began to feel the agony of holding both her arms up. Lowering her arms to relieve the pain caused the mattress to wobble, setting Matt out of balance. "Are you okay back there?" he called as he stopped walking.

"No. My arms are killing me."

"Yep, mine too. But if we put this thing down, we'll never get it up again."

Sighing, Barb agreed. "Okay, let's get moving. The sooner we get to the cabin, the sooner my arms will stop screaming in my ears."

More than two hours after leaving the camper with their mattress on their heads, they reached the porch of the cabin. Stopping at the edge of the porch, Matt suggested, "Okay, let's lower it to the right. It will fall, but we can catch it. I will catch it. Easy now . . ."

Lowering the mattress started slowly and smoothly. Both bearers bent to the side trying to maintain some control. When the edge was about four feet off the ground, the mattress took control and crashed down to the earth. Matt reached out and grabbed the upper edge, preventing it from toppling over, however the linen and bread, which had been traveling on top, rolled across the ground.

Seeing her husband grimace in pain, Barb responded, "I feel your pain, Lover. Trust me, I DO feel your pain."

As they maneuvered the bulky box through the door, Barb groaned, "Know what we forgot?"

"WHAT?" Matt growled.

"The broom."

Matt paused before replying, "You're right. Let's lean it against the wall and we'll get the broom next trip."

"Deal!" Barb agreed and lifted her end as Matt guided their bed to the closest wall.

Winding his arms around like a broken windmill, as he retrieved the bread and linen, Matt eased most of the pain from his shoulders. He then produced lunch meats and condiments from his pack. Without thinking, Matt placed the lunch fixings on the rickety old table.

"Always thinking about food," Barb teased, and began making sandwiches. Being suspicious of the table, she brushed off the counter with her hand and moved lunch supplies there.

"Not just food," Matt replied and wrapped his arms around his favorite person, making her task a bit difficult but definitely more pleasant.

When Barb handed Matt a ham and cheese sandwich wrapped in a paper towel, he turned to the table and chairs. Testing one of the chairs with his hand, he commented, "We need to bring the chairs back next trip, too." He then retrieved a bottle of water from their packs and stepped out to the lake. A minute later, Barb dropped down into the grass next to him.

Lunch was quiet as both campers looked out across the lake in front of them. The scene was tranquil, inviting, and perfect for a late spring picnic had they not been prisoners of a maniac.

Finishing her sandwich and sipping on her water, Barb sighed, "I miss Dee-O-Gee."

"You mean Prince Albert," Matt corrected. "Don't worry, I have a feeling we'll be seeing him again before too long." Pausing in his own thoughts, Matt also sighed, then stood with his hand extended to Barb. "Ready to head back for another load?"

"Not really." Barb looked up at her husband then accepted his hand and stood. "Let's get going."

Arriving at their trailer, Barb spied their red tablecloth. "We could use our red flag at the cabin. Think you can get it down without hurting yourself?"

"I got it up there, I'll get it down." Without another thought, Matt climbed the tree and pulled the flag down, dropping it to his wife. Back on the ground, merely fifteen minutes after starting his climb, Matt wiped his hands on the cloth and started listing things they needed this trip. "Chairs, broom, stove, gas, and . . ."

"Eating and kitchen utensils," Barb added.

Matt collected the chairs from the bushes, where their captors, pretending to be Grumpy, had tossed them. Placing them against the SUV, he then climbed up the camper and unlocked the storage bin. Seeing everything piled on the far side, out of reach, he moved to the camper door and climbed inside, where he made his way to the bed. Being on its side and without a mattress, Matt had no problem opening the storage beneath the bed.

Surveying the mess, Matt found their old portable stove and tugged on it till it came free. Using the edge of the counter as a walkway, he lugged the stove back to the door and heaved it up. As it flopped through the door to the side, above his head, Matt called, "Barb. When was the last time we used this stove?"

"Two or three years, I guess."

"Hmm, not good. I need to make sure it works before we carry all that weight back to the cabin." Looking around the interior, Matt spied and retrieved the broom before climbing out. Back on the ground, he proceeded to check the stove.

This stove was essentially a self-contained unit with legs stored in a compartment below the burners and a hose fixed to the regulator, which fed two burners. Not bothering to attach the legs, Matt pulled the hose out and set the stove on the ground beside their SUV. Stepping over to retrieve the propane tank, Matt realized he had not seen it since they returned from town. Looking around the campsite, he found nothing but the two tanks on the camper tongue, which were now essentially empty.

Seeing Matt puzzled, Barb asked, "What's the matter, now?"

"Where's the propane tank? The one they delivered with the second grocery box."

Not seeing it, herself, Barb replied, "You don't suppose they took it back, do you?"

"Wouldn't put it past them, but not really." Matt then started looking toward the bushes. "There it is," he called, pointing toward a clump of growth fifty feet downhill from their camper. Lifting the tank, Matt was relieved that it was heavy and full. Connecting it to the stove, his relief faded quickly.

Holding a butane lighter ready, he turned on the gas and tried to light the first burner. The gas flashed and burned on only one side. Turning the first burner off, he lit the second, with much the same result. "Damn. Burners are dirty and essentially useless. I'm going to try to clean this thing before we lug it back to the cabin. Don't want to carry all this weight if it's going to be useless."

Opening the rear of their Durango, Matt retrieved a small tool box, which contained several screwdrivers, pliers, vice-grips, tape measure, wire cutters, and a small steel brush. Using the brush, Matt went to work on the burners of stove, removing debris which filled holes meant to provide flame.

Not wanting to stand around useless, Barb tossed their empty knapsacks up on the camper, then took one of the plastic bins used for grocery deliveries and made her own way up onto and then inside the trailer. Heartbroken by the condition of their little house-on-wheels, she went to work. Starting with the refrigerator, she emptied it, placing some food into the bin, other stuff into knapsacks. She then retrieved pots, pans, plates, cups, all the essentials for preparing and enjoying a meal. Having very little room left in any of the containers, she took what she could from the pantry. Her work done, she tried to lift the first backpack out the door.

"MATT! I NEED SOME HELP!"

Matt had just finished testing one burner, getting the ring of flame to a usable 90% burn. Turning the burner off, he looked around for his wife. "Barb? Where are you?"

"In the camper! I need help getting stuff out the door."

Matt quickly scaled the camper and kneeling beside the door, reached down for the first backpack. "I had no idea you were doing this."

"I know. I got what I could. Will probably need another trip with two bins to finish clearing everything out." She then handed him the second backpack, which Matt took and put aside.

Seeing the bin coming next and how Barb was struggling, Matt flattened himself and reached in with both arms fully extended. Both Barb and Matt groaned under the weight of the cookware. Propping the bin on the side of the door, Matt exclaimed, "You shouldn't have loaded it this heavy!"

"Now you tell me," Barb agreed as she let Matt take the weight from her.

After pushing the bin to the side, Matt raised up on his knees and put a hand down to his wife, who accepted the assist.

Once she was out of the camper, Matt flipped the door to a closed position, realizing as he did this it was pointless, and carried the cookware bin to the front, then to the ground. Barb dropped the knapsacks down to him, one at a time, then ambled down herself as she had seen Matt do several times.

"How's the stove?" She asked, brushing her hands against one another.

"One burner's good. About to test the second." Matt then lit his butane lighter and released gas into the second burner. A ring of blue flames appeared, using all but one of the holes in the burner. "That'll do. Now, time to get organized and head back to the cabin."

Seeing Matt put his tool box on top of the cookware bin, Barb asked, "What about the solar panel, it doesn't weigh much."

Without considering why they might need it, Matt walked around to the back door behind the driver's seat. Opening it he saw the panel had been destroyed. Drawing a deep breath, slowly, he controlled his rage. "Bastards smashed it! Guess we don't really need to charge the battery."

Returning to their pile of goods, he asked, "Do we have any water?"

Barb silently retrieved a bottle from one of the knapsacks. After downing nearly half the contents, Matt, his voice extremely tense, sighed, "It's going to be another slow trek back. Ready to get started?"

Each silently donned a backpack, then Matt loaded the chairs on top of the bin with his tool box and the red table cloth. Each took one end of the bin in one hand. Seeing the broom had not been added, Matt cupped it in his hand with the propane tank while Barb carried the stove.

"Good thing we didn't bring walking sticks this time," Barb commented as they started back.

The trip back went slightly faster than the previous trip, with the mattress. Reaching the cabin in under two hours, they ducked into the porch just as rain returned. Exhausted, Matt announced, "That's it for today. No third trip."

"Sounds good," Barb agreed, opening a chair and flopping into it. "I did get the coffee pot."

Twenty-Six

Day Twenty-Six

Matt lay on the mattress next to Barbara, gently holding her hand as she slept. Looking to the dark ceiling above him, he needed her touch to strengthen him for the day ahead. His eyes followed ancient smoke lines from the center of the cabin down to the fireplace. Looking elsewhere about the ceiling he saw mildew growing around open holes in the roof and other dark spots that looked like water had been seeping through but not dripping. He recalled how he had seen moss was growing on the cedar shingles and Jerry telling him there was a supply of replacement shingles somewhere. As first rays of a new day filtered through these holes, he silently pondered their new and ever-changing situation.

Who, what, when, where, why, and how. Now we know those answers, but lot of good it does us. Seems a bit stupid to ask questions when acquiring the answers only brings more trouble and grief. Jerry is going to try to get us out of here, but what power does he have against that idiot who put us here and the entire U.S. Army? We have got to get ourselves out . . . over the ridge and beyond that community. It will be a long walk to freedom, but when we get out I'm going to alert the media and bring that egomaniac to his knees! . . . Step one, make sure we have the tools ready that we'll need to get through the fence, if there is one, then out of here!

Armed with a new resolve and a plan, Matt sat up, kissed his sleeping wife's hand, and rolled off the mattress. His first task of his new challenge was to fix two cups of coffee. Taking their kettle, he went out the back of the cabin to the cold house and dipped it into the trough, filling it from the stream running through the stone building. Returning to a makeshift kitchen area, he lit the portable gas stove and put the kettle on. Rummaging around for instant coffee, he made a bit more noise than he thought.

"What are you looking for?" Barb called gruffly from the mattress, propped on one elbow and stifling a yawn.

"Instant coffee."

"Look on the shelf above the cabinet, left of the window. About the height of your eyeballs, if you'd bother to open them." Barb then flopped back into the bed, her head on a pillow, and began to rub sleep from her eyes. She lay there, trying to organize random thoughts. Hearing the kettle whistle, she sat up, slipped on shoes, and stood. "I'm heading for the loo. Be right back."

Matt lifted the noisy kettle and smiled at his wife as she shuffled out the door and down the path to the left, wearing only a ruffled sleep shirt that barely covered her panties. Feeling heat surrounding his hand, he realized he was holding the kettle and poured hot water into two prepared mugs. Stirring the second cup, he mumbled, "Forgot the milk." Dropping the spoon in a mug, he crossed the cabin and returned to the spring house.

"I much prefer our camper toilet to this arrangement," Barb complained when she returned.

Matt held a cup of hot coffee out for her, which she took with an appreciative smile and sat in one of their folding chairs.

"So, what are the plans for today?" Barb asked, after two healthy gulps of restorative caffeine.

"First, breakfast. Don't know what yet, but breakfast. Then, back to the camper for whatever we might need to survive here." Matt then whispered, "maybe up to a week. . . ."

Startled, Barb replied in a soft whisper, "What do you mean a week? You have a plan?"

Returning to a more normal but soft voice, Matt continued. "I was just about to get to that. After we go to the camper, I'd like to rest a bit this afternoon." He then paused and silently mouthed the words, "Talk when we walk."

Barb looked puzzled then realized what Matt was saying. In confirmation, she nodded and whispered, "Bugs?"

Matt nodded with a grin and drank his coffee. After another gulp of her own, she asked, "Breakfast?"

"Well, that is another story. I thought we had bacon, eggs, cereal, milk . . . all the usual good stuff. But, when I got the milk for our coffee, the bacon was grey, which makes me not so sure about the eggs. Milk is a bit edgy, too. How do you feel about instant grits?"

Barb thought for a moment, sipping on her coffee, then got up and went to the door and looked toward the lake. A smile slowly crept across her face and she looked back at Matt. "I believe we have groceries."

Matt stepped from the kitchen area, where he had been leaning against the cabinet, and looked out the door from behind

Barb. Seeing two bins at the end of the path, he commented, "Now that's what I call customer service. We didn't even have to file a change of address and our weekly rations still found us." Exhaling heavily he stepped around Barb and retrieved the bins.

Eating the last of her pancakes, made with fresh milk and eggs, Barb asked, "What do you suppose made the food go bad and what did you do with it?"

Wiping syrup off his lip, Matt replied, "Nothing yet; was planing to drop it into the latrine. Only place I can think of where critters wouldn't get into it. Don't want to make them sick. As for what made it go bad? Not sure, something in the water maybe?"

"The water we are drinking?!" Barb exclaimed.

"The only water that has come from the spring has been boiled for coffee. No worry there, but what could be in the water?"

Absentmindedly licking syrup from her fork, Barb pondered, "That spring comes from under ground, no telling what it picked up. Now, was there anything that didn't go bad?"

"One pack of ham that hasn't been opened yet."

"There's the answer. Don't put open meat in the spring. It needs to be in a sealed bag or container. The water is definitely cold enough to keep it for several days, but we don't want water running over the meat." Barb pondered a few seconds. "Eggs might still be okay. How many?"

"Four, I think. And milk was almost gone, too. Could have been a natural degradation." Matt thought through their new predicament. "Okay, I'll go ahead and dump the meat and milk, but save the eggs. When we get to the camper, pull every plastic storage container and every resealable bag. Instead of resting this afternoon, I'll go to the waterfall and fill our jugs. Need to bring them from the camper, too."

Barb shook her head and stood to put her plate in the sink, then realized they did not have a sink. "Need to get our dish washing bins."

"Dinette seats," Matt chirped. "Stored under the dinette seats. No room to leave them on the counter. We better take one of our grocery bins with us to carry the smaller stuff."

Twenty minutes after finishing breakfast, Matt and Barb were heading toward their camper. Both wore empty back packs; Matt carried the larger of the two grocery bins. Walking sticks were left behind to free their hands. Entering the forest path leaving the lake, Matt commented, "You know, I didn't hear the grocery delivery today. They must have just dropped it off. I'll bet we could even meet them if we got up early enough. Maybe even share a cup of coffee."

Barb looked over at her husband, replying with a less than friendly tone, "Let's just focus on getting out of here. . . . Speaking of which, you have a plan that starts with an afternoon nap?"

"Not a nap so much as just resting, because I'd like to check out the ridge after dark. See if they have really fenced us in and if so, start making a gate."

"Why does it have to be done in the dark?"

"Don't want to be seen going up the mountain. We'll need as much lead time as we can muster to get over the mountain and past that community, Benmill. As soon as they know we are gone, they'll be heading straight there and I want to be well past that before they wake up."

"And where, pray tell, are we going?"

"No idea, just away from here. Find the nearest community not controlled by these idiots. I'm hoping there will be some kind of highway marker near the feed store. You know, a post with signs that say something like, Not Here 6 miles and Over There 8 miles."

Barb squelched a grin at Matt's attempted humor. "Okay. So we clean out the camper, go back to the cabin and rest, then after supper we climb through Grumpy's thicket to the ridge."

"Let's just call it 'the thicket,' if you don't mind. Don't want to think too much about Ole Grumpy."

"New subject," Barb responded. "Bugs. Are you going to get rid of their bugs in the cabin?"

"Not sure at this point. I get rid of them, they put more back. It's a stupid game. As long as they don't have cameras inside the cabin, I'm not sure it's worth the effort."

"Have you looked for cameras?" Barb asked, feeling very self-conscious.

"Didn't see any lights this morning, but I think we should both look this evening, or whenever it's dark enough that we can see them glow. I'll look for little black boxes while we rest this afternoon."

Barb grimaced at the thought of more surveillance equipment intruding upon their not-so-private moments. She was distressed with feeling like a test subject in a fish bowl. Conversation was minimal the remainder of the journey to their camper. Once there, Matt climbed inside and began retrieving all the gear he could find from cabinets and under the bed. Fortunately, most of the outside storage was accessible through the bed box, which was easy to reach now the mattress was out of the way.

Scrounging through equipment which was now a pile due to the orientation of the camper, Matt found their gas lantern and two small bottles of propane. He shook each bottle. Feeling something inside, he was confident they would now have light in the cabin when they needed it. Continued digging rewarded them with an old hammer, a folding camp saw, and a large canvas bag of rope and twine. After lifting this booty out of the camper, he went to work on the cabinets around the kitchen, where he found another pot, some cooking utensils Barb had missed, and two boxes of plastic storage bags. Looking under the dinette benches he retrieved two plastic wash basins, a dish drainer, half-dozen plastic storage containers of different sizes, and a cast-iron Dutch oven.

"Hey Barb, do you see any reason to carry this iron Dutch Oven back to the cabin?"

"That thing weighs a ton, but it is good for cooking chilli and pies. You decide."

Matt hefted the oven in his hand, judging its weight. Scrunching his lips with indecision, he called back, "Not today. If we need it, we know where it is." He then put it back inside the dinette seat.

"Matt! While you're in there, check the cabinets and wardrobes by the bed. See if we left any books or clothes in there."

After hefting his most recent finds up through the door, Matt clambered back to the bed. First he checked his side and found a pair of old shoes, which he tossed toward the bathroom. Then by reflex, he opened the cabinet over his side of the bed, which was now the higher side. Looking inside he instantly felt more than a bit foolish realizing anything that had been behind that door would now be accessible only through the door on

Barb's side, near what was now the floor. Shaking his head, he looked in the lower door where he found a collection of books, playing cards, and another small pillow. Retrieving everything, he checked her wardrobe, where he found a sweater and the Celtic fantasy book she had been reading, *Vrenessbith*. Looking at the cover he recalled the Army doctor had given her this book when he, Matt, had been mistaken for a bear and shot.

Hands full, Matt made his way back toward the door and started lifting treasures through the hatch above his head. Everything needed for this expedition now out of the trailer, he stood on the side of the dinette and lifted himself through the door. Once outside, he began dropping supplies to Barb, who waited below.

"I went through the front of the car while you were in the camper," Barb reported when Matt was back on the ground.

"Find anything useful?"

"Not really, but you need to check the back end."

Matt followed Barb's suggestion and found a few more tools, another pair of pliers and a couple screwdrivers. He had already taken the main tool bag, but these were loose. Checking all the bins and hidden compartments, he found a roadside emergency kit, two eight-foot ratchet straps, and a small hydraulic jack. He didn't want to leave these behind but none of it was of any real value in their current situation. Exhaling heavily with frustration, he reached up to close the back of their Durango, then stopped. Retrieving the two straps, he closed the tailgate and turned to survey what they were taking with them. Realizing what was missing, Matt circled the camper and found both water jugs behind it.

Most of what they found packed easily into the large grocery bin or their backpacks. After donning their packs, they lifted the bin between them as they had done before, and each grabbed a water jug with their empty hand. Before stepping off, Barb commented, "Glad you didn't bring that Dutch Oven."

Matt chuckled agreement and they began their journey back to the cabin. Barb looked back as they left, however Matt kept his eyes forward. This trip was difficult, but strengthened their resolve that it was past time to go home.

While Barb stored everything they had retrieved from their camper, Matt searched inside the cabin for electronic devices. He didn't find any cameras but located two microphones. Walking around the outside of the cabin, he found two new cameras. One behind the cabin watching the door to the spring house, the other in front of the porch and aimed at the front door. Barb's shirt had been removed from the camera watching the lake and now hung on a branch below it.

While making sandwiches, Barb made sure everything going into the spring house was either in a plastic bin or a plastic bag. Both she and Matt marveled at how cold their bottles of water were, having left them in the cooling stream that morning. Lunch completed and cleaned, Matt picked up both water jugs from the front porch and started up the path toward the lake.

"Wait!" Barb called. She grabbed both walking sticks and caught up with Matt lakeside.

He smiled and swapped the collapsible jug for his walking stick. Side by side they began their journey to the waterfall. Not far from the cabin, Matt noticed an algae bloom along the banks of the lake. He didn't say anything about it, but made a mental note to check it later.

Saturday, on Scott Mountain in California, was relaxing and filled with wonder as Steven and Susan explored favorite haunts from her childhood. While enjoying a breakfast of ham, eggs, and English muffins, Susan described a nearby glen filled with magic. While en route to this wondrous location, they got lost three times and Susan had to admit it had been about fifteen years since she was last there. Steven openly wondered if this place truly existed and if her memory was playing tricks on her. Susan dismissed Steven's chiding and continued her search. Eventually arriving at a remote pool with a small cascading waterfall, she quickly removed her shoes and socks and waded into the bone chilling water. Between shivers she threw her arms into the air, declaring, "I told you it was wonderful!"

Steven waded out and wrapped his arms around her, making his own declaration amidst delighted laughter. "I do love you!"

The two young adults spent most of the afternoon splashing in the pool, chasing salamanders, and eventually making love surrounded by ferns. Basking in the sunshine and the privacy of their own company, they found their world free of worries, concerns, and problems. That evening, as they enjoyed cold beers while grilling steaks at the cabin, Steven looked at Susan with something more than awe and wonder.

"Miss Susan Scott, would you do me the great honor of sharing my life?"

"Isn't that what we are doing?" she replied, a sparkle in her eye.

"In a more formal, lasting manner. As husband and wife."

Susan put her beer on the cabin porch and sidled up to Steven, taking his hand in hers. "Are you asking me to marry you?" Seeing Steven smile silently with his eyes and his lips, she replied, "Not now. Wait until you get everything sorted about your parents, then ask me."

The sparkle left Steven's eyes and his lips straightened just a bit. Seeing this change in his demeanor, Susan asked, "What is going on with your parents' estate?"

Steven looked deeply into Susan's eyes and understood. She had not said, "No." She had said, "Let's remove some problems from our lives, then maybe." Looking at the grill he realized the steaks were ready to come off. As they ate fresh salad, not quite fresh rolls, and hot steak, he explained what he understood.

"I told you my folks were hit by a tractor-trailer rig and for some unexplained reason, the government has locked up their house and won't let Angela or me inside. Last time I talked with Uncle Jim . . ."

"Your dad's detective friend. He's not really your uncle," Susan clarified.

"Right. But he is like family so we called him 'Uncle Jim.' Anyway, when I told him what was going on, he got suspicious. Contacted the Highway Patrol and finally got a copy of the accident report. Last thing he told me was there was something fishy with the report and he was going to go check out the camper and SUV this weekend."

"Was your dad working on something top secret or something the feds don't want leaking out?"

"NO! He was a safety engineer, head of security for a company that did have government contracts but he didn't do any research or work on any projects. He basically kept the plant safe from *idiots who worked there*. His words, not mine."

"Hmm. Maybe Uncle Jim will find out something useful this weekend and you can find out what's going on." Leaning over to kiss Steven, she whispered, "THEN, you can ask me again."

That evening they sat close and held hands as they watched the heavens display an incredible array of stellar beauty.

While Barb added seasoning to ground beef sizzling in a pan on the two burner portable gas stove, Matt hung towels over the two cameras in front of the log cabin. He then stepped up to the lake where he found an ounce of peace watching fish nab insects that landed on the water's surface. Looking across the lake, he watched shadow engulf the western mountain and pondered how to go about their next task.

Barb silently joined him, slipping an arm around his waist. "Supper's ready."

Without a word, he took her hand and they returned to the cabin for a dinner of seasoned ground beef mixed with rice and cheese. Cut green beans and fresh apples filled out their menu. Matt didn't have much to say beyond compliments to the chef for creative cooking under difficult circumstances. Barb just smiled. After dinner they cleaned the dishes, using boiled water from the spring house, and quietly made ready to climb to the ridge.

Darkness was chasing last traces of dusk away as they walked around the lake, following the path Dee-O-Gee had shown them days before. Reaching the mouth of the tunnel into the rhododendron, Barb hesitated, just as before.

"You can wait here, if that will make you feel safer," Matt told her. Preparing to enter the tunnel, he removed the pack filled with tools he might need to open the fence.

"No. It's just that knowing this is Grumpy's territory bothers me. We never know where he is and we don't have Prince Albert here to sniff him out."

"Barb, do you want to go home?"

Barb looked at Matt's expectant face, barely visible in the light of a half-moon. Taking a deep breath, she dropped to her hands and knees and began crawling through Grumpy's tunnel. Having experienced this tunnel before, it did not take Barb quite as long to negotiate this torturous obstacle. Fifteen minutes after getting on her knees, she stood tall on the far side of the rhododendron thicket and drew a deep breath.

"I didn't think you could move that fast!" Matt chuckled as he emerged behind her.

Shuddering slightly, she looked squarely at her husband. "Let's get this over with before that bear comes home." Without another word, she turned and trudged up the hill to the ridge.

"Well, they fenced us in," Matt declared, placing a hand on an eight-foot commercial chain link fence running along the ridge. Looking down the fence line he added, "And it appears we don't have to worry about Grumpy. See how the fence has been attacked from the OTHER side?"

Barb looked and did see that the fence had been assaulted and was bent toward them. Without another word, Matt pulled a pair of vice grip pliers from his backpack and began examining the fence. To his dismay, this fence was galvanized after weaving, which would usually make it more difficult to remove a single strand. Fortunately, Grumpy had solved that problem. His assault against the fence broke most of the zinc coating joining separate wires. Without further delay, Matt selected a strand to remove and locked his pliers on the twist at the bottom of the fence.

Freeing two steel wires twisted together proved more difficult than Matt had anticipated. Working in the dirt, he had to release and relock his vice grips several times, achieving less than a half turn each time. Eventually the wires released their grip on one another and he stood to consider his next step.

"If I try to remove the strand completely," he mused to Barb, "the fence will fall apart. Be easy to spot. And I have to reach up eight feet, ugh. BUT, if I cut the wire in the middle, the hole will be less obvious. Now, how hard is it going to be to break this wire?"

Barb watched, without comment, as Matt locked the cutting edge of his pliers on the wire, about five feet above the ground, and twisted them back and forth. After resetting the tension of the pliers and twisting them on the wire for a third time, it snapped. Matt smiled back at his wife and clamped his vice-grips on the cut wire. Twisting the wire out also proved to be a daunting challenge. Tension on the fence fabric held it firmly in place. Without pondering the problem, he reached into the backpack and pulled out one of the ratchet straps.

"What are you going to do with that?" Barb asked, genuinely perplexed.

"I need to reduce tension on the fence." Separating the strap into two pieces, Matt hooked the shorter section of strap, with the ratchet, onto the fence near the ground. He then wrapped the longer section through the fence, starting just below the cut and allowing three sections on either side of the cut wire. When the woven line reached the ratchet, Matt was faced with a new problem. The woven section of fence was too narrow to accommodate the ratchet. Believing she had a simple solution, Barb unhooked the short strap and moved it over several sections until the ratchet was flat against the fence fabric.

Matt smiled at his wife. "We'll see. Simple solutions are often the best." He then fed the woven strap through the ratchet and began cranking. After four full cycles of pulling the fence, the ratchet became too hard to work and the fence was just beginning to lose its tension. Matt tried to turn the wire out. It wiggled, a bit, but could not make a full turn needed to wind out. Determined to not be beaten, Matt put his vice-grips on the ratchet lever and tried to crank. It worked, though he could not get full closure of the handle due to the grips being in the way. Applying all his strength to the vice-grips, he watched the fabric of the fence loosen inside the weave of the strap. Once again, he tried to twist the cut wire out. Pulling against itself, the wire resisted then snapped around. It was working. After two more twists, Matt tried to tighten the ratchet once more. He achieved less than a quarter turn, but it was enough to allow the wire to twist out, with resistance. More than an hour later, Matt pulled the wire free and released the ratchet.

"This might have been more difficult without Ole Grumpy's help," Matt declared as he reached down and pulled the fence open. "Plenty of room for us to slip through," he smiled. "Now, let's do it again."

"What?" Barb asked, confused as to why they might need two holes.

Matt picked up his vice grips and strap and moved some twenty yards down the fence, where he began making a second hole.

"You still haven't told me why a second hole," Barb pushed as Matt untwisted the bottom of a weave.

Talking as he worked, Matt explained. "If they find the first hole, they will definitely repair it but, and this is a big BUT, they might not think to look for a second. Even if they do, it will be easier to remove next time because there won't be any zinc welds in the wire. Besides, it's tough but not as difficult as I expected. Would be a lot easier with bolt cutters, but I left them in the garage back home." With that he began clamping and twisting each union of two specific wires, breaking the galvanizing weld. To further improve their chances that this second hole might not be discovered, he cut the wire closer to the ground at a height of about two and a half feet. Learning from his previous experience he wove the strap in a slightly wider pattern, grabbing four sections on either side of the cut wire. The added width proved beneficial, allowing the cut wire to turn with less effort once the tension was removed. When he finished, the resulting hole was not as accommodating as the first, but was still passable, providing one person held the fence open while the other crawled through.

Satisfied with his results this night, Matt checked his watch. "Hmm, we have just enough time to get back to the cabin and grab some sleep before they wonder where we are."

Twenty-Seven

Day Twenty-Seven

Matt stretched out and took a deep breath. Filtered light of a late morning sun warmed the cabin. *I never really thought about it, but this cabin does warm up as the day wears on. Hope that's not important,* Matt pondered as he raised his arm so he could see his watch. *9:45, guess it's time to get up.* Sitting up he saw that Barb was still asleep. Rolling off the mattress he slipped on shoes and moseyed to the outhouse. Returning a few minutes later, he smiled when he noticed both front cameras were still covered with towels. Once inside he set to fixing coffee, then cheerfully uncovered all cameras while the water heated.

Barb was not disturbed when the pot whistled, so Matt fixed a single cup of coffee and took his chair out to the front porch. Settling and enjoying his first sip of rejuvenation, he looked through the trees, across the lake to the hillside beyond. The sun was now high enough that the hillside and half the lake were in full sun. "Need to get some fishing in today," he said to himself.

"What?" Barb asked, standing just inside the door and stretching with a yawn.

"Don't' come out 'till you get more clothes on, sweetheart. Cameras are live and I don't like sharing you with those weirdos lurking in the caves."

"Thanks for the warning. Have you had breakfast?"

"No. But I thought I'd take the easy way out and just have cereal again. Maybe grits."

"Sounds good," she yawned and turned back into the cabin. She returned a moment later wearing shorts, t-shirt, and sandals. Stepping toward the outhouse, she paused. "Last night, when do we get to do it again?"

"I don't know . . . maybe tomorrow or the next day. Night fishing is fun, but I need my beauty sleep."

Barely understanding what Matt had told her, she resumed her journey to the facility. Stepping back onto the porch, several minutes later, she squirmed as she adjusted her pants. "You don't suppose our hosts would supply us with a new toilet seat in the next grocery delivery, do you?"

"Possibly, if they knew you wanted one."

Barb moved to the front door, then stepped to the edge of the porch. Staring straight at the camera that monitored this area, she screamed, "TOILET SEAT! . . . AND NOT ONE OF THOSE CHEAP PLASTIC ONES!"

Smiling from ear to ear, Matt responded, "I think they heard you. Not sure they got the message, but I'm sure they heard you. Now, breakfast?"

"Yeah, grits. Don't want cold cereal again."

"You want coffee first? I think there is enough hot water."

"Please."

Matt stood, placed a peck of a kiss on Barb's cheek as he slipped past her, and began to make her coffee. After handing her the cup, he refilled the kettle from the jug they had filled at the waterfall. Minutes later it was whistling and they each had instant grits, with added salt, pepper, and butter.

Finishing her breakfast, Barb asked, "Plans for today?"

"Thought I would try some fishing. Last night was interesting, but we didn't catch anything. I think I'd like fish for supper tonight."

Thinking about their conversation, Barb asked, "Fish don't sleep at night. You said they eat, so why didn't you catch anything?"

Smiling at her continuing the ruse, Matt replied, "Only thing I can think of is the lure has to be more bug-like. Not a spoon that runs along the bottom but something more like a surface fly."

"Like those little ones Steven makes?"

"Precisely. . . . Or," Matt hesitated, "It could be you swimming in starlight. Distracted me. Probably the fish as well."

Standing and leaning over her husband, Barb kissed him seductively. "You are welcome to join me anytime . . . just cover those cameras."

Steven and Susan cleaned the Scott Mountain cabin as they loaded everything back into the Jeep. Making a final pass through each of the rooms, they found a bag of trash on the porch. Picking it up, Steven laughed heartily, "In plain sight and we almost missed it! Your dad would have been irate!"

Wrapping her arms around Steven, Susan chuckled. "Naw, he left a sleeping bag up here once and Mom forgot to clean out the sink on another trip. He would probably yell for a few seconds, then break down and laugh." She then kissed him smartly and without letting him go, turned to look at the view one more time. Taking a deep breath, she released Steven, took his hand, and tugged. "C'mon, time to return to civilization."

"Yep, I guess so," he responded and followed her to their chariot.

The trip off the mountain was far easier than the climb up. Both Steven and Susan were more relaxed and in good spirits. Puffy clouds blocked sunshine at critical moments, making it easier to see difficult passages. Susan joked, "God's making it real easy to leave my mountain, He wants you to come back." Steven shook his head slightly and smiled appreciatively.

Arriving at a convenience store, Susan pulled her phone out and turned it on. Expecting, or hoping for, a message from Jim Thompson, Steven turned his phone back on as well. Both left their phones in the jeep, out of sight under their seats. Returning ten minutes later with snacks and cold drinks, each was alerted to new text messages.

Steven had two from associates at work plus one from Uncle Jim, which he opened immediately. Susan had fourteen new text messages and was flipping through them when Steven gave her bad news. "Uncle Jim didn't get to Mom and Dad's car this weekend. Had a double homicide and it rained all weekend. Maybe next week. Did you get anything interesting?"

Susan was quiet so Steven started the Jeep and pulled out on the road. Two minutes down the road, Susan erupted, "Steven pull over! NOW!"

Seeing she was excited about something, Steven pulled off the road and put the car in park but did not run the engine off. Susan handed him her phone, "Look at this text message!"

Steven took the phone and read aloud, "Tell Steven his parents are alive. Project Gumdrop." Steven's face went blank and all color drained from it. "Who sent you this? Do you recognize the number?"

"I have no idea who sent it, but there is a number. Do you want to call it or should I?"

Steven thought for a minute. "If you call, they might recognize your number. That could be good or bad. Maybe I should call and have it in my log." Seconds later, Steven was punching the number into his phone. After several rings, the line went dead. Checking his signal strength he thought aloud, "That's odd. Call went dead as though a line was cut. We have three bars, so plenty of strength. Let's try again on your phone."

Looking back at the text message on Susan's phone, Steven pressed the "call" icon. After several rings, the call was answered by voice mail so Steven left a message. "This is Steven Harper. I got your message but don't understand. What is Gumdrop? Please call me on my phone, the number is 369-239-2123." Ending the call, Steven immediately switched back to his phone and looked up Jim Thompson in his contact list. This call also went to voice mail. "Uncle Jim, Steven Harper. I just got a message that Mom and Dad are alive and something about a 'Project Gumdrop'. On the road right now, will call again later this evening."

Handing Susan her phone, Steven looked into her eyes then without restraint leaned across the seats and kissed her passionately. The embrace was cut short when Steven's foot hit the accelerator and the engine raced almost as fast as his heart. "They're going to love you! Now, we just have to find them!"

Whooping with joy, Steven pulled the Jeep back onto the road and sped toward home.

Recalling their adventures along the ridge, Matt retrieved his fishing gear from the end of the porch and walked up to the lake. Thinking he had always fished the same area, the end opposite the stream from the waterfall, he turned toward the stream. Looking for an area clear of trees where he would have plenty of room to cast, he noticed the algae bloom he had seen the day before.

Standing above the green growth, which extended about six feet in a semicircle, he pondered silently. *It seems to have appeared recently, wasn't here before. Doesn't seem to have grown any since yesterday, but why is it here and nowhere else?* He then scanned the visible shoreline, confirming it was indeed only in this one location. Seeing a pine branch nearby, he put his fishing gear down, retrieved the branch, and began poking around in the bloom. Swishing the stick around moved the slime and he discovered what appeared to be a stone drain pipe. Poking the stone structure, which surrounded an opening about eight inches across, he also found iron bars cris-crossing the opening. Standing, he looked back to the cabin. "The cold house," he said aloud. "This drain feeds the stream in the cold house and . . ."

Tossing his stick into the middle of the slimy bloom, Matt stopped his pondering and returned to the cabin. Finding Barbara on the porch, reading *Vrenessbith*, he grabbed her hand and dragged her around the far end of the lake where he normally fished. Not seeing any red lights from hidden surveillance devices, he exploded in a constrained voice.

"We need to get out of here TOMORROW! WITHOUT FAIL!"

"That's what you said last night, or this morning. Whatever. What has happened?"

"First they force us into the cabin, then they poison us."

"WHAT?!"

"They've planted algae around the drain that feeds the cold house. We can't drink that water, not even sure we should wash dishes with it."

"What about fish and the water from the stream?"

"Near as I can tell the algae bloom is restricted to the area that feeds the cold house."

Barbara looked at the strain on her husband's face then turned toward the lake. Looking at ripples sparkling with reflected sunlight, she asked, "Why can't we leave tonight?"

"I'm not sure. Something tells me it would be a bad idea, but I can't tell you why." Matt thought for a moment. "This whole situation is like a multidimensional chess game. If I read that idiot commander correctly, he has no life and will spend all weekend in his office. Some of their staff may have the weekend off, so he will spend more time looking at us on his monitors. Anything we do today will trigger his suspicion and an irrational reaction. No, we need to be more careful about covering the cameras. Count on the probability that the worker bees are more sane and less likely to sound an alarm just because they can't see us. . . . I need to find a way to get a message to Jerry about the algae. I'll bet he doesn't know about it."

Barb stared at her husband as he spoke. She could see he was strategizing, brainstorming, building a plan for escape.

Rather than feel sick about the algae, she felt a new confidence growing that they would soon be home.

Looking down into his wife's eyes, Matt relaxed. He had blown up and now had a plan. "I need to get my fishing rod and catch some supper."

"Where you going to fish that we can eat what you catch?" Barb replied, taking his hand and walking back toward the cottage.

"I'll try Grumpy's fishing spot. If he shows up, I'll yield and move on around the lake, toward the waterfall."

Barb laughed once, loudly. "You and that bear!"

Steven pulled into the parking lot of *EdeBee's Snack Shack* on Highway 101 north of Trinidad, California at 4:13 p.m. This restaurant had become a traditional lunch spot for campers returning from the Redwood Forest. Still early for supper, neither he nor Susan could resist their specialty burgers. One other customer waited as Steven picked up their bag of unique gastronomic delights and settled to one of the outside picnic tables.

"Are you going to call your detective uncle?" Susan asked as she unwrapped her "Baby Bigfoot" burger.

Steven had already sunk his teeth into his "Elk Burger" so she had to wait a moment for his reply. "As soon as I get home." Their conversation continued between mouth watering bites of oversized burgers and shared fries.

"What about calling your sister?"

"I think I want to talk to Uncle Jim first. Don't want to get Angela too excited just yet."

"You ought to at least tell her husband. Let him decide when to tell her."

"Good idea. Might do just that . . . also gets me off the hook of her hysteria."

As they were finishing their dinner, the owner of the Snack Shak stopped by their table. "I'm leaving now. You folks please clean up after yourselves. Thanks."

"Will do," Susan and Steven replied in unison.

Finishing his burger, Steven stretched then grabbed another fry before opening his phone.

Detective Jim Thompson answered before the second ring. "Steven, I'd like to talk but I'm trying to wrap up an on-site investigation."

"Real quick, Uncle Jim, some very important information about Mom and Dad. They're alive. Somehow part of a 'Project Gumdrop'."

"Damn, son, you sure know how to grab someone's attention. What have you learned?"

"We got a text, actually Susan did, telling us Mom and Dad are alive and to look into this 'Project Gumdrop'. Don't know the person who sent it but I have called . . ."

Jim interrupted, "Is that the voice message you left me? I haven't had time to check."

"Yes, sir. We don't know anything more right now. I was hoping you might have heard something about this 'gumdrop' business."

"Never heard of it. What happened when you returned the call?"

"That was weird. When I called from my phone the call wouldn't go through but Susan got voice mail and I left a message asking them to call my phone."

"How did you get the text?" Jim's voice now echoed a bit of confusion.

"It came on Susan's phone, not mine."

Jim was quiet as he considered the pieces Steven had just given him. "Don't be surprised if you don't get a callback but Susan might. I'll see what I can find out about this 'Project Gumdrop'. Anything else?"

"Not right now. Thanks, Uncle Jim. I'll keep in touch."

When the call ended, Steven looked to Susan. "Jim says you might get the call back from whoever sent the text. Not sure why . . ."

Having no idea how to respond, Susan shook her head. "Let's clean up and get home. You still have a ways to go and need to call your sister."

Reaching Susan's parents' bungalow, Steven lingered only a few minutes. Before leaving, he reminded Susan of the question he had asked. "Don't forget what we talked about."

"What we talked about?" Susan taunted him.

"That question no man wants hanging in the air!"

"Hasn't left my mind for a second." She then kissed him smartly and pushed him gently into the driver's seat of his vehicle.

The hour of driving alone in his Jeep Wrangler with wind blowing around him, gave Steven time to think about what was going on. *Yes, I do want to marry Susan and build a life with her, but this business about Mom and Dad being alive . . . what is this all about? Who texted her? Why her and not me? Why did her phone call get through when mine didn't? We use the same service. And above all, what is "Project Gumdrop"?*

Parking in front of his duplex apartment, he took the first load of gear inside and dumped it in a spare room. Returning for the cooler, he closed up the jeep in case it rained. After emptying the cooler he stored it with his other gear and took care of personal business. He then retrieved a beer from the fridge, plopped down on a well-worn sofa, and opened his phone.

Reggie answered on the fourth ring. "Hey, Steven. Angela's not up to talking right now. Seems morning sickness can last all day."

"That's okay, you're the one I need to talk with. Morning sickness, huh? So you have news to share?"

"Sorry, I didn't mean to leak that. What's up?"

"This is going to sound strange and you need to decide how to tell my sister . . . I got news today that Mom and Dad are alive. We don't know where or anything other than that but I've talked with Uncle Jim and we are both going to try to figure out what a 'Project Gumdrop' is all about."

" 'Project Gumdrop'? What's that?"

"We don't know, but it may have something to do with where Mom and Dad are. You now know as much as I do. Tell Ange when you think she can handle it without freakin out. So, when is the baby due?"

"Wow! This is a lot to take in . . . oh, sorry, delayed reaction. We just found out right before your parent's accident, which I guess didn't really happen?"

"Don't know. Uncle Jim is looking into it. He thinks there's something fishy about the accident report. So, that means I'm going to be an uncle around November?"

"Well, actually late September or early October. You keep us posted on what you find out?"

"Of course. Go take care of my sister and be nice to her."

"Always. Ciao."

Taking a large glug from his bottle of beer, Steven pondered the big question for a minute before turning his computer on. After scanning his email, dumping two-thirds of it as junk or spam, he opened one from Susan sent half-an-hour before. He smiled inside and out when he read, "Great weekend. Love You."

Closing his email, he opened Firefox and thought for a second before starting his search for 'project gumdrop' on google.com. He was quickly frustrated by all the candy links and changed to another search engine, StartPage. Seeing much the same as before, he considered what to do next when his eyes caught a non-candy link: Clinical Trials for Genito-Urinary Cancer - GUMDROP. Without opening the link he perceived this as a government-sponsored project. Shifting in his seat he entered a new search phrase: government projects. The results on this search were both encouraging and discouraging at the same time. Hundreds of links led to different government projects, each targeting something unique. Adding "gumdrop" to the search phrase took him back to candy land.

Draining his beer, Steven restarted his search on government projects, this time clicking on different links. An hour and another beer later, his mind was a muddle and he had no answers, other than there are too many government projects dealing with too many different ideas. Somebody needed to trim some of the fat off this beast.

Staring at the cluttered screen with sixteen search windows open, Steven remembered he had a friend in the U S Government. Retrieving his phone, he scanned his contacts, stopping with Thom Strong and pressing the call icon.

"Thom, Steven Harper."

"Wow, haven't heard from you in a while."

"Come on, not that long, what four months?"

"Four months? That would be what, January?"

"Yea. We did that cross-country skiing and camping trip, in very wet snow."

"Oh, yea. I remember that one. As I recall, you were all about helping some young lady who took a tumble. What was her name . . . Susan?"

"Good memory, in fact I shouldn't say too much but this weekend I asked her to marry me."

"WOW! Big move there my man. What'd she say?"

"Said I have to resolve some issues with my parents before she can answer."

"What issues? I thought you and your folks were close."

"Well, yes, but they are missing. Supposedly killed in an accident about three or four weeks ago. That's why I called you. You still work for the government?"

"Sorry to hear that, but, yes. U S Forest Service. Why?"

"Do you have access to searching government project databases?"

"I believe so. Don't use them very often. Why?"

"I need a big favor. Would you see if you can find something on a 'Project Gumdrop'? It has something to do with why my parents are missing."

"Sure. I'll have to use one of the systems at work, can't do it from home. I'll be in the office tomorrow and let you know. One thing, though. If this is some secret project, my security level might not find it or read about it."

"I understand; thanks, man. Please call me when you find out something, even if it's nothing."

"Will do. Bye."

Twenty-Eight

Day Twenty-Eight

Jerry Tanner sat at his desk, Monday morning, staring at reports on his screen. The "game" he and two other economists had been playing was turned into reality by Brian Bard. This "reality" was now a nightmare for Matthew and Barbara Harper and two other families.

Staring at the reports on his screen, Jerry struggled with the nil effect the Harper's isolation had on his predicted results, his mind whirling with questions. The "game" scenario still predicted near global economic collapse on the not-to-distant horizon and all indicators still pointed to these three couples. Had they already done that something that triggered future events? Had Bard somehow identified the wrong people, or was something about to happen that was not in his field of vision?

"Doctor Tanner, the commander would like to see you right away."

Jerry's thoughts were interrupted. Looking up, he saw the Project Manager's secretary standing in his doorway, waiting for him. Heaving a sigh, Jerry drank the last third of his cold coffee and stood. "What kind of a mood is he in today?" Jerry asked as he followed the soldier through the hallways.

"Not good, sir. Been engaged with a rather heated phone call."

Resigned to the coming conflict, Jerry remained quiet as they made their way to the commander's office. Colonel Prescott stormed out of Bard's inner office as they entered the project manager's suite, mumbling something about accountability. Bard's secretary, a corporal, immediately snapped to attention and saluted the officer, who stormed out without response. Relaxing his posture, the corporal stopped at his desk in the outer office, extending his hand toward the open door to Brian Bard's office. Continuing to the inner sanctum, Jerry looked to the corporal and grimaced. The secretary reflected the emotion.

"Close the door!" the 'commander' barked without looking away from his computer screen.

Jerry did as directed and sat in the nearest of two chairs, waiting quietly.

Turning his head and looking directly at Jerry, Bard asked in a strained voice, "Do you like your job?"

"I've had better," Jerry replied, shifting in his seat.

"But you do like the paycheck," Bard affirmed. "Which brings me to the point. I make weekly reports to our benefactors. Those nice people in the government who are paying your salary as well as all other expenses of this project. They like to see that our 'guests' are being treated properly and we are making progress identifying how our world economy is fairing in their absence. They were not happy when *someone*, not me mind you, but *SOMEONE* told them about the shooting incident! I had a helluva time convincing them we were still okay after the Harper's stroll downtown! We are on very thin ice here Mister Tanner, which brings me to my next question. How did Steven Harper find out his parents are alive and who the hell is Heather Thropshire?"

"My answer to both questions is I have no idea what you are talking about." Jerry strained to not reply in the same tone Bard used in his attack. With great difficulty, he kept his voice calm, yet could not conceal his apprehension.

The Commander took a deep breath and let it out slowly. "I suppose since you look only at your economic trends and analysis you have no knowledge of what my, excuse me, our tech folks captured yesterday."

Breathing fast and shallow, Jerry shook his head with bewilderment. "Sir?"

"It seems Steven Harper has a girlfriend, a Miss Susan Scott, who got a text over the weekend informing her that the Harper's are alive and in the custody of 'Project Gumdrop.' He responded by calling someone named Heather Thropshire. Any idea who this Heather Thropshire is? Perhaps a client of your wife's company?"

Hearing his wife being accused of interference, Jerry's voice took a defensive tone, barely suppressing his anger. "I have no idea. Never heard the name before just now."

"Well, it's a good thing at least one of us is on top of this project. My research team has found Heather Thropshire IS a client of your wife's employer. Now, why the hell is she in contact with the Harper's son?"

Fed up with Bard's attitude, Jerry snapped back, "You seem to have all the answers, you tell me!"

Drawing another deep breath, Bard exploded. "I have already put a regional block on Scott's phone and a monitor on this Thropshire woman. Any further attempts to contact the families of our guests and your family will be put under house arrest! Violation of the National Security Act, which could lead to charges of treason! Do I make myself clearly understood?"

Jerry swallowed hard. He wanted to correct this pompous idiot but decided not to, thinking to himself, *Homeland Security Act you imbecile.* Standing to leave, Jerry opened the door and paused, turning back toward The Commander. "Just so you know the latest findings. There has been no significant shift in economic indicators since you kidnaped our guests. Whatever our simulation suggested might happen is still going to happen and there is absolutely NO CHANGE in the Harper indicators." Turning once more to leave, he stopped again. "I'll be gone the rest of this morning, on matters of Homeland Security."

Shaking his head as he left the Project Manager's offices, he failed to see the restrained smile on the secretary's face.

An hour after leaving Brian Bard's office, Jerry knocked on the door frame to his wife's office. "Hey, beautiful. You have time for a cup of coffee?"

Surprised and caught off-guard, Linda replied, "Sure, what are you doing here?"

"We need to talk. The sooner the better."

"Okay. Here or down the street?"

"Doesn't matter. Just need to avoid interruption for a few minutes."

"Fine. We can get some coffee in the break area and come back here. Close the door for privacy." As Linda picked up her coffee cup, which had not been filled since Friday, her desk phone rang. Seeing Heather Thropsire's name come up on the caller ID, she put a finger up to signal her husband and punched the speaker button to answer the call. "Heather, what news do you have today?" She then whispered to Jerry, "Close the door."

"Linda, I've had a strange morning. Got a voice message from your son using his girlfriend's phone."

"Not my son, but a friend. What did it say?"

"That's where things get really strange. He asked about this gumdrop project and gave me his phone number. Said he would call me directly. Since I had a few minutes, I tried calling him but the call wouldn't go through. Thinking I had written the number down wrong, I tried to replay the message, but it was gone. What's going on?"

"Miss Thropshire, this is Jerry Tanner, Linda's husband. This may sound a bit like a spy novel, but do NOT try the numbers for Steven Harper or his girlfriend again. If you can, I suggest you delete any and all records of contacting them. And one more thing that might be a bit scary . . . if representatives claiming to be with Homeland Security show up, verify their credentials and answer their questions honestly. Do not let them bully you, just tell them you were making the call for a friend. You can even admit it was for Linda, should they ask."

"HOMELAND SECURITY? Linda what have you got me mixed up in?" Before Linda or Jerry could respond, Heather added, "Is this something we will be laughing about later and I'll be able to share with my grandchildren?"

Chuckling, Jerry responded, "Yes, I believe we will be laughing about this later. But for now please understand, and please do not repeat this, that Linda has been trying to help a family that an egomaniac is trying to control. I am trying to help them as well. You should have nothing to worry about as long as you are honest with your answers and do not try to hide anything, except the 'egomaniac' remark. Are we good?"

Chucking, Heather replied, "Linda, as soon as this thing blows over, you are coming to my shop on a client service call. Bring a bottle of wine and an explanation."

"Sounds good, Heather. Keep smiling and thank you for all your help. Bye." Linda tapped the speaker button and put her coffee cup back on her desk. Looking to Jerry, she said, "Okay, Mister Tanner, we are going down the street and you are going to tell me everything." Following her husband out the door of her office she quipped, "Homeland Security, huh?"

Matt and Barbara watched the sun rising in a cloudless sky, it's light sliding down the western slope across the lake, and finished their second cup of coffee.

"It is pretty, but I won't miss it," Barb whispered. Turning her head toward her husband, away from the intrusive camera, and concealing the side of her head with her hand, she continued softly. "What do we need to do to get ready for tonight?"

"ACHOO!" Matt sneezed, covering Barb's faint words. "Let's go see if Grumpy has been to the lake."

Putting their cups down on the porch, they walked hand in hand around the lake to where there were no microphones or cameras. Once in a safe place to talk, Matt replied, "Work under the assumption that we will not be coming back. We can't take anything we can't carry in our backpacks, but whatever we leave behind will be left for good. I'll take my phone because of the contact information, but I should probably check it for tracking chips and spy software before we go."

"How will you check for software?" Barb asked, her face covered with deep concern.

"Easy, turn it on and check the apps list. See what's been recently added or updated."

"Won't they see it if they have added anything?"

"Probably, but we are still in the cabin. They know we are here and it needs to be removed *before* we aren't here."

Barb smiled at the thought of not being *here*. "What about money? Will our credit cards still work?"

"Don't even think about the plastic cards. I bet they would set off alarms from coast to coast before they get denied. I have some cash and as I recall I had some emergency money stashed in a secret pocket of my wallet. Won't be much, but I'll check on that as well. We'll need clothes and some food and water, but keep in mind that we need to be able to travel fast. I'd like to be twenty miles from here before they even realize we're gone."

Dumbfounded, Barb looked at her husband. They were going home! Matt had finally worked out a plan for their escape, with military-like precision. Knowing this is the way he did things, stewing on problems for a while until he came up with a 'workable' solution then acting on them, she was a bit miffed at not being included in the final planning. Not knowing what to say or how to argue his reasoning, she quietly accepted his plan and followed Matt as he strolled casually to the far side of the lake where they had previously seen Grumpy.

Thom Strong arrived at his desk in the U.S. Forest Service Shasta-Trinity Regional Office a few minutes early and quickly checked work sheets for daily assignments. Not finding anything that required his immediate attention, he sat and turned on his computer. After thirty-five minutes of frustrating searches, he pushed away and went for a second cup of coffee.

"You're looking for something you can't seem to find," Jack Blackfish commented as he took the coffee pot from Thom. "Is this something for work that I might have missed?"

Groaning softly as he fixed his mug of coffee, Thom confessed. "No, sir. A friend of mine is searching for information on a 'Project Gumdrop.' Could be a government operation and somehow involves his parents, who may have been killed or might be simply missing. Something to do with this project."

"I should write you up for using USDA resources for a private search, but this sounds important. Let me see if I can help you . . . just so you can get to your job with a clear mind." Jack Blackfish was a Native American, born and raised in Northern California. He was also Thom's immediate supervisor and had extensive experience in finding the unfindable, in the forest and elsewhere. Returning to Thom's desk, Jack asked, "What databases have you been searching?"

"All the USDA, Forest Service, and open military reference systems. I can't find anything."

"Okay. Let me use your computer. You watch and try to remember where I go because I can't officially tell you anything about what I am about to do." Taking Thom's seat, Jack typed a long string of names and numbers into the address bar, with ".gov" and multiple "/" included. Almost instantly a text-based search screen appeared. "What is this project you are looking for?"

"Gumdrop," Thom replied, amazed at how Jack could possibly remember this address.

"G U M D R O P," Jack repeated as he typed. Once again the screen displayed information within seconds. "Sorry, dead end, Thom, but here is something curious. 'Gumdrop' is only the project nickname, actual initials are GMDRP - Global Monetary Decline and Repair Prevention. Sounds important but says this was a project proposed and denied by the United States Department of Defense and Clandestine Services Division of the NSA. I never heard of them before, but . . ." Jack then paused and stared at the screen for several seconds before getting up. "General Alexander Keith. That name sounds familiar. Come with me, I might have something that could help you." The two men went into Jack's office.

Sitting to his own desk, Jack rapped the keys on his computer, clicking his mouse several times then pausing. "Thom, the general who denied that project is coming here to do some fishing. Let me see, later this week. I'll forward you these details. They aren't classified."

"Thank you, sir! You are a miracle worker!" Thom praised as he went to his desk, only to return a minute later, after reading the email. "Sir, this general is wanting a guide for trout fishing. I know a great spot on the Trinity River that could be both challenging and rewarding."

"When?"

"Wednesday, sir."

"Okay, fine. I'll send the invitation and let you know if he accepts. Now, get to work."

"Yes, sir." Thom practically danced back to his desk.

Matt remained quiet the entire time he and Barb strolled a third the way around the lake before turning back. He paused twice, where he had seen Grumpy at the water's edge and again at the same place on their return. Squatting down, on the return, he examined the mud for paw prints. Barb watched with wonder, taking his hand when they resumed their walk. Turning down the short path from the lake to the cabin, he broke his silence.

"Doesn't look like Ole Grumpy has been around for a few days. I wonder if he has a fishin' hole at the river."

"How would he get to the water?" Barb asked, trying to follow Matt's train of thought. "The river banks are awfully steep."

"Not sure, but I bet he knows a place. This is HIS domain, after all and HE is master. You saw what he did to our camper and that was just to get his back scratched." Matt snickered a bit as he continued, "How about some lunch? Will you fix us a couple sandwiches, please?"

"Sure," Barb replied, somewhat put out and not amused by the camper reference. Her mood changed when she saw her husband cross the cabin to their stash of personal gear. Realizing what he was up to, she prepared lunch.

Matt went through his clothes bag, toiletry bag, both backpacks, a fanny pack he had not used, and even checked pants that needed washing. Frustrated by not finding what he was searching for, he looked to Barb. "After lunch, how would you like to go to the camper?"

"I thought we got everything out of there, are you sure we need to?"

"Yes, afraid so. I finished 'Digital Fortress' a couple days ago and can't find that second book I wanted to read, 'Treasured Adversaries.' Long book, as I recall. Should keep me busy for quite a while."

"You don't read very fast, do you?"

"Typically, I breeze through technical papers, but I've had so much on my mind this trip that reading doesn't come easy. I'll look again after we eat. While you finish fixing sandwiches, I'll go get some water from the cold house."

Matt and Barbara settled quietly on the porch with ham, salami, and cheese sandwiches. Bottled water stored in the cold house trough was icy cold and refreshing. Barb wiped her bottle with a clean cloth before opening it, then wiped the top of her bottle before every sip. Matt just wiped his off once. After lunch, Matt resumed his search, which was interrupted when Barb pointed to his wallet under the edge of their mattress. After retrieving the wallet he pulled 'Treasured Adversaries' from his clothes bag and dropped it on the table. "I must be going blind," he commented. "Going to the cold house for a minute; you want more water?"

"No, thank you. I'm going to the ladies' room."

After a quick peck of a kiss, Barb went out the front and Matt went out the back. Once in the privacy of the cold house, he opened the wallet, examining every pocket. Counting out thirty-six dollars in bills, he moaned, "Really should have taken time to get more cash before we left home." Ignoring two grocery store cards, two credit cards, and one bank debit card, he lifted a flap under his driver's license where he found his "emergency stash," a fifty-dollar bill.

Slipping his wallet into his back pocket, he bounced out of the cold house. Wanting to relax and rest a bit, he grabbed his fishing gear and started up the path to the lake.

"MATTHEW! HELP!"

Barb's bloodcurdling scream froze Matt in mid-step. Dropping his fishing gear where he stood, he turned and launched himself toward the outhouse. Yanking the door open he found Barb bent over, pants around her ankles, and one hand on her right bare buttock.

"I've been stung!"

Looking around the outhouse, Matt saw a yellow jacket on the bench beside Barb. "You got your assailant, let's get you back into the cottage and see what we can do to ease the pain."

Matt helped Barb lift her pants then supported her as she hobbled to the bed. Pulling her pants down to examine the sting, Matt saw it had already welted and was growing bright red. His mind raced, *Poison - swelling. Get the poison out first!*

"First aid kit?"

"On the fireplace mantle," Barb whimpered in reply.

Matt raced across the cabin, grabbed a large green vinyl pouch, and opened it as he returned to Barb. Looking inside he flustered for a few seconds before removing a snake bite kit. Popping the rubber cups apart, he squeezed one as hard as he could and pressed it against the wasp sting.

"OW! WHAT ARE YOU DOING?"

"Trying to get the poison out, then I'll get a bottle of water to reduce the swelling. He got you good!"

Removing the suction cup when it was about half inflated, Matt checked the sting area. Seeing a stinger projecting from the wound, he found tweezers in the first aid kit and yanked the bayonet out. Seeing the mound was still swelling, he squeezed the suction cup once more and pushed it against the site. Barb cried softly as the cup slowly inflated. When Matt popped it off, the site showed a bit of blood where the stinger had been. After wiping the sting off with an alcohol pad, he went to the cold house, returning with three icy cold bottles. Without celebration or explanation, he opened one and wet a wash cloth which he wrapped around the other two bottles and pressed against his wife's swelling butt.

Matt rubbed the cold wet cloth gently across Barb's injury for nearly twenty minutes, pausing when she asked for an aspirin.

"Aspirin? Why would you want an aspirin?"

"Ibuprofen would be better. How's she doing?" a strong female voice broadcast across the cabin.

Turning, Matt saw the female doctor who had treated him when he was shot with tranquilizers. A corpsman accompanied her but stopped at the cottage door. Pushing Matt aside, she looked at Barb's rump. Seeing the remains of a red ring around the sting site, she quickly looked about the bed. Lifting the snake bite kit, she asked, "Ma'am, are you allergic to epinephrine?"

"I don't think so. I had it once before."

Without another word, the doctor slammed an epipen into Barb's thigh. Turning to Matt, she held up the suction cup and asked, "Snake bite kit?"

"Got the stinger and poison out."

"Good trick, don't know that I've seen that technique before. Did you get much poison out?"

"I guess so. Only used it twice. First time pulled the stinger almost out, then I stopped when it began to bleed."

"Cold water bottles, okay. What about the ice packs we sent you?"

"Weren't with the first aid kit. Don't know where they got put. May still be in the camper."

"Randy, an ice pack, please."

The corpsman, Cpl. Randall Walters, opened the doctor's medical bag and pulled out two ice packs. He smashed one to activate it before handing it to the doctor. While pressing the ice pack against the sting, the doctor looked at Matt. "Where did this happen?"

"Outhouse."

Raising one eyebrow, the doctor directed her assistant. "Check the outhouse. Make sure there are no nests and be sure you check under the seat."

Watching the corpsman leave, Matt asked, "How are you here? Won't your commander shoot you for interacting with us? Isn't this treasonous?"

"Oh, Bard might consider me coming to your aid as and act of treason, but I happened to be in the observation room when your wife screamed. The boss is out of the office right now so I didn't have to waste time arguing with him." Looking back at Barb, she asked, "How are you doing, ma'am?"

"It hurts."

"Aching or throbbing?"

"Throbbing."

"Found the culprit, Ma'am," the corpsman reported. Handing the corpse of the wasp to the doctor, he continued, "Over grown yellow-jacket. No signs of a nest."

Handing the wasp back to the corpsman, the doctor sighed. "Well, Missus Harper, you are going to have to lie still for a couple hours. Keep that ice pack on it till it is no longer cold. Wait about an hour, then apply the second one. You may find it hard to walk for the next couple days. Sorry, I know how much you like to roam the woods."

Standing to leave, she reached into her medical bag and pulled out another ice pack. Handing it to Matt, she explained, "A spare, just in case. Find the others and please keep them handy. You never know when you might need one. I'll come back in a day or two for follow-up. Should you need me sooner, just call. The front porch camera has the best pickup." Looking back to Barbara, she continued, "Remember, Missus Harper, stay down today. If you feel up to it, you can walk around a bit tomorrow, but no long hikes. Maybe you can get back to exploring on Wednesday."

Looking around as she moved toward the door, she commented. "Not as bad as I thought. You have a couple holes in the roof."

Matt looked at the holes before responding. "Yep, and I'm not a very good carpenter."

"Take care, sir. Oh, and give your wife some ibuprofen."

Matt watched as the doctor and her assistant got onto an ATV and drove off around the lake, disappearing into the woods just past where Grumpy liked to fish. Turning back into the cabin, he retrieved an ibuprofen from the first aid kit. By the time the first ice pak lost its cold, Barb had fallen asleep. Matt covered her with a blanket and went fishing, staying away from the algae growth yet close to the cabin. He caught only one small trout.

Twenty-Nine

Day 29 - Tuesday

Barb woke Tuesday morning in mild agony. Bending her leg at the hip tightened swelling across her buttocks, which made walking painful and sitting impossible. Matt made her breakfast in bed, delivered coffee - which, not being able to sit up, she had great difficulty drinking - and saw to her needs as best he could. Her response to his kindness and care was, "I want to go home."

Matt's response was, "It's raining outside. Looks like we are socked in; could be days before we see sunshine again."

Project Manager Brian Bard stormed into the medical clinic bellowing, "WHO GAVE YOU AUTHORITY TO MAKE CONTACT? YOU KNOW THE RULES! NOBODY, AND THAT INCLUDES YOU DOCTOR, NOBODY MAKES CONTACT WITH OUR GUESTS WITHOUT MY PERSONAL PRIOR APPROVAL!"

Seeing the battalion commander, Colonel Prescott, come in behind Bard, the doctor swallowed hard and responded calmly. "Sir, I am not privy to all the purposes of this project but I do know that the health and welfare of our *guests* is MY responsibility. I will NOT allow their lives to be put in jeopardy for YOU or anyone else. Missus Harper was in distress and I responded accordingly. Further more, I will check up on her if and when I deem it necessary. Do I make myself clear, sir?"

"Insubordination will not be tolerated in my camp, doctor. You either adhere to published standards of behavior for this project or I will have you replaced. There are other doctors who would love this posting."

Her eyes growing hard and cold, the red-haired physician replied confidently, "I am quite sure, sir, that there are any number of physicians who could replace me, and every one would tell you that as a military officer we answer to our commanding officer, however, as a physician we answer only to the health and welfare of our patients. In THAT, sir, I outrank you."

Bard drew a long hard breath then turned and stormed out of the clinic, pushing his colonel aside. Prescott looked at the doctor and shook his head as he turned to leave.

"Colonel Prescott," the doctor called.

"Doctor?"

"According to my corpsman, the Harpers' outhouse needs a new toilet seat, sir. I'm certain if it could be dropped off, sooner rather than later, Mister Harper could find a way to install it."

The colonel looked to the doctor and heaving a huge sigh, replied, "I'll see to it. Anything else?"

"More instant ice paks sir. They seem to have misplaced or used what we sent them weeks ago."

Nodding, the general left the clinic.

Drawn by Brian Bard's explosion, Jerry Tanner raced from his office toward the clinic. Standing two doors down, he heard the entire exchange between Bard and the doctor. Inspired and energized by the doctor's responses, he returned to his office and began a new line of investigation.

"Given that every individual impacts local economies every day, by what they spend or do not spend, it is conceivable that departures from established routines might have a broader, more far-reaching impact."

Jerry read the project statement, which he had helped to craft, three times. Two words suddenly jumped out at him. "Local economies." Picking up a pen and pulling a yellow note pad to the center of his desk, he thought. *We have isolated three couples, watching for a global impact. What has happened to their local economies?* Pondering the problem, he created a column on the left edge, writing, "30 days, 31 - 60 days, 61 to 90 days, 365 - 395 days, 396 - 426 days, 427 - 457 days" Across the top of the pad, he created three more columns labeled, "Morrisville, NC; Aurora, Il; Corrales, NM."

"Okay, let's get started," he said to himself and turned to his computer. An hour later he studied numbers generated by data mining. There was no significant difference in any of the date periods in any of the locations. Removing three couples from their homes had had zero impact on the towns where they lived. Thinking aloud he murmured, "I'm looking too far out, let's try again restricting the zones to one mile radius from their homes."

Returning to his computer he reformulated his data searches, writing the refined results next to those he had just acquired.

"Now we're getting somewhere," he said with a bit of excitement in his voice. Once more he refined his search parameters and let his search engine run. Results began trickling in after fourteen minutes and built a disturbing picture. Jerry let the engine continue to run and went to lunch.

Returning from his break, Jerry found more disturbing news in his search results and began assembling a document. "Project Results Interim Evaluation." At 3:45 p.m., Jerry lifted the seventy-four pages, primarily tables of raw data and a few graphs, from his printer, punched holes in the margin, and dropped them into an official binder. Wasting no time preparing a formal cover letter, he paraded down to the project manager's office. Seeing that the commander's secretary was away from his desk, Jerry knocked on the open door frame of Bard's office.

"What?" Bard responded, in his typical foul mood.

"Sir, I have run an interim analysis on the local economies of our three subjects and it is my strong belief that we should release each of them, NOW."

"This had better be good. What do you have?" Bard extended his hand for the notebook Jerry carried.

Jerry handed his findings to the Project Manager and began his explanation. "Removing our subjects has had no effect on the Internet nor on global, national, or even their local economies. It has however caused considerable impact on a number of other families and businesses.

"The Harper's neighbor had an offer on their house that fell through citing the fact that the Harper's house is now vacant and is not being maintained."

"I'll get a crew to clean up all three yards. Good call," Bard interrupted.

"One lives in an apartment, sir. But, continuing. Spending by their neighbors has suffered significantly, in all three cases. Their neighbors are concerned by the sudden disappearance and reported deaths. None of it has made sense, sir.

"Look, when a neighbor dies or is killed in an accident or losses their job, the community rallies around for support. They fix dinners, and find ways to help. In our three communities, there is nobody to help, we have created a void, a vacuum. There isn't even any mention of their disappearance or deaths on the Internet. THAT is virtually impossible!

"Many neighbors have stopped going out for dining and entertainment, the purchase of alcohol has increased, and these changes may have caused one dry cleaner, which many neighbors used, to default on a loan. The pennies that are not being spent, because we have our subjects in isolation, are causing trickle down failures in every case. Nothing large, except the one dry cleaner in Albuquerque who was barely hanging on before, but their absence is causing a negative impact.

"Matt Harper's company is now facing a law suit as a result of a report that was not filed because he was not there."

"I appreciate your diligence in bringing this information to me, Jerry, but how is any of this different than if they had actually been killed?"

"Had they actually been killed in accidents, as was eventually reported, employers would have immediately begun replacing them. But reports did not reach their employers immediately and were worded in such a way that there was some doubt or there was a hope that they might return."

"Preposterous!" Bard exclaimed. "Each was notified within three days with the news that their employees were now deceased."

"No, sir, they were not. Two were, yes, but Matt Harper's employer was not told for seven days because he was on vacation. The notice then read, and I know because I checked the official record, 'the Harpers suffered a fatal traffic accident.' 'The HARPERS', not Matthew Harper, but THE Harpers. Nor does it say WHO the fatality was. Matt's boss tried to get confirmation and was blown off, not told any specifics or details such that he could accept Matt as being killed in the accident. They delayed action for three days trying to get confirmation from proper authorities, during which time the filing deadline was missed. Had Matt Harper returned, as they had planned, the report would have been filed appropriately. Follow-up by your agent leads me to believe their initial response was hope that he would return, then suspicion of his disappearance when there were no bodies. They were in turmoil because of your sloppy notifications."

Seething at the insult, Bard growled, "What else?"

"You have not allowed families to enter the residences. You have locked them up as crime scenes, which casts all sorts of doubts and suspicions with neighbors and families. Retrievals of the subjects did not go as smoothly as planned and others have taken notice."

"Has there been any change to our primary goal?" Bard asked coldly.

"None whatsoever!"

"Then the project continues . . . until you can show me how to avoid the anticipated event."

Jerry stared at Brian for several seconds before storming out of the office. He continued to mumble to himself until he reached home.

Seeing a friendly name appear on his phone Tuesday afternoon, Steven Harper pushed away from his computer. "Hello Uncle Jim, have you found some news?"

"Yes and no, do you have a couple minutes?" Detective Thompson replied, his voice heavy and lingering.

"Sure. Let me save this file and I'm all yours." Steven tapped a few keys on his keyboard, saving his current work. "Okay, what's up? Please tell me you've learned something about 'Gumdrop'."

"As I said, yes and no. A project labeled 'Gumdrop' was proposed to the Army, but it was dumped. Too radical and too expensive, near as I can find out. I cannot see where it was ever picked up by another government agency. Sorry."

"No, actually that does help. Especially that it hasn't been picked up. Turns out a friend of mine with the U.S. Forest Service found out this project was denied by some clandestine branch of the NSA, just like you found out. But, tomorrow I get to go fishing with the general who denied it. I'm hoping he will be able to tell me what's happened to Mom and Dad."

"NSA? How did you wrangle this catch?" Jim responded with delight and disbelief.

"By pure coincidence this general likes to fish and my friend is going to be his guide to a great spot we use from time to time. I'm taking the day off to join them."

"Sounds like your parents' angels are lending a helping hand."

"Yes, sir, and I hope to not let them down. I'll let you know what I find out. Any luck on getting to examine the car and camper?"

"Not yet. I have a couple more days on this murder case. Hope to have the culprit in cuffs tomorrow or the next day, then a day of paperwork. Should be able to head to the mountains on Thursday or Friday. Please keep me posted on your visit with this general."

"Will do. Thanks for calling." Steven pressed "End Call" with his thumb and sat in his chair staring into the space between himself and his computer.

Day Thirty - Wednesday

Matt stood in the doorway to the cabin, sipping his third cup of coffee, and watching rain drizzle onto the lake. Feeling a pair of warm arms wrap around him, he looked over his shoulder and smiled. "You had a good long sleep. Feeling any better?"

"Not bad, actually. Hip's only a bit tender." Barb slid around to Matt's side as she reached up and took his coffee cup. Sipping the hot brew, she looked toward the western slope and smiled. "Might even be up to a walk later today."

Still looking at his wife, Matt responded, "What? In the rain?"

"Look again. Sun just came out. Looks like it's going to be a beautiful day."

Turning his head, Matt witnessed last drops of rain being replaced by midmorning sunshine spreading across the lake. "Yes, indeed. Looks like it will be a great day for an afternoon stroll down to the river. We haven't been there for a while." Smiling at his bride, he took his coffee cup back. "I'll fix you a cup if you want."

"That and some bacon and eggs would be nice."

Turning to follow Barb inside, Matt paused and nodded his head toward the porch beside the door. "By the by, we got a package this morning."

Barb looked around the door frame and smiled when she saw a new toilet seat. "Nice. Maybe you can get it installed before we go to the river."

Thom Strong and General Keith, Deputy Director of Clandestine Services Division of the National Security Agency, met at Thom's office early Tuesday afternoon and drove up to the Hobo Gulch Campground on the North Fork of the Trinity River in the Shasta-Trinity National Forest.

Steven had planned to join them, but he had to work late Tuesday evening to get Wednesday off. Waking at 4:30 a.m. Wednesday, he made the three hour drive, watching the sun rise before getting to the river. Arriving at the campground, he found only three of the ten sites occupied so it was easy to locate his friend.

"Where's your guest?" Steven asked as he walked into Thom's campsite.

"Already on the river. He wants fresh trout for breakfast," Thom replied, offering Steven a cup of coffee.

"Yeah, I could use some breakfast," Steven responded, accepting the steaming mug. "Thank you."

"Two trout! How long before we eat? I'm starved!" A man wearing chest waders strode up to the campfire, carrying two beautiful speckled trout, each about fourteen inches long. He appeared to be fifty years or so with an athletic build and hints of grey in dark brown hair. Seeing Steven, he asked, "Who's your friend?"

"General Keith, this is Steven Harper. He knows this river even better than I do," Thom responded.

"Al Keith, no 'General' today." Keith handed his fish to Thom and reached across to greet Steven. "Thom said he might have a friend join us. Welcome to paradise."

"Yes, sir, this is a beautiful place. How do you like our river?" Steven acknowledged.

The Trinity River near the campground was roughly twenty to thirty feet wide, lined on the camp side with stones that were easy to traverse. The riverbed was rock with random larger stones poking through the clear, swift running, cold water. Recent rains insured the river depth allowed plenty of swimming room for trout. Mature hardwoods and evergreens lined both banks, with occasional rock faces reinforcing this natural waterway.

"Wonderful, absolutely wonderful. But right now, I have a couple fish to clean if we're going to eat them for breakfast. Would one of you young men care to give me a hand?" Keith reached over and took the fish back from Thom, implying he was off the hook.

Steven led Keith to a cleaning station, two campsites over, provided by the Forest Service. Their conversation centered on the catching of these beautiful fish. When they returned, Thom had an iron skillet heating and waiting on a gas stove.

"What? We aren't going to cook them over the fire?" Keith objected.

"Not if you want to eat before lunch. It takes longer to cook them over the fire than in a hot skillet," Thom responded. "Maybe we can smoke a few this evening."

"I do want to get back on the river, so that's a deal," Keith agreed, handing his cleaned catch to Thom.

While Thom cooked the fish and some fresh cornbread on sticks over the nearby fire, General Keith talked with Steven. "What brings you up here?"

Seeing Thom shaking his head slightly, Steven avoided his primary purpose. "Thom and I have a sort of ongoing contest fishing this river. It's not just who can catch the biggest or the most, keep in mind that we release most of the fish we catch, but who gets the best 'fight'."

"I'm intrigued. Which of you is the standing champion of this contest?"

"I am," both replied without hesitation.

"Ah, true fishermen. And I bet at least one of you has a story that will tell of a battle that lasted an hour, or longer, and ended with the beast getting away as you dipped your net?"

"That's Steven's story," Thom laughed. "I netted mine successfully and it fed both of us two full meals."

"That sounds like a 'fish story'," the general laughed. "Does this contest take place on this river or will any river do?"

"Oh, no, sir. THIS river," Steven affirmed.

"And I bet you have a spot where the fish are begging to challenge you." General Keith looked at Steven with excitement in his eyes.

Steven smiled conspiratorially and looked once more to Thom who rolled his eyes. "Yes, sir, I do. But if you want my spot, it'll cost you."

"Ah, a fisherman with an agenda," Keith replied, cautiously. "And what is the price for your secret?"

"You fish, then I'll share my secret desire over lunch if your morning is successful. If not . . . well, I don't think we'll have to cross that bridge."

"Once again, I'm intrigued. Tell me, Steven, what type of work do you do?"

"Software engineer . . ."

The conversation continued over breakfast of fresh caught trout and hot smoky cornbread twists. Thom was careful to not open any doors that would offend their guest. Steven continued to tease with secrets and fishing fables. All pitched in to clean up and they made ready to engage wild trout.

Walking down a shaded tree lined, dirt and stone trail, just wide enough for two abreast, Thom prodded Steven, "So, are you going to share your spot or hog it for yourself?"

Passing through a line of trees and stepping into sunshine and onto grapefruit sized river stones, Steven replied, "We'll see."

"So, where is your spot, Steven?" Keith asked as they stepped from dry rocks into the river.

"Let's just start here, by the campground. Loosen up our shoulders and wet our flies. Once I appraise your style, I'll consider taking you to an overlooked treasure." Steven winked slyly, then entered the river ahead of the other two, gaining an upstream advantage.

All three men wore chest waders, GORE-tex waterproof fabric with integrated boots. Thom's had lined boots to keep his feet warm, while Steven wore heavy socks inside his steel-soled boots. Keith's waders were the latest in lightweight high-tech nylon fabric, fully lined for warmth and ease of movement. Each man carried a small fly box in a chest pocket and a net attached to a waist belt.

An hour into their fishing, Thom and Steven had each caught and released three large fish while the general had caught and released only one modest trout. None had experienced any appreciable challenge.

"Okay, sir, play time is over; it's time to do some fishing," Steven called. "Thom, you going to join us?"

"I'll follow part way, but I don't believe there will be room for all three of us," Thom replied with a snicker in his voice.

The general looked from Steven to Thom and wondered if he were being "played." When Steven began wading upstream, he and Thom followed. The force of the river and stone bottom encouraged each man to move slowly and with great care. Steven stopped about two hundred yards from where they began and motioned the general to join him. Standing beside Steven, the general took in the beauty of majestic fir trees and sugar pines filling both banks and crystal clear water tumbling over stones. The air was void of any contaminants and the aromas of nature filled his soul.

Pointing to an oxbow in the river, Steven explained, "Okay, here's the situation with this spot. Right now the river is still somewhat swollen from snow runoff. Two or three weeks ago you wouldn't have been able to stand here. The fish get tired fighting the swollen river and come to rest in that pool over there."

"I don't see a pool," Keith interrupted.

"No, sir, you don't, but there is a pool hiding in the bend there. A sandbar just below the surface deflects the current, hiding it. The trick is to let your fly float just to the side of the sandbar, toward the bank, not the river. If your fly drifts on the river side of the bar, you won't get a hit. As it drifts along the edge of the pool, give it a little action to attract whoever is napping down there. And be ready, because I have never had one play with me; they grab dinner and run!"

"Are we both going to fish this hidden pool?"

"No, sir. Right now, this is your treat, or possibly your challenge. I'll work the other riverbank; it can be fun as well."

General Keith looked at the bank opposite the hidden pool, exposed rocks and the river tumbling toward where they were standing. Satisfied he should try Steven's suggestion, he moved upstream another five yards and began casting his fly. As soon as it landed on the inside of the rill above the sandbar Steven had described, he began slowly pulling his line in and watching his fly. Steven smiled and cast his fly close to the opposite bank.

It took ten minutes, or so, for Keith's fly to drift down the oxbow. Steven recast his line three times. Resettling his feet on the rocky river bottom, Keith cast his line upstream for the second time. This time his fly sat still, so he tickled the line to get it moving. Slowly the lure slipped into the rill and began drifting around the pool.

"Remember to make your fly dance to entice those sleeping giants," Steven whispered.

Following Steven's advice, Keith began tickling his line, wiggling the tip of his rod to give the line just a little action so that the fly danced around in the water. At one point, the lure seemed to drift into the pool and just sit there. Frustrated, Keith wiggled his rod with more animation, giving more action to the line and thus the lure. As he pulled the excess line back, the water exploded and his line went taut. Instinctively, Keith snapped his rod and the line went berserk, running all over the quiet pool.

Steven and Thom retrieved their lines so they could enjoy the show that was now unfolding with General Keith, who was doing his best to keep his line taut. The fish on the other end, however, had other ideas. The wily trout ran back and forth across the pool, confounding the fisherman with the rod. It then ran upstream, as expected, only to reverse and run downstream out of the pool and into the main body of the river. Having experience with fish in a running river, Keith thought he now had the upper hand, until the fish ran back into the pool and out the upper end. Confounded, Keith worked himself into a frenzy trying to keep his line straight and tight as his adversary now came down river toward him. Keith watched helplessly as he watched the largest trout he had ever seen race past his leg.

Realizing what was happening, Thom called out, "As soon as he passes you again, tighten the line and net him!"

Following the advice, Keith pulled his line in as fast as he could. It tightened when the fish was some fifteen feet downstream. The fight then became one of river current and stones. Being pulled back upstream, the fish tried darting under and around several large rocks, however Keith kept his rod high, preventing potential snags. Forty-two minutes after engaging this challenge, Keith lifted a beautiful speckled trout from the water in his net.

Steven stepped over and pulled a tape measure from his fishing vest. "Sixteen and a quarter. Well done, sir."

Thom and Steven both admired the catch. Keith handed his rod to Thom and carefully reached inside the mouth of his captive. Seeing the fly just beyond reach of his fingers, he pulled a pair of long nose pliers from his own vest and gingerly removed the hook. Slipping the pliers back into his pocket, he washed his hands in the river and carefully lifted the trout from his net. "Thank you," he said and slipped the fish back into the river.

Taking his rod from Thom, he said, "Gentlemen, that is possibly the best fresh water challenge I have ever enjoyed. Thank you."

"Fresh water, sir?" Thom asked.

"I once hooked a sword fish. Took three hours to land him . . . but, to be honest . . . I think I liked this one better."

"Well, if you want smoked fish for supper, we had better get to the job at hand," Steven laughed. "I think I'll go up to the creek." He then quietly waded upstream a little further to where a small creek joined the river. By lunch, each fisherman had caught and released several more fine trout, keeping only their last for supper.

Lunch was cold-cut sandwiches, potato chips, and soft drinks. After lunch, all three fishermen cleaned their own catch and put them on ice. Keith and Steven went back into the river for a couple more hours of catch and release. There were no more challenges as they experienced that morning, but General Keith loved every minute on the river.

Returning to camp, after four o'clock, Keith watched as Thom arranged the fire for cooking. Once happy with the wall of hot coals, Thom retrieved the fish and began placing them in a wire basket.

"What, you aren't going to smoke them?" Keith challenged again.

"Yes, sir. This is a gizmo I rigged up for just that," Thom replied. He then opened each fish along the back and spread them gently across the wire grill. Once arranged, he locked a second grill across the back and hung the filled basket on an iron stake in front of the glowing coals. "Dinner will be ready in about an hour or so."

Seeing Keith raise his eyebrows, Steven patted him on the shoulder. "You'll love this. Trust me."

Steven then helped Thom make more cornbread twists and all three settled around the fire with a cold beer. Keith couldn't stop talking about his experience with the trout that morning until he suddenly went quiet and looked at Steven.

"What was it you wanted to ask me, Steven?"

Thom nodded as Steven took a sip from his beer and looked at General Keith. " 'Project Gumdrop.' You squashed this project as being unrealistic and too expensive. What's it all about?"

Thinking for nearly half a minute before answering, Keith stared straight at Steven and responded calmly, "It was, as I recall. Why is this important to you?"

"My folks were supposedly killed in a traffic incident about a month ago. Then last week, I got a text, through my girlfriend, that they were alive and to check out 'Project Gumdrop'."

The General's face went cold, white, and stern. "Where did this text originate?"

"As near as we can figure, West Virginia. At least it is a West Virginia area code."

Keith drew hard on his beer, growing visibly tense. After a moment of silence, he responded with a voice that was cold and harsh. "Thom, when we get back to your office, make sure I get Steven's contact information." Once again, he drew down on his beer, emptying the bottle. Looking across at the fire, he asked, "How much longer till supper?"

Thom checked the fish, and turned them around for the third time. "Just a few more minutes. Steven, you want to help me get the rest of supper ready?"

Seven nodded and removed sticks holding their cornbread twists from the fire. Supper that night was smoked trout, fresh baby green salad, and hot cornbread twists. Keith talked with both Thom and Steven about their jobs and kept the conversation light. After supper, Steven stood and excused himself.

"General Keith, it was a delight to share my secret river with you. I believe you are the current champion of the fight. However, I do have to be back at my desk at seven o'clock tomorrow morning, so I must be off. Sleep well."

Shaking Steven's hand firmly, Keith responded, "Thank you for the thrill of a fantastic challenge." He looked into Seven's eyes with another message, a silent message which Steven understood and acknowledged with a silent nod.

Matt and Barb took it easy most of the day, Wednesday. At Barb's request, he mounted the toilet seat in the outhouse then enjoyed a light lunch of ham and cheese sandwiches. His mind racing through the journey ahead of them, Matt strolled up to the lake and fished for an hour or so. Having not caught anything, he returned to the cabin and stretched out on the bed next to Barb.

Waking from their afternoon siesta around four o'clock, Matt checked their gear and they each packed essentials into haversacks; a change of clothes, water, first aid supplies, matches, granola bars (which Matt did not like but would eat if he had to), and they left room for food yet to be prepared. As shadows began to creep down the western slope, Barb heated up two cans of Brunswick Stew. After supper, Matt put all their dinner ware and the stew pot into a bucket which he filled with water. Barb fixed more sandwiches, using up all their bread and sliced meat.

Matt checked one final time to make sure he had his phone and wallet in his pack, and each had a flashlight that worked. He then casually went out to the porch and put a towel over the two cameras, telling those watching, "Good night boys." A minute later, with packs on and walking sticks in hand, they left the cabin laughing.

Barb called out, "That water is going to feel great tonight." When they reached the lake, Matt tossed a log into the water, making a loud splash. Their deception played, the campers slipped quickly and silently around the lake.

Dusk was settling into the valley when they reached Grumpy's tunnel through the rhododendron thicket. Taking a deep breath for courage, Matt dropped to his hands and knees and began crawling. Barb shuddered slightly as she drew a deep breath, then followed her husband. Not knowing where the old bear was, both tried to move quickly, which caused troubles. Carrying his pack on his chest, Matt caught straps on his back twice on rhododendron branches. Barb had to crawl over him the second time to effect his release. Seeing her husband's problems,

Barb elected to push and toss her pack ahead of her. When they reached a side tunnel going to Grumpy's den, both froze hearing an undescribable moaning sound. Deciding that the noise was not ahead of them, both moved more quickly.

Arriving at the exit, Matt immediately scrambled to his feet and offered his hand to Barb, who welcomed the assist back to her feet. Barb took just a moment to rub her sore knees before continuing to the fence in silence. To their surprise the hole Matt had made in the chain link was wide open, decorated with tufts of black fur at several spots.

"Let's go!" Matt whispered as he held the fence back so Barb could scoot through. He quickly followed and they raced for the ridge. Sky beyond the eastern slope still held a bit of pink and the hillside was lit with dusky light as they began weaving their way down the mountain. Successfully reaching the trail, both stopped to catch their breath. Breathing heavily and looking right, they longed to visit Gram. She provided a safe haven before, but both knew it would be unwise to expect this of her again.

Straightening up and taking a deep breath, Matt pointed toward town. Neither said anything for the first hour. Barb eventually broke the silence with a concern.

"Hey boy scout, where are we going when we reach town?"

"I've been working on that and I think the solution is right beside us."

Barb looked around and seeing nothing but forest, she replied, "I give up. What?"

"The stream. As I recall, the stream turned before we got to the meadow. Stay with the stream, even walk in it if we have to, but follow the stream to the other side of the village, maybe even further."

"So, you're thinking stay with the stream and reach the ocean?"

"Or the next community, whichever comes first." Matt then leaned over and kissed Barb smartly. "Don't forget that I love you."

Finding an old barn near the stream on the west side of Benmill, Matt and Barb settled for a brief rest. Matt was so exhausted from the pace of their escape that he even ate a much disdained granola bar, washing it down with half a bottle of water. Barb laughed and nibbled hers away. Glad to finally be heading home, she dozed. Unsure of what the new day would hold, Matt lay next to her, staring at the sky through a hole in the barn's roof.

Thirty

Day Thirty-One - Thursday

Feeling rested enough to continue, Matt woke Barb around three o'clock, in the dead of the night. Continuing down a trail beside the stream, they followed the water, its gurgle the only sound of the night. This trail never moved more than three yards from the waterway, passing through dark copses of trees, and often winding down to the stream itself. Three times they heard trucks or cars and watched headlights on the road less than sixty feet to their left. Each time they froze, not breathing until the vehicle had passed and no longer posed a threat to their freedom. Relieved when the only sound they heard was the gentle gurgling of the creek, they resumed their walk beneath the starlit moonless sky.

As dawn began to offer a new day, they came to a bridge over the creek. Noting that this was a road of some significance, Matt suggested they check it out; see if they could find a marker or some direction. Following this secondary road to the main highway, which paralleled the creek, they found a post with two direction signs pointing along the main road. Benmill was nine miles east and Acorn was one mile west. A third sign, which pointed down the secondary road, offered Acorn in three miles.

Looking to his wife and companion in adventure, Matt asked, "What will it be madam? Been there, back nine miles, or Let's See? Let's See can be reached in three miles or one."

Smiling at Matt's attempt at humor, Barb replied, "Let's See, the shorter route. I'm feelin' somewhat peckish."

Confident there would be little or no traffic this time of day, Matt took Barb's hand and strolled toward Acorn, taking the shorter route along the highway.

Acorn was much like Benmill, a small mountain community which offered little for adventurous tourists. The first establishment they came to, however, doubled as a service station and diner. Seeing interior lights, Matthew and Barbara ventured inside, where they found a room measuring about twelve feet wide and sixteen feet long. A counter with cash register was in front of them, beyond which was a door to two auto service bays. Behind the register sat one table large enough for four people, then a doorway with café doors, then a coffee station, and three more tables. Along the wall closest to them were six booths, each large enough for four people. A door to restrooms was centered on the wall at the end of the booths. The only window was a wall of glass on the highway side, opposite the cash register.

"Morning folks, coffee'll be ready in a bit." A man about sixty, wearing coveralls, olive green t-shirt, and John Deere hat welcomed them. "Y'all just find a sit anywhere ya like. Menus on the table. I'll take yer order just as soon as I get the grill turned on."

Both Barb and Matt headed to the table furthest from the door, next to the restrooms. The menu was situated in a rack which also held salt and pepper, and sugar and sweetener packets. After looking at the menu, Barb told Matt, "I'll take the Farmer's Wife - two scrambled, sausage, grits, and coffee." She then stood to go into the ladies' room but paused. "No, whole wheat toast instead of grits." She then disappeared behind a door marked "Gals."

"Welcome to Chester's, I'm not Chester, he was my dad. I go by Junior." The man in coveralls smiled as he looked down at Matt. "What can I get for you two fine morning folks?"

Matt smiled at their host's warmth and placed their order. "My wife would like the Farmer's Wife plate with whole wheat toast instead of grits. I'd like the country ham, two fried eggs, grits, and coffee."

"Yes, sir. One 'Wife' and one 'Hand' comin' up."

"Sir," Matt called as Junior turned to leave. "Does that phone work?"

"Yep, as long as you got quarters." He then disappeared into the kitchen.

"What's wrong?" Barb asked as she slid into the booth opposite Matt. "You look worried."

"No. I was just thinking about calling Steven. Junior says that phone works and I do know his number. I'd rather call Jim Thompson, but I don't know his number. He's speed dial six."

"And you don't want to turn your phone on," Barb confirmed. Seeing Matt nod, she added, "It's awfully early in California."

Matt looked at a clock over the kitchen door. 6:45. "Yeah, you're right. I'll wait until we leave." Looking at his wife, who had stuck with him without flinching through this entire bizarre

ordeal, Matt rapped his hands on the table and stood. "My turn."
He then stepped through the door marked "Guys."

Returning to the table, Matt noticed that more customers
had arrived, filling two tables. Sliding into their booth, he gasped
at the breakfast waiting for him. "If this is what a 'Farmer's
Hand' eats? I bet he works hard all day!" Cutting into the large
slab of ham, he smiled with anticipation. His second bite
included the runny yellow of his fried egg, then steaming hot
grits. His coffee was included in the mix but it was the ham that
was the star of this show. Barb delighted in every bite as well.

"Would you care for more coffee?" an attractive young lady,
about twenty-four, asked.

"Please," Barb replied.

"Are you part of the 'Chester' family?" Matt asked, flirting
just slightly.

"Junior is my grand." She smiled as she refilled both coffee
cups, then turned and attended to the other tables, slapping one
of the regulars lightly on his shoulder.

"Nice place," Barb commented as she finished her breakfast
and settled into finishing her coffee.

Moments later, the waitress returned. "Will there be
anything else?"

"No, just the check," Matt replied.

The waitress removed a pad from her apron and pulled a
ticket off the top. "You can leave it on the table or pay at the
door. Y'all have a nice day."

Seeing the ticket was $16.85, Matt counted out $21.00 from
his wallet and left it on the table. He then walked to the phone
and lifting the handset, tapped the lever several times and waited
for several long seconds.

"Operator, I'd like to place a collect call. The number is 369-
239-2123." Matt listened as the phone rang then went dead.

"I'm sorry, sir. There seems to be a problem with that
number. Is there another you would like to try?"

Matt thought for a second before responding, "No, operator.
Thank you." Looking around he asked the waitress, "Excuse me,
is there someplace nearby where I can purchase a cell phone?"

"If you're talking about those throw away type things,
Bobby usually has them. He has a convenience store service
station just up the road, middle of Acorn."

"Thank you, breakfast was delightful," Barb responded. She and Matt then left and resumed their journey.

Ignoring and violating Brian Bard's orders to not check up on Barbara, Doctor Olivia Adams and her corpsman, Randy, parked their ATV in front of the cabin. Collecting her medical bag from the cargo carrier, she marched smartly down the path. Noticing towels over the cameras, she wondered but knocked on the door anyway. When there was no reply, she knocked a second time, this time calling, "Missus Harper, it's Doctor Adams. I need to check on your bee sting." There was no reply.

Looking back at the draped cameras, Doctor Adams lifted the door latch and stepped inside. Finding the cabin empty, she strolled around. Plates and a pot sat in a pail of cold water. Touching the stove, she found it cold. Looking in a trash bag, she saw a brunswick stew can on top of other miscellaneous garbage. Looking around once more, she realized what she did not see and considered how this information affected her.

"They left last night," she whispered to herself. "Now, do I report this?"

Pondering her dilemma, the doctor stepped outside, closing the door behind her. Looking once more at the two cameras draped by towels, she grinned slightly and returned to her ATV. "Back to base, Randy."

"Yes, ma'am."

Walking through the hallways inside the mountain, the doctor happened upon Jerry Tanner, who was leaving the observation room. "Mister Tanner . . . Jerry, could you step into my office for a minute, please?"

Surprised slightly by the doctor's familiarity, Jerry replied, "Sure, what's up, Olivia?"

Closing her door before speaking, she looked to Jerry and spoke just above a whisper. "They've run off, again."

Smiling, Jerry replied, "Interesting. I guess my son was right."

"Sir?"

"My son and several of his friends were out rather late last night. Didn't get home 'till after seven this morning, but he told me he thought he saw them going into a restaurant near Acorn."

"Did he stop?"

"No. He wasn't driving and was still suffering a touch of hangover."

"WHAT? On a Wednesday night?"

"Yep. I should be angry but it is an unofficial school tradition. End of year celebration for seniors. It was after noon before I got home from mine."

"What should we do?" Doctor Adams asked, snickering about Jerry's story.

"About what?" Jerry responded, cocking his head to the side.

Smiling conspiratorially, the doctor opened her office door. "Thank you for visiting, Mister Tanner. I need to speak with my corpsman."

Walking past the observation room toward his office, Jerry stopped when he heard Bard challenging a report. Curious, Jerry stepped inside.

"What do you mean he got a call from the valley but it was a Las Vegas number?"

A technical specialist tried to explain. "Sir, as you know we have both children's numbers flagged in the local telephone system. At 7:21 this morning, a call was placed to Steven Harper's telephone from somewhere in the valley. When we retrieved the calling number, it came back as 702-992-9550, which is a Las Vegas exchange."

"How did we get a Las Vegas call from this area?"

"An older payphone, sir. Many old payphones transmit that same caller id, from all across the country. We know the call was placed from this region but have no way to tell from which phone."

Turning to the bank of screens linked to cameras within the project, Bard saw two were blank. "What's wrong with those two cameras?"

A soldier assigned to log events replied, "Log says they were draped last night, when the Harpers went swimming. They were heard entering the water and laughing, sir. We assumed they wanted some private time and had not yet removed the towels."

"Get somebody over there NOW!" Bard was agitated by his soldiers' casual attitude. Looking at other screens, he asked,

"What's wrong with the patio camera in New Mexico? I don't see anyone in the living area there, either."

"No, sir. They did just take breakfast out to their patio. Camera was knocked out by a storm last night at 11:23."

"Schedule a crew to repair it, TONIGHT! Should have been fixed last night!" Bard turned to leave the room, but stopped at the door. "Get somebody to the Harper's cabin NOW and have them report to me immediately when they get there." Looking at his watch as he stomped out, noting the time. 9:15.

Stepping into the Convenience Mart in downtown Acorn, Matt walked to the register. Seeing the man behind the counter was wearing the name "Bobby" on his shirt, he asked, "I am looking for a disposable cell phone. What do you have?"

"Sorry, sir, we don't have them phones any longer. Nearest place I know of where you might find one is at Wally's."

Matt heaved a sigh and looked at his wife. Turning back to Bobby, he asked, "Where is 'Wally's'?"

"Oh, he's just up the road about five miles. Name on the building is 'Toliver's Appliances'."

Looking back at Barb, Matt asked, "Do you want a drink or anything?"

"No. Let's just keep going."

Turning toward the door, Matt looked back to Bobby. "Thank you for your help. Have a good day."

"You, too, sir. Sorry I couldn't help ya."

Standing beside the Convenience Mart, Barb and Matt looked around. The road paralleled the creek, which had now grown to a small river, but there was no trail beside it. Beyond the river was forest and both banks were steep and not easily negotiable. A steep nonnegotiable hillside covered by trees lined the far side of the road. A footpath followed the road on their side, eight feet or so off the pavement.

"How do we go?" Barb asked.

"Seems like we have only one choice. I'd really like to get on the other side of that river, but don't see an easy crossing."

"Let's just stick to this path. Maybe we'll find a bridge." Taking Matt's hand, they stepped off.

Four soldiers riding on two ATVs arrived at the cabin, whereupon two men stood guard at the vehicles while the other two went to the door. Rapping loudly on the door, the men waited silently for a response. Hearing nothing within five seconds, they opened the door and entered. Finding nobody inside, they surveyed the room. Seeing dirty dishes in a pail of water, one soldier took charge.

"I'll go check the cold house out back; you check the outhouse and front."

Both men moved immediately in opposite directions. A minute later they met again on the front porch. Pointing to the camera watching the front door, the one in charge directed, "You get the drape off that camera, I'll get the other one. Leave the drape on a branch below the unit."

Returning to their ATVs, the leader removed a cell phone from his pocket and placed a call. "Commander, there is no sign of our guests." . . . "No, sir. I cannot determine how long they have been gone nor where they went." . . . "A pot and bowls are in a wash basin. I cannot tell whether it was supper last night or breakfast this morning." . . . "Yes, sir, we have uncovered the cameras." . . . "Yes, sir. We will check the camper and then southeastern quadrant, down to the river." . . . "Sir, yes sir."

"Well, gentlemen, you heard the orders. Let's ride through the woods."

Bursting from his office, Brian Bard stormed to the observation room. Finding Colonel Prescott, he ordered a search and retrieval expedition. "Prescott, the Harpers are not at the cabin. I must assume they have taken off. Again! I want four groups out right now. Two to canvas the town, store by store. The other two to head east and west. Show their pictures at every gas station, diner, any place these folks might have stopped for help, food, drink. Anything! If they are not found in town, those two groups should follow the others and assist the east and west searches."

"How far should we search, sir?"

"Until you find them!" Turning to leave the room, Bard stopped. "One more thing. Send a group of your men to the ridge and check the fence. If they got out, find out how!"

Having heard only part of the new directive while refilling his coffee, Jerry Tanner pondered his next move. Should he give aid to the Harpers? His puzzle was shattered when Bard saw him.

"Tanner, I need an update on the project status. I like what you did on the local impacts; now see just how far that influence reaches. All three locations, on my desk before lunch."

Inserting his ear piece as he climbed into his car, Steven started the engine, placed a call to Jim Thompson, and put his Jeep in gear. He reached the first stop sign before the call was answered. Pulling out, he heard, "Hello, Steven. News? How was the fishing trip?"

"The trip was great and yes, a bit of news. General Keith is quite the fisherman and was not too happy when I asked him about 'Gumdrop'."

"Is he going to look into it?"

"He didn't say so exactly, however . . . the look in his eyes . . . well, I wouldn't want to be on the receiving end when he gets hold of them. He's a cautious man, guess he has to be, but I trust that he will find out what's going on."

"That sounds good. Now, I will be heading toward the mountains after lunch. Still have a few loose ends to tie up and my wife, Marsha, will be traveling with me. She's packing a suitcase as we speak. With an ounce of luck I should have eyes on your folks' camper by end of the day."

"Thanks, Uncle Jim. I'm not ready to give up just yet."

"I don't expect you too. I'll call when I get to the camper."

Steven tapped his earpiece, ending the call. Thinking aloud, he whispered, "Hang on Mom and Dad. We're coming."

Walking as far off the highway as they could, Matt and Barb continued their journey. Cars and trucks passed without slowing. Two hours after leaving the Convenience Mart they encountered their first bridge crossing the river. Standing in the middle of the bridge, Matt looked to the opposite bank.

"Looks like locals ride dirt bikes along the river." He then looked back in the direction they had come. "Trail must start here. What do you think, time to get away from the highway?"

Looking down the road and the river, Barb offered a different suggestion. "Looks like Toliver's is only half a mile, or so, and appears there's another bridge just the other side. You want to stay on the road to the store or get off now?"

"The next bridge appears to be at the store, so let's get off now. I'm certain they know we're gone; let's not tempt fate."

Leaving the highway provided little relief for Matt's tension. He could still see the road through a narrow line of trees, so he knew they were visible as well. "I hope this path continues far enough that we can reach another town by evening."

"I'd like some lunch," Barb replied. "You reckon this Toliver's has lunch food?"

"We'll find out shortly," Matt replied, squeezing her hand.

Barely fifteen minutes later, Matt held the door at Toliver's so Barb could enter first. While the name on the building did say "Toliver's Appliances," inside was a larger version of the Convenience Mart. A lunch counter offered three varieties of hot dogs cooking on hot rotating bars. Coolers filled with drinks from soda to beer and wine lined one wall. Another section was dedicated to sporting goods, offering both fishing and hunting gear. The center of the store was filled with grocery items. Looking to the right of the door they entered, Matt saw a man, he assumed was Wally, ringing another customer's purchases. Behind and around the register was an array of electronic gadgetry, including phones.

Seeing Matt looking at the phones, Barb told him, "I'm going to get us a couple dogs, what do you want? They have all beef, hot, and sausage."

"Sausage, and a Coke," Matt replied. Seeing the previous customer leave, Matt stepped up to the counter. "I need a cheap phone."

"How cheap do you want to go? I have them for $14.95," the man behind the counter replied. He stood almost six feet tall, a full dark brown beard, and was dressed in freshly pressed shirt and jeans with stars and stripes suspenders.

"Only need it for a couple days, till I can get mine fixed."

"In that case, I suggest the cheapy with our lowest calling card. Package would be $27.35 plus tax."

"That'll do, and please add two bottle drinks and two dogs."

Placing a phone shrink-wrapped with an instruction card on the counter, the man said, "That will be $36.29 total. You need help activating that thing?"

Looking at the back of the card, Matt replied, "Instructions seem good enough, but thank you." He then removed the fifty-dollar bill from his wallet and handed it to the man. Turning to check on Barb, he saw she had her hands full. "Do you have a bag?"

"Yeah, your girlfriend should use the bags with the cooker. They're better for not messing up the dogs."

"Got it!" Barb called.

After receiving his change, Matt waited for Barb to join him and they headed for the door, freezing in a panic. An Army Humvee had pulled up and two men wearing MP arm bands climbed out. Looking around, Matt told Barb, "Back door. Out the back door, fast."

The two Military Police entered the front door as Matt and Barbara escaped out the back door. Seeing them running, one MP grabbed the microphone on his shoulder. "Suspects fleeing Toliver's Store. Out the back. In pursuit." Both soldiers raced to the back door, but could not see Matt or Barb when they got outside. Squeezing his microphone, one MP called for help. "Lost sight of our suspects, but they have to be nearby. Request immediate support."

Hiding in leaves behind a fallen tree, Matt and Barb waited breathlessly for what seemed an eternity. Still holding the phone in his hand, he unbuttoned his shirt and stuffed it inside, then pushed the buttons back through the holes. As soon as the MP left, one going inside, the other walking around the outside back toward the road, Matt grabbed Barb's hand and tugged her to her feet.

Running as hard as they could for the bridge, Matt stumbled on loose gravel. Barb paused to help him, but he yelled, "GO!" As she reached the bridge, another Army Humvee screeched to a halt just a few yards away. One MP jumped out and ran after her, another went after Matt.

Seeing the MP grab his wife and hold her with excessive force, Matt exploded. Like a football lineman opening up the opposition's defensive line, he bowled his pursuer over, sending him flying backwards. Reaching the MP holding his wife, he jabbed him in the back with his walking stick. When the MP turned, releasing Barb, Matt brought the stick down on his shoulder, breaking the stick and sending the MP to his knees. Another soldier arrived and tried to grab Matt. Adrenaline pumping out of control, Matt spun around and planted his fist into the MP's face. With the soldier rolling backwards, blood spewing from his nose, Matt grabbed Barb's hand and they ran around the vehicle. Trying to reach the bridge, they were quickly blocked by the arrival of the first Humvee, which threw gravel in every direction as it sped around the building in pursuit. The first man, whom Matt had bowled over, ran up behind Matt and wrapped an arm around him, forcing him to his knees.

"That will be enough Mister Harper," the restraining MP said. "I don't want to hurt you, but I will."

Matt looked up at Barb who stood helplessly with her walking stick hanging from one hand and their bag of hot dogs hanging from the other. The driver of the vehicle blocking their escape took Barbara's stick and guided her respectfully into the back seat of his vehicle. Defeated, Matt allowed his shoulders to fall, whereupon his MP helped him to his feet and guided him into the vehicle as well. As soon as Matt and Barb were safely locked inside the Humvee, both guards went to the aid of their companions.

Seeing the amount of blood flowing from one man's nose, an MP went into the store and purchased a roll of paper towels. The other able bodied MP checked on guard number four and found his shoulder in severe condition; he was unable to move his arm.

Assessing the situation, the soldier who had purchased the paper towels began directing the others. Handing towels to the soldier with the bloody nose, he told him, "Tommy, you get into my vehicle with our guests. Bob, you take Will in their vehicle. I'll call this in as we head back."

"Shouldn't we get Will to a hospital?" Bob challenged.

"Nearest medical care is going to be back at post. Do you need help getting him into the vehicle?"

"No. We'll get it. You get going and tell them to have the doc waiting for us."

As soon as Bob got Will into the second vehicle, the first Humvee, with the Harpers on board, left the parking lot heading east.

Jerry walked into Project Manager Bard's office and dropped a report on his desk.

"What's the short story?" Bard asked, looking away from his screen.

"Influence extends a little over a mile, excluding employers," Jerry responded. Rolling his jaw and looking toward the floor he continued. "Sir, when my friends and I developed this hypothesis, it was purely theoretical. Out of curiosity, we applied sound economic principle and . . . well, you know what we came up with, actions of one family or individual could impact global economy. Butterfly Effect. However, after studying the results of the past month, I need help analyzing what we've learned. You ran the other two developers off, but I'm going to contact them with real world results and see if we can determine where we might have faulted in our determinations."

Turning to leave Bard's office, Tanner added, "Enjoy reading the data."

"Doctor Tanner, before you go, you might want to read this joint bulletin from Homeland Security on behalf of the FBI and SEC." Bard extended his hand, offering a paper to Jerry.

Jerry took the paper with an air of exasperation, looking at the headline, "Cyber Terrorism Alert." He then scanned the first paragraph. Staring back at Bard with contempt, he responded, "This is pure nonsense."

"Nope. It seems that while our guests were out in the world not long ago, Mister Harper accessed his email and released a worm into the NY Stock Exchange. That worm corrupted one trading company then leapt to three others. Major players on the Exchange shut down for the better part of a day. Even the SEC was impacted. Now, you want to tell me how innocent these Harpers are?"

"Couldn't have been them, they never had access to any computers!"

"Your son showed them the computers at the Inn, didn't he? FBI investigators found the source of the worm and identified it as an email from Matthew Harper. Didn't you tell me his profile pegged him as angry about how the Internet was taking over the world? Could've been something Harper was considering all along, just hadn't sent the email . . . till he did."

The two men stared coldly at one another. Dropping the paper on Bard's desk, Jerry turned and silently left the office. He knew the truth, that this was the result of that email Bard had sent Harper in an attempt to trap him. "An exclusive trading opportunity" was loaded with an invasive worm. Matt's system had caught the infected email and trashed it. Somehow, Bard had forwarded the infection under Matt's ID and now Homeland Security labeled him and Barb as 'cyber terrorists.' They were now criminals and setting them free had become a lot more difficult.

Steven reviewed his notes, studied his computer screen, then began closing files. Trying to make up for going fishing, he had put in a long day without breaks. It was finally time to go home and relax; maybe call Susan. Thinking about Susan, he smiled and began walking toward the door. Halfway to his Jeep, his phone rang.

"Good evening, Uncle Jim. You must have news to be calling this late."

"Yes, and I'd like to say it's good news but to be honest I can't say that it is. I saw your parent's car and camper. . . . " Jim Thompson paused as he structured his thoughts.

"Uncle Jim, what's wrong?" Steven stopped at his Jeep without getting in.

"Steven, my detective senses are all screaming at me. First, when we got there, both the camper and car were on a truck about to be taken to a compactor. The yard manager told me they had a rush order to crush them, which is unusual. Fortunately the compactor had locked up and has been down for several days. Has just been put back into service. They had been loaded for transport just before we arrived. This just isn't normal . . . they had vehicles that had been on that lot for months, possibly years, but he let me examine them on the truck.

"Anyway, both the camper and car were in really bad shape, burned and smashed, but to be blunt, Steven, I don't think it is theirs and I'll tell you why. When I borrowed the camper, we had a rainy spell so I looked at that notebook the previous owner made. That engineer was a bit strange but quite creative. Anyway, I was fascinated by that sewage tank arrangement he made. I couldn't find that notebook and this camper, the one they say is your parents', had a standard black tank, not removable. The body of the camper was a mess but the rear undercarriage was intact . . . "

"Tell him about the books," a woman interrupted.

"Yeah, that too. Personal belongings were still in the wreckage and we found a book in the bathroom, which was in the back and not burned up like the front. Marsha, my wife, knows Barbara fairly well. She says your mother wouldn't be caught dead reading a book like that."

"Interesting. What about the car? Anything unusual about the car?" Steven asked, growing somewhat excited as Jim talked.

"That car they showed me was the same make and model as what your dad drives and it was pretty much burned up, except that . . . keep in mind that this is not my area of expertise, but one of the seat covers, the front passenger seat, survived the fire, somewhat. I saw no impression of a body having been burned in that seat. . . . Steven, I have no idea why but in my opinion, somebody has gone to a lot of trouble to make it look like your parents were killed in an accident and now they want to destroy the evidence."

"And they weren't," Steven responded. "What now, Uncle Jim?"

"I almost hate to bring this up because I know it is bogus, but my partner back at the office knows what I'm doing and forwarded a Homeland Security bulletin to me. It seems your parents are suspected of cyber terrorism."

"That has got to be a joke because Dad barely knows how to use a computer."

"Yeah, you and I both know that, just another piece in this bizarre puzzle. . . . Well, it's late so Marsha and I are going to get a room and go to the campground tomorrow morning. I want to

talk with the hosts and see if they remember Matt and Barb
getting in. I'll call you as soon as I talk with them."

"Thank you. You don't know how much this means to me."

"I think I do. Remember, your parents are our best friends.
I'll talk with you tomorrow."

Thirty-One

Arriving back at the mountain, the MPs assisted Matt and Barb from the Humvee and hooded them. They were then led into a tunnel, through office hallways, and released on the opposite side of the mountain, in the same spot where Matt had been shot. Barb still had her walking stick and the food from Toliver's, so swallowing their anger and disappointment, they had a picnic beside the waterfall before making their way along the stream back to the lake and around to the cabin. Nobody had said a word to them. Nobody checked them for injuries. Nobody checked to see if they had acquired any new toys.

Neither felt like doing anything when they got back, so supper was sandwiches they had made and put in their haversacks. Exhausted from their escape, they stretched out on their mattress as the sun set.

Day 32 - Friday
Hearing what sounded like a swarm of basketball-size bees, Matt opened his eyes. Light above and around him was a bit hazy but he could affirm that he was indeed back in the cabin. Sighing heavily, he rolled over, sat up, and put shoes on his feet. Shuffling to the door, he looked out.

"Rain and groceries. Another day in paradise," he mumbled sarcastically to himself. Stepping forward, he turned left and made his way to the outhouse. Returning several minutes later he retrieved one of the two grocery containers, leaving it on the porch. Shuffling back to the bed he kicked his shoes off and stretched out next to Barb.

"Did I hear you say it was raining?" she asked, barely awake enough to speak.

"Yes, but it isn't really. At least not at the moment, more of a heavy mist . . . just enough to spit on us."

"Wonderful. I need to make a trip to the loo." Barb then followed the same steps as Matt had, putting on shoes, shuffling out to the facility, and back again. Flopping down onto the mattress, next to Matt, she said, "Thank you for the toilet seat. We got groceries."

It was another hour before either Matt or Barb got motivated enough to climb out of bed and get dressed. While water heated on the gas stove, Matt retrieved the second grocery bin. Finding a box of Entenmann's blueberry muffins, he commented, "They must be trying to appease us." Turning his head up he exclaimed in a rather loud voice, "The missus appreciates the muffins but I don't care for them. Try raspberry Danish if you want me to smile." He then collected eggs, bacon, and English muffins from the bins and began preparing breakfast.

"Do you have any plans for today?" Barb asked as she finished eating and pondered another cup of coffee.

"I may need to go check on Grumpy. Haven't seen him for a while. I'd like to know that Prince Albert is okay as well."

Barb looked at her husband with wonder, thinking, *I know he isn't going looking for that bear, and I miss Dee-O-Gee, too. Ah, he wants to go up on the ridge!* His intent understood, Barb responded, "Any idea what time?"

"Not right now. I have some reading I want to do first, then I'll let you know."

Barb stared at him totally befuddled this time. Seeing her expression, he mouthed the word "Phone."

Barb smiled and nodded, asking, "Another cup of coffee? I'll fix while you read."

Matt smiled and went over to where he took his clothes off the night before. Digging around through his shirt and jacket, Matt found two packages he had stuffed inside his shirt while hiding behind Toliver's. Crossing to the table, he dropped the card with "purchased minutes" on the table and began reading the back of the phone package. A minute later he opened the package and turned the phone on.

"Three-quarters charge . . . I guess that's okay," he said softly, in case Barb was interested in his progress. "Needs activation code, that is on the paper in the package." . . . "Here we go." Typing in the code, he whispered to himself, "F 9 W K Y Z 7 5." After entering the code, Matt exclaimed with frustration, "Oh great, now we need a zip code. Barb do we have the receipt from yesterday? That'll have a zipcode on it."

"Try 24949," a female voice suggested from the door.

"Doctor, what brings you by today?" Barb asked, panicking that she saw what Matt was doing.

"I wanted to make sure the two of you were okay. You really sent our Project Manager off the deep end." Strolling over to where Matt had placed the phone on the table, she commented softly, as though whispering. "Not sure that phone will have enough power to reach public towers from here. You may have to take a hike to the ridge, but please don't run away again. At least not for a few days. Bard, our PM, is a real ass whenever you folks don't behave."

Matt looked at the doctor's face and nodded slightly. Turning around toward Barb, the doctor spoke loudly and clearly, "Missus Harper, how is your hip doing? You had a nasty reaction to that bee; any side effects?"

"It's still a bit stiff, but nothing I can't manage."

"Okay. You might try an Ibuprofen if it gets too uncomfortable. Exercise will be good for it as well. In fact, if you aren't up to climbing, maybe stroll down to the river?" Doctor Adams looked to Matt to see if he understood. He nodded with a smile. "By the way, you have become something of a legend among the military police."

"What?" Matt asked, suspicious of what Doctor Adams was about to tell him.

"You, sir, took down three of four trained soldiers. One you simply knocked the wind out of. Did you play football when you were younger? Doesn't matter, the man you slugged has a broken nose; he'll be okay, however your third victim has a broken collarbone. I don't know what you hit him with, but you did some damage. He'll be out of service for a couple weeks. You earned a lot of 'street cred' yesterday."

"Please tell the men I'm not sorry. They were unnecessarily rough with Barbara and I'd do it again." Looking down at his phone, Matt announced, "I think we will need to take a walk, Barb. Maybe as soon as it stops raining."

"Weatherman called for rain till about noon," Doctor Adams responded. "Take care of yourselves." She then left. A moment later Matt and Barb heard her ATV scooting around the lake.

Barb finished fixing two cups of coffee, which were delayed by the doctor's visit. Matt took food that needed to be kept cool to the cold house, then joined Barb on the front porch. While looking across the lake, Barb noticed something had changed.

"Cameras are gone!"

Standing and looking into the trees, where their drape towels still hung on lower branches, Matt spotted the cameras. "Nope. Just moved higher so we can't cover them. No more skinny dipping, my love."

Both settled into their chairs and watched the rain fall across the lake, hiding the western slope.

Rain did stop shortly after noon, as Doctor Adams had suggested. Having had sandwiches while waiting, Matt and Barb prepared themselves for a walk.

"You need to find yourself another walking stick," Barb commented as they started out around the lake. Matt nodded with a shrug of his shoulders.

"Halt!" a soldier called as Mat and Barb began climbing toward Grumpy's tunnel. Turning, they found two young soldiers, rifles slung over their shoulders. One informed them, "You are no longer allowed on this hillside."

"What?" Matt asked. "You are saying we aren't allowed to walk in this valley?"

"Walk wherever you like, sir, just not up this hill," the second soldier replied.

"And if we continue, will you shoot us?" Barb challenged.

Bringing their rifles to shooting position, both replied, "Yes, ma'am."

Matt took Barb's hand and led her away from the hill. "Come on, sweetheart. It's too wet to climb the hill anyway." Without looking back, they walked back toward the cabin, but turned off on the path down toward their camper.

Twenty yards down the trail, two young soldiers jumped from logs they had been sitting on and brought rifles across their chests, prepared to act if required. "Sorry, folks. This area of the valley has been declared off limits."

"So we can't go to our camper?" Barb asked, feigning innocence.

"No ma'am. If there is something you would like from the camper, you need to write a note to Commander Bard and someone will retrieve it for you."

"Well, Missus Harper, it appears our exercise must be restricted to excursions around the lake or up to the waterfalls," Matt suggested, smiling only slightly.

"I don't feel like walking now, anyway. I'm going back to the cabin!" Barb exclaimed. Her face pouting, she turned and began walking. When she was about fifty yards away from the guards and Matt had caught up with her, she said bluntly, "This is totally absurd."

Laughing, Matt replied, "You gotta admit, we've messed up their plans. Now, do you really want to call it a day or are you ready for a new adventure?"

"Let's go!" Barb's face lit up like a child on Christmas morning.

Before they reached the cabin, Matt turned into the woods and made a new trail behind the outhouse and well out of range of the camera watching the rear of the cabin. They continued in an east-southeasterly direction until they came to the river. Seeing a clearing and hilltop not far ahead, Matt continued pushing through the light undergrowth. Once on top of the hill, he opened his burner phone and turned it on. Seeing instructions to activate on the screen, he pressed the enter key. Seconds ticked by slowly until the notice disappeared and a blank phone screen appeared. He had two bars of service. Before he could start a call, the phone displayed, "You have 0 minutes of airtime."

Sighing, Matt dug the minutes card from his pocket and entered the code. When the phone displayed, "You have 300 minutes of airtime," he began entering Steven's number but stopped before hitting "Call."

Recalling the failed connection to Steven the day before, Matt pulled out his personal cell phone and turned it on. As soon as it was up, he went to contacts and looked up Jim Thompson. Copying Jim's number into his burner phone, Matt hit enter and held the phone to his ear. While he waited, he turned his personal phone off.

The call rang three times before it was answered. "Jim Thompson."

"Jim this is Matt Harper. Barb and I are alive and . . ." The call ended. Looking at the phone and growing angry, Matt pressed redial. He heard a click then nothing.

Looking to Barb, Matt sighed, "I don't know if he heard me and it appears that this phone is now blocked."

Taking Matt's hand, Barb returned Matt's sigh and frustration. "Maybe he did hear you and will do something about finding us. Let's go back. I think I saw some beer in the groceries this morning." Dropping Matt's hand, she wiped a tear from her cheek.

Matt carefully picked his way through the forest, going back the way they had come. Approaching the cabin from the downhill river side, he saw a stone structure he hadn't noticed before. A large round moss-covered rock, roughly fifteen inches across and five inches thick. What caught his eye was the way it sat just above the ground, just a couple inches. Curious, he walked over and tried to lift it. It barely moved.

"Barb, let me use your walking stick."

Reluctantly, she handed her stick over, warning him, "You break it you'll have to make TWO sticks."

Smiling appreciation, Matt placed the stick under one edge and lifted carefully. Hearing moss tearing away, he stopped and tried to lift the stone again. This time, the rock gave way, revealing a square of old metal, slightly smaller than the rock. Grabbing the metal on opposite sides, he wiggled it until it lifted up. Holding the old tin in his hand, he became even more puzzled. Measuring twelve inches square and four inches deep, it appeared to be very well tooled and soldered on the corners. Looking to the ground, he realized this unexpected piece of metal was a cover to a bin buried in the ground, illuminated by afternoon sunshine. Looking inside, Matt could see a square metal box. While the opening was only about twelve inches square with a four-inch raised lip, the bin itself was about twenty-six to thirty inches wide and filled with paper and a bucket of something. Looking to the corners of the bin, Matt could see that they were riveted and soldered, like the lid. This bin, was completely buried, except for the concealed opening.

Lying on the ground, Matt reached into the box, down to his elbow. Grabbing a pack of paper, he rolled over as he lifted it out. Staring at the old printed paper, he realized it was money, currency more than one hundred years old. And it was dry. The entire bin was bone dry. Replacing the money, he reached into a bucket and removed a coin.

next. I considered going to the park admin office, but I'm confident that would be a dead end as well."

"Look, right now just knowing they are alive is more than I could hope for. If I don't hear from the general within twenty-four hours, I'll track him down."

"Sounds like a plan. Not a great one, but the only one we have at present. Call me as soon as you hear anything, anything at all! Have you talked with your girlfriend?"

"Yep. She's coming down tomorrow."

"Okay, take care. Bye."

Thirty-Two

Day 33 - Saturday

Unable to sleep, Matt Harper lay on their camper mattress next to his wife and stared through a hole in the roof across the cabin. He had awakened multiple times during the night contemplating their current situation.

More than a month had passed since he and Barb were kidnaped, presumably to avoid some undefined *economic catastrophe*. . . . Family, friends and employers were told they were killed in a traffic accident! Their camper had been destroyed and they now lived almost like caged animals in an old log cabin with holes in the roof. Multiple attempts to escape had failed. . . . they did escape the valley twice, but were found and brought back. Now military guards kept them corralled in a restricted area! Phone calls to their son had failed and Matt wasn't sure if a call to his best friend had delivered an important message - he and Barb were alive.

Staring through the hole in the roof, Matt watched the sky gradually begin to lighten. Feeling totally isolated, he dismissed a faint and unfamiliar sound. When his stomach called for attention, he decided fresh fish would make a delightful breakfast. After checking on Barb, he got up and quietly dressed before leaving the cabin, letting her sleep a while longer.

Walking toward the lake, he looked up at the camera set to watch the front porch. The activity light glared at him like an evil demon. He paused for a few seconds, then turned and walked over to the outhouse. After a brief visit, he walked around the back of the privy and made his way to the lake out of range of the camera.

Arriving at his preferred fishing spot, where there were no cameras or microphones, Matt looked toward the west. Not seeing any guards at the base of the hill, he made his first cast. The silver spoon with green skirt sailed over the glassy surface of the lake, dropping into the water more than thirty yards away. He had shied away from using spoons when he first fished this lake, fearful of snagging on roots and other debris along the bottom. Today, he was more frustrated than fearful, thinking if it snagged, it snagged.

Reeling the lure in, he felt an immediate strike, then another. "Somebody's hungry," he said softly to himself, his mood improving. Seconds later he felt a solid hit and jerked the line just like his father had taught him so many years before. The lake came alive with activity as Matt worked the fish on the other end of his line, slowly bringing him closer to shore. It was a short battle, only about five minutes, but Matt landed a healthy ten-inch trout. Hooking his catch on the stringer and putting it back into the water, Matt caught a glimpse of something golden racing through the trees.

"Dee-O-Gee! You're back!" Matt dropped to his knees and lavished affection on the Golden Retriever, who soaked it in. After a minute, the dog jumped back, whoofed, and ran toward the cottage. Matt called, "Don't wake her up just yet!"

Delighted with the visit from a friend, Matt returned to fishing. Twenty minutes later, he landed a second trout. Feeling lucky, he continued to cast.

"How's the fishing? Anything biting this morning?"

Hearing a strange voice so close to him, Matt stumbled as he turned around. Heart racing, he looked at the man approaching him, now only ten feet away. Wearing a sand colored camouflage uniform with a tan brimmed hat similar to a baseball cap, this visitor was fifty years or so with an athletic build and hints of grey in dark brown hair. Seeing a patch on his shoulder, Matt read "National Security Agency." A reflection of early morning sunlight from his collar, led Matt's eyes to three stars. Matt did not notice he held a fishing rod in his right hand.

Still unsure as to who was calling nor how he got there, Matt looked behind his visitor. Two men in similar attire stood about thirty feet away. Behind them, at the path to the camper, were two soldiers in tan camouflage wearing tan berets and armed with serious weapons. The two guards who had blocked Barb and Matt from going to their camper the day before were sitting on the ground in front of these soldiers. Spinning around to look toward the western hill, Matt smiled when he saw two more soldiers, also armed and wearing tan berets. The hillside guards also sat in front of these visitors.

Not knowing whether he was being taken hostage again or being rescued, Matt looked back to his visitor. Now seeing the fishing rod he carried, Matt took a deep breath before replying.

"Well, I have two so far and was about to go fix breakfast. If you want to join my wife and me, you're welcome to share what we have or catch your own."

Stepping forward, the visitor, prepared his own rod for casting. "I recently had a great fishing experience in California. A young man named Steven took me to a fantastic and unexpected treat. Not sure I will get the same here, but let's give it a try." Just before casting, the man extended his hand. "My apologies. Al Keith."

"Matthew Harper, but friends call me Matt."

"Good to meet you, Matt. Now, let me try a couple casts then we can see about breakfast."

Matt finished reeling his last cast in, which had been interrupted. Feeling it hang slightly, he jerked his rod a bit harder than needed. His spoon popped out of the water, landing back in the water twenty feet from the bank.

"Get a hit from a root bass?" Keith joked.

Matt finished reeling his spoon in and the two men cast together quietly. Keith got a strike on his third cast, reeling in a handsome eleven-inch trout.

"Where do we clean?" Keith asked, pleased with his catch.

Matt lifted his stringer with two trout and led Keith over to the stone steps in front of the cottage. As they cleaned their catch, Matt asked, "So when are you going to tell me why you are here? You should be aware that we are being watched."

"Watched? How?"

"Cameras in the trees. One watches the lake, the other our front porch."

Turning to one of the officers accompanying him, Keith called, "Mike, check surveillance, please. Make sure everything is out." Turning to Matt, he replied, "We suspected as much and have been running an electronic jammer since before we arrived. Mike will check it just the same. As for why I am here . . ."

"MATT!" Barbara screamed from the door of the cabin. She was dressed only in a t-shirt, underwear, and sandals.

Standing so Barb could see him, Matt called, "It's okay. We have company for breakfast. You might want to get dressed."

"My apologies, Matt. I didn't realize your wife was still sleeping."

"We've had a tough couple of days. I was letting her sleep as much as she needed. You were saying?"

"Yes. Steven asked me about a project that I had turned down, yet appeared to be in full operational status. I thought I'd check it out for myself."

Turning to go toward the cabin, Keith noticed the algae bloom. "What's that over there?"

"Just what it looks like. Algae, but doesn't seem to be expanding beyond that small cove. Problem is, that is where water draws for our cold house. Can't drink water from inside and any food it touches spoils . . . but it does cool very nicely."

"Where do you get drinking water?"

"Waterfall. About half an hour walk from here."

Barbara hesitantly welcomed General Keith into the cottage after she got dressed. Matt started a pot of coffee using one of the gas stove burners and proceeded to fry trout over the other. Matt, Barb, and Al Keith discussed their unexpected vacation while breakfast cooked and they ate.

Finishing his second cup of coffee, Keith stood and quietly walked to the door, where his officers waited. "I've heard enough. Call our men in and have Bard and . . ." Turning back to Matt and Barb he asked, "Who was the man who dreamed this thing up?"

"Jerry Tanner," Matt replied. "He's a good guy and helped us. I think he's the one who got the message to Steven somehow."

Turning back to his officers, Keith continued, "Collect Bard, Tanner, and whatever officers you can find. Especially the CO. Have them escorted here."

Watching the officer remove an unusual phone device from his belt and initiate a call, Matt added with some concern on his face. "Al, you do realize there is a full army battalion housed inside that mountain?"

"Yeah, so I heard. But don't worry, my men are better. They know what to do, how to do it, and will do it correctly."

"I'm familiar with the green and burgundy berets, I see them on the news frequently. What are the tan berets your men wear?"

Smiling with pride, Keith replied, "Elite of the elite." Seeing a puzzled look on Matt's face, he explained further. "The

National Security Agency deals primarily with intelligence gathering and analysis. We don't have our own army, but we do work with all branches of the military. These men, under my command, are the highest echelon of special forces. Some are Army, Navy, Marines, and two from the Air Force. And no, you probably haven't seen them on the news. We don't seek recognition, our only goal is to keep our government and country safe from all threats, internal and external."

"Wow, I know about Special Forces but I guess you guys are pretty special," Barb interjected, wrapping an arm around Matt.

"Yes, ma'am," Keith responded, still smiling. Shifting his posture to be more casual, he added, "But, it may be a while until everyone is assembled. Can I help with the dishes or anything?"

"No, thank you," Barb responded with an appreciative smile of her own. "If Matt will put some water on to heat, I'll take care of the dishes shortly. Did you have enough to eat?"

"Yes, ma'am. I do enjoy fresh fish and Matt did a fine job with it."

"How did you meet Steven?" Barb asked as Matt emptied one of the large water jugs into a pot and put it on the stove.

Hearing Barb's question, Matt turned and asked, "I want to know how you found us. I'm still not sure where we are."

"How I found you will have to wait. However, about your son. I arranged to go fishing while in California last week. It turns out the ranger who served as my guide is a close friend of your son. Thom Strong, I believe. When I came back to camp with breakfast, Steven was there. I could tell something was up, he even admitted as much, but he kept quiet until I had my fun. When he told me about a text he had received, I had my own suspicions about what was going on. Returning to Washington, I did a bit of quick research and, well, here I am." Seeing a strange look on Barb's face, Keith offered, "Would you like to call him?"

"How can you? Phones don't work in the valley; they have everything locked up," Matt challenged.

Pulling a phone from the side pocket on his pants, he replied, "Satellite phone." Looking at both Matt and Barb, he handed the phone to Barb, who immediately tapped in Steven's number.

"General Keith? Is this good news?" Steven answered, responding to the caller id.

"This is your mother, and yes, I think it is going to be a good day, today."

"MOM?! Are you and Dad okay? Uncle Jim told me you tried to call!"

"Later. Right now, I just wanted you to know that your father and I are alive and . . . well, as I said it looks like today is going to be a VERY good day! I hope to be home by tomorrow . . ." She paused and looked at Keith, who nodded. "Yes, General Keith says we should be home tomorrow. Please call . . . no never mind. I'll call your sister."

"That would be great, she has some news for you. Love you Mom. Give my love to Dad, too."

Ending the call with Steven, she quickly called their daughter, Angela.

"H e l l o?" Angela answered slowly with a great deal of suspicion.

"Angela, this is your mother. Your Dad and I are okay and hope to be home tomorrow. You have some news?"

"You called Steven first?"

Seeing men gathering outside the cabin, Barb pushed, "Angela, news? I only have a minute."

"Where are you?"

"Missus Harper, we have to go outside." Keith extended his hand for the phone.

"We'll talk later, I have to go." Barb ended the call and returned the phone to Keith. "Thank you!"

Nodding acknowledgment, Keith turned and left the cabin. Matt turned the gas off under the water, which was just becoming hot enough to wash the morning dishes, and followed Keith. Barb was right behind him.

"WHAT IS THE MEANING OF THIS?!" Brian Bard bellowed as Keith, Barb, and Matt arrived. Recognizing the general, he rolled his eyes and grew quiet.

Barb and Matt looked around at the assembly of men and women standing between the cabin and lake with their backs toward the trail to the camper. Four NSA soldiers flanked Bard, Tanner, Colonel Prescott, Doctor Adams, and another man they had not seen before. Six more NSA soldiers stood ready behind Keith's two officers and an NSA Lieutenant.

Keith looked to the Lieutenant who immediately responded, "Facility is secure, sir."

Keith nodded, then turned to the assembly from the mountain. "Brian Bard, I told you no when you pitched this absurd project, but you apparently shopped it around. Who picked it up?"

"Economic Development." Bard replied coldly.

"No, they cut you off as well. May have given you enough to get started, but they stopped writing checks months ago. So, let me guess, you tapped into that whacko consortium who likes to pull strings all around the world?" Seeing Bard's expression affirm his suspicion, Keith explained to Matt and Barb. "There is a group of financially powerful men and women who like to have things their way. They have very deep pockets and have the connections to exert control on anything and everything from how your Internet works down to local politics. Some people in the know believe they actually control elections around the world, but that is another problem. What is pertinent to our current situation is their control over the Internet. Mister Bard, here, uses quite a bit of Internet bandwidth. Don't you?"

"Yes, and this project would not succeed without their assistance." Bard glared at the general.

" 'Succeed.' Interesting word choice. Is the consortium happy with your progress so far?"

"We're getting there. Latest data reports are encouraging that we are on the right track," Bard replied, puffing up with an air of importance. "My investors are satisfied."

Keith raised both eyebrows at the word 'satisfied' and drew a deep breath before continuing. " 'Data reports,' another interesting phrase. Tell me about Data Retrieval Dynamics, Mister Bard. I believe you own sixty-five percent of this communications company. Is this correct?"

"Yes."

"And Colonel Prescott, let's talk with you for just a minute. You stepped down from Battalion Commander to command a company? I appreciate you are running out the clock until you can retire with full benefits, but how did you manage to bring a company of U.S. Army soldiers into this project?"

"We are on field exercise, sir, and are in full compliance with our directive," Prescott responded; his voice filled with contempt but still respectful of military tradition and protocol.

"And that directive?" Keith pursued.

"To establish and maintain a remote monitoring post to test our readiness should our borders be breached by a foreign power."

"Okay, I'll buy that, fits with the project description. Now, I believe I saw your name on the roster of Data Retrieval Dynamics owners. How much?"

"Twelve percent, sir. A personal investment."

"Yes, I appreciate that. No conflict of interest there, I suppose. . . . Now, let's look at this Data Retrieval Dynamics." Turning to his assistant, he accepted a folder and opened it. "Data Retrieval Dynamics provides high speed high density data farming and transfer across the internet. Each transaction by this project costs one tenth of a penny. Your simulations and analysis registers over five million transactions each and every day. That's five thousand dollars a day into your corporate pockets. Basically clear profit since the U.S. Army is paying for the Internet service."

Shifting his stance to better view Bard and the others, General Keith continued. "Since the start of this project, your company, Mister Bard, has gone from $126,000 in the red to $750,000 profit. That's quite a chunk of data retrieval, don't you think? Quite a bit of change in your pocket. Now, Geoffrey Bard, this is your son?" Seeing Bard shrink, Keith continued. "Does he know he has an account with a current value of . . ." Keith paused to look at his notes, "One point four million dollars? It seems six companies have been billing your benefactors and funneling their proceeds into this offshore account." Looking at the notes again, Keith looked squarely at Bard before continuing. "Judging by the date of the first deposit, you have not only been defrauding the consortium, but also the U. S. Government. That isn't going to go over well. You left a bit of a paper trail. Consortium might not find it but specialists at the NSA had no trouble."

Turning toward Jerry he said, "Now, here is something I find very interesting. Mister Tanner, you've been quiet through all this."

"Sir?" Tanner responded respectfully.

"You and two other economists developed the model and
the utility for retrieving all this data. Is that correct?"

"In a roundabout way, yes sir. However, we never put it
into practice. It was all on paper as hypothesis until we came to
work on this project."

"And where are your partners, the other two economists?"

"Bard ran them off. When we recognized the technology
Bard was using as what we developed, my friends wanted their
cut. Brian paid each of them a fraction of what it is worth and
threatened professional ruin if they ever disclosed their
participation."

"I dare say he could do it, too. Why did you stay?"

"This valley belongs to my family. I've been trying to keep
an eye on it."

"Is he paying you anything for its use?"

"Five thousand dollars a month plus my job. The lease
money goes into a family trust which will someday pass on to my
children and their cousins."

"Matt, what is that smell?" Barb whispered, trying to not
interrupt the general.

"Fish. We didn't get back to clean up and now the sun's
baking the heads," Matt replied, shrugging his shoulders with
apology.

Not hearing Matt and Barb, General Keith continued
questioning Jerry Tanner. "I understand that you are the one who
broke the confidence clause in your contract with Mister Bard
and sent word to Steven Harper that his parents are alive."

"No, sir. My wife did."

Smiling for the first time since the review began, Keith
responded, "Good for her. Very creative under the
circumstances. I also understand that you have provided
assistance to the Harpers?"

"Only when they showed up in town. Since talking with
them I have been doing project reviews trying to bring an end to
this nonsense."

" 'Nonsense?' Wasn't this your idea?"

"A hypothesis . . . no a puzzle really, conjured by three
economists over a lunch at a symposium."

"I am sure you now realize that this project is not so much
about predicting economic disasters as it is about making money

for Brian Bard." Keith took delight in seeing Bard shifting his posture, squirming a bit. "Mister Tanner, would you be willing to continue . . ." Keith's question was cut short by a loud noise behind him.

"G R O A R!" emerging from the trail to the camper, fifty feet behind the assemblage, Grumpy interrupted Keith's question to Tanner. Raising up to his hind legs, he sniffed the breeze.

Multiple soldiers brought assault rifles from their shoulders to firing position.

"STOP! DON'T SHOOT!" Matt yelled. "Get out of his way and he won't hurt you. That's Grumpy and he's never hurt anybody."

Seeing the assembly of men part, providing clear passage, Grumpy dropped on all fours and lumbered forward. Just before he reached the steps into the lake, where Matt and Keith had cleaned fish earlier that day, Bard panicked and reached for a soldier's rifle.

Alarmed by the tussle between the soldier and Bard, the bear rose again on his hind legs. Turning toward the two men, he was hit by a golden thunderbolt.

Seeing Grumpy become aggressive, Prince Albert shot out of the log cabin and launched himself at the bear's neck. Now off balance with eighty pounds of dog around his neck, Grumpy stumbled and rolled into the lake. Smashing into the water, Prince Albert released Grumpy and swam back to shore. Righting himself, about eight feet from shore, Grumpy quickly began swimming across the lake, away from all the bothersome people.

Seeking to take advantage of the confusion caused by Grumpy, Brian Bard turned toward the forest and ran past Keith. Two NSA Soldiers turned to give chase, however Matthew Harper, who had been standing to the side closer to the cabin, launched into action even faster. Bard had covered about fifty feet when Matt leapt forward planting his left shoulder into Bard's right shoulder. Bard spun around and flew into the air, landing in the algae bloom. Matt placed one hand down, catching himself, and stumbled back to his feet.

When Matt returned to Barb and General Keith, Keith reached out with his hand, chuckling. "Nice play, but you do realize clipping is a ten-yard penalty."

"I'll take the penalty if that stuff does to him what it did to our food."

General Keith looked toward Bard and the slime and smiled. Smiling himself at Keith's reaction, Matt asked, "Now what?"

Keith watched Barb fawning over Prince Albert. "Who's the dog?"

Kneeling down to pet the wet dog, Matt replied, "Prince Albert, he belongs with Jerry's grandmother who lives on the other side of the mountain. He tends to show up when we need him."

Chuckling at the unexpected events of the past minute or two, Keith looked to Matt and Barb. "Well, I guess you folks would like to go home and resume your lives." Seeing Barb nodding and Matt analyzing him suspiciously, he continued. "Matt, I spoke with your office yesterday. They have scheduled interviews with three candidates to replace you. I suggested they wait a week. Barb, your desk is still open. I guess somebody will need to replace your Durango and camper . . . I hope you are still interested in camping."

Matt and Barb both sighed and shook their heads with indecision.

"Well, somebody owes you a new camper and truck and before I forget, you said phones don't work here in the valley. If you will get your phones, I'll have one of my techs look at them and remove any bugs Bard has put there. I'm sure you'll need a few minutes to collect your belongings and I would like to see this installation they built in the mountain." Looking around, he called, "Mister Tanner!"

"General . . .," Matt interjected. "Al, if you don't mind we have something we need to show Jerry."

Keith thought for a moment before replying, "Not yet. I have some legal business I need to tend to and Mister Tanner should be present. This will also answer your question about how I found you." Strolling over to where Bard was climbing out of the algae-covered water, General Keith addressed him formally. "Brian Bard, I am placing you under arrest cyber terrorism . . ."

"WHAT?" Bard exploded. "I didn't send those emails, THEY DID!"

"Mister Bard, I will admit you have some pretty good tech folks, but my forensic team is better. When I saw the Harper's name come across on a Home Security bulletin, I acquired the original message. You didn't bounce it enough, because the transmission path led back to this valley . . ."

"YES!" Bard interrupted, again. "Harper sent it from the library in the village!"

General Keith immediately turned toward Jerry. "Mister Tanner, I believe you worked with the Harpers during their first escape. Is it possible that Matthew Harper sent an email while they were in the village?"

"No, sir," Jerry replied. "My son told me that he showed them the computers at the inn, but they never touched one. I do believe the email in question was sent by Mister Bard but I have no way to prove it."

"Thank you, that is all I needed to know," Keith confirmed with a nod. Turning to Bard he continued, "No, Mister Bard, the originating IP address is from your facility in the mountain. I told you my team is good. I do suspect the resolving address with point to your desk, but we'll have to confirm that." Turning to the Harpers and Tanner, he nodded and winked. Seeing they got the message and turned to leave, he resumed his legal duty. "Now, Brian Bard, in addition to cyber terrorism, you are charged with unlawful abduction and detention of the Harpers and the other two families you have been using as pawns in your stupid game. I am certain the US Attorney General will be adding charges for fraud and misappropriation of U.S. Military resources. If I were you, I'd keep my mouth shut until you are formally interviewed by the A.G. and have counsel present." Turning to two of his men, he casually told them, "Gentlemen, confine him . . . after he cleans that gunk off himself. Be careful to not get any on you, it could be toxic." Smiling at Bard's panicked expression, he turned to Prescott. "Colonel, I'm not quite sure what to do about you, but I believe everything will go better if you direct your company to assist my men in packing this operation up. Also, the Harpers informed me that you installed a barrier fence on the ridge of the mountain, which is now a problem for our favorite bear. See to it that that fence is removed by sunset." Looking around, he saw Jerry Tanner and the

Harpers going down into the woods behind the cabin. Catching sight of a familiar face he called, "Doctor Adams . . ."

She responded with a smile. "General, good to see you again."

"Olivia, you should have called me when you saw what was going on here."

"Call you? When? Al, I had no idea who was financing this shootin' match and you are never in your office. You want me to be your watchdog, give me your cell number." Adams stared coldly at the general, then softened and with a bit of a smile continued. "Besides, I was keeping an eye on the Harpers. . . ."

"Jerry, what was that about? Cyber terrorism?" Matt asked as they moved a short distance from General Keith's men.

"I guess you didn't know. You and Missus Harper are accused of sending a virus laden email to the NY Stock Exchange and have been classified as cyber terrorists. You are on multiple watch lists. I knew Bard had done it but had no way to prove it. I imagine you will be cleared by the time you get home." Taking a deep breath and exhaling heavily, he asked, "Now, what did you want to see me about?"

Matt looked to Barb, then shook his head and grinned. "You remember how you told us about how your great-great-grandfather came up here and returned flush with money?"

"Yes. Dozens of people have looked for a stash of treasure, but nobody, including me as a teenager, ever found anything."

"Hold out your hand," Matt requested. When Jerry complied, somewhat hesitantly, Matt placed the gold coin on his palm.

Seeing Jerry's eyes double in size, Barb wiggled her finger, her eyes sparkling tauntingly. "Come with us."

Barb and Matt led Jerry around the cabin. When they had gone a short way down the hill, Matt stopped and turned around. "There it is!" he then went back up the hill about ten feet and stood over a large stone. "Give me a hand."

Together, Jerry and Matt removed the stone, revealing the metal vault. Seeing Jerry's face fill with puzzle and disbelief, Matt told him, "That's the lid. Lift it."

Jerry got down on his knees and lifted the metal lid from the vault. Unable to see inside, he retrieved his phone from his pocket and turned on the flashlight, exclaiming softly, "Damn!" Reaching down he tried to lift the bucket of coins, asking for Matt's help as it came into the light of day. Jerry then began retrieving papers that had been stacked around the coins.

After removing all the money, Jerry checked the vault again with his phone light. The bottom of the vault was lined with gold bars stamped "C.S.A." General Keith's aid arrived as Jerry removed the first bar.

Examining the coins and paper bills, which included Silver Certificates in $1, $2, $5, $10, $20 denominations - lots of them, the aid said, "One of my hobbies is Civil War mysteries. I'll bet that what you have here are stolen Confederate and Union payrolls. Each of these bills is worth at least ten times the face value and you seem to have what, ten to twelve thousand dollars here. I have no idea what those coins are worth but that bar in your hand, half a million dollars if it's pure, and I bet it is. Where did all this come from?"

"My great whatever grandfather inherited it from the old hermit who built this cabin," Jerry replied, softly. Looking at the mound of old money surrounding him, he found it difficult to breathe.

Epilog

Hearing his phone ringing, a twenty-six-year-old safety engineer in Billings, Montana looked away from his computer screen. Realizing the call was from his cousin, he answered it. "Hey cuz, whatsup?"

"Mister Matthew Harper, today is your lucky day. I just got some info and I need help with an internet stock trade that could make us both a lot of money. Now before you hang up, listen for a minute. This is insider information and I'm not supposed to share it, but knowing you need some cash, I can't resist." The caller paused.

"Okay, you didn't hang up, good. Here's the deal. A pharmacy company, who is a client of our sister company, is about to go public with an announcement of a new drug they are supposed to be working on. I stumbled across a confidential internal report that says they are hemorrhaging money 'cause the drug don't work. We need to buy their stock TODAY and be ready to unload it within thirty days, before the real news leaks out."

"I don't know. I trust you to handle my small stock list but this sounds fishy. I don't want to risk what little I have."

"Hey. This is a last ditch effort for them to stay afloat. When they announce a release schedule for this drug, their value will skyrocket. We want to ride that rocket, then get out before the bad news becomes public. Who knows, maybe they fix it and you become rich on dividends."

"Like most of your schemes, Larry, this sounds too good to be true. What if it goes wrong? Economic depressions have been caused by schemes gone awry."

"Collapses happen all the time. Could cause a black hole in the stock market, maybe just a small one for a few days, but not if we move smart. We buy, then get out ahead of the explosion. We just need to buy the right amount of stock. Not too much, but enough to be profitable, which is what I want you to do."

"But won't selling cause questions?"

"Look, Matty, your company has a leg in the pharmacy industry so this information could have come to you from another source. That would squash any suspicions but we don't have much time. If you are in, I need you to log into that online account I set up for you and . . ."

www.ingramcontent.com/pod-product-compliance
Lightning Source LLC
Chambersburg PA
CBHW011030190726
48290CB00011B/2782